O9-AHW-996

Thieves' World™

Turning Points

Edited by **Lynn Abbey**

TOR®
fantasy

A TOM DOHERTY ASSOCIATES BOOK
NEW YORK

This is a work of fiction. All the characters and events portrayed in these stories are either fictitious or are used fictitiously.

THIEVES' WORLD™: TURNING POINTS

Copyright © 2002 by Lynn Abbey and Thieves' World 2000

Thieve's World™ and Sanctuary™ are registered trademarks belonging to Lynn Abbey and are used with permission.

A Tor Book
Published by Tom Doherty Associates, LLC
175 Fifth Avenue
New York, NY 10010

www.tor.com

Tor® is a registered trademark of Tom Doherty Associates, LLC.

ISBN: 0-765-34517-X

First edition: November 2002
First mass market edition: December 2003

Printed in the United States of America

0 9 8 7 6 5 4 3 2 1

Copyright Acknowledgments

In memory of

Poul Anderson
Marion Zimmer Bradley
John Brunner
A. E. van Vogt
and
Gordon R. Dickson

Contents

x   Contents

Introduction

Lynn Abbey

Cauvin thought he'd made himself froggin' clear: He was a workingman, a stonemason who liked the feel of a heavy mallet in his hand, not some froggin' songbird caged up in the palace.

"He says he'll beat me, if you don't come," the stranger—a youth not out of his teens—insisted flatly, desperately.

That didn't sound like Arizak perMizhur. Sanctuary's froggin' tyrant was a hard man, not a cruel or vindictive one, or so Cauvin remembered. Cauvin had a thousand froggin' memories of Arizak perMizhur, all of them clamoring for his attention. Problem was, almost none of those memories were his. Five months earlier, on his way to smash some old bricks, he'd gotten his sheep-shite self caught up in the death-wishes of Molin Torchholder, an old man who'd had his froggin' finger on every worthwhile pulse in Sanctuary for a half-century. Everyone knew the froggin' Torch was a liar, a schemer, a hero, and the priest of a vanquished god. What they hadn't known was that the old pud was a witch, too, and before he breathed his froggin' last, he managed to cast all his lifetime's worth of memories into Cauvin's skull.

If he'd had the power, Cauvin would have summoned the Torch's shade and forced him to take back his froggin' gift. If he'd had the power, which he didn't. Cauvin *remembered* the ways of witchcraft but he couldn't *do* anything with them, not yet anyway. Along with his memories, the Torch had managed to bequeath his god to Cauvin. Vashanka now skulked in Cauvin's dreams.

Cauvin could handle the memories and Vashanka's bitter prophecy. He'd survived a childhood on the streets of Sanctuary and adolescence in the grasp of the Bloody Hand of Dyareela. He was a froggin' master at ignoring the unignorable. But he wasn't the only one who knew about the Torch's legacy. Arizak perMizhur knew it, too. Sanctuary's tyrant had relied upon the Torch's cunning to govern the city his Irrune tribesmen had conquered ten years ago and would never understand. Arizak was getting old himself and crippled by a rotting foot, but his mind remained sharp. He knew exactly how to get Cauvin—and his inherited memories—moving.

"I'm off to the froggin' palace," Cauvin called across the stoneyard to his foster father, Grabar.

"Be careful," Grabar replied nicely, as if Cauvin's absence wouldn't wreak havoc on the day's labor.

Then again, why wouldn't Grabar bend over backward for him? Tucked away among all the Torch's memories were the hundred-odd boltholes where the old pud had stashed his considerable wealth and Sanctuary's treasures, beside. Shite for sure, with a little effort, Cauvin could have bought his foster father out of the stoneyard. He could have bought himself a magnate's mansion fronting on the Processional or resurrected one of the abandoned estates ringing the town, even the great Land's End estate of the exiled Serripines. Frog all—Cauvin could have bought Arizak out of the palace—if he'd wanted any part of the life that went with wealth.

Cauvin did have a clean shirt in his quarters over the shed where they stowed their tools and stabled the mule, but pulling on a clean shirt halfway through a workday was just the sort of thing he refused to do. He did pause by the water trough to sluice himself off. The water was breathtakingly frigid, but midway through winter, it *was* water, not ice.

Sanctuary had had a few bitter days, but nothing like its usual winter. The old folks—older than Grabar—who remembered before the Irrune, before the Bloody Hand of Dyareela, and all the way back to the days when the Rankan Empire had thought to make something of this city stuck on its backside, they whispered that magic must be returning to the city, as though the presence of a few wizards could change the weather . . .

They once had, the Torch's memories rippled through Cauvin's mind. *They might again. Be careful.*

Cauvin shrugged away a dead man's thoughts and followed the youthful servant onto Pyrtanis street.

"**J**ust so! Just so! You move now. Quick!"

Cauvin waited alone in the shadows of the audience chamber. The servant had melted into the tangled corridors, first froggin' chance he got. Arizak sat in his cushioned chair at the center of the chamber—not his usual place, which was on the dais at the rear. His bandaged and blanketed foot was propped up on a separate, higher stool. He'd twisted sideways over his hip—a posture that had to be painful, though not as painful as a slowly rotting limb. A servant stood behind him struggling with the butt end of a long spear from which three lanterns—all lit and smoking—dangled.

The man doing the speaking, the mud-covered man in tattered fur and leather, was the tyrant's brother, Zarzakhan, the Irrune's sole shaman. The way his mud shone in the lamplight, Zarzakhan was fresh from a spirit walk with *his* god, Irrunega, and considering what the shaman mixed into his mud—blood, horse dung, and stinkweed oil—Cauvin was froggin' glad to be upwind and watching as Zarzakhan seized sixteen-year-old Raith, the most able of Arizak's sons and potential heirs, and stood him face-to-face with an older Irrune warrior, whose back was to Arizak.

"See? See?" Zarzakhan chirped. "Tentinok blocks the sun. His shadow falls on Raith. The moon is hidden from Tentinok's eyes."

From his chair, Arizak grunted and rearranged himself. Zarzakhan immediately grabbed Raith by the shoulders again and guided him into a new position between Tentinok and Arizak, with his back to Arizak. The shaman then spun Tentinok around to face both Raith and his father.

"Now, Raith blocks the sun and *his* shadow falls on Tentinok. For Tentinok, it was day, but becomes night"—Zarzakhan gave Raith a shove that sent him staggering toward Cauvin—"then the shadow is gone. It is day again."

Another grunt from Arizak. "If this were true," the tyrant decreed, "then each month as the moon grew full, it would disappear and later, instead of resting, it would sneak into the heavens to swallow the sun. My own eyes have seen that this is not so. The sun and moon move above us bringing the light of day and the light of night. The makers of light do not hurl *shadows* at our eyes, brother. This is nonsense."

Zarzakhan slammed his staff against the stone tiles. The servant started at the noise and nearly lost his grip on the lantern-hung spear.

"It is Irrunega!" The shaman shouted the name of the one god of the Irrune through the swaying light. "The vision Irrunega shared with me, to warn me—to warn *you*, my brother, that twice, soon, the shadows are coming! Prepare! Mischief hides in the shadows. Sorcerers—wizards, magicians, priests of lesser gods, and *witches*. Irrunega has seen them creeping—slouching—toward Sanctuary. Prepare!"

Arizak wasn't comfortable. He writhed on the cushions, turning away from the shaman and spotting Cauvin, finally.

"Hah! You're here. Have you heard this nonsense?" Arizak beckoned Cauvin closer and, cautiously, he entered the lamplight. "My brother says that the next time we have a full moon, it will turn red, then disappear, and later the sun will do the same." His face tightened into a scowl. "Have you ever heard of such a thing?"

Cauvin flinched. It wasn't his answer the Irrune wanted, it was the Torch's. He braced himself for the sensation, a half-breath shy of pain, that came with a dive into a dead man's memories.

"No," he croaked, then, "Yes," as, in his mind's eye, rippling draperies the color of dried blood fell slowly over a round, silvery moon and—alongside the moon, as it could only be in recollection, never in life—a black disk sliced into the sun. The Torch's memories held nothing of shadows, but the Rankan priests had known the eclipses—that was the word Cauvin found with the images—were coming and that they would be over quickly, without damaging either the sun or the moon.

Cauvin fought his way back to his own mind. From Arizak to the guard holding the spear, everyone in the audience chamber was staring at him. "It could be," his tongue told the tyrant while his thoughts cursed the Torch to greater torments. "If— If Irrunega says it could."

"Wise man," Zarzakhan crowed, rushing to Cauvin's side. "Wise man."

Cauvin held his breath, but that trick failed when the shaman clapped him hard between the shoulder blades. Odor as thick as smoke filled Cauvin's chest and there was nothing he could do to keep himself from gagging. Zarzakhan clapped Cauvin a second time before retreating a pace. Cauvin couldn't stop coughing. Arizak couldn't stop laughing. The tyrant shook so much the stool beneath his rotting foot toppled and his foot dropped to the floor like a stone.

Cauvin froze mid-cough and stayed that way while Tentinok darted to Arizak's aid. The older man righted the stool and gently—oh-so-froggin'-gently— lifted the tyrant's foot onto it.

"Better," Arizak said through clenched teeth. "Leave us." He dismissed Tentinok with a flick of his hand.

Tentinok dropped to one knee instead. *"Sakkim,"* he pleaded, giving the tyrant his Irrune-language title. "I ask—I beg—*She* has done it again—"

"Kadasah?"

Tentinok nodded. "There was much damage. Many complaints. They want *money.*"

Cauvin was too close. He could hear the conversation he was not meant to hear.

Money was a sore subject between the Irrune war-

riors and the city they ruled. Bluntly, they froggin'
refused to use it, said it broke their honor, and
they'd have risen up against Arizak perMizhur if
he'd been fool enough to argue with them. The tyrant was not a fool. He let his warriors keep their
honor intact and quietly paid their bills from the
palace. Shite for sure, since he could scarcely leave
his cushioned chair, paying those bills—especially
the bills run up by his own sons—was the joy of
Arizak's life. Tentinok's problem was that he didn't
have a wild son; he had a wild daughter who drank
and fought from one end of Sanctuary to the other
and back again.

Cauvin slid one foot back, prepared to get out of
earshot—but retreat would only prove that he'd
been listening, so he stayed put.

"I said, last time was the last time. You said there'd
be a marriage."

Tentinok hung his head like a bullied child. "I
have tried, *Sakkim.*"

Cauvin had seen—not met, merely seen across
the common room at the Vulgar Unicorn—the lady
in question. She was attractive enough, even had a
few dogged admirers—the timid sort of men who
needed a froggin' strong arm to back them in their
brawls—none of them Irrune or worth marrying.

Arizak understood. He laid a hand on Tentinok's
arm and promised that he'd have his Wrigglies—
Cauvin and his neighbors, the native blood of Sanctuary, had been called Wrigglies so long that they
no longer considered it an insult and used it among
themselves—settle Tentinok's debts . . . again.

"Now, go," the tyrant concluded and pointed toward the chamber doors.

Tentinok mumbled his appreciation and escaped.
Cauvin wished he could have followed, but Arizak

had already caught his eye and motioned him—or, more properly, his froggin' memories—into confidence range. Like Tentinok, Cauvin dropped to one knee beside the cushioned chair. Raith joined them—he had the itch for governing a city—and so—the gods all be froggin' damned—did the reeking Zarzakhan.

"It has gone as you predicted," Arizak confided once his circle had drawn close around him.

He fished among the cushions and withdrew a parchment coil with a broken seal that he handed to Cauvin who unrolled it. Only a few froggin' months earlier and Cauvin wouldn't have known which end of the scroll was top and which was bottom, much less that it was written in the elegant hand of an Ilsigi court scribe. Reading—even reading languages he couldn't froggin' speak or understand—was another of the Torch's froggin' legacies.

But read Cauvin could and read he did, while Arizak explained to his brother and Raith.

"The Ilsigi king hears his rival, the Rankan emperor, has sent a tournament to Sanctuary—to honor our role in his recent victories. The Ilsigi king suspects his rival has other reasons. He does not say so, of course, but he has sent us the emissary who brought this, a golden statue of a horse my grandmother would not stoop to ride, and eight fighters to—what?—'uphold our ancestors' glory'?"

Cauvin nodded: Those were the words and the gist of the letter King Sepheris IV had signed and sealed himself.

"So," Arizak continued, "now we have them both in Sanctuary, suspecting each other while they pry after our secrets. What *are* our secrets, my friend?" The tyrant scowled down at Cauvin. "Why are they here?"

"War," Cauvin replied with his own wits. He'd had enough time with the Torch's memories to learn some things for himself. "The Nis in the north are finished. Caronne is in revolt and devouring itself. There's nothing to keep Sepheris and Jamasharem"—the Rankan emperor—"from each other's throats."

"Of course, war," Arizak snapped. "They are young and strong and the world is too small. But why *here?* Why Sanctuary?"

A twinge of almost-pain squeezed Cauvin's heart. He couldn't speak until it had passed and, by then, it was all clear in his mind.

"Sorcery—magic, prayer, *and* witchcraft." He listed all three branches, of which witchcraft was the most feared, the most reviled. "They know about the eclipses . . . When the moon is swallowed, everyone from Ilsig to Ranke will know, but the disappearance of the sun"—Cauvin swallowed hard: The Torch's memories were no match for his own dread—"that will happen *here.* And between the two"—he shook his head, but the images of fire, blood, and things he could not name would not dissolve—"great sorceries will be possible."

"This tournament is diversion," Arizak mused. He was a wily, farsighted man. "An excuse to flood Sanctuary with strangers . . . sorcerous strangers."

"Irrunega!" Zarzakhan shouted and slammed his staff to the floor.

"What manner of sorcery is possible between the eclipses?" Raith asked.

Cauvin got along well with Raith. He would have answered the young man's questions without a goad from the Torch's memories, but memory was no fair guide to the future. "Powerful sorcery, that's all I know," he admitted. "The sort of sorcery no one's seen for forty years or more. Worse than ten years ago, when the Bloody Hand tried to summon Dyareela. *Doors* could get opened, and left open. We can't be too careful."

Arizak stroked his chin and nodded. "We need someone *in* that tournament, someone who'll win—"

"And someone who'll attract trouble," Raith added, and they all turned toward him. "Naimun," he suggested with a guileful smile. "Who better than my brother?"

"Anyone would be better than Naimun!" Cauvin answered. "He can't be trusted!" Raith's slow-witted but ambitious elder brother had already been caught treating with the outlawed remnants of the Bloody Hand, not to mention every foreign schemer who washed ashore.

"We don't need to *trust* him," Raith snarled coldly. "We need only *follow* him."

"**R**aith said that?" the black-clad man asked with the raised eyebrows of surprise and new-found respect.

Cauvin nodded. "Everything went dead quiet—you could hear the froggin' flies buzzing around Zarzakhan. But that's not the strangest part—"

"I might have guessed."

The two men were alone on a hill outside Sanctuary, their conversation lit by the faint light of a silver moon.

The black-clad man's name was Soldt and he was a duelist—an assassin—who'd come to the city years ago to solve a problem called Lord Molin Torchholder. The Torch—no froggin' spring chicken then, either—had outwitted him and Soldt had wound up staying on as the old pud's eyes, ears, and, sometimes, his sword. He was another part of Cauvin's legacy.

"While I knelt there," Cauvin went on, "not daring to froggin' *breathe*, the light began to shimmer—"

"Zarzakhan catching fire?"

"No—not that froggin' strange. The guard—the spear man who'd played the part of the sun? I looked up and he was shaking all over—*laughing*. Shite, I'd forgotten he was even there; we *all* had—and that's the way he meant it."

Another arch of eyebrows.

"I blinked and the man's eyes were glowing red."

"Ah, Yorl again, Enas Yorl. Spying on everyone. How long do you suppose *he's* known we were fated for two eclipses in quick succession?"

"I didn't get a chance to ask. I blinked again, and he was gone."

"And *then* Zarzakhan caught fire?"

"No, the *guard* was still there—looking like he'd just awakened from a nightmare; *Yorl* was gone."

"That's new. He's finding a way to turn that shape-shifting curse to his own advantage. You've got to ask yourself—who would benefit more from a little sky sorcery? Doesn't want any competition, that's for sure. Figure he'll show up in the tournament?"

Cauvin cleared his throat. "All the more reason we've got to have someone there . . . and it can't be one of the Irrune, even though Raith volunteered, of course, and you know the Young Dragon would eat dirt for the chance."

Soldt recoiled. He stood up, stomped away, then turned on his heel. "I don't work in Sanctuary, you know that. It's bad enough, with everything that happened with Lord Torchholder's death, that my name is known. But a common tournament? I will *not*."

"Shite! I understand!" Cauvin couldn't meet the other man's eyes. "That's why I'm putting my name in."

"You?! It's a *steel* tournament, pud. You can't even draw a sword properly. You're—" Soldt stopped, mid-rant, then finished in a far more thoughtful tone: "You're getting more like him every day."

Home Is Where the Hate Is

Mickey Zucker Reichert

A dense fog blurred the long-ruined temples of
the Promise of Heaven and dimmed the early afternoon sunlight to a dusk-like gray. Light rain stung
Dysan's face as he slouched along the Avenue of
Temples that led to the shattered ruin he alone
called home. The dampness added volume and curl
to raven hair already too thick to comb. It fell to his
shoulders in a chaotic snarl that he clipped only
when it persistently fell into his eyes. Few bothered
with this quarter of the city, though Dysan guessed
it had once bustled with priests and their pious. In
the ten years since Arizak and his Irrune warriors
had destroyed the Bloody Hand of Dyareela and
banished all but their own religion from the inner
regions of Sanctuary, no one had bothered to pick
up the desecrated pieces the Dyareelans had left of
their former temples. Instead, the buildings fell prey
to ten years of disrepair, beset by Sanctuary's infer-
nal storms and soggy climate.

At sixteen, Dysan was only just beginning to learn
his way around the city that bred, bore, and ne-

glected to raise him. He recalled only flashes of his first four years, when he, his mother, and his brother, Kharmael, had lived in a hovel near the Street of Red Lanterns. Only in the last few years had he figured out what so many must have known all along: Kharmael's father, Ilmaris, the man Dysan had once blindly believed his own, had died three years before his birth. Their mother had supported them with her body. Dysan's father might be any man who had lived in or passed through Sanctuary, and his mother, in what the Rankans had proclaimed was the 86th year of their crumbling empire and the Ilsigis called the 3,553rd year of theirs.

Dysan flicked water from his lashes and wiped his dripping nose with the back of a grimy, tattered sleeve. He had managed to swipe a handful of bread and some lumps of fish from an unwatched stew pot, enough to fill his small belly. Tonight, he planned to use his meager store of wood to light a fire in the Yard—his name for the roofless two-walled main room of his home—beneath an overhang sheltered from the rain. It was a luxury he did not often allow himself. The flames sometimes managed to chase away the chill that had haunted his heart for every one of the ten years he had lived without his brother, but it was a bittersweet trade-off. Even small, controlled fires sometimes stirred flashbacks to the worst moments of his life.

Tears rose, unbidden, mingling with the rain-water dribbling down Dysan's face. Kharmael and the Dyareelans had raised him from a toddler to a child in a world of pain and blood that no one should ever have to endure. Lightning flashed, ig-niting the sky and a memory of a stranger: skinned and mutilated by laughing children trained to kill with cruel and guiltless pleasure. Dysan had personally suffered the lash of the whip only once. Small and frail, half the size of a normal four-year-old, he had passed out at the agony of the first strike. Only the scars that striped his shoulders and back, and the aches that had assailed him on awakening, made it clear that his lack of mental presence had not ended the torture. The Hand had labeled him as weak, a sure sacrifice to their blood-loving, hermaphrodite god/goddess; and he would have become one in his first few weeks had Kharmael not been there to comfort him, to rally and bully him, when necessary, into moving when he would rather have surrendered to whatever death the Hand pronounced.

Kharmael had been the survivor: large, strong, swarthy with health, and handsome with a magnificent shock of strawberry-blond hair inherited from their father. *His father*, Dysan reminded himself. Dysan had shared nothing with his brother but love and a mother, dead from a disease one of her clients had given her. Later, Dysan discovered, that same illness had afflicted him in the womb, the cause of his poor growth, his delicate health, and the oddities of his mind. Oddities that had proven both curse and blessing. Social conventions and small talk baffled him. He could not count his own digits, yet languages came to him with an eerie golden clarity that the rest of the world lacked. At first, his companions in the Pits, and the Hand alike, believed him hopelessly simple-minded. At five years old, he barely looked three; and only Kharmael could wholly understand his speech. It was the orphans who figured out that Dysan used words from the languages of every man who had come to visit his mother, of every child in the Pits, interchangeably, switching at random. But once the Hand heard of this ability, Dysan's life had irrevocably changed.

Dysan turned onto the crude path that led to his home, sinking ankle-deep into mud that sucked the last shreds of cloth from his feet. He would have to steal a pair of shoes or boots, or the money to buy them, before colder days set in. Already, the wind turned his damp skin to gooseflesh; his sodden hair and the wet tatters of his clothing felt like ice when they brushed against him. But the thought of shopping sent a shiver through Dysan that transcended cold. No matter how hard he tried, counting padpols confounded him. Most thieves would celebrate the discovery of something large and silver, but he dreaded the day his thieving netted him a horde of soldats or shaboozh. He could never figure out how to change it or spend it, and it would taunt him until some better thief relieved him of the burden.

A gruff voice speaking rapid Wrigglie froze Dysan just at the boundary between the dilapidated skeleton of some unused Ilsigi temple and the one he called his own.

"Frog your sheep-shite arse, I'm done for the day. My froggin' left hand can't see what my froggin' right hand is froggin' doing."

An older man snapped back. "Watch your language, boy! There's a lady present."

The aforementioned lady spoke next. Unlike the men, clearly Sanctuary natives, she spoke Ilsigi with a musical, Imperial accent. "Don't worry about his language, Mason. I don't understand a word that boy says."

Dysan peeked around the corner. However else being born with the clap had affected him, it had not damaged his eyesight or his ears, at least not when soggy shadows and darkness covered the city, which was most of the time. He spotted three figures in his Yard, standing around a fresh stack of stone blocks. They had worked quickly. He had seen no sign of them when he left the ruins that morning. *Gods-all-be-damned. What in the froggin' hell*—? The goosebumps faded as curiosity warmed to anger. *That's my home. MY HOME!* Dysan's hands balled to fists, but he remained in place. He had seen plenty of fights in his lifetime, enough to know he could barely take on the plump, gray-haired woman, let alone the two strapping men beside her.

The mason translated for his apprentice, eliminating the curses, which did not leave much. "He says it's quitting time. We'll finish staging the wall tomorrow, then start mortaring." Mopping his brow, he straightened, then plucked a lantern from the ground.

"Fine. Fine." The woman glanced at the piled stone from every direction, stroking her strong, Rankan chin as she did so.

The fish churned in Dysan's gut, and he thought he might vomit. He swallowed hard, tasting acid, wishing he had not fought the lurching in his stomach. The sour taste reminded him too much of the End. This time, he struggled against the memory, but it surged over him too quickly and with a strength he could never hope to banish. Once again, he found himself in the Pits, surrounded by dead-eyed orphans lost to that empty internal world that numbed them to any morality their parents might have managed to drive into their thick skulls before the Dyareelans snatched them. The Hand molded them like clay puppets to fit their own image of normalcy: soulless brutality, bitter mistrust, and blood. Dysan knew that place, an empty hideaway for the mind while the body performed unbearable evil. In time, the orphans either severed that place or escaped into it. The first left them forever stranded from their consciences, the latter steeped in madness.

When the Bloody Hand finally fell, an old man they called the Torch had interviewed each of them separately. Dysan had dodged dark eyes keener than any man that age had a right to and said he wished to remain in the palace with the Hand forever. At the time, he had meant it. His brother was there, and Dysan recalled no other family, no other life. He knew the Hand was evil, that they gleefully sated their goddess with the blood of innocents, that they tore down the orphans with brutal words, torture, and slave labor. Yet, Dysan had suffered far less than the others. Once the priests gave him the organizational skills to tame his runaway talent with languages, he became proficient down to the accent in every tongue they threw at him. He slipped effortlessly from perfect Ilsigi to a melodious and Imperial Rankene to the rapid, broken Wrigglie that was his birthright. They had taught him others as well, most of which they never named and none of which posed much difficulty, written or spoken. They had taught him to steal, to climb, to bend, wrap, and twist his scrawny, underdeveloped body into positions that allowed access into the tiniest cracks and rat holes. They had taken him to houses and temples, to gatherings and inns, where he had only to sip a bowl of goat milk and report the conversations of strangers, who seldom bothered with discretion in front of a young boy. In short, the Hand rewarded him for next to nothing and taught him to survive.

Dysan had used those skills to rescue his brother from the solitary confinement into which the Torch had placed him. Together, they had returned to the

Pits to gather their scant belongings, all the while planning grand futures that six- and nine-year-old brothers could never really hope to attain. There, they found their companions feasting on a bounty of raw horsemeat. Kharmael joined them. Nursing the end of a stomach virus and accustomed to richer foods than his companions, who supplemented their meals with the bony rats they could catch, Dysan refused his share. Worried for his little brother's strength, Kharmael forced a mouthful on him. Many of the orphans had come to prefer their food raw, the bloodier the better; but Dysan's never-strong stomach could not handle it. He started vomiting almost immediately. By midnight, all of the others had joined him. One by one, he watched them fall into what he thought was peaceful sleep. But, when a jagged agony in his gut awakened him in the night, he found his brother eerily cold beside him.

Now, with a desperate surge, Dysan managed to throw off the memories that had assailed him. Again. Slipping into the shadows, he watched the men and woman navigate the mucky pathway to the road, shaking slime from their boots with every step. The woman's features pinched. "We'll need to cobble that. Can't have us swimming through a stinking swamp every time it rains."

My mud. My swamp. Dysan remained unmoving, watching the retreating backs and resenting every word. Though he had long cursed that same quagmire, it was a familiar quagmire. It was *his* quagmire.

"Always froggin' raining," the apprentice muttered, and the others ignored him. "Shite-for-sure, I can't wait to get out of this cess of a city."

"Gravel might be better," the mason started. "Dump a few cartloads of broken . . ." His voice and the figures disappeared into the night, the lantern light visible like a distant star long after they had vanished.

Dysan's fists tightened in increments, until his nails bit painful impressions into his palms. Once certain they were not returning, he glided to the piled stones and examined them. Their position told him everything. These strangers planned to re-build the missing walls, which might have pleased Dysan had it not clearly meant that someone ex-pected to take over his home. *More than five froggin' ruins in this froggin' run-down quarter, and they have to pick mine.* There were a lot more than five, but that was the highest number Dysan could reliably iden-tify.

Seized by sudden rage, Dysan hurled himself against the piled stones. Pain arched through his shoulder, and his head snapped sideways. He slid to the ground rubbing his bruised, abraded skin, feel-ing like a fool. The mason and his foul-mouthed apprentice had not mortared yet, which meant the wall would come down, even if Dysan had to do it block by heavy block.

Dysan set straight to work. It had not taken the men long, but Dysan harbored no illusions that he could work as quickly. Strength had never been his asset. The Hand had made him understand that his frailty, the strange workings and malfunctions of his mind, his notched front teeth and bow-shaped shins were all a god-inflicted curse visited upon his mother for her sins. If the Hand had intended to drive him toward worship, their words had had the opposite effect. Dysan would never throw his sup-port to any deity who punished infants for their parents' wrongdoing. More likely, the priests had intended the insults as a substitute for the "sheep-shite stupid" label they gave to most of the other orphans. They could hardly call Dysan brainless and still expect him to learn the language lessons they bombarded him with for much of the day.

Sometimes, in his dreams, Dysan taunted his teachers, driving them to a raw rage they dared not sate with coiled fists, whips, and blades for fear of losing their delicately constitutioned secret weapon. In his dreams, he could triumph where, in real life, he had miserably failed. Then, Dysan had done whatever they asked because he had seen the price others paid for disobedience. He had been desperately, utterly afraid, terrified to the core of his being, dependent on the praise and approval that he received from a brother who, though only three years older, was the only parent figure Dysan had ever known. Certain her undersized, sallow baby with his protuberant belly and persistent river of snot would die, his mother had not even bothered to name him. He had turned two, by the grace of Kharmael, before she dared to invest any attachment in him. By then, the disease had damaged her physically and mentally, and she relied nearly as much on her older son as Dysan did.

Dysan examined the stonework from every angle, ideas churning through his mind. Though willing to spend the night dismantling the structure, he sought an easier and faster way. Well-placed and wedged, the gray stone seemed to mock him, a solid testament to another stolen love. He had one possession in this life that he saw as permanent, and no one was going to take it from him without a fight. He examined the base, knowing that it ultimately supported the entire pile. If he could remove a significant piece from the bottom, the whole day's labor might collapse. He had only to find one stone, one low-placed weak point.

Anger receded as Dysan focused on the wall, here studying, there wiggling, until he found an essential rock that shifted slightly when he pressed against it. Dysan flexed his fingers, planted them firmly against the rock, and shoved with all his strength. A sheeting sound grated through his hearing, but he felt much less movement than the noise suggested. Not for the first time, he cursed his lack of size. He had stopped growing, in any direction, since he had eaten, albeit lightly, of the poisoned feast and had met more than one seven-year-old who topped him in height and breadth.

Damn it! Dysan pounded a fist against the wall, which only succeeded in slamming pain through the side of his hand. He had long ago learned that legs were stronger than arms, so he lay on his back and braced his bare feet against the rock he had selected. Dampness permeated the frayed linen of his shirt, chilling his back to the spine. Closing his eyes, he attempted to focus his mind in one direction, though the effort proved taxing. His thoughts preferred to stray, especially when it came to anything involving counting, and it took a great effort of will to keep his mind engaged on any one task. The Hand had taught him to use anger as an anchor, and he turned to that technique now. Dysan closed his eyes and directed his thoughts. *They want to take away my home.* His muscles coiled. *They battered and broke my friends.* It was a different "they," but it had the same effect. *Those sheep-shite bastards killed my brother!* Images flashed through Dysan's mind: maimed women screaming in mindless terror and agony, grown men streaming blood like spilled wine and pleading for mercy, a broken fevered child begging the others to kill him so he would not have to face the tortures of Dyareela alive.

Bombarded by rage, vision a red fog, Dysan drove his feet against his chosen stone. It gave way beneath his assault, grinding free of its position in the wall. For a hovering instant, nothing happened. Dysan opened his eyes, immediately assaulted by lime and rain. His anger dispersed with the suddenness of a startled flock of birds, and he abruptly realized his danger. "Shite!" He scrambled backward as the entire wall collapsed, and stone exploded around him.

A boulder crashed against Dysan's wrist, sparing his face but sending pain screaming through his arm. More rumbled onto his legs, one caught him on the hip, and another smashed into his abdomen with enough force to drive air through his teeth. Then, the assault ended. The world descended into an unnatural silence, gradually broken by a growing chorus of night insects.

Dysan assessed his injuries. His arm hurt, the rubble pinned his legs, and pain ached through his hip. Cautiously, he wriggled from beneath the pile, stones rolling from his legs and raising a new crop of dust. Gingerly, he rose, careful not to put any weight on his left hand. His legs held him, though his weight ground pain through his right shin. Teeth gritted, he limped toward his bed, unable to fully savor what had become a bitter victory, and wished he had chosen the slower course.

Dysan awakened to a string of coarse swearing. He lay still, heart pounding, limbs aching, and forced himself to remember the previous night. Wedged into his blanketed crevice between the ceiling beams, he looked down on the Yard. The stoneworkers stood surveying the scattered stones that had once formed the beginnings of a wall far sturdier than the previous adobe. This time, two women accompanied them: one the gray-haired matron he had seen yesterday, the other a middle-aged dark blonde with a bewildered expression.

The apprentice paced with balled fists. "Gods all be froggin' sure damn! I don't froggin' believe this!"

"Watch your tongue, boy. There're ladies present." The mason's familiar words had become a mantra.

"The wind?" the younger woman suggested softly, with the same Imperial accent as her companion. "Perhaps it—"

The apprentice stopped pacing to whirl and face the women. He seemed beyond controlling his language. "Shite-for-sure, this ain't done by no wind. There weren't enough froggin' wind last night to take down a froggin' hay pile."

Apparently giving up on curbing his apprentice's swearing, the mason leaned against one of the solid walls. "Don't pay him any mind, ladies. Lost his mother young and raised by a foul-mouthed father."

The gray-haired woman ran her gaze around the entire area. "I don't hire builders for their sweet manners. And, like I keep saying, I don't understand a word he says anyway."

The younger woman blushed. Apparently, she did. "So how did it come down?"

The mason ran a meaty hand through black hair liberally flecked with gray. "Someone worked, and worked hard, to bring this down."

The younger woman glanced at the older, who pulled at her lower lip and examined the carnage thoughtfully. "Who?"

The apprentice threw up his hands and walked toward the mule cart, filled with new building stone.

"Don't know," the mason admitted. "It's never happened before, and I'm not sure what anyone would get out of it except the pleasure of watching me and Makla do the whole thing again."

The older woman looked up suddenly, hazel eyes darting, gaze sweeping the ceiling. Dysan froze, hoping she could not make out his shadow against the cracks, that his eyes were not as visible to her as hers to him. He had the benefits of darkness, of solid wood and blankets, of familiarity and utter stillness; but he could not help feeling as if the woman's cold eyes pinned him solidly to the beams. Yet, if the woman noticed him, she gave no sign.

The mason set to regathering stones, and the apprentice swiftly joined him.

"A prank?" the younger woman suggested.

"Sheep—" the apprentice started, cut off by the mason's abrupt gesture.

The mason turned to her, head shaking. "Possible. But a lot of effort for some dumb pud out looking for a frayed purse string." He went back to his work, straightening those base stones still in place.

For several moments, the men worked in silence before the younger woman tried again. "An enemy, perhaps?"

The mason checked the alignment while his young apprentice hurled the most widely scattered rocks back toward the damaged wall. "Haven't got any I know of." He rose, walked to the other side, and eyeballed the construction from the opposite side. "Got a son who's made a few, but he's out smashing stone for another project. His are the type who'd walk right up and plant a fist in your face, not ruin a day's work then hide like cess rats."

"Froggin' cowards," the apprentice muttered, barely loud enough for Dysan to hear.

Dysan smiled at the insult. He was used to worse.

The mason finally gave his full attention to the women again. "Begging your pardons, but not everyone's happy to see someone new come to the Promise of Heaven. Memories of . . . the Hand and all."

Though not his motive, Dysan had to agree. He hated the Dyareelans and mistrusted the ruling Irrune, the victims of most of his spying; but he had no grievance with the established religions of Ilsigi and Ranke. He remained unmoving, watching the interaction unfold beneath him.

The gray-haired woman stiffened. The other's mouth dropped open, and no words emerged for several moments. Finally, she managed, "But we're not a temple—"

The older woman took her arm. "No, SaMavis, but we are dedicated believers. A passerby could assume." She smiled at the mason—at least Dysan thought she did. Her mouth pulled outward more than upward. "Whoever did it seems like an opportunist rather than someone willing to take credit or blame for his actions. Despite his presentation, I believe the young man is right. Our vandal is a coward. He wouldn't dare bother our mason, and he's not likely to touch the wall while we're here either."

"Ma'am," the mason started. "It might not be safe for a group of women . . ." As the older woman's attention settled grimly upon him, he trailed off. "I just mean it—"

The woman's tone held ice. "I know what you mean. But we've bought this place, and here we will build. We'll eventually have to live here, women that we are. What will we have then that we don't have now?"

"Walls?" the apprentice suggested.

Dysan swallowed a laugh, his course already clear.

He would let the stoneworkers build their walls and repair the leaky ceiling. Once he chased the newcomers away, he would have a fine home for which he did not have to pay a padpol.

"We have the blessing of sweet Sabellia. She chose this place for us, and She does nothing without reason."

Dysan did not recall a visit from any goddess. In fact, they had not answered the prayers of any of the orphans trapped in the Dyareelan Pits. He wondered how so many fanatical worshipers convinced themselves that their god or goddess held a personal interest in the mundane doings of any human's day. Had he not committed himself to statue-like stillness, he would have rolled his eyes in disdain.

The mason went back to work without another word. To argue his point would only anger his clients, which tended to hamper payment. Dysan remained stock-still and planned his next strike.

Dysan watched the women move basic packs and provisions to the Yard, counting five, all with Imperial accents. The youngest appeared a decade older than Dysan, the oldest the solemn woman who had handled their business with the stonemason and his apprentice. Their hair colors ranged from gray to medium brown, their features chiseled and fine, their skin Rankan ivory without a hint of Ilsigi swarthiness. Dysan waited until the stoneworkers took a break and the women disappeared to gather more of their belongings. Their conversation had revealed that they did not expect the vandal to return until after nightfall, so Dysan seized the opportunity.

Slipping from his hiding place as quietly as any cat, Dysan glided around the crawl space, which al-

lowed him a bird's eye view of every angle in and
near the ruins. No one hovered around the two still-
standing adobe walls, behind the new construction,
around the collected stones where the mule grazed
on twisted shoots jutting between the debris. Attuned to the slightest sound, Dysan spiraled through
shadows toward the packs. He trusted his senses to
warn him of any traps and his intuition of any
magic. Those things alone had never failed him.

No stranger to thievery, Dysan scanned through
the packs quicker than most people could pour out
their contents, disturbing little in the process. He
discovered blankets with embroidered patterns,
dresses of simple design yet without holes or fraying,
dried travel foods that might suffice for sustenance
but little more, not worth stealing. He did find three
soldats and a scattering of padpols. Dysan shoveled
these into one purse without counting, which always
gave him a headache. When others occasionally
hired him and asked his charge, he always answered,
"Five," leaving the denomination to the client. So
far, he had received only padpols. If a man ever paid
him in anything bigger, he would know it reflected
a more difficult, valuable, or dangerous assignment.
He tucked the purse in his waist band, covered it
with the remnants of his shirt, and tried to minimize
the bulge.

Finishing in scant moments, Dysan slipped
around the walls and onto the Avenue of Temples.
Even in broad daylight, he found little company on
the street. Every altar desecrated, every priest bru-
tally massacred, every wall blood-splattered or
smashed reminded the inhabitants of the worst of
Dyareela. The inner shards of the broken walls of
Dysan's home still held paint that had once probably fit together as a mural depicting some pantheon

and its miracles. The altar contained stains that reeked of urine and sex, blood and death; and he had disposed of lumps of animal and human feces left where valuables had once sat as offerings. Even those gods who might bother returning to Sanctuary could want nothing to do with the defiled remnants of their once great temples. Except, apparently, a small, confused group of Rankan women.

Dysan kept to the smaller alleyways, preferring to risk robbery over the need to exchange small talk. Though he had lived his entire life here, few knew his face and only a handful his name. Though he had kept "Dysan" throughout his life, a tribute to Kharmael, he could see no reason why anyone from his past would recognize it. He had seen the corpses of the other orphans buried by strangers. If others had survived the Pits, and he had heard rumors that a few had, they must have escaped before the poisoning and the fire. Reportedly, the Dyareelans had been destroyed to a man; and good riddance. He only wished they could have suffered the same terror, the same protracted and agonizing deaths they had inflicted on so many others.

A cold breeze touched sweat trickling along Dysan's spine, shocking him with an icy shiver. He shoved the thoughts aside before they could spark to flashback. He had suffered enough of that in the years following his escape; they had plagued him nearly to suicide. Grim focus had finally given him dominion over the leaps and lapses of his thoughts, but it required him to become attuned with body and mind, with the first indications that memory was rising toward rebellion. Only in his dreams could it still catch him unprotected, but even those had become rare in the last several years.

Dark men hidden deeply in shadow paid less at-

tention to Dysan than he did to them. He seemed
a most unlikely and unnecessary target in his bare
feet and tattered clothing. He knew how to draw
attention away from his hidden purse, how to let the
others know he saw them without giving away their
concealment, how to listen while seeming distant
and disinterested. This language, too, he knew, the
one that kept a small man alive on dangerous
streets.

Dysan also knew where to take his money, the
only place he trusted to give him a fair exchange
for his coins or for the merchandise he acquired.
As he trotted past the Maze, he realized the time
had come to enter it again, too. He had spent a lot
of time there with the Hand, usually in the Vulgar
Unicorn; but, in the last ten years, he went only often enough to keep tabs on the shifting landscape,
or when hired business brought him there. Though
great places for information, he otherwise found taverns boring. Strangers saw him as a child. He rarely
found himself invited directly into discussions or
games of chance, and the barmaids usually diluted
his drinks to water. He had learned to appreciate
that, as his slightness gave him little body mass to
offset even one full-strength beer, but it also gave
him nothing much to savor.

Dysan turned onto Wriggle Way and headed for
the shop of Bezul the Changer. A pair of women
passed him, discussing intended purchases in the
market. He heard more than watched a dark-clad
figure slink into the Maze. Ignoring them, Dysan
tripped the gate latch and headed into the shop
yard. He had taken only three steps when an enormous, muddy goose waddled from behind a bush
with a snake-like hiss followed by a honk loud
enough to wake the dead. More geese answered in

ringing echoes from the back courtyard. Dysan turned his quiet saunter into a run for the door, the goose honking, flapping, and biting at his heels.

Dysan charged into the changer's shop, attempting to slam the door without breaking the goose's neck. But the huge bird crashed in behind him, and the door banged shut an instant too late. Loose in the shop, the goose ran in crazed circles, huge wings walloping the air into whirlwinds and sweeping a line of crockery from a low table. Clay pots spilled to the floor, some smashing, some clomping hollowly against wood and tile. Shards scattered like frightened spiders.

Bezul scrambled from behind a table where he had been servicing a customer. "No! No!" His sandy disarray of hair looked even more tousled than usual, and he moved spryly for a man in his late thirties. He rushed the goose.

Dysan threw the door back open, hoping no one expected him to pay for the damage. He had no idea of the value of such things, but he had enough trouble keeping himself in food and clothing.

The customer back-stepped, presumably to steer clear of the growing wreckage, but stepped on a crockery shard. Balance teetering, he flailed, lost the battle, and landed on his backside. A thrown-out arm barely missed the row of empty jars and vials he had been examining a moment earlier.

The fall drew Dysan's attention even more than the goose, now hissing and squealing as it raced back into the yard, a step ahead of Bezul's broom. The stranger appeared to be nearing thirty, tall, with wiry black hair veined with white. Unlike most graying men, the lighter hairs did not congregate at his temples but seemed chaotically sprinkled, as if someone had dumped a scoop of wheat flour on his head. He had blue eyes, brighter than Dysan's own but cast into shadow by prominent ridges. The long face and solemn features looked familiar, and Dysan took an involuntary, shocked step backward. He knew this man, or would have, had he sported a seething cacophony of tattoos. Like all of the Dyareelan priests, the man Dysan thought he recognized would have had arms as red as the blood ritually and gleefully splattered in the name of his goddess. That man had also worn permanent swirls of flame, numbers, and names plastered across his face and body.

Stop it! Dysan chastised his imagination. He had not projected an image of the Hand over an innocent in years. He shook his head to clear it, just as Bezul returned, leaving the door open as a welcome to customers. Dysan tried to apologize for letting the goose in, but his tongue stuck to the roof of his mouth.

As if nothing had happened, Bezul leaned his broom against a display and approached the stranger. "Were we finished, Pel?"

"Yes," Pel said, his gaze on Dysan, his voice too gentle and deliberate to have ever served the Hand. "We're finished."

Dysan knelt and started picking up pieces of broken crockery, feigning excessive interest in his work.

"I think the boy's a bit shaken by your deadly man-eating attack goose."

"Who, Dysan?" Bezul's attention turned to him, much to Dysan's chagrin. "He's a regular. Not the first goose he's tangled with, eh Dys?"

Dysan hated when Bezul shortened his name. It reminded him that the first two letters matched those of the goddess he despised.

When Dysan did not back-banter, Bezul's tone

changed to one of concern. "You all right, boy?"

"Eh, Bez," Dysan returned belatedly, though Bezul was already a shortened form of the man's name: Bezulshash. "I thought you locked those nasty critters up during the day."

"Must have missed one." It was the standard answer. It seemed like Bezul always forgot a goose or two when he shooed them from the main yard in the morning. Usually, they had the common sense not to follow someone inside the shop.

Dysan swept the clay shards into a pile so he did not have to force a smile. He owed no one an explanation, especially not in Sanctuary, but he still felt obligated to say something. He forced himself to look up. Then, uncertain what to do with his now-free hands, he rubbed his nose with a not-quite casual gesture. "It wasn't the goose. It was the thought of who's going to have to pay for this." He made a gesture that encompassed those shards that had escaped his crude attempt at cleaning.

Bezul shrugged off the concern. "My goose. My mistake."

Pel headed for the door, and Dysan gave him plenty of space. "We'll all pay for it, ultimately." He looked down at the younger man from a frame at least a third again as tall as Dysan's and winked. "You, me, everyone. Believe me."

Bezul neither confirmed nor contradicted as Pel left the shop. He watched the man down the pathway and through the gate before turning to Dysan, who had slowly risen. "So, what can I get for you today?"

Dysan knew he ought to make small talk before launching into business, but jokes about shins bruised by the goose might force him to display the real ones he had gotten from falling building stones.

He could ask about Bezul's mother, wife, and children; but he always sounded nervous when he did. Chatter made him uncomfortable; and, under the circumstances, he preferred to stick with the familiar. "I need something to put on my feet." He raised a bare foot, then returned it to the floor, careful to avoid the piled shards of clay. "Some live rats or mice. A couple of snakes."

Bezul's brows crept upward. "You're keeping odd pets these days, Dysan." He did not question; Bezul never questioned. But he left the point hanging if Dysan wished to discuss it further.

Dysan gave an evasive answer. "Need more meat in my diet." Knowing what he could buy depended on what he had to exchange for it, Dysan untied the purse and spilled its contents on the counter.

Bezul's head bent over the coins, revealing pale scalp where his hair had begun its southward march. He picked up the soldats, separating them from the padpols. "Not pure, but decent. Worth about—"

Dysan stayed the Changer with a raised hand. "Just tell me what I can get with it. Something for my feet. And those critters I mentioned."

Bezul straightened. "Right." An almost imperceptible grin touched the corners of his mouth. By now, he had to know Dysan preferred not to count money or deal with much in the way of change. They both scanned the outer shelves, filled with an assortment of bric-a-brac that spanned the length and breadth of Dysan's imagination. Pots and mugs sat beside foodstuffs, trinkets, books, and artwork, much of it filmed with a layer of dust. As he headed for the back room, Bezul made a quick grab that knocked a neat pile of linen askew. He emerged with a writhing black snake clutched behind the head. He held it up in triumph, then took it with him as he disappeared into the back.

Dysan planted his elbows on the table and buried his face in his hands. Too tired even to glance around the shop, he closed his eyes and savored the moments of dark aloneness. His mind glided toward those empty moments prior to sleep.

Safely ensconced in his hiding place above the Yard ceiling, Dysan watched the drama unfolding beneath him. The stonemason and his apprentice had finished, leaving the beginnings of a wall a bit bigger than the one from the night before and securely mortared. The women sat around a controlled circle of fire, the flickering oranges, reds, and ambers casting dancing shadows along the walls and their faces.

In the firelight, the oldest looked more world-weary than wise and dangerous. The middle-aged, dark blonde she had called SaMavis moved with jerky motions that seemed nervous, and she glanced around the Yard as if she expected an abrupt visit from a pack of starved and wild dogs. Dysan examined the others, gleaning their names from occasional bursts that rose above their quiet conversation. They called the old woman SaVell or Raivay SaVell or just the Raivay, which was, apparently, a title of respect. The youngest was a pretty brunette in her twenties named SaKimarza. The last two were non-descript, heavyset women in their early thirties who could have passed for twins: SaShayka and SaParnith.

Dysan had to strain to catch even spatterings of their conversations. They talked softly, mostly in Rankene. Occasionally, they spoke more intimately in a self-styled syntax that resembled the Court style of Rankan aristocrats, one of the first languages the

Hand had taught him. Most Wrigglies would find those portions of their talks incomprehensible, though anything based on Rankene came as easily to Dysan as counting did not. The only languages that had given him any trouble at all were the cryptic, unnamed, and evolving dialects of spies and thieves. However, when the women slipped into their personal tongue, they also tended to drop their volume. What Dysan did manage to catch concerned watches and guarding, fears about an attack, speculation about the person or people who had destroyed their wall in the night.

Though Dysan tried to stay above it all, in attitude as well as position, he could not help smiling. He had only received this much attention when he reported conversations overheard in various tunnels and taverns to his handlers. Normally, he shied from notice, preferring anonymity. But, perhaps because these were women and he had never managed to win over his mother, this felt right. The fact that he had had to commit a crime to attract them did send a twinge through him. Kharmael would not approve, yet Dysan knew he had to keep focused on his mission. These women were invaders; and, one way or another, he would repel them.

The aromas of roasting spiced tubers and venison brought saliva to Dysan's mouth despite the full meal, cold and tasteless, that the women's money had bought him. He had gotten his boots, scuffed outside and smoothed inside by the child who had worn them before him, but still the best footgear he had ever owned. A new linen shirt, at least three sizes too big, joined the tatters of his regular clothing, along with britches he had to tie up with a belt looped three times around his waist. He had exchanged the women's purse for another, in case he had to deny the theft. Even with the five padpols change, Bezul said Dysan had squared the cheap pottery and its thorough clean-up. Apparently, he had stolen a fortune from these women, yet they seemed not to have noticed. Or, if they did, they had done their screaming and shouting in his absence.

The blankets felt snug and greasy against Dysan's skin, warmed by the fire. He closed his eyes, limiting his concentration to one sense, the one he so often wholly relied upon, his hearing. The women's conversations turned to the mundane. Desperately shy on rest, Dysan slid into sleep without realizing it, awakened moments later by a shrill scream of terror. Only well-ingrained training kept him from springing to his feet and braining himself on the crawl space. Instead, he jerked opened his eyes and aimed them at the sound. Movement caught his vision first, a mouse scampering for freedom and a snake sidling with surprising speed for a creature lacking legs. SaShayka clutched her gear in trembling hands, her features paler than usual, her gaze locked on the fleeing snake. SaMavis stood on the stones surrounding the fire, hand clutched to her chest. The other three women stared at them.

As usual, the Raivay took control, clapping her hands for attention. "Ladies, please! Control yourselves. They're just little animals."

SaShayka hurled her things to the ground, and another mouse scrambled out, running jerkily into the night. "Those aren't little animals," she said, with a yip. "They're horrid little vermin and slimy, repulsive serpents." She shuddered. "Disgusting."

Once again, Raivay SaVell's sharp yellow gaze swept the interior and seemed to ferret out Dysan where he lay. He scarcely dared to breathe but could not stop a cold shiver that twisted through him despite blankets that still held his body heat. "Disgusting they may be, but we'll see many more, I'd warrant. Now, ladies. Each of you take an end of your bedrolls and shake. And don't be surprised if you find valuables missing."

The women obeyed, some with clear timidity and others with the apparent intent of dislodging a herd of mules. Clothing and foodstuffs, blankets, personal toiletries, sacks, and even jewelry flew through the partially enclosed room, along with the mice, lizards, frogs, and snakes that had not skittered out of their own accord since Dysan had placed them there. All of the animals ran scared, disappearing into the darkness while the women unfolded every shift and emptied every pouch to assure they would not deliberately share their beds with creatures of the creeping variety.

The youngest, SaKimarza, switched to their private dialect. "Our invader?"

SaVell nodded once. "Undoubtedly."

SaMavis sorted her things back together and ran a comb through her locks. She returned the conversation to standard Rankene. "If the excitement is over for the night, I suggest we get some sleep."

"Indeed," SaVell said, gesturing to the others to collect their belongings and find a suitable location. "Watches as discussed. The guard will be mostly responsible for tending the fire, as I think our welcoming party has performed his cowardly evil for the night."

Dysan suffered a flash of angry pain at the insult. He did not like the words *cowardly* or *evil* ascribed to him, though both currently fit. They had left him little choice, five against one, commandeering his home without so much as an apology. Though women, every one stood taller and heavier than him, and it might take him forever to earn the money to buy them out. He did work the occasional odd job, but no one would hire his scrawny self for manual labor. They could always find someone larger, stronger, more personable to do the job. The anonymity necessary to perform Dysan's true calling well also kept the vast majority of people from knowing he existed for hire. Even those who learned of him often balked when they saw him, assuming him an unsophisticated child, unsuitable for such intricate assignments. In a life where his clothes wore out faster than he could replace them, where he went to bed hungry as often as not, where a grimy blanket worn threadbare served as his only constant source of warmth, he could scarcely help turning to the darker side of himself for sustenance and solace. At the worst of times, he sometimes wondered if the Irrune had done him any favors by destroying the Dyareelans. At least they had kept him alive with a daily warm meal, a place by the fire, and herbs when the raw fogs of Sanctuary crept deep into his lungs.

Dysan always knew he had reached bottom when those thoughts oozed into his mind. At those times, he warmed himself with rage. Those few and regular comforts had come at an unbearable price. And, he knew, the Hand only tended his illnesses because they found use for his talent. If it had ever failed him, if they had found another who could do it better, if they had no longer needed his services, they would have sacrificed him as blithely and easily as any goat and taken ruthless pleasure in the experience.

Dysan watched the women preen and dress for bed. The girls among the orphans had taught him propriety by slapping or kicking him when he dared to peek at them unclothed. The more jaded ones either did not care or might charge him in a murderous rage. It became vitally important to discern which and, after his brother had rescued him twice, easier not to look at any of them in a vulnerable state. Dysan had finally grown old enough to find women more than just a curiosity, but his body had not caught up to his mind and probably never would. He had long ago resigned himself to the permanent height of a seven-year-old but found himself wistful again as he passed into the second half of his teens. He doubted any woman would ever take him seriously as a partner, not even the girls in the Unicorn; and anyway, the idea of paying for it reminded him too much of his mother.

At length, all the women, except SaParnith, settled in for the night. She kept herself busy throwing an occasional log on the fire, staring out at the stars, and laboring over a knot of rope work in her lap. Dysan had no trouble sneaking down from his loft to the outside, then creeping soundlessly behind SaParnith. He distinguished the breathing of each woman, four naturally and blissfully asleep and one calmly awake. Cautiously, he dipped the end of SaParnith's bedroll into the fire. She took no notice of him either when he slipped away, clambered back into position, and watched the results through a space in the ceiling timbers.

The cloth took longer than he expected to ignite. Gradually, wisps of smoke condensed into a billow. He watched long enough to see a flame appear amidst the smoke. Smiling, he settled back into position, with every intention of observing the drama unfolding beneath him. Then, exhaustion ambushed Dysan, claiming watchfulness and consciousness alike.

Dysan dreamt of another fire. The past flooded into
a dawn memory of men dragging out the bodies of
dead orphans, speaking sorrowfully about these
soulless babies, hopelessness, and parental dreams
dashed. Several cried or made gestures he did not
understand. Somehow, he managed to drag his un-
responsive brother to a crevice, to cram Kharmael
inside, to hide himself in a nearby hole. He watched
in horror as the men gathered the children's meager possessions, the remainder of their feast, the bits
and shards of remaining Dyareelan might, and set
the pile ablaze. Finally, the men retreated.

Only then did Dysan dare to squirm from his
hiding place. Those flames had roared to life with
a suddenness that caught him wholly off-guard.
Smoke funneled into his lungs like a living thing,
solid and suffocating. He ran for the nearest exit,
dragging Kharmael into a wild column of flame
consuming the doorway, searing his face, wringing
tears from his eyes only to dry them with heat
an instant later. Gasping like a beached fish, he
sprinted blindly back the way he had come, losing
his grip on his brother.

Kharmael! Dysan tried to shout, but the flames
burned his lungs, and his throat felt as raw as cin-
ders. He took a step forward, tripping over something solid. *Kharmael?* He reached for the body,
blistering his hands on blazing linen. He jerked
backward, sobbing, trying to find bearings that the
now impenetrable smoke would not allow. His mind
grew desperately fuzzy. He ran in a tight circle, then
forced himself to struggle onward, to leave Kharmael's flaming body behind. *He's dead. Dead.* Dysan's
overwhelmed mind could not comprehend that any
more than the realization that the only existence he

knew had ended. He waded through smoke and flame, guided only by instinct that sent him always to where the smoke thinned, where the air felt coolest. His brother's death had only just penetrated when he realized that he, too, would die.

Dysan struggled forward into another wall of fire that ignited his clothes.

Dysan awakened screaming for the first time in seven years. He heard the echoes of his own cry bouncing from the loft and clamped a hand over his mouth to keep from loosing another. His heart slammed in his chest, and his breath wheezed out in frenzied gasps. *It's all right. I found the window. I'm alive.* Dysan measured his breathing, felt his heart rate slow. Then, another sound trickled to his ears, familiar but unplaceable. Just as he finally recognized it as priestly magic, the floor collapsed beneath him.

Air surged around Dysan, and he felt himself falling. Before he could think to do anything, before he could even untangle himself from the blanket, he hit the ground with an impact that shot pain through his shoulder, hip, and gut, stealing his breath. For a moment his eyes and lungs refused to work. Darkness closed over him, filled with spots and squiggles. Then, a sharp spiral of agony swung through him. His lungs spasmed open, taking in air, and his gaze revealed a circle of five women amidst a shattered fire and a pile of billowing ash.

"It's a child," SaParnith said.

SaMavis's sooty face softened, and she made a high-pitched syrupy noise. "He's so cute."

"Adorable," SaShayka agreed.

Too stunned and hurt to move, Dysan remained still and let them talk around him.

SaKimarza brushed back the knotted clump of his hair to look into his face. "You're injured, little boy. Tell me where it hurts?"

Dysan found himself unable to focus on that. Pain seemed to envelop all his parts, and he was more concerned with what these women planned to do with him. Nothing made sense, especially his captors cooing over him like a flock of mother hens. He rolled his eyes to Raivay SaVell, who studied him with equal intent and silence.

The other four began to talk at once, while SaKimarza rummaged through a cloth sack. "Poor little one." "I hope we didn't hurt him too badly." "You don't think he's really the one—"

The Raivay broke in. "Of course he's the one. Remember, sisters, child or not, he's the rat we caught in our trap."

"He's the one who—" SaShayka started.

"Yes."

"This child—" she started again.

"Yes."

All of the women went quiet, studying Dysan. Still uncertain what to do or say, he remained still. He measured the distance to the door with his gaze but knew pain would slow him too much to try. Sleep, slight as it was, had stiffened his wounds from the collapsed stonework; and the fall had reawakened every ache. He had landed on the same hip the toppling rocks had pummeled, and he worried for the bone. Bruises mottled his legs, his wrist ached, and his shoulder felt on fire.

The women switched to their private language; but, this time, Dysan could hear each word. He darted glances in every direction, only partially feigning fear and pretending not to understand them.

SaMavis never took her eyes from Dysan. "What do we do now?"

SaKimarza continued to search her sack. "Find out why he did it. Fix him up. Go from there." She laid out a row of crocks and bottles, and a mouse skittered from the linen. She jerked backward, and a frown scored a face pretty with youth.

SaParnith dropped to her haunches. "I say we scare him off for good. Threaten to . . . sacrifice him to Sabellia or something."

SaMavis gasped. "Sacrilege! Sabellia doesn't take blood—"

A grin stretched SaParnith's face. Though probably intended to appear wicked, it did not measure up to what the Hand priests could manage with the rise of a single brow. Their eyes had always given them away, and SaParnith's pale brown orbs lacked that dangerous gleam of cruelty. "He won't know that. After what the people here have suffered, he won't doubt—"

Raivay SaVell interrupted. "That's exactly what we don't want. Any comparison to the evil that nearly destroyed this place, nearly turned them all against the gods. Sabellia sent us here." She made a stabbing motion at the ground to indicate the building, then a broader gesture that encompassed all of Sanctuary. "Here—to spread the word and greatness of Sabellia to the women of this . . . this city."

Dysan thought he caught a hint of contempt in her tone, a common reaction of foreigners to Sanctuary for reasons he did not have the information to understand.

"I just—" SaParnith started.

But SaVell had not finished. "Money has corrupted the highest priestesses in Ranke, and Sabellia sent us here to win over the hearts of Sanctuary's women honestly—with selflessness and good deeds, not by terrorizing children."

SaMavis stirred a finger through the sodden ashes. "Imagine what this boy would tell his parents. The Dyareelans have left these people suspicious enough of religion inside their walls. Remember, those bloodthirsty monsters, too, started with good works and charity."

SaShayka leapt to her feet. "But ours is genuine!"

"I'm sure the Dyareelans' seemed that way, too—at first." SaMavis looked up at SaShayka. "Otherwise, they couldn't have grabbed so much power so quickly."

SaVell still studied Dysan, her yellow eyes vital for one so old and their intensity unnerving. "We can discuss this later. We have another matter to deal with now." Finally, she switched to Ilsigi. "Boy, why did you set our things on fire?"

"Maybe I didn't." Dysan restored the brisk stop-and-start inflection to the bastard Wrigglie language. "Maybe you just put your old junk too close to the flames." Fatigue slowed his thoughts and pain made him hostile; yet, at the same time, he felt dangerously vulnerable.

"Maybe nothing." SaVell's gaze remained unwavering. "Ah, so you want to do this the hard way." She raised an arm.

Dysan flinched.

As the old woman came no closer, and she did not strike him, Dysan turned his attention to her. A tingle passed through him, and he recognized it instantly as priestly sorcery. He had seen his share of it in front of altars writhing with human bodies or dripping with their blood. This time, he saw no illusions, felt none of the crushing evil that accompanied the summoning of Dyareela's power. This time, it seemed to cleanse him, to strip away the layers of grime that darkened and protected him. His thoughts floated backward, not to the blows, physical and verbal, of his handlers but to the warm solace of his brother's arms.

The whole proved too much for Dysan. Tears stung his eyes, and he confessed in a whisper, "I live here." The words raised a power and anger all his own, and he rammed through the pain to make his point. "You're going to take away my home. My home!" He rolled his gaze to the ceiling, where the boards hung in jagged disarray, revealing the hole that had once served as his bed. Those timbers had remained solid all this time; he tested them daily. Only sorcery could have caused them to fail instantaneously and without a hint of warning. SaVell had made him fall, and Sabellia had granted her the power, had sanctioned that decision.

Before Dysan knew it, he found himself cocooned in warm arms, pressed against an ample bosom, and rocked like an infant. He did not fight, just went limp in the embrace, let her body heat wash over him in a wave of soothing he would not have imagined contact with some stranger might fulfill. She smelled clean and of some sweet spice he could not identify.

The Raivay's voice shattered the sanctity of the moment, struggling to mimic his coarse Wrigglie dialect. "We are building our Sisterhood here."

Dysan anticipated a flash of anger that never came. He knew better than to trust himself to make significant decisions when fatigue and pain muffled his thoughts, just as he knew better than to fall asleep in a house with an uncontrolled fire. Yet, tonight, he did both. Adopting the Rankene variation the women had used, he spoke in a perfect rendition of an Imperial accent. "I know Sabellia doesn't take human sacrifices, and I don't have parents to which to tell anything."

Startled, the woman dropped Dysan. He tensed to keep his balance, the abrupt movement driving pain through him. Cold air washed over Dysan, and he realized SaMavis had been the one embracing him.

Even SaVell's nostrils flared, though she gave no other sign of her surprise.

"How . . . ?" SaParnith stammered. "How . . . ?" When the words still did not follow, she changed the question. "You don't . . . look . . . Rankan."

Dysan glanced between the women's shocked faces and wondered if he had made the right decision. "I'm Wrigglie. But I do all right with pretty much any language." He could tell by the bewilderment still pasted on their faces that his explanation had not wholly satisfied them.

Finally, SaKimarza explained, "But that language belongs to our Sisterhood. Only us and Sabellia—"

SaVell leapt in, as she so often did. "Sabellia picked this city, this building." Though not a real explanation, it served well enough. Even Dysan understood that she believed Sabellia had cast his lot with theirs on purpose, had filled in any blanks between his natural bent toward languages and the Rankene code-speech that served this order.

Dysan shivered at the loss of control. That anyone might take over his mind and actions chilled him to the marrow, and the understanding that she was a goddess did not make him any more comfortable. He had been so young when the Bloody Hand, and perhaps Dyareela, owned and shaped him; and he had spent the last decade assuring himself that he answered to no one unless he freely chose to do so.

He had done some stupid things in the last two days: positioning himself to get crushed by stones, falling asleep near fire, allowing a dream to take over his common sense. Yet, he felt certain all of those mistakes were his own, not attempts by anyone to consume him. The association felt right, secure. Five mothers for the one he had never really known and Grandmother Sabellia. None of these could ever truly take the place of the brother he so desperately missed, but any seemed better than ten more years of loneliness.

"So what do we do?" SaShayka finally said. Though soft and gentle, her voice seemed to boom into the lengthy silence.

They all looked at Dysan.

"I think," he said carefully, "I could be talked into sharing." He had no real power in this negotiation. Ten years of living in this ruin meant absolutely nothing compared with the money the women had spent to buy and restore it. Nevertheless, he continued to bargain. "I don't do heavy labor, but I can crawl into small spaces that need checking or fixing. And I'm very good at listening."

SaVcll smiled. This time, her face opened fully, and her eyes sparkled. Beneath the gruff exterior, apparently, lurked a good heart. "I don't suppose you could use a few hot meals a day, a home with walls, and a bed without a gaping hole in the bottom."

"I might find use for such things." Dysan managed a smile of his own. "Welcome to my home."

"Our home," Raivay SaVell corrected as Sa-Kimarza examined Dysan's wounds. "Our home."

Role Model
A Tale of Apprentices

Andrew Offutt

"Better that all such cocky snotty stealthy arrogant bravos
were stillborn."
—Shive the Changer

"Me and my Shadowspawn, skulkin' down the
Serpentine . . ."
—Bill Sutton

High of ceiling and sparse of furnishings, the
room was half again as long as it was wide. Its illumination was provided by a pair of matching oil
lamps, each cast in bronze and resting on a three-
legged table at an opposite end of the chamber. The
failure of the yellowish light they provided to do
more than hint at the arcane drawings and runes
on the two longer walls seemed a tease. Both were
covered with a medley of intricate, often grotesque
ornamentation. Included were fanciful fauna and
ornately overblown flora, some with elaborately,
even impossibly twining foliage; birds real and un-

lewdly portrayed lovers with bodies and limbs twining but a little less intricately than floral vines; serpents' flowers; medallions and completely untranslatable runic designs. The lamps were fashioned in the likeness of gargoyles so preposterously hideous that no sensible person could believe they were anything but fanciful.

Yet perhaps not, for one of the two men in the room was their owner, and his trade and life's work was sorcery. Such a one might be capable of summoning up such demons from one of the Seven Hells, might he not? He—Kusharlonikas—was a few months past his one-hundred-first birthday, with a face like a wizened large prune bleached to the color of parchment tastelessly decorated with orangey-brown spots. On the vain side as well as still a sexual being, Kusharlonikas the mage chose, understandably, not to show his true likeness—except when he elected to "wear" the age-overused face as a disguise.

On this auspicious night in his keep of keeps the master mage affected the likeness of a man of forty, neither handsome nor un-, with luxurious and wavy auburn hair above eyes like chips of greenest jade and a bushy, droopy mustache. Yet he wore a long robe, a deep rich green bordered with gold at hem and neck and sleeve-ends, for even an intemperate devotee of the arcane did have the devil's own time disguising his ancient legs with their knobby knees and varicose veins.

The other man in this, Kusharlonikas's Chamber of Reflection and Divination, was aware of the mage's age and appearance, for he was Kusharlonikas's apprentice. He was a long-faced and lamentably homely fellow with hair the color of straw— old straw, and subjected to dampness—who was close onto but not quite five-and-twenty years of age. His seeming copy-cat robe of lime green did not require much cloth, for he was both short and slight of build. Indeed, the largest thing about him was his name, which was Komodoflorensal.

His master stood at one end of a long table of polished hardwood topped with a narrow runner of olive green cloth, well napped and tasseled in gold at either hanging end. He stood moveless, with his hands behind his back, bony left wrist clasped in a right hand burdened with three rings, one of them outsize. Its large brown set seemed to be, oddly, a buckeye. As if listening intently, he stood gazing down at the table, which bore three objects.

One was a large, two-handled flagon of some greenish metal that appeared to have little worth. Another was a wooden stick not quite the thickness of a little finger and some two feet long. It bore no bark, and yet did not have a peeled appearance. The third object was fashioned in the shape of an hourglass, but it was not; its sand was but a quarter-hour's worth.

The younger man with the name too long and the robe too bright stood opposite his master, at the opposite end of the table. A film of perspiration glistened on his face and hands. He had been muttering and gesturing arcanely for over a minute. The hand with which he did most of his gesturing bore a ring with a large setting: an object that was at least the color and shape of a buckeye.

"Let us hope no one menaces you when you are at your spelling," his master said, with no seeming regard for distracting the young man, "for you have given an intruder or foeman plenty of time to lay you low."

Had a third person been present in the room, the

sudden seeming shiver of the wooden stick would surely have attracted his attention, not to have mentioned raised a few nape hairs. Inanimate object or no, it appeared almost to writhe. A moment later the master mage winced, seemingly at one of his apprentice's gestures or words. At the same time, a drop of sweat fell from the tip of the nose of that effortful mage-to-be. And Komodoflorensal uttered a final word rather explosively, at the same time jerking his gesture-hand, and visibly sagged, as if having exhausted himself.

"*Iffets!*"

The wooden stick returned to motionlessness, but the quarter-hourglass fell over onto its side.

Komodoflorensal sighed and sagged even more pronouncedly, and watched his master gesture.

"Idiot!" Kusharlonikas said, while in response to his single, almost casual gesture, the wooden stick on the table between them accomplished the fundamentally impossible feat of becoming a slender, yellowish, two-foot snake that wriggled toward him as if dutifully.

"Shit!" Komodoflorensal snapped.

Seven blocks away toward the western wall, Fumarilis the Gatho opened his larder to take out the small, precious bag of sugar he had skimped to purchase, and was shocked to find a torn and empty sack. Furthermore he was staring into the eyes of a small, sugar-stuffed honey badger. It did not even snarl before it pounced, and not at his eyes.

The room that Nim rented was in a building three blocks away from the house of Kusharlonikas the mage, in the direction of the north wall. Popular and confident in her voluptuousness, Nim hummed as she prepared. This nocturnal assignation was one of extra importance. She was careful not to spill so much as a drop of the far-too-expensive Lover's Moon perfume as she opened the vial. She half smiled, and inhaled luxuriously, and gasped at the ghastly odor she had loosed, and with a choked cry fled her home. It remained empty for three days, the inexplicably horrid stench holding at bay anyone and anything so foolish as to enter.

Not too far from that building, Semaj Numisgatt was hand-feeding his beloved blossoms when his favorite orchid, the violet-and-white Aurvestan Autumn Queen, opened wide and nipped off his right index finger to the first knuckle.

Deleteria Palungas was combing her rich mass of midnight-hued hair with the jewel-encrusted comb that dear Shih'med had given her three namedays back when the errant spell of a would-be mage she had never heard of wafted through her modest dwelling on Red Olive Street. Too numb with horror and disbelief to shriek, she watched the flashing comb become laden and then clogged with the gleaming black treasure of her scalp. And then it was piling up on the floor, and her shrieking began.

The tavern named The Bottomless Well—not infrequently fondly referred to as "The Bottomless Cesspool" by regulars—was on Tumult Street, a name that had made all too much sense fifteen or twenty years ago. The staff of The Bottomless Well was, unusually, not from Sanctuary and not conquerors, but a family from Mrsevada. The Bottomless Well was not a dive and yet more than a watering hole. At the same time, it was not an inn much frequented by the wealthy and/or pretentious. The walls and ceiling of the family-run establishment were not painted dark and yet were only a little darkened by grease and the smoke of lamps and candles. That smoke and the odor of frying fat rode the air; not heavily, but sufficiently to cause this or that patron occasionally to rub an eye or two.

The furniture and surroundings were decent enough, with lots of rounded edges, and rails and legs of blond wood, the ale and wine unwatered except on request, and the food acceptable and sometimes better than that. A modest statue of Rander Rehabilitatis perched on a stoutly braced shelf on the wall behind the proprietor/counterman. No one had to squint or look too closely to see that it was well tended and kept free of dust and grease.

In a reasonably well-lit area against the back wall, two men of age sat at a three-cornered table. Neither was young. The hawk-nosed one with more lines in his face than his companion wore all black, unrelieved black. That included his eyes and his hair, whose growth started well back of his forehead and was surely too black for a man of his seeming years. On the back of his chair hung a cane of plain hardwood, thicker than a thumb and with a crooked grip.

By contrast the hair of his companion—in his forties?—was cloud white. He wore it short, and in short bangs that were trimmed well above dark brown eyebrows. He was decorated with a gold chain and a couple of rings. His imported, brushed-fabric robe of Croyite blue formed a veritable tent about him, for he was passing large of height and chest, and especially belly. His face and hands, however, showed little fat. His goblet was nice enough, and contained thick red wine, while the hand of the man in black surrounded a plain crockery mug of oddly pale beer.

He had requested that it be watered. That raised eyebrows but no one made fun of him, for despite his years and his cane he had the look about him of a man not much given to jocularities, a man who would not take denigration with grace, and perhaps not simple joshing, either. Besides, a few minutes ago everyone's attention had been *distracted* by an abrupt weirdness: the thick, quality wine in one patron's chalice-like cup had suddenly burst into flames. They shot up a foot above the table of the worse than startled fat man for several seconds before a young fellow at a nearby table plopped his big personal beer mug down over the offending goblet. With apologies, the proprietor had bustled over to grasp the cup—using a towel to shield his hands—and hurried to the door to sling its contents outside.

"What in the cold hell—" the dark-clad man with the too-black hair began, but his companion interrupted.

"Some wizard has lost his touch or is training an apprentice," he muttered, wagging his head.

The two old friends had discussed the fact that the white-haired man had narrowly avoided worse than retribution when Noble Arizak's horse fell and damaged Arizak's leg. He sent to the white-haired man for help, but his considerable skills succeeded only in *reducing* the pain of the high-placed nobleman. He felt reasonably certain that this was because Arizak was no good man and he—the white-haired man—despised him.

"At any rate, his Noble Self did not forgive me for failing to work sufficient magic to end all trace of his injuries."

His friend cocked his head. "Ignoble self, I'd say.
You are lucky to have escaped with your life!"

That did not seem to cheer the white-haired man.
"It was an act of cowardice that I returned his gold
and eased the other charge—the Price."

"What was that?"

"We will not discuss that, Chance."

"Hmm. Damn it! Once again I wish I was younger
and still had four good limbs! It would be such fun
to visit the palace one night and bring you exactly
the amount of the charge in gold coin!"

The white-haired man smiled, only smiled and
nodded a few times. Perhaps he understood the occasional wistfulness of old age but surely not fully,
for he was a year past his fortieth birthday and his
friend, who had been the friend of his adopted father, was seven and sixty. Too, he well knew that
Chance had never truly been happy, especially so
after parting from the love of his life, a S'Danzo
named Mignureal, and years later his large and de-
cidedly strange cat. To his friend that was truly horrible.

His reverie gave way to interest in a very young
patron of The Bottomless Well who had not advanced far past the door, and who chose not to seat
himself.

Interestingly, he also wore black, tunic and leggings and boots and, on a chill night, a cloak. When
he threw it back—a trifle too dramatically, perhaps—he showed some color: He had decorated
himself with a broad sash of blood-red. Neither tall
nor short and the beautiful natural tan color of
mixed races, he wore his jet hair long but pulled
back into a horse-tail passed through a short, narrow
sheath of dark red leather. His feet and calves were
sheathed in buskins, soft boots of a dull black

sueded leather that made next to no sound when he walked. He was well armed with at least three knives and a sword. The sight of a knife worn upside down on each upper arm was an odd one. He also swaggered, and flirted mildly with the teenaged female server, Esmiria, calling her Esmy.

Quietly the dark, dark-haired elder with the nose of a hawk asked, "Strick—who is that swaggering pup who is so intent on looking so tough?"

His companion chuckled. "Uh . . . the one called Shadowspawn?" he said, putting on a face of complete innocence as he named a youthful thief-cat burglar of time past, though not out of mind. "Hanse, I believe his name was?"

His companion gave him a dark look. "In your ear and out your nose, O Spellmaster," he said, without rancor. "I see no resemblance."

"Amazing! I'd wager our next dinner that yon youth is working as hard as he can for just that—a resemblance. In fact I do know who he is. And a little about him. He calls himself Lone."

"*Lone!*" The echo was heavy with the emphasis of incredulity, but not so loud as to be heard by the bravo they discussed.

The snowy head nodded. "Aye—and not the monetary kind. But say it a little louder and he'll be right here, looking down at us. And ready to fight, Chance, believe me."

The black-clad man he called Chance glanced back along the room. The black-clad youngster he called pup had not moved from the bar just a few feet from the door. He was not looking their way. He bent close as he spoke to their host, Aristokrates.

Without turning, black-clad Chance said, "I wonder; is he old enough to shave?"

Strick snorted. "From the darkness of that hair I'd

say he likely started at age twelve or so," he said, and lifted his goblet to his lips.

Even as he spoke, broad-shouldered Aristokrates moved his plain green-tunicked self away to tend to business—with a casual glance at the two men at the back wall—and the object of their interest turned and set his elbows on the bar behind him. Thus the lean, lean youngster stood, casually and yet poised as a cat, while he surveyed the room from low-lidded eyes the color of anthracite. Defiantly accentuating his dangerousness, he looked as confident as a prince, or an army facing a stick-armed rabble.

Chance's mouth moved as if it considered smiling but changed its mind. "He's got the look. Knows how to do it. I'll never forget Cudget's counsel before I had lived twenty summers: 'Wear weapons openly and try to look mean. People see the weapons and believe the look and you don't have to use them.' You say you know something about him?"

The robed man called Strick nodded. "I do. Lone was one of the orphans the Dyareelan scum kept in concealment under the palace to turn them into kill-slaves. During the major bloodletting that removed the Dyar heel from Sanctuary, the men who discovered them considered him and a few others salvageable, and so allowed him to be claimed by his 'parents.' "

"Ah. He has parents, then."

Strick sighed. His companion claimed not to have known his parents, who were little more than nodding acquaintances. But by his power Strick knew that at some long-ago time Chance had once at least known who his father was. Strick knew too, but never said so.

"All of us have parents, Chance, whether we knew them or not. But no, these two who claimed him to

raise were not his. They were a childless couple who
wanted him to be theirs. Although the people who
... uh ... *rescued* what few children they did not
murder as hopeless servants of Dyareela accepted
them as his parents, I believe Lone really was an
orphan. I believe he has no knowledge of his parentage, or the name they gave him. Nor do I know
what his step-parents called him. They are dead, and
he decided to call himself Lone. So ..." He gestured. "Lone he is."

"I didn't ask for his life story, Strick. But all that
black he's wearing, at his tender age, and at those
buskins—he's a roach, isn't he." It was not a question, but an observation by a man who was sure of
his surmise that Lone was a thief; that is, a creature
who went abroad only by night, like a roach.

"Absolutely. He's addicted to it. After the death
of his stepfather, he supported his mother with his
thieving. His stepmother, I mean."

"He must be good at it, then."

"Must be. Word is that she never questioned the
source of her sustenance, meaning she probably
knew and did not want to deal with it."

Chance snorted. "Or endanger her source of in-
come and food!"

"Probably. Oh—I was told that he said that what
they called him in the Dyareeling Pits was 'Flea-
shit.' "

"Charming. Those Dyar scum ... ah! Sorry,
Strick. No offense."

The man called Strick shrugged. "None taken, old
friend and friend of my mentor."

His attention was distracted by the emergence of
a spider from a crack in the wall above and to the
right of his companion. Abruptly it sprouted lovely
wings the color of an Aurvestan Autumn Queen or-

chid and soared awkwardly down to alight on the
table between them. The dark man moved with surprising rapidity for one of his years. Under his cup
the secret of the spider's sudden winged state was
forever lost.

The white-haired man gave his head a slow, solemn wag. "That's the third abrupt total impossibility
I've seen in three days," he murmured, watching a
frowning Chance gingerly lift his cup to examine
the total impossibility of a winged arachnid.

"Like the flaming wine," he said in a deliberately
dull way. Then, cocking his too dark-haired head to
one side, "Since when is total impossibility unusual
in Sanctuary?"

Strick's smile showed rue, not mirth. "Just what
this town needs! Somewhere in town an incompetent is attempting to cast spells." He sighed, and
shook his head again. "But . . . Chance . . . do you
have some sort of interest in that, uh, swaggering
pup?"

"You know I have."

"Because you have been offered a mission that
you believe in but that is beyond you now, and because yon smart-ass reminds you of you, forty or
more years agone."

His companion chose not to acknowledge that.
Time was when he would never have—could never
have acknowledged that anything was beyond his
ability. But he had lost that along with his physical
swagger and the use of a limb. He said, "Interesting.
He is trying to be me, f—uh, a few years back. In
fact he is only pretending to be . . ." He trailed off,
looking puzzled. "Sorry. Can't think of the word.
Oh! Casual!—he is only pretending to be casual in
challenging the room. His main interest is right
here, at this table."

"You?"

"Maybe. Maybe it's you. You do look prosperous, you know—and no fast mover. Listen, Strick, you know surprisingly much about him. But always there is more to be known about a person. Will you do me the favor of learning what it is?"

"I can understand that you want the upper hand, Chance. But believe me, he is a smart youngster. He will know he is being investigated."

The elderly man with the too-black hair shrugged, slightly. "So he knows. Use a double go-between so that he makes no connection to you." Then he looked away from the one called Lone and gave his companion a small smile. "Damn! Sorry again! As if you didn't know how to do that!"

His smile was returned. "As if I didn't," Strick said.

As the man he called Chance looked in the direction of the one called Lone again, the one named Strick and called Spellmaster looked whimsical and wagged his head, however slightly. His companion had just said *sorry* twice, and the first man named Strick had told this, the heir he had chosen and coached and trained to carry on his good work, that hawk-nosed Chance had in his younger years given no indication that he knew the word *sorry*.

Even some swaggering pups matured and mellowed, if they were lucky . . .

The first Strick, the White Mage from Firaqa up north, was an ex-swordslinger who had become the strangeling called Spellmaster. He was unbound by gods and locale, or by spells or anti-spells. His was true empathy; he truly Cared about each person who came seeking his help. Part of his curse for being given the power was that he *had to* care. This curse—and so he called it—of being unable not to care for and about others was part of his pact with whatever god or Force he had bargained with, and it was not always a pleasant trait to possess. He was unable to do magic of the variety referred to as "black"—meaning that his spells were good or "white" magic, only.

Strick also did well. Sanctuary's Spellmaster, sometimes called "Hero of the People," became a wealthy man and remained well off despite losses over the years in the various properties he had acquired. The losses resulted from the "natural disasters" that had plagued poor little Sanctuary-on-the-sea, as well as the thefts of conquerors—thefts that they called "confiscations," of course.

Over forty years ago he had married a noble-woman of an old Ilsigi family. She died, as too many women did, in childbirth. The unpredictable twists and turns of love being what they were, the Spell-master had taken as second wife a "reformed" Dy-areeling. He was able to make her ritually imposed scars invisible, although of course she paid a physical price—the Price. It was bearable to them both, and to the Spellmaster's adopted daughter, and to the two children this second wife bore him. He had been abroad oversea, making certain arrangements with some people of the Inception Island group, when the Irrune "rescued" Sanctuary from the horror that had been the Dyareeling cult's rule of the gods-despised city.

The latest foreigners to take over here also did their best to put an end to every member of the cult of the Blood Goddess Dyareela, with a great deal of success. Victims included the wife and children of the renowned white mage Spellmaster. All, including his adopted daughter, died in the Irrunekindled fire that claimed his luxurious country home.

He was never the same man after . . .

But he did take in a skinny young orphan and train him as apprentice. Only that lucky lad—whose name was Chance—knew that his "father" had paid a great deal of money to have various punishments inflicted on various Irrunes, because his talent allowed him to wreak white magic only. When years later the adopted son made his bargain with the unknown that made *him* a white mage, his dark brown mop of hair turned white overnight *and* he gained girth with a rapidity that was a boon for the makers of breeches and tunics and belts. It was the Price he paid for the ability.

The Spellmaster, who had never ceased his grieving, named Chance son and heir, and bade him use the name Strick and never, never charge greedily for his services. And when he thought his successor was ready and he had done this and that with the properties he owned in and about the town, Strick killed himself.

The new Strick had long since become the friend of the strange dark man who was a longtime friend of the almost legendary Spellmaster. The day Chance changed his name to Strick, their friend changed his to Chance, and moved into a better area of town than any he had previously tenanted. They met frequently to dine and drain a few cups, and The Bottomless Well was one of their favorite places.

Leaning well in toward the aproned, balding Aristokrates of Mrsevada, Lone said, "Whatever you do, do not so much as glance at the men I am about to ask you about. At the back of the room—look only at me, Aris!—is the man in the blue robe with the white hair the one called Spellmaster?"

Looking at his questioner as if to assess the stability of the chip the youngster wore on each shoulder, the counterman said, "Yes."

Strick and Chance had forbidden him to reveal that he and Chance owned this place, a fact known to perhaps seven people, three of them city clerks. Strick was known to own or have a stake in several commercial establishments, including, in a lesser part of town, the Vulgar Unicorn. That was a dive he'd had lovingly restored to what it had been before one of the onslaughts of nature that Sanctuary had suffered. The Golden Gourd was his, too, and other places and properties.

Lone asked, "And what of the man with him? Is he a cripple?"

The thickset proprietor and supposed owner of The Bottomless Well blinked medium brown eyes. "He walks with a cane, and limps." The mustache adorning his well-rounded face like a semi-trimmed bramble bush was no minor growth, brown and thick, and always its trailing ends wiggled when he talked. As to his reply, he was always careful with Lone, considering it simple wisdom and perhaps self-protection. The chips on the shoulders of the aptly self-named Lone were big enough to challenge a wood-splitter. While the lad possessed a certain . . . basic integrity, his opinion of himself was inviolate.

Lone nodded. "Do you know his name?"

"Aye. He is Chance. Of the old race, I think."

"Ilsigi, like me. But . . ." Lone was frowning, and on a dusky face with such black eyes under hair as black as the heart of a money changer, that was a sight to give pause even to a bold man. Although Lone was not of the Ilsigi, his idol was, and so Lone

called himself. "Are you sure about his name?
Maybe he has a nickname?"

The non-aristocrat named Aristokrates made a
small gesture with a ringless hand and tapped his
chest with the other in the manner of a devotee of
Rander. "His name is Chance, Lone. I have never
heard him called anything else."

Lone looked disappointed, but said, "When I
draw back my hand you will see an earring that
came from afar and is not cheap but also not as
valuable as it looks. Call it a gift to your wife or your
daughter. You choose which, Aris."

The taller, meatier man looked down at the object glittering in silver and green on his countertop.
His glance around did not seem furtive and yet was.
When he saw that no one was looking their way, he
made the earring disappear.

"Falmiria or Esmiria will be grateful, Lone. It is
surely worth more than the single cup you just
drank."

"I said it was a gift."

A well-maintained mustache of major proportions
writhed with Aristokrates' smile. "So is the cup you
just drank!"

"Aris!" That, sharply in a female voice, from the
kitchen.

"Ah. His master's voice," Lone said.

Aristokrates rolled his eyes. "Go to hell, Lone."

"Be patient," Lone said with a wink. "Surely I'll
not be making that journey for a while yet!" With
that he put on another expression altogether before
turning away to stand and pretend to survey everyone. His manner was that of a man of supreme confidence; the commander of an army facing a mob
armed with staves.

The watching Strick's mutter was only for the ears

of his companion. "He seems to have the stance right!"

Chance snorted. "Well, he knows how to posture!"

After a couple of minutes of such posturing, Lone swaggered to the door and outside into the darkness, where he seemed to belong. He was heard to snap a curse when a seriously warped plank in the boardwalk paralleling Tumult Street forced him to execute a little hop-skip step. And then he . . . well, droop-eyed Cajerlain the Twitchy, lounging at the mouth of Angry Alley not far away, later swore by Theba's Immortal Crotch that the cat-walking lad just disappeared.

The woman who stood with her back against a wall while he groped her bore out his story, too.

A little under an hour later Chance and Strick also settled up and departed amid the tap-step-tap of Chance's cane and right foot. About a half-block along, one of those embarrassingly little yellow and brown and high-voiced dogs began yip-yapping before they were anywhere near the territory he considered his. His frail-looking little body bounced with each yap.

"Yip-yap yip-yap yip-yap," Chance said. "What a temptation to introduce that imitation of a dog to a throwing star!"

"Ah, that little beast is not worth it."

"Just a little one," Chance persisted, tap-step . . .

Strick paused and addressed the animal directly. "Imitation Dog with the voice of a bird, you are never going to be able to understand what happened, but hereafter you are not going to be able to bark again unless someone is within three steps of you *and* headed your way."

Chance smiled broadly. The yip-yapper's mouth continued to move but no sound emerged. Wearing a distinctly puzzled look, the dog dropped back onto his tail and sat staring at the passersby from wet eyes. Neither so much as glanced at him. The dark one was chuckling as they went on their way.

Even though gold showed here and there on his person, a master mage had little to fear when abroad at night in a neighborhood that, while not the worst, was also not wholly safe. His lack of fear of being accosted was bolstered even more when he was in company of the man now called Chance. In fact that proved to be the case this night, when not even a block and a half from the inn not one but two were so foolish as to accost them.

The burly one addressed them in a cultivated snarl that unfortunately made him sound sillier than it did deadly. "Let's see the sight of your purses and them rings, whitey, or you two old farts are going to get stuck with sharp steel!"

Strick spoke very quietly. "I am the Spellmaster," he said. "You boys don't want to do this. You had better run along."

"I don't give a shit if you're the Shadow God hisself," the thinner man with the long knife said, as if anxious to prove his fundamental stupidity and perilous lack of judgment. "Do what my friend says."

Since the attention of both accosters was now focused on Strick, his black-clad companion proved that his limp was false, and too that he was left-handed. His cane, startlingly heavy for the last eight or so inches of its length, became a weapon that all but brained the one with the bigger knife and drove deeply into the midsection of his burly companion. With a spin that proved him no cripple, Chance whacked the side of that one's head, too. The sound of impact was alarmingly loud. Both would-be thieves went straight down and lay moveless half on the boardwalk and half in the street.

The friends exchanged a smile.

Strick shook his head. "A pair of men with a staggeringly bad grasp on reality," he said.

"Old fart indeed!" The offended sixty-seven-year-old kicked one of the men he had knocked unconscious, but in the leg and with not all that much force. "Candlelight!"

"What?"

"I called him Candlelight. One blow and he's out!"

Strick laughed. "No question: You've still got it."

Chance had used his left arm only, and the right continued to hang as if asleep, or dead. That had been the case since that horrible occasion when the man who had always been left-handed had awakened from . . . something; sleep?—he had no memory of what had gone before the waking—to discover the disconcerting fact that he was looking up into concerned faces, most of which belonged to strangers, and that his right arm no longer did what he wanted it to do. It continued in that worse than distressing behavior, and was often cursed by its possessor.

"You had a stroke," a medical type or shaman improbably called Changjoy told him. Whatever in the coldest hell that meant—a stroke of what?—struck by whom or what?—it essentially ended the career of the seemingly invisible Shadowspawn, the world's most brilliant cat-burglar.

Now he of the disrupted arm, livelihood and lifestyle went on his way homeward with his friend Strick, at home in the night and its shadows . . . without knowing that every moment of his violent reaction to a robbery attempt had been witnessed

from an overhanging roof just above them by a vitally interested young man whose all-black attire
helped to conceal him in the shadows.

"So his legs are not crippled and the cane is
weighted as a weapon," he muttered, only to himself. "But that right arm must be useless or nearly.
And it is him!—it has to be!—he *is* Shadowspawn!"

The young man, smiling and nodding only to
himself, would see to it that a man named Treggi-
nain had a new nickname . . .

Candlelight.

Komodoflorensal paid little attention to the countryside here, north of Sanctuary. Sometimes pictur-
esquely beautiful, it seemed unexcited about the
imminent arrival of spring and the colors it would
bring to decorate the land. On his way back to Sanctuary after making a little delivery for his master, the
apprentice mage rode a medium-size horse of a medium rust color. The animal and its accouterments
belonged to Kusharlonikas. Its bridle and saddle
with its high back braced and shaped by carved
wood, were of old, tired-looking brown leather. Komodoflorensal wore a pair of aged long-riding pants
of similar brown leather, and a high-necked, sleeved
tunic vertically striped in burnt orange and off-
white. The sun had made a belated appearance
along about midmorning, its heat persuading him
to roll up his lime green cloak and lash it behind
the saddle with its cantle of leather over wood.

His thoughts were on his life and his brilliant but
cruel master. They were soulful thoughts, and some
of them were tinged with sadness.

It was a difficult life, being apprenticed to a man
who was often worse than "merely" difficult. Komodoflorensal, however, was born to nothing of no

one whose name was remembered a few moments beyond death. Naturally such a youth considered himself lucky to be in the service of Kusharlonikas. His master was the man he most respected and admired, and the apprentice's only aspiration was to be as exactly like him as he could make himself—with the aid of his master, however painful. To that end, the diminutive mage-to-be swallowed the bitter fruits the old man served up, and tried not to dread the next manifestation of impatience.

He was not sure what prompted him to glance up. But he did, and saw a bird. No, not just a bird, but one of incredible size. In fact it was growing larger by the second. For a moment the apprentice mage froze, staring at the oncoming creature. His first thought was of the bow on his saddle. He realized that would not work; the bird was practically hurtling down. If it were some demon-thing bent on attack, he would never have the bow strung and nocked in time. Although he was no swordsman and in fact better with the foot and a half of steel on his right hip, Komodoflorensal reached across his lean belly for his sword . . .

And the huge diving bird swept over him, on the ascent.

The youth felt his hair ruffle and his clothing ripple in the heavy draft from mighty wings and he squinted, thinking how beautiful this enormous denizen of the air was, all deep emerald and turquoise and pale yellow. It flew on, climbing the air, while Komodoflorensal twisted about in the saddle. His hand merely rested on the undecorated hilt of the sword he had not drawn. He was frowning now, thinking, watching the bird that could not be natural. It flapped on, climbing until it was smaller and seemed darker against the clear sky.

Then it banked and came swooping back. It was beautiful in flight, which was bringing it directly at him. Never mind its beauty; Komodoflorensal reined his horse about and drew his sword. Again the bird passed over, in beauty and with a rush of air and slapping of wings little smaller than lateen sails. Kusharlonikas's apprentice had not even begun to swing his sword.

Why, it means me no harm at all! he told himself. *Foolish Komodoflorensal! This is surely sorcery, Ah—probably a Sending of my wily master to keep watch on me! Either that or it meant to tell me something, show me something, and I have stupidly frightened it off.*

The young man let the half-drawn sword slip back into its sheath and kept a tight grip on the rein of a mount that had grown increasing restless. Again the great bird of green and green and cream yellow banked, and again it came back his way, flapping gently this time. Though he was sore nervous, Komodoflorensal put a smile upon his face—and spoke quietly to his horse. All was well . . .

A hundred or so paces from him, the outsized bird swept back its wings and held them so. It came hurtling down in a plunging dive, and by the time Komodoflorensal saw the terrible curved beak and talons as long as his hands, he had no time to take action. The monster raptor's impact drove him backward off his horse, which reared and swerved, screaming. Its mouth was torn, for its unseated rider had clung to the rein until it was torn from its grasp. He fell with bloodied fingers.

The horse galloped in a desperate fear that would not allow it to slow for miles. After a time it did turn, to return to the land it knew. Someone was about to be made very happy.

Its former rider-not-master, meanwhile, was kept

in unrelenting agony as he was torn and clawed and bitten to bloody shreds and gobbets. Still he was carried up, and up, in agony and blood loss. And then his unnatural assailant dropped him. Screaming, Komodoflorensal fell and fell and fell and actually *heard* the terrible thump as his torn form struck the earth.

But he did not feel that impact, and when he awoke in his home—that is, the home of his master—he realized that the sorcerer had used a spell to punish him for last night's failure. Even as Komodoflorensal gave silent thanks that he was not only not dead but unharmed, a huge soldier in full armor came rushing at him and his battle-ax came rushing at the terrified young man's face and—

After that horrible and horribly painful death the apprentice mage awoke again—to open his eyes and see his master gazing down at him.

"So, fool," Kusharlonikas said. "Practice, and think, and next time *try harder!*"

The haughty people of Ranke, self-styled conquerors of the world, expressed their disdain for the town named Sanctuary by its founders, the Ilsigi—people of the god Ils. It was the *former* Rankan overlords who coined the insulting term Thieves' World for the town. The once almost important coastal city had fallen so low, the imperious invaders from imperial Ranke had been wont to say, that only thieves remained, and so the thieves were reduced to stealing from each other.

Not that the Rankans had not done their share of stealing, along with despoiling and tyrannizing . . .

Important or not, Sanctuary's outdoor market seemed no less bustling than those of cities that were aprosper, and/or still on the rise. Two senses

were kept close to the point of overload by the great
Sanctuarite marketplace. Even in winter the air was
freighted unto crowding with overlapping scents,
aromas, even odors. The competing of fragrances
was emphasized at this time of year by those hopeful
vendors who earned the price of their bread by serving hot drinks and cooking hot treats to warm the
buyers. Each scent separated itself from the others
as prospective buyers approached the source,
whether fruits or vegetables or (ugh) fish, and receded after their passage, when another scent was
competing and, at least for a time, winning domi-
nance.

A third sense was kept busy, but not to the point
of being whelmed. That was vision. Many colors and
hues marked the clothing and tents and stalls of
both sellers and buyers, though the color of their
hair differed only a little.

Ah, but that second, nigh overwhelmed sense!
The sprawling collection of stalls, tents, and wagons,
drab and colorful, was *noisy*. Even in the open air
hundreds of people, nearly all talking at the same
time, did not create merely the "buzz" so often used
by storytellers. It was bedlam. In fact, the noisiness
of Sanctuary's market defined bedlam.

Yet two people were quite able to carry on a conversation, provided that they paused now and again,
reluctantly or in anger, while wending their way
through the mass of people, scents, and colors of
both produce and of garments. The two older men,
for instance, on this cool but sunny day. The one
was portly under his veritable mane of hair the color
of whitewash, his shorter companion his senior
though his hair was blacker than black, and who
walked with a cane.

Abroad in daytime, the man called Chance did

not envelop himself in the concealing black garb of
the man he had been, the infamous shadow-
spawned thief and cat burglar. The lightweight
cloak he wore over an off-white tunic and medium
blue leggings was a sun-sucking dark red, for a
man's blood was thinner at the age of seven and
sixty, if not his arteries. This day they wended their
way among stalls, booths, tents, and shoppers, while
Strick relayed to Chance a few additional facts and
beliefs about the youth called Lone gained through
the Spellmaster's quiet and judicial questioning of
a few selected persons. It was Strick's belief that he
was discreet... and then their attention was demanded by a woman excitedly talking, with gestic-
ulations, with a vendor who was apparently her
friend.

The semi-attractive woman with the hair dyed red
under the fluttery green scarf was not well off, but
she was erect and carried herself well and with
pride. Too, she did know how to dress, and it was
pretty clear to anyone who saw her that she spent
what money she could on decorating her well-kept
body. She was talking wildly, shrilly, and with a lot
of gesticulating at the shortish, thin and thin-haired
seller of inexpensive body decorations.

"But I live on the third floor!" she squealed. "That
must be—what? Sixty feet up?"

The man in the booth under the orange and violet awning shrugged and made a gesture to indicate his uncertainty but desire to be agreeable.
"Uh-huh, about that, uh-huh, I reckon..."

She was babbling on as if he had not spoken, making it obvious that he need not have done. "So
somebody *climbed up the wall* all the way up there,
Cleggis, and then he broke into my place through
my window while I was right there sleeping"—with

a sudden shiver, she clutched each of her upper arms with the opposite hand—"and he knew where to find my earrings, or he's so experienced at thievery that he guessed, and he took them out of my shoe *about one foot below my head, Cleggis!*"

Cleggis shook his head. "Wackle! What a sneak! That sumbitch is *good!*"

"Yes! And then ... and then ... he left one of them in the other shoe, just to—to ... to taunt me, I guess."

Cleggis shook his head. "Wackle!"

Strick had moved to place his mouth near Chance's ear. "Reckon we're hearing about our boy Lone?" he asked, *sotto voce.*

"Sounds that way. And it sounds like he's even better than we thought we knew."

"Not in need of a lot of training," Strick said, wickedly teasing.

"Just climb off it, Strick," his friend said, changing course in the smallish throng to head for the savory aroma of cooking meat. "No one is ever, ever going to be as good as I was."

He was happy to order a fat, juice-dripping sausage. With the seven-inch cylinder of meat in hand, he made a flamboyant gesture that silently invited Strick to join him in having one. The Spellmaster, however, preferred to cross the aisle between rows of vendors and purchase a smallish wedge of cheese. Chance knew the reason. Strick's vast girth was part of the Price extracted from him in exchange for his ability, but still he had to be careful of his diet, lest he add to that girth and run his weight right on up past three hundred pounds.

"To continue about you know who," he said, as they ambled on, munching, "sometimes called the cat-walker. He is naturally right-handed, but to em-

ulate his idol, that Shadowspawn fellow, he has put
in a lot of time training himself to use his left arm
and hand. So long, in fact, that he is about equally
as good with either arm-hand by now."

"Brilliant fellow," Chance said, as drily as a man
could when his mouth was full of greasy sausage. He
smiled and nodded at the end of the shelf of the
next vendor's booth along the way.

Comfily curled and snoozing there was a smallish
cat about the color of charcoal except for the small
white area on his left ear and another back of his
left rear "ankle."

And somewhere, someone triumphantly pronounced his word of power.

"*Iffets!*"

Even as Strick turned his gaze in the direction
indicated by Chance, every hair on the slumbering
animal whipped erect and its eyes flared huge. With
a hideous yowl of alarming volume, the cat did not
just leap to its feet, but straight up to an elevation
that was beyond impressive and in fact appeared beyond possible. Landing as only a cat could, it spun
around three times at almost incredible speed,
pounced onto the canvas side of the adjacent stall,
and ascended as if someone had set its tail afire. It
set a record for speed of climbing, surely, for a cat
without a flaming tail and not being chased either.
Reaching the top of that dingy tent, it ruined the
"roof" by spinning completely around—three times
at speed, as before, just as if it could count.

By now the performance of the suddenly demented feline had attracted a good number of wit-
nesses, all gawking and ejaculating in excited voices.
By the end of its third rotation atop that vendor's
tent, the object of their attention looked bigger by
twice. Surely an illusion . . .

It was at about that moment that several people screamed, including Strick, and hurled from them newly bought cheese suddenly become too hot to handle.

Without pausing or even slowing, meanwhile, the dark gray kitty pounced from the top of the dingy tent onto the top of the neighboring one where it had lately slept so peacefully, presumably its home. But! Its destination changed en route. Flattening in air with all four feet extended, as well as neck and tail, the presumably ensorceled animal took on kinship with a flying squirrel.

"Sorcery!" a high-voiced man squealed.

"Oh Ils father of us all," Chance muttered, "how I hate sorcery!"

The sorcerer standing beside him said nothing, but only stared, as so many were doing.

A charcoal gray streak and still growing, the cat soared completely over the booth of its befuddled mistress, a permanent site constructed of wood. It struck the flat roof of the next stall in line, one of gold-hued canvas with a russet awning. The impact was heavy.

At the instant of that impact the flying feline smashed through the flat canvas roof, at the same time messily *exploding* into revolting components, without sound other than stomach-turning juicy noises. From within came the sound of yells and screams, one of either sex.

Some vendors and every visitor to the market stood as if frozen, staring at what had been. Abruptly one person detached itself from the crowd. The long skirt of the loosely girt blue tunic worn by the more than portly man with white hair flapped as he strode to the aerially invaded stall. From it emerged no cat or person, but only increasingly muffled screams. Both Strick's ringed hands slapped down onto the wooden counter and, on tiptoes, he bent forward to peer inside.

"Oh, *fart!*" he barked, which was as profane as the Spellmaster got. He turned. "Chance! I need your help."

His friend's unhurried compliance with the urgent request clearly lacked enthusiasm. He learned Strick's desire and waylaid a burly woman to help him. Together, they assisted the beyond burly man with the stocky legs onto the counter, and over it. A few moments later they were joined by a wide-eyed fellow who came hurrying around the left side of the stall, and the equally goggle-eyed woman who closely followed. Dark, dark they were, desert people whose place of business had been invaded by the ghastly components of the product of sorcery. In desperation and charged with adrenaline, they had hoisted the canvas in back and crawled out.

Together, the four of them watched Strick ritualistically bestow a touch on each of the several wet pieces of fresh meat lying here and there on the earthen floor, most bearing at least a trace of hair the color of charcoal. Without wiping those begored and lymph-shining hands, he unfolded a caravaneer's wooden stool and seated himself slowly and with care.

"Here," the owner said, slapping the counter with one of her thin, veined hands and pointing with the other. "Break that stool under your vast butt and pay for it, fat man!"

"Hush," the coal-haired cripple beside her snapped. "He is a mage at work—a good and honorable mage and the best man you're likely to meet, *skinny woman,* but I'd not be testing my luck if I was you . . . and beside, if that crappy little stool breaks he will *offer* payment!"

The woman, her presumed husband who had preceded her in fleeing their marketplace tent, and a few others so daring as to have joined them, all directed their stares at the man who had spoken so harshly. But no one responded vocally. Even old and leaning on a cane as he was, there was something about the fellow . . .

Strick, meanwhile, had uttered not a word, but only besat the stool with legs wide apart in the way that comforted men with great bellies. He seemed to be fondling or perhaps kneading a chunk of fresh cat—the only large piece, which was about the size the animal had been before it commenced its unnatural growth.

"Not a word," Chance murmured to his fellow watchers, and put on his meanest menacing look.

No one spoke a word.

Abruptly the seated Spellmaster snapped up his head and startled those watching with an aspirated "Ah!" that sounded pleased. He followed that with several nods of his snowy head. Then he glanced round, and his audience heard his grunt without being able to translate it.

Chance knew the man, and recognized the sound of effort. Strick's divining was at an end; he had just made an effort to hoist his bulk off the low stool, and failed. He who had been Shadowspawn leaned against the counter.

"Strick."

The white head turned and the white mage looked over at his audience.

"For you," Chance said, and with care, tossed his cane over the colorful array of mingled peppers and onto the ground that floored the cluttered little

room. It fell with little sound and rolled only about
three-quarters of a revolution before it fetched up
against Strick's left foot. He grunted anew in bending to pick it up, and with its aid and another gasping grunt he came to his feet. The stool had
survived. It did creak as if with gratitude at his departure.

More effortful grunts accompanied the Spellmaster's departing the booth in the same way the vendors had. He came round the tent a few seconds
later and handed Chance his cane. By that time the
two desert people had used their counter to reoc-
cupy their tent. With clear distaste, they were collecting gobbets of deceased cat and dropping them
into a large urn.

"Hope they aren't meaning to clean that meat
and try to sell it," the burly woman who had helped
Chance boost Strick into the tent said, and he
flashed her a smile. He was revolted by the sorcerous occurrence, and a little angry. Years and years
ago, a cat had been the best friend he could claim.

Strick addressed the vendors across their counter.
"I will pay asking price for a basket of peppers, as-
sorted but without the hottest ones." He pointed to
a medium-sized basket.

At that marvelous and in fact unparalleled offer
the vendors bustled to fill the basket with colors and
shapes; the peppers they judged best of the lot, all
without a word about the doubtless weakened stool.

"What . . . happened?" the woman asked, as without attempting to negotiate he paid her the price
she named.

"It was a cat," Chance provided, and received no
thanks for being so kind as to provide the information.

"A cat of normal size," Strick added, "until an incompetent someone somewhere not too far away cast a spell that he botched. An apprentice mage whose talent I suspect is worse than limited. I know whose he is, but it's best that I don't tell you. It was an accident."

The overly earringed vendor in the adjoining booth, whose cat the deceased had been, had been told what had befallen her pet, since the action had taken place out of her view. Now Strick was so kind as to purchase some of her vegetables, which were hardly among the best available in the market, even at this out-of-season time.

"You are the one called Spellmaster," she said.

Strick was hardy unaccustomed to that same non-question. "I am."

"Can you bring back my dear Sleeks?"

He shook his head.

"Huh!" a nearby shopper snorted. "Can't bring back a little old dead cat! Some kind of 'spellmaster' you are!"

Strick smiled. Never, never could his friend, who had been a model of truculence all his life, understand why Strick was so accepting, so understanding, so extremely slow to take offense. "Restoring a dead cat to life," the white mage said quietly and without turning, "would not be an act for good, and I can perform only that kind of magic. And besides, cats make a point of breeding quite well enough that we need not help increase their number by granting immortality to some. I hope you soon adopt one, or more likely, that one adopts you," he told the vendor.

"Sleeks was one of a kind," she said wistfully, "but you are a great man, Spellmaster. You did a great service for my sister-in-law when you dispelled the wart off her nose."

His smile was small, a slight change in the shape of his mouth. "Apparently whatever inconvenience or thorn in the flesh she had to accept in return for her improved appearance is bearable," he said.

The woman smiled across the counter at him. "Something else did happen just like you warned her it would, and she is marked—but neither she nor her husband my brother minds as much as they did that damned wart!"

Naturally Strick asked no questions, and nodded. Having paid for and accepted a small packet of vegetables, he turned to walk away. He was brought up short. The fellow who had spoken from behind him and been all but ignored moved swiftly to bar his way. "So you can't do nothing that ain't good, huh?" His chest was out and his hands were balled into fists the size of small loaves.

"Putting a wart on that snotty bully's nose of yours," the dark man just behind Strick's shoulder said, bracing the considerably larger accoster with a very steady gaze, "would be no bad act."

"Why, you little piece of cat sh—"

The bully was interrupted by a third male voice, from behind him. "Say, citizen, do you really think it's smart to go messin' around with a real live *wizard?*"

The bully wheeled on his accoster, who was a burly swordslinger hired by the market manager to police the place and protect its users. No longer a young man, he was intelligent enough to be standing about a yard back, holding a one-handed crossbow aimed at the bully's middle. It was cocked.

"Huh! *Big man!* Tough when you've got that sticker aimed at my gut, arencha, old fart!"

Again Sirrah Hostility heard a hostile voice from behind: "Argalo, would you have to arrest me if I was to crack the skull around this ugly little fellow's big noise-hole with my little walking stick?"

The security man moved his head a little to look past the man he accosted. "Oh, hello there, Hanse— I mean Chance! Killed anybody so far this week?"

Hanse-I-mean-Chance laughed. The former bravo he called Argalo laughed. Strick laughed. Several others nearby laughed. The heavily intimidated bully proved that he retained a modicum of intelligence by suddenly remembering his urgent need to be somewhere else.

Thanks and good wishes were exchanged, and Strick bought some fish that smelled good enough to eat provided he didn't put it off, and he and Chance made their way to the east entry to the marketplace. There, just inside, they had time to sit down and, without incident, knock back a small measure of wine. Then it was about time to step outside and look for transportation.

It had arrived: here was Strick's man Samoff with the one-mule-cart which the Spellmaster chose over a carriage, in order not to look as well off as he was. It was in accord with Strick's desire that Samoff of the thick, droopy, rust-colored moustache wore nothing that even approached livery. He who had named the mule "Killer" dressed as he wished and wore arms as he wished. In his case that meant he was well armed with sword and dagger and crossbow and back-up knife, and as mean-looking as he could look in mostly leathers with boots well up his thighs and his big wide-brimmed old desert hat with a sweat-stain about the size of some small animals. He was a much wrinkled man of one and fifty who had put in a lot of years traveling from town to town across the desert as a caravan scout. The job meant keeping to himself and riding ahead and on the flanks all along the way, on the alert for possible menace.

Samoff was a man of few words and considerable respect who knew how to use his weapons, although he was handicapped by an old leg injury.

He knew he was lucky to be employed by the Spellmaster, too, who also provided food and housing, and had spelled away the personal problem that Samoff called the worst: a pair of feet whose sweat had smelled worse than a hound-dog's mouth. Samoff was also privy to the former life of his boss's dark, unfriendly looking friend. One afternoon a couple of years back he had heard an old acquaintance of Chance ask him if the change of name really worked; what about people who had known him as Hanse the roach for many years?

"They are mostly all dead," Chance replied, and no one could disbelieve that, for nearly everyone who had lived in Sanctuary a half-century ago no longer lived anywhere.

Today Samoff greeted that man, along with his employer, with respect. He was pleased to accept with a low nod of his head the half-measure of beer that Chance had been so thoughtful as to purchase for him, saw the two men seated in the cart, and mounted its forward seat to make the long drive to the much better area of town and the Spellmaster's home. The drive was leisurely and without incident of any significance.

The door of that spacious dwelling was opened from within and they were greeted by a quite shapely, thin-faced woman in her late thirties or early forties. She was Linnana, who was as always rather garishly attired in several items of jewelry and at least as many colors, not all of which were compatible.

Chance was one of the very few who knew that this S'danzo "housekeeper" was Strick's woman. Since her people tended to shun liaisons with outsiders and frown upon those who broke that unwritten "rule," she pretended to be no more than his housekeeper, and they maintained the fiction that she dwelled in the small building attached to his large home.

In fact, long ago a S'danzo had been the one true love of the hardly lovable thief named Hanse and called Shadowspawn, and he had lost her because he had persisted in being Hanse called Shadowspawn—and never ceased to blame himself. It was because of his lost Mignureal that he had long secretly channeled money to one Elemi, a widow, because she was S'danzo and he was sentimental—a fact that even now, so close to the end of his life, he would never admit, even to Strick.

Linnana was more than civil and showed no long face as she apprised them that while cleaning she had discovered that someone had broken in last night, without causing damage to door or window or—apparently—taking anything except the mostly purple raw gemstone that Strick kept lying on one end of the table in his divinery and office.

"But he left this," she said, handing her lover a tiny tablet of hard clay and soft wax. It had been sealed with Strick's wax and seal.

He gave Chance a look. "Want to risk a wager as to who left this?"

"I like him more and more," Shadowspawn said. "It's what I would have done!"

Smiling—rather tightly—Strick broke the seal and lifted the tablet's cover. *Very* neatly scratched into the soft wax coating the inside of the tablet were the words "Why not just ask me stead of them uthers?"

Strick chuckled. "That would be Lone, all right. All is well, Linnie. We are in no danger from this intruder."

While she showed visible relief, she also remained close to her man.

Chance added his assurance: "A certain youngster just wanted to show us he could do it."

"Wants to be like his idol," Strick appended, now with an arm about his woman. "You remember hearing about a certain Shadowspawn, don't you Linnie?"

She heaved a sigh and showed the two men a wan smile. "Never heard of him," she said. "But I do smell something that needs to be taken outside and cleaned."

"Sorry," Chance grinned. "Strick did do some sweating . . ."

With an indulgent smile she took over the fish. The Spellmaster headed for his private sanctuary, his home office-divinery, while Linnana took charge of the market purchases. She presented no real argument when Chance said it should be his job to clean the fish. Strick was still in his sanctuary when he finished, so Chance went out to visit with Samoff and "maybe lend a hand in tending to the mule and cart."

He and the former caravan scout sat in the barn and reminisced, as they had on several other occasions. Most of what each told the other was true.

Over dinner, Strick surprised no one by advising that he had been at a little private divination, an ability enhanced by a few things he had learned not from his stepfather, but from a friend of his, a dauntingly large man named Ahdio.

"The lad who continues to cast bad spells over Sanctuary is named Komodoflorensal," he told Chance and Linnana.

Chance paused over a slice of onion-rubbed bread the color of old leather. "Now that," he said, "is a lot of name!"

Strick nodded, using his tongue to explore the morsel of fish in his mouth for bone. "He is apprentice to a master mage named Kusharlonikas, who is older than dirt. Do you know of him, Chance?"

"Why ask me? Because I am older than dirt?"

So many years he has lived, Strick thought, *and still so defensive and quick to take offense!* For him not to be happy, and so low of self-esteem as to feel it, especially for a man so very good at his life's work, was to Strick one more miscarriage of justice—and proof once again that the whole "justice" concept came not from the gods but was solely a human invention, and did not exist in any natural state.

Or so believed Strick, Spellmaster.

"No," he told Chance, "because I believe this Kusharlonikas to be old enough to have whelped you."

Chance jerked erect in his chair. "All gods forbid!"

"No argument offered," Strick said.

Linnana chuckled. "What an irony *that* would be!"

Strick went on, "I should not have much trouble learning where Kusharlonikas lives, since I have seen the neighborhood behind my eyes. I intend to have a talk with him. Sorcerers are wont to claim— even believe, in some cases—that any and every event that takes place—or fails to take place, as expected!—is demonstration of their magnificent abil-

ity. This one needs to accept responsibility for the
bad, too. The incompetence of his apprentice is a
danger to everyone. And certainly his master owes
that couple in the market for the tent destroyed by
that excrementitious spell."

While Chance was wondering what the grundoon
that meant, Linnana was aborting the lifting of
nicely peppered fish to her mouth. Strick and
Chance had given the shapely woman a brief description of the outré mis-happening in the open
market. Now she said, "And that poor woman's cat?"

"Cats," Strick announced with uncharacteristic
portentousness, "are plentiful and not at all expensive."

But the man called Chance was staring at a blank
wall blankly, remembering, and he said nothing.

The quite spartan apartment that Chance kept was
not at all far from the considerably nobler estate of
his friend, but as sometimes happened, the retired
Shadowspawn spent the night at Strick's. When he
entered his two rented rooms next morning, he discovered that he had been visited. Someone had
neatly arranged on his bedspread the amethyst off
Strick's desk and another little clay tablet.

"While yur frend was trying to learn about me,"
the note said, "I was learning about you, Shados-
pawn. Sign me if yu hap to be at same table at Bottomless Well this night."

He who had been the ultra-cocky Shadowspawn,
invader of so many dwellings not his own, felt vio-
lated and was righteously outraged, but that night
he was at the table he had shared with Strick the
night the spider sprouted wings and the "professional barker" outside became a "good dog."

The boy, as Chance thought of Lone, was not

present, and Aristokrates understood the reason of this influential patron for drinking "wine" that contained more of the well than the grape.

The ever-patriot and former professional thief had lived a long time, and played many games, mind and otherwise, and so was not surprised when after the turn of the hourglass on the counter *the boy* had still made no appearance. Neither had he sent a message, which admittedly Chance had half-expected. He rose, step-thudded to the counter, paid, and leaned close to the host to murmur a number of words for his ears only. Aristokrates agreed, and Chance departed the establishment.

Time passed. Aristokrates and his modestly dressed daughter Esmiria stayed busy serving beer and wine and food. The wife of the proprietor and supposed owner of The Bottomless Well, a woman meatier and thicker-set than he was, emerged from the kitchen in response to a customer's special request. She listened, and nodded her agreement, and responded with a few words; why mention that one of the spices the interfering ass requested was already in the stew, and his other suggestion would spoil it? On her way back out of sight—where Falmiria repeatedly made it clear that she preferred to be—she paused, watched the last grain of sand disappear from the top of the hourglass, and turned it.

And time passed in The Bottomless Well. At last through the arched doorway he came, in his gliding gait called catlike, a lean young man of no great height but at least five lengths of sharp steel that showed. He wore black, black, and black, tonight unalleviated even by the red sash, and the soles of his soft buskins made not a sound on the hardwood floor. From arrestingly dark eyes beneath rather thick, black brows he scanned the place as if in a casual way, but which his host knew was quite purposeful indeed.

The catwalker wore no happy look when he turned to the counter and those nearly black eyes bored into the mild, medium brown ones of his host.

"I was to meet the man who calls himself Chance here," he said. "I don't see him . . ."

Aristokrates bobbed his head in such a way as to make it obvious that he was attempting to be ingratiating. "Yes. He was here, Lone. Alone. He sat at the back wall, and sipped a mug very slowly like a man waiting for someone to join him. After more than an hour he had still not bought another cup and I despaired of ever selling him one. Then he came up here on that cane of his, and paid, and looking not at all pleased, told me that if you came in I was to say these words, and I repeat them exactly, Lone: 'I waited a long time; too long for a boy so young and inexperienced.' "

Immediately he had spoken, the balding man from Mrsevada took a step back from the counter and the stormy face on its other side. That face had darkened, and its features were writhing, and the eyes seemed ready to emit flashes of fire.

"That *bas*tard!" Lone blazed, and louder than Aristokrates had ever heard him speak.

"I . . . think you are right," the bigger man said mildly, while judiciously reserving all comment on Lone's lack of parentage.

Lone slammed a fist down on the counter. "That blag-dagged blaggard! This is—this is—you said his words *exactly*, Aris?"

"Absolutely! D'you think I would say such a thing to you?"

"That blag-dagged *bas*tard!" Lone spun about as if in hopes that someone would hurry to pick a fight with him, or that he could find an excuse to assault someone. Anyone.

No such opportunity knocked.

"I can understand that you are not amused," Aristokrates said. "Let me pour you something."

Lone wheeled back to him with such speed and such a stormy face that the other man bethought himself of the thick hardwood club he kept under the counter. But Lone proved not the sort to take out his anger on the message-bearer.

"Not tonight, Aris. Damn! Damn him for an arrogant blaggard!"

Aristokrates considered that his wisest course was to say nothing.

"Shit!" the young man snapped, face still writhing, and with a swish of cloak dark as midnight he whirled away toward the door.

"Oh, Lone," the man behind the counter said. "Wait a moment. He did bid me give you a few words of council when you were about to leave."

Dark clothing did not rustle despite the speed of Lone's turn. Wickedly menacing eyes met those paler ones of Aristokrates. "Council?"

"He bade me do you a favor," the proprietor of The Bottomless Well reported.

"I'll just bet!"

"Umm. He said to warn you not to enter Angry Alley."

Lone stared. "Huh! That's all?"

"Yes." Aristokrates nodded solemnly.

"Hey, Aris! How about another mug over here!" That call sounded in a voice with a bit of surliness in it.

Aristokrates waved a hand at the patron, one of

several at his table. Two of them also signed for another. "Oh oh. Sorry, Lone. Uh . . . good night . . ."

Lone did not return that ritual well-wishing as he glided to the door and in a second as much as vanished into the darkness outside.

Naturally, being angry and more, being Lone, he headed directly for the dark, dark opening between two close-set walls—a passage that too often reeked of urine. Although he saw no one in Angry Alley, someone was.

"The carelessness of rash-brash youth," a voice quiet as a tiptoe in shadow said, "is not bravery, Lone. The *real* Shadowspawn would not be so rash as to charge in when such a clear warning was issued."

"Shadowspawn!" Lone gasped, cloak swept back and hand frozen to hilt. It was as if the darkness had spoken, for still he saw no hint of person or even movement.

"The same. And well armed, and vexed at you with reason, but only talking instead of letting steel speak for me."

Lone of the prickling scalp and armpits considered that, and swallowed, and actually devoted a few seconds to thought, and for once he answered from his brain, not his bravado.

"You left word that I must stay out of this alley only because you knew I would have to accept the challenge!"

"It was a safe assumption," the darkness said. "You have just restrained yourself. You must learn to do that much more often, which is to learn to think. Else you will die a very young man, and who could possibly give a damn."

The final words were no question, really, but spoken flatly as a statement of fact. And once again

Lone felt assaulted . . . and once again, somehow, he found discipline within himself, and exercised it.

"I will try, Master of Thieves."

"I doubt it. And just 'master' will do, if you intend to apprentice yourself to Shadowspawn and succeed him."

"You do not make it easy, do you."

"I have had no easy life, Lone. My mentor was hanged when I was only a boy, younger than you. I was a cocky little piece of cat shit, but I learned that I must learn, and so I tried, and I learned."

Lone swallowed and, even in pitch darkness, blinked. It had not occurred to him that his idol was capable of such profundity.

"Doubtless you think that was profound," the darkness said, in the shadow-quiet voice of the master thief of Sanctuary.

Lone swallowed and managed to make no reply.

"If you can learn, I know things that you don't and can still do things that you can't."

As I can do things that you no longer can, poor crippled Shadowspawn, Lone mused, but again he strengthened himself to hold silent.

Then it occurred to him that the unseen owner of the ever-challenging voice was also saying nothing, and he steeled himself to pronounce the simple words:

"I can learn, Master."

The man called Chance had not been so elated in a long, long time. But none of that was apparent in his shadow-quiet voice: "You must be tested. To begin with you have not I hope forgot the location of the home of the Spellmaster."

"I remember," Lone said, trying hard not to sound sheepish. *What an idiot I was, breaking into that mansion! What a friend such a man as Strick could be!*

"Good," the shadows said. "Then we will meet there. Your first test is to reach his door before I do."

After a time Lone realized that although he had heard no sound of movement, he was alone in Angry Alley. With a slight smile, he began walking. Rapidly.

With a fleet and eager horse hitched to the mule-cart and a pass to show any law enforcement types who might stop him, Samoff made very, very good time driving through the night to the home of his master. Simple matter to wait near the end of the alley Chance had specified, say nothing when the black-clad man appeared and climbed aboard, and set off. From time to time as he guided the more than spirited young horse through the night he heard a chuckle from the man seated behind him, and Samoff made a vow to ask Chance—at a more opportune, meaning safer, time—if he had wet his underpants in his gurgling glee.

If the younger cat-burglar wet his pants that momentous night, it was not in glee. He was not short of breath but his legs were afflicted with spikes of ice when he reached the estate of the Spellmaster . . . and stared, blinking. Strick was right there outside, seated on the front steps of the carefully elevated house, apparently awaiting Lone's arrival. Moreover and far more awesomely, beside him sat a black-clad figure. That one threw up a hand as the other man in black approached on weary legs that he had pushed close to the limit of their endurance.

"Lone!" Chance called jubilantly. "Good to see you at last, lad!"

"Shit!" Lone muttered. Then, reprovingly as a schoolmaster: "You cheated!"

"True! I used my brain instead of my legs!"

While Lone ground his teeth, Strick spoke. "Not to mention a horse. Promise never to enter this house again unless invited, Lone, and we will go in for some refreshment."

"I promise," Lone said. "I even . . . uh . . . I had something to prove."

"Still have," Chance said, rising with the apparent aid of his cane.

Lone heaved a sigh and nodded. He had aborted, saying, "I even apologize," because it was hard, so hard for him to say such words. They went inside, and Lone learned what it was like to have the wherewithal to have a fast runner fetch ice from the mountains down to Sanctuary.

Or, in this case, for a certain old master cat burglar to find a way to relieve Arizak's runner of his burden and make a gift of such rich bounty to a friend . . .

Ice weakened good ale a bit, but how good to a sweatily exercised man it was with a bit of coolth added!

And then a bit more without the ice, as the three men talked. The woman present talked but little, as was her habit, but she gazed much on the cocky youngster working so hard to control his natural cockiness and truculence. What a fascinating boy! How strangely . . . *akin* to him she felt!

Linnana knew already the story of Strick's non-payment by Lord Arizak, even to the amount. Now she heard Chance lay out his desire to steal into Arizak's less than modest dwelling and relieve him of that exact amount.

"Not a quarter-ounce of copper more," Chance said, one finger upraised, "and not a quarter-ounce less."

"Yet," Linnana put in, "there is or should be the matter of interest . . ."

Strick smiled. "I have little doubt that opportunity will one day arise for me to extract that from the great Arizak."

She chuckled.

Chance did not. Meeting the eyes of no one, he said, "How I long to do it! But my age and leg make me unable to undertake that exciting piece of night work . . ."

"Your age and arm, you mean, Master," Lone said, lest Chance think the youth still believed that he was crippled in the leg, that the walking stick was necessary. "But the work will be done. I need only bethink myself of what I will need, and make a little list . . ."

"You need make no list," Chance assured him. "I know exactly what you need, for in past I completed an almost identical mission."

"Hmp," the Spellmaster said, without the hint of a smile. "Mission? Not on my behalf. Must have kept the swag to yourself!"

His friend also did not smile. "Nah, nah. Gave it all to the poor and the Temple of Him Whose Name We Do Not Pronounce, I did!"

Strick laughed with him, and continued to keep his peace about what he knew: his friend was indeed spawn of the shadows . . . or rather of the shadow god, Shalpa, usually referred to namelessly, as Chance just had.

"By four nights hence," Linnana suggested into the laughter, "we will have full dark of the moon, surely the perfect time for such a wicked venture . . ."

"But too easy," Chance said firmly. "By night after next the moon will be a mere tiny sliver—a fine working night for an excellent roach anxious to prove his talent and ability!"

Lone shrugged and endeavored to look relaxed and, above all, casually confident. Whatever the Shadowspawn said. At last he had achieved his goal, and here he sat, in the company of the man he most respected and admired. Naturally a youth with such a goal considered himself lucky to be in the service of Shadowspawn, no matter how much in his shadow! The only aspiration of the orphan Lone was to be as exactly like his idol as he could make himself—which meant doing things Shadowspawn's way, however dangerous.

"For one thing," Chance said, "you will need an archer."

Lone cocked his head. "An archer?"

"Someone good with a bow," Strick said, as if it were the meaning of the word that Lone did not grasp. "And arrows."

Without taking his gaze off Chance, Lone said, "Oh."

"An archer who can loft an arrow upward, trailing a rope," Chance explained. "That gets you over the Lord Arizak's wall, and maybe farther, as in higher."

"Ah!" Lone bobbed his head, acknowledging something he had not thought of.

"I, ah, know a girl who is expert with bow and arrow," Linnana said, and received strange looks from the men, all thinking: *a girl?!*

Strick said, "Would that be that teen daughter of Churga and Filixia?"

She nodded. "Jinsy, aye. She practices every day behind their house, and the girl is *good.*"

Chance was looking uncomfortable, and wishing he were having this meeting with his apprentice elsewhere, and just the two of them. "Uh . . . you sound like you're talking about a neighbor . . ."

"Right," Linnana said, smiling brightly. "And very good friends. Jinsy will be thirteen next month."

"Pardon me," Chance said, "but we are not going to use the child-daughter of well-off neighbors to help break into the keep of the lord of Sanctuary."

"Their financial status has nothing to do with it," Strick said. "They are Ilsigi, and love Lord Arizak no more than you do."

"Lone and I thank you," Chance said, "and we will recruit someone from within the Maze—" he broke off, and a little smile tugged at his lips. "Or maybe in what remains of Downwind relocated to the Hill. Remember: I come from there."

Having tried to help and been rejected, Linnana and her almost-husband sat back and looked grim.

"You will want to take rope with you, too," the master said. "Lightweight, thin, and tough. Test it yourself at your weight, *plus*. For me it was best to wind it around myself."

"And something to bring out the coins in," Strick suggested.

Two experienced thieves gave him the sort of look he was not accustomed to: disdain. Strick and Linnana offered no more advice or help, and the plan was made. The offer was made and repeated, but the catwalker repeatedly turned down opportunity to spend the night in the manse. Then the man he had apprenticed himself to nodded and made the decision for him.

"We thank you three times, friends, for such kindness. You have two overnight guests: Shadowspawn and Catwalker."

Later, very quietly in a darkened room, Chance furthered the education of his apprentice: "We made them unhappy by accepting no help or advice from them. When people really want to do you a favor, let them if you can. That is doing them a favor. We are making them feel good by staying here tonight."

"Thank you, Master. Ah . . . Shadowspawn . . . I need all such advice you can give me."

"Here's another piece, then. Never call me that again."

"Yes sir."

Father Ils save us all, Chance thought, just before he fell asleep, *for the ocean may go dry. Me, giving advice!*

Two nights later three men in dark clothing stood in the dark area below the wall of the lordly keep of the master of Sanctuary. Two were clad all in black, the third only a shade less somberly. He alone wore headgear, a soft cap of dark gray. The oldest among them had relieved the youngest of his cloak and sword, in the interest of better mobility. With Lone ready to set off on the mission that neither of them considered the least bit dishonest, the trio watched the arrow go up, and up, and a grin of pride rearranged the beard of the rag-tag former soldier Chance had recruited. He had proved his mettle. It was a perfect shot or appeared to be: the shaft caught, and here dangled the rope for Lone's use.

And no matter what plans the ocean might or might not have to go dry, Chance proved to have more advice to impart to his newfound apprentice. "If it's possible without overmuch danger," he counseled, "bring out the rope with you. *Absolutely* bring out the arrow, no matter what. And . . . Lone."

The younger man was gazing up at the wall, and

the place where arrow and rope had disappeared. "Aye."

"Look at me."

Instantly, Lone did.

With the portentousness of master to assistant, Chance said, "You are going to be very proud, and you will want to leave some sign that you have been there. *Do not.*"

Lone nodded. "Aye. May . . . may I ask why . . . Master?"

"Once in my weening pride I left proof to the man who then ruled this poor foreigners-saddled city, and after I was out it occurred to me that it was a bad idea to let him know how easily I could break into his palace, and out."

"Ah." Lone's dark, dark head was bobbing. "And did ill come of that?"

"No, except extra time and labor for me, for I felt obliged to steal back into the palace and remove the signal I had left of my presence . . . and then I had to get myself back out again."

Lone smiled, and then chuckled, and apologized for laughing. Then he noted that his mentor was also chuckling . . .

As the young man began to make his way sinuously up the rope, the watching Chance felt a touch at his sleeve. He turned to face his archer.

"The rope's in place and there he goes, yer lordship," the bearded man said. "About my payment?"

Chance pressed three coins into the waiting, grime-etched hand. The old soldier raised it to examine the contents of his palm, then gave his temporary employer a look.

"That is half," Chance told him. "So far the rope has not worked loose or broken. When he tops the wall and we know the rope has held, you will have earned the full amount we agreed on."

The archer looked crestfallen. "Aw . . ."

"If you don't think you can trust me, come with me to a place called The Bottomless Well."

Acorn-colored eyes shone in the darkness. "Are you buyin', yer lordship?"

"We will see," Chance said. "And stop calling me that."

He and the fellow, whose name he had given as Kantos, were on their second cup when through the doorway came a smug-faced young man all in black, in quest of his cloak and sword. Reaching the table, he produced Kantos's arrow and, with a flourish, handed it to him. Lone was reaching into his tunic as he removed his sword and cloak from a third chair and seated his smiling self with his mentor and the hired help.

"Done," he announced.

Chance shoved his mug over in front of his apprentice, who bobbed his head in gratitude.

"Well done!" Chance said, and immediately diverted his attention from the pridesome youth. "Kantos, the other half of your payment for a job well done," he said, and pressed the coppers into Kantos's ready hand. "As a bonus, I am paying for your beer. Do have a good night."

Kantos was smart enough to recognize dismissal. "Thankin' ye both," he smiled, touching his forelock as he rose, and he all but louted out.

When he was gone Lone withdrew from within his tunic a soft cloth sack that he had partially burdened with earth before he went up the wall. The purpose of that strangeness was to absorb the sound of clinking coins while he took his leave. With great pride and smugness he set it on the table before Chance. They both heard a muted clink.

Chance directed his dark gaze into the dark eyes across the table from him. "The exact amount?"

Lone nodded. "The exact amount."

"Strick is going to crow! And what did you take for yourself, Catwalker?"

Lone looked offended. "Nothing!"

"Well done. Did you have any trouble?"

Lone compressed his lips and flared his nostrils with a sigh. "I did. I was on my way out when a servant appeared out of nowhere. Nothing I did had attracted him. He just happened along and there was nothing I could do about it. He saw me, but I had the scarf across my face. His mouth went wider'n his eyes, and I hit him, hard. He fell down and just stayed there. On his back with his eyes closed. I got out of there as fast as I could. He could never recognize me."

Chance sighed and looked unhappy. It was the way of masters.

Part of the problem had nothing to do with the fact that Lord A. now knew that someone had breached his keep. As disturbing to the man who so despised sorcery was the fact that this afternoon an unduly nervous Linnana had told him that she'd had an unfamiliar experience: for the first time in her life, she had Seen, in the way of the S'danzo. What she Saw had to do with Lone's entry into Arizak's keep: a man lying on the floor on his back, with his eyes closed.

The successful apprentice thief sat erect in his new less-than-finery, *so* filled with pride that he had been complimented—but not much!—by his idol. He had rejected Strick's insistence that he accept the coins he had *liberated*, until he caught the sharp look directed at him by his chosen mentor and master.

He accepted the spellmaster's "too kind" offer as he said, head bowed, with great gratitude ... that Chance later told him was overdone.

Lone had also agreed and acceded to Chance's wise suggestion that during his "off-duty hours," he wear much less somber clothing and perhaps even fewer weapons. Lone had even been gracious enough in accepting Linnana's offer to help him find a more colorful tunic and leggings. Now he sat comfortably in a medium-blue tunic over dark yellow or "old gold" leggings and soft tan boots with heels. The four of them once again sat together, at Strick's. This time they were out back, in a yard full of flowers and ornamental shrubs that the Spellmaster had caused to be surrounded by a strange fence made of vertical slats with spaces between.

Strick had told them of his contacting the ancient mage whose apprentice he had determined was responsible for the many mis-sent spells in Sanctuary of late, and they had met. At first Strick's only report was a terse, "He and I are not going to be friends."

Chance and Linnana prevailed upon him to tell the story of their meeting, however brief. The Spellmaster's reaction to the reaction of Kusharlonikas to the news, and his attitude, was, all but grinding his teeth, to call himself "appalled." The sorcerer not only refused all responsibility for both his spells and those of his less-than-competent apprentice, but was positively obscene in his dismissal of the woman who had lost her sole companion—the cat—and the couple who had been forced to the expense of replacing their tent.

Chance did have to like Strick's characterization of Kusharlonikas as "that pompously overblown droplet of ant excrement!"

Now he who had been Shadowspawn had told the

blue-tunicked youngster that he "seemed" ready for the real job; a deed of true importance. This news was more than welcome to Lone, who was immediately all attention.

"When the Dyareelans desecrated the main temple of Father Ils," Chance said, quietly in the pre-insect twilight, "they committed the heresy of stealing the Sacred Left Sandal of the Father. I have all but begged to learn its whereabouts, and retrieve it." He made an unhappy face. "In times past, I needed help for the first task only. Now, I must have others perform both."

"Only respect for you, Linnana," a suddenly grim-faced Lone said, "stops me from spitting on your grass at mere mention of the Dyareela swine. It's even hard for me to say the name. But a chance to undo something *they* did—*one* of their many evils—I can count only as a gift. And to do a service for the Ilsigi and our god of gods at the same time . . . what have I done to merit such a pile of riches?"

The master thief shot him a look. "Don't overdo it, Catwalker."

But then he saw that the lad who called himself an Ilsigi in emulation of Shadowspawn was sincere or at least mostly, and Chance was almost embarrassed.

Lone either did not notice that or affected not to. He was, after all, a boy—however bad a boy. "Do we yet know where the Sandal is?"

Chance was nodding as he said, "Strick has just located it."

Lone looked pleased. "Ah!" He looked expectantly at Strick. After a moment, when no one had spoken, Lone prompted, "Well?"

Quietly Strick told him: "The Dyareeling destroyed it. But! A precise copy of it has been fabricated, imbued with its essence, and coated with a SeeNot Spell."

Lone looked dubious. "Will a copy do?"

"The priest says so," Chance told him.

"Ah! Then where—?"

"It's in the keep of the mage Kusharlonikas," Strick said, and was interrupted by the youth.

"Sorcery! Shit!"

"Lone, damn it," Chance snapped, "are you going to blither, or let us tell you what you have to know?"

Lone put on a chastised look. "Apologies, Strick. Please tell me all of it."

Strick nodded amiably, something he did well. "It's in the spell room of that dot of ant excrement. His Chamber of Reflection and Divination, the pompous scum calls it."

Lone managed to curb a blurt, but rolled his eyes. So cute, Linnana thought . . .

"The spell disguises it," Strick went on. "I believe that what I Saw around the Sandal is a large, two-handled flagon. On his divination table."

This time Lone was unable to hold back an entirely natural reaction to such unwelcome news: "Shit!"

With the piece of special beef folded in an enormous leaf to contain its greasiness, Lone was just about to depart on the biggest night of his life when Strick appeared. The bulky man was winded from hurrying from his home to Chance's apartment, where Lone had reported a couple of hours ago.

"Something strange just happened," the man in the long-skirted tunic said, panting a little. "Until she Saw a man on the floor on his back with his eyes closed during your Arizak adventure, Linnana had never showed any evidence of having that peculiarly

S'danzo ability—which is certainly not granted to all her people. Now she and I have both had a vision of you and your destination this night."

"Good. I hope it wasn't about me lying on a floor with my eyes open!" a cocky youngster said.

"Nothing so final, but something very unpleasant, I think. Kusharlonikas has laid a spell on more than one item in his innermost chamber. We were unable to See specifics because of wards on the room, but two menaces to an intruder are there. They are disguised with a SeeNot *and* a binding spell. I think the scum has trapped a pair of demons as guardians of his divining chamber."

"Demons!" Lone blurted his reaction because he was unable to disguise the fact that he was shaken by such news.

"So I *think*, I said. Now stand still, close your eyes, and try to think of nothing while I make some silly noises."

Lone was right willing to go along. The "silly noises" the Spellmaster referred to apparently comprised a spell, and Lone certainly hoped that it was effectual. He thought he recognized some of the sounds as words, but he could never be certain. If the oral spelling was accompanied by gestures, he saw none, for he kept his eyes closed as bidden.

"Good," Strick said. "Let's hope for the best. Naturally I place a lot of faith in spells, but nothing is certain when I'm not sure what I'm trying to combat. Here, Lone, wear this."

With his own hands the Spellmaster slipped the shortish thong over Lone's dark, dark head and let the medallion flop onto the black-clad chest. Lone peered downward. He was not able to make out any details of what he was wearing, and was unwilling to touch the thing. It appeared to be ceramic, rather than metal.

"Uh ... Spellmaster ... this thing swinging and sliding around on my chest is going to be a distraction and maybe worse ..."

Strick nodded. "Good point. I've got to find a way to secure some kind of locking pins to the back of such a ward-medal, for you *active* types. Here, be still a moment."

Lone was not a person who took kindly to being touched, but he curbed the movement of his hands while the white-haired man slid the ward-medallion down into his tunic.

Strick stepped back. "I can't think of anything else to try, other than to tell you what you must already know: Breaking into the keep of a master mage is a bad idea, and I advise you not to do it."

"Thanks, Spellmaster. And you already know that I am going."

And so he went, ghosting through a nighted city in his jet clothing under a pallid crescent of a moon just on the point of being swallowed by the demons of the night sky. He was all unaware that his mentor was already at the scene, to observe whatever of his apprentice's actions he could.

Not a lot, as it turned out, and that did not displease the spawn of the shadows. First Lone went close to the fence that surrounded the sorcerer's sizable estate, flapped his arms to attract the dog, and threw the drugged meat over the wall. Then he faded into the shadows. Tempted by the aroma of beef, the big dark red animal redirected his attentions to the good-sized morsel. He was peacefully snoozing in less than a minute, and Chance smiled without showing his teeth. Strick did know his potions!

What the youth did with cloak and sword Chance did not see, but he watched him take the fence as if it were mere inches high, go up an outbuilding wall with seeming ease, and onto the roof of that building. Chance saw him make the leap from there onto the roof of the large keep—home of the man that Chance, thanks to Strick, could not help but think of as "ant excrement." He neither saw nor heard—good!—the landing of the buskin-shod lad, and saw nothing further except the distinctly handsome and nonmenacing structure. After a while he realized that Lone must have unwound his rope to go in through a window not visible to his mentor.

So Lone had. While his mentor was tying to convince himself to walk away and await the youth as agreed, Lone's soft-soled boots were padding silently along a corridor little less dark than his clothing. He heard no sound until he came to the second-floor room he assumed was his destination, at least according to Strick. There he paused and pressed himself flat against the wall. Holding his breath with throwing knife in hand, he rolled his eyes this way and that—and heard nothing.

He swung to the door, opened it, slithered into the smallish and completely windowless room beyond, and closed the door all in one fluid motion that took but a moment. How very kind of Kusharlonikas to keep a little oil lamp burning here, in his keep of keeps! Odd, that it rested on a side table while at either end of the long green-draped one that dominated the centenarian mage's Chamber of Reflection and Divination rested an ornate brass lamp in the shape of a preposterously hideous gargoyle. Each was about the size of a lap-dog, and partially supported by its thickish tail. Neither was lit.

Glad they're not the real thing, Lone mused, staring

in curiosity at the third object on the divination table: a large, two-handled flagon of an unrecogniza-
ble greenish metal that appeared to be of little
value. He moved silently round one end of the table
so that he faced the door. It was time to open the
small vial that Strick had given him.

The youthful man called Catwalker opened his
pouch, removed the vial of medium green glass, and
uncorked it. According to instructions, he slung its
contents into the air above the table and backed
away, holding his breath. The dark powder proved
very nearly lighter than air. A few grains floated down
onto the flagon, and onto each of the gargoyle
lamps. Almost in a moment Lone was gazing at what
looked like an ancient sandal of rust-hued leather—
and two gargoyles were looking at Lone from eyes
large as those of calves. Every hair on his scalp and
nape tingled as it rose. As if they had practiced, the
twin horrors snarled in unison.

The intruder into the domain that they had been
set to guard had his long Ilbarsi knife out in less
than two seconds. At the same time, he backed another couple of steps from the table. It occurred to
him to draw the medallion out of his tunic and let
it lie on his chest. Maybe sight of it would affright
these trapped demons back into being lamps again?
He'd be happy to light them . . .

No, and furthermore with a slight rustling as in
unison they scuttled to the edge of the table, they
launched themselves at him. Simultaneously, one
from his left and the other from the opposite direction, and all he saw was huge inimical eyes, and
fangs—lots and lots of sharp teeth. For wingless
monstrosities, they certainly flew well enough! Lone
squatted low, did some crablike scuttling of his own
to the side, and was on his feet again quick as

breath. Already he was swinging the long almost-sword at the pair of brainless monsters that hurtled past his former location and crashed into the wall.

Speed and skill abetted by plain good luck enabled him to cut one of the hell-sent things completely in two—bloodlessly. That was when he heard the door open behind him. He did not turn to greet the new menace for the simple reason that the intact demon was hurtling up at him from the floor. Lone moved so fast that the ward-medallion swung—and a claw tore through its thong as the demon hurtled past. Disgruntled was a mild term for what the apprentice cat burglar felt when he heard the ceramic medallion shatter on the floor.

Instantly and simultaneously someone behind Lone snapped out a "Shit," and the two halves of the slain gargoyle fused. So. Strick's medallion had been more effective than its wearer had anticipated, and now he was totally unprotected, with *three* foes intent that he never leave this place on his feet!

"Off me, beast!" the voice behind the intruder said, seemingly as fearfully as in anger, and those words were followed by other ones in a language older than Sanctuary.

So the one that missed me attacked whoever came in— or at least struck him in its flight! Lone thought, desperately kicking at the reincarnated gargoyle number one again, *and now he is putting a curse on me, or worse!* And then he spun and his right arm snapped forward to send a flat leaf-shaped blade in the direction of the voice. When it swerved away from the homely, very young man in the icky green robe, Lone shuddered at knowledge that he was in the presence of a sorcerous enemy with a better protective spell than his. Kusharlonikas's apprentice, surely. And his fellow apprentice hardly appeared incompetent, up close!

Kusharlonikas's apprentice slung gargoyle number two at Shadowspawn's apprentice and began gesturing and muttering. This time Lone successfully skewered the thing—which slid right along his blade and clawed his hand.

He made a sound of pain just as Komodoflorensal finished casting his spell and added his personal word of power: *"Iffets!"*

Immediately the tan sandal became a green flagon and the monsters from hell became handsomely wrought but hideous oil lamps, and Komodoflorensal was staring across the divining table at a thoroughly angry young man all in black.

One of the apprentices present said, "Shit!" and the other said, "You'd better start running, Komo-duh-whatever!"

The high priest of the pitifully diminished temple of Ils Father of All was unsparing in heaping praise and blessings on the two who surreptitiously brought him the long-missing Sacred Left Sandal of the Father. And yes, he acceded to the wish of the master and his apprentice that he tell no one whence came the great gift.

The two well-dressed men were on their way to meet Strick when somewhere a savagely punished young man in a green robe said, *"Iffets!"*

The shattered shards of ceramic on the floor of the Chamber of Reflection and Divination of Kusharlonikas the mage did not reassemble into a circle, but a shadow passed between Sanctuary and the sun.

"Shit," Komodoflorensal muttered.

"Damn," Lone muttered. "How convenient! Darkness at noon!" And he abandoned his mentor to head for the alley beside the nearest well-to-do apartment building . . .

The Prisoner in the Jewel

Diana L. Paxson

---

*H*ere, there is no time.

She turns, meeting herself in a hundred refractions, always shifting, but never changing, for there is no time here.

She turns and sees herself, always and only herself. It is this, she thinks, that will drive her mad. Perhaps it has done so already.

Once she walked beneath the sun, clad in silk and jewels. Now she is the bright spark in the heart of a jewel. When Time had a meaning, a mage imprisoned her here. She fought, but now she would welcome even that rape of the psyche. Only those who are alive can feel pain.

Light and Dark succeed one another, so she knows that in the world outside, night still follows day.

But here, there is no time.

The board above the door to the inn turned in the wind that blew in from the sea. As it swung back, it caught the thin sunlight, and the golden eye of the phoenix that gave the inn its name appeared to blink. Latilla paused for a moment, squinting, to see if it would happen again, then shook her head and sloshed the bucket of water across the worn stone steps. Her husband would have seen that momentary flicker as an omen. Her father could have made the bird come alive and fly away. But to Latilla it meant it was going to be another damp day in late winter. And every morning when she rolled out of the bed in which she slept (alone) she prayed that nothing would happen to change this from one more ordinary day.

When she was a little girl, magic had been a wonder. Later, it had become a horror. Both she and Sanctuary, she thought sourly, were far better off without magic, magi, or gods.

Phoenix Lane was waking around her. Far down the road she could see a horseman ambling slowly along. Water gurgled and added itself to the remains of Latilla's pail as the fuller down the road poured out the stinking contents of a bleaching vat. For a moment the acrid reek of aged urine filled the air. Long ago, when her father had built Phoenix House from stone left over from the new City wall, the street had been clean and inviting.

But concepts like safety and respectability seemed to be alien to her hometown. Wealth and corruption, yes—those might survive—but there was something in the air of Sanctuary that corroded peace as the stink of the fuller's vat was fouling the air. Her father was gone, and the pleasant home he had built now supported what remained of his family as an inn.

Still, whether the smell was dissipating or she was simply becoming used to it, with each moment Latilla's awareness of it grew less.

Sanctuary never really changes, she thought with a sigh, *but even here, life goes on.*

What ought to be going on, or at least getting up,

was her brother Alfi, whose job it was to feed the animals stabled in the shed at the rear of the inn. She could hear the trader's donkey braying impatiently. The empty bucket banged against her calf as she strode around the building to see.

By the time she had gotten Alfi going, the rider she had seen earlier was coming up the lane, peering about him as if not quite sure of his road. He was either a very tall man, she thought, watching, or he was riding a small horse. It was early in the day for an incoming traveler to have reached Sanctuary. She wondered what he was looking for.

It was not only the beasts who protested when breakfast was not forthcoming, Latilla thought as she pushed open the door of the cook shed they had added onto the back when they turned the house into an inn. Her daughter Sula was bending over the hearth, stirring a pot. That was a relief— her twin brother Taran had never come in last night at all.

Then she caught sight of the breakfast tray still waiting patiently, and emptily, on the table.

"Sula! You've not taken that tray up to your grandmother yet? What were you thinking of?"

Boys, most likely, Latilla realized as Sula turned, coloring up to the roots of her fair hair. She was a good girl, or had been until adolescence had turned her brains to mush.

"The porridge is done, so get that bowl filled and upstairs! The other guests will be coming down to breakfast any moment now."

"Oh Mother, Gram always complains so! She'll ask me who I've been seeing, and come out with some dire warning because his grandfather, or his father, or his uncle, came to some ghastly end. Doesn't she know anything good about anyone?"

Latilla snorted. "In this town? Get up there, child—You won't sweeten her temper by starving it."

"I'm not your servant, or hers, either . . ." Sula muttered as she took the bowl from the tray and ladled a dollop of porridge into it.

"No—a servant would be grateful!" Latilla replied tartly. "Now go—disaster is only deepened by delay!"

"Oh mother, does everything you say have to have a proverb?" Sula complained, pouring tea into the cup.

Whatever Latilla was going to say was interrupted by a clangor at the front door. As Latilla started forward, Sula made her escape up the stairs, laden tray in hand.

𝕋he horseman stood on the step, still holding the rein of his mount. She looked up at him, in one swift glance noting the lines graven by patience and perhaps suppressed passion as well. His life had not been easy, but she thought he was younger than he at first appeared.

"They say you have rooms. Clean, and not too expensive."

His voice was very deep. A swiftly suppressed spurt of awareness identified it as the kind of voice she liked in a man. Her husband, Darios, had spoken thus, although the two men were unlike in all other ways. The stranger sounded as if he had come from Ranke, though the accent had been worn smooth by years of exile.

"And stabling for my horse."

"I've a room on the second floor," she said slowly, "though I don't know where I'll find a bed to fit you. The horse will be easier."

She let her awareness extend towards him in the

way Darios had taught her. The ability to "read" her guests had proved useful before now. This time, however, her probe met a blank wall. No one expected a widow who kept an inn to know any magecraft. Latilla had worked hard to keep it that way—it was not worth jeopardizing that concealment by probing further.

"Give me a few padpols off the price and I'll sleep on a pallet on the floor . . ." he was saying, as if he had not noticed. Perhaps the shields were natural, then, and the man was no more than he seemed.

Questions might be unwise, but speculation was another matter. The stranger's clothing was worn, but he wore it with an elegance that suggested there might have been a time when he slept in a bed built to match his inches. She would have to decide on the basis of that air of faded nobility, and the pain she had seen in his eyes.

"Two shaboozh the week, with board for you and the mare." She spat in her palm and held it out to him. "My name is Latilla. Welcome to the Phoenix Inn."

He looked a little taken aback, but he clasped her hand. She could feel the warmth within him, like a hidden fire. "You may call me Shamesh."

Well, that was one way to let her know it was not really his name. But that was no concern of hers, Latilla told herself firmly, so long as he paid his rent on time. Now if Taran would only get home, the whole family would be accounted for, and as safe as anyone could be, in these times.

Taran was, at that point, only a few backstreets away, reflecting on how much he hated mornings. He hated them even more when he saw them from the other side, with no sleep to soften the breaking day.

A bleached, thinned quality always seemed to weaken the blue of the sky, as if some forgetful god had left a translucent veil to obscure the night. Taran tried not to dwell on such thoughts. They wakened childhood nightmares best left alone.

On this particular morning his apprehensions were particularly acute.

Mama's going to kill me if she finds out! he thought miserably,

Latilla disapproved of the company Taran chose to keep, a mixed gang of youths who haunted the marketplace led by Griff, a boy two years Taran's senior. Griff had grown up in the Maze, and had a scar for every lesson he'd learned there. But Griff had humor in him too, which gave him a certain charm that drew Taran and others to him. It was that charisma that inspired them to go looking for trouble. Where many in Sanctuary simply sought to survive, Griff and his boys wanted to thrive.

Damn you, Griff! thought Taran. *What the hell were you thinking?*

A sharp yelp stopped him. Up ahead, a half-dozen boys had tied a mongrel dog to a stake they'd hammered into the ground. They were throwing rocks at it, and from the look of it they'd been at it for awhile. The soft scent of blood mixed with the city smells of urine and dirt.

The dog was too tired even to defend itself, and staggered back and forth behind the inadequate cover of the stake. Occasionally a particularly sharp rock would gouge it and the dog would muster enough strength for another whimper. All this did was to make the ragged boys cheer whoever had made the shot and inspire the others to imitate him.

Taran's eyes blurred, and for a moment he saw Griff surrounded by men with clubs. Up and down the clubs went, blood splattering behind them.

Taran shuddered. He had not been able to help Griff. He could not help the dog now. He turned and dashed past the boys and their victim, trying to ignore the pity that welled within him. And the fear.

Once Shamesh had arranged his scant luggage in his chamber, and every morning thereafter, he would leave the Phoenix and head towards the residences of the Rankan exiles at Lands' End, or in the other direction, towards the town. Taran, who had shown an unusual willingness to stay home lately and thus had been pressed into service as a guide, reported that the man's purpose was not commerce, for he took no goods with him, nor was he carrying anything in the evening when he came back again. Whatever his business was, it was not proving successful. With each day, Latilla could sense his frustration mounting.

At the end of the week, when Shamesh came to her to pay his accounting, she could stand it no longer.

"Will you be wanting the room for a week longer, or have you completed your business here?"

He gave her a quick look, as if suspecting sarcasm. But Latilla had good shields too. The pain, and the passion, were closer to the surface now. It needed no magic to sense the moment when desperation breached his defenses.

"I have not even begun!"

"Come—sit down. I have just made tea." Her smile invited confidence. When the house was new, her mother had hoped to hold feasts in the dining room. Large enough to hold all the guests for a communal meal, it was empty now. Morning sunlight filtered through the high windows and glowed on the frescoes, the only remnant of past splendor that had survived the hard times when anything that could bring in a few padpols had to be sold.

"Nothing in this town is where I was told to seek it—even the Vulgar Unicorn has moved!" Shamesh exclaimed.

"The past few years have been troubled," Latilla agreed. "Much has been destroyed, and many died." She waited a little, watching him. "Is it a person or a place that you are looking for?"

"A person . . ." he said at last. "A noblewoman of Ranke who came with the household of Prince Kadakithis when he was sent here as governor."

"The Prince left Sanctuary thirty years ago! The only Rankans remaining here are the old families—I suppose you have asked among them?"

"Exhaustively. A few of the older folk remember her, but they believe she went with the Prince to the Beysin isles . . ."

Something about the way he said it alerted her. Clearly, Shamesh knew that Prince Kadakithis had returned to Ranke instead of sailing away with his Beysib queen. Was he dead, or was it he who had told this man about Sanctuary?

"My older sister was one of the Beysa's ladies," Latilla said instead. "So I can tell you that there were only a few women from Sanctuary on those ships, and none of them was Rankene." Watching, she saw the light fade from his eyes, and repressed the impulse to reach out and comfort him. "She never arrived in the capital?"

Shamesh shook his head. "Do you think I would have come all the way to this miserable hole if she had?"

For a moment Latilla bristled. Then she sighed. It was, after all, true. Even her own father had left in the end, and though he had promised to be back in a year's time, he had never returned. She took a calming breath.

"What was her name?"

"Elisandra. She was the older sister of the lady who is now Empress of Ranke. I have been sent to look for her."

Latilla sat back, understanding many things. Though Ranke no longer dared claim Sanctuary as a possession, rumor of events in the Empire still reached them. The throne had been seized by a northern general some years back, who appeared to be ruling well. To legitimize his reign he had married into a family which was, if not quite imperial, ancient enough to make him socially acceptable.

Had Shamesh taken on this search for money, or was there some more pressing motive? She could not ask, but he had gained her sympathy.

"When I was a child, my father was often in and out of the palace. I was acquainted with many of those who served there. If they can be found, there might be someone who would know what had become of her . . ."

The sudden light in his face made it for a moment beautiful. Latilla's breath caught, and she was abruptly conscious of him as a physical being, and at the same time remembered how long it had been since she had felt that kind of awareness of a man.

He is at least a decade younger than I am, despite the silver threads in his hair, she told herself, *and whatever beauty I might have had is long gone!*

"That's true!" he exclaimed. "But I would not know how to begin asking. Mistress Latilla, will you help me?"

———

In the morning it had rained, and the streets were still muddy. Latilla held up the skirts of her second best robe and picked her way along Pyrtanis Street with care, very conscious of the tall man at her side, who was glancing from side to side, his expression an uneasy mix of disgust and caution.

"Who is this woman we're going to see?" Shamesh asked as they turned the corner to Camdelon Street. The buildings here were even shabbier, but the steps were swept and here and there a plant in a pot made a pathetic attempt at gentility. *Like me—* thought Latilla, remembering how Sula had stared at the unaccustomed finery. *The girl is too filled with her own dreams to imagine that her mother might also cherish a few fantasies. . . .* She realized the subject of her current fantasy had spoken and forced a smile.

"Her name is Mistress Patrin. In the old days, she was chief housekeeper at the Palace, and the terror of the servants there. When I was a little girl she certainly terrified *me.* She will probably inform you that her father was a Rankene lord, and it would be best to pretend to believe her. My mother always doubted that story, but at least while they could still get out and about, the two of them stayed on visiting terms. So I know the old bat survived the Troubles, though whether she's alive now I couldn't say."

It had taken a week of patient inquiry to get this far. Most of the Palace servants she had thought of first were dead or disappeared, and even Taran's network of scruffy layabouts, motivated by the promise of Rankene coin, had run out of options by the time she remembered her mother's old friend.

"And you think this Patrin can help us?"

"Well, she knew everyone who was at court in those days—and all the gossip as well. She'll have known this Elisandra of yours."

And Elisandra, if we find her, will be at least ten years older than I, thought Latilla with a grim satisfaction. She would be no rival, even in fantasy.

A gaggle of yelling children shot out from an alley, gave Latilla and her companion a practiced once-over, and having decided they looked too alert to try a little purse snatching, pelted off down the road.

Latilla, who had been counting the houses down from the corner, paused, eyeing the dwelling before her dubiously. The potted plant on the step had clearly died some time ago.

Shamesh, less sensitive to nuances, took a step forward and banged on the door.

They waited in the street for what seemed an endless moment, Latilla feeling more foolish as it extended. But Shamesh had only just lifted his hand to knock again when a crack widened at the edge of the door. Metal glinted—the chain was still on. Above it she glimpsed the glitter of an eye.

"Mistress Patrin? It's Latilla, come to see you. It's been several years, but I used to come with my mother. Do you remember me?" She moved closer. "You used to bake such nice little cakes when we visited, so I've brought you some pastries and a little fruit—"

The chain glittered and swung as the door was pulled open.

"Who's this?" the old woman barked as she saw Shamesh. "Not your husband!" She looked him up and down in an appraisal which her age saved from being insulting.

"A . . . friend, who volunteered to escort me through the town—" answered Latilla as they had agreed.

"Please, good mistress, I am quite well behaved, I assure you!" said Shamesh, smiling.

"A Rankan lord, by your accent! Did you think I would not know? I wonder what such a one is doing here?" She sniffed, but she pulled the door the rest of the way open.

It was just as well they had brought their own food, thought Latilla, wrinkling her nose a little at the faint sour smell in the room. It was dusty, too. From the way Mistress Patrin moved, she guessed that the old woman's sight was failing. She must have recognized her by voice rather than vision.

"And how does your mother?"

"Her health is good," said Latilla, "but she cannot walk very well anymore."

"Too fat!" Mistress Patrin exclaimed triumphantly. "I told her that her joints would give out one day! I flatter myself that I have kept my own figure tolerably well!" She added, smoothing shawls draped over a frame like a rack of bones. Her wig, pinned in a style that had been fashionable a generation ago, bore a spider web between two stiff curls.

For a moment Shamesh caught Latilla's glance and she fought to keep her composure. Mistress Patrin's vague gaze slid towards the corner where she had told him to sit and she simpered.

"And you, my lord, are from the great city? How I should love to see it! My father, you know was an exile, but he often used to speak of its splendors."

Shamesh cleared his throat. "The recent wars have left their mark, but the new Emperor is rebuilding, and one day it will be more magnificent than before."

Latilla blinked as she heard the rougher accent he had used give way to a drawling intonation that reminded her of court speech long ago. For the first time, she believed absolutely that the story of his quest was true.

The old woman had recognized it too, and was reviving like a withered flower in the rain.

"And why have you come to Sanctuary?" Her voice fell to a conspiratorial whisper. Hope made the dim eyes gleam. "Are the Rankans returning? Will the Emperor send a Prince to govern us again?"

Shamesh flinched from her intensity, then rallied, eyes glinting with amusement. "My lady," he said softly, "I am on a quest."

Latilla stifled a smile. Mistress Patrin was leaning towards him, an unaccustomed excitement spotting her cheeks with color. Shamesh knew just how to appeal to the old woman's romantic yearnings.

And what honesty forced the question about yours?

I . . . am simply enjoying his company!

Feeling her own cheeks hot, Latilla forced her attention back to the conversation.

"Her Serenity loved her sister," Shamesh was saying now, "and will grieve until she knows Elisandra's fate. And so I have come to Sanctuary to search for her."

"Elisandra . . ." Mistress Patrin echoed, her vague gaze growing even more abstracted. "She was a slender girl, with fair hair?"

"Her Serenity is a woman of queenly figure," Shamesh said carefully, "and her sister would no doubt by now be the same, but the family does tend towards fair hair."

"I remember her. Sweet-natured, she was, not like some of them, but rather flighty . . . always fancying herself in love with someone, and wept like a watering pot when they disappointed her." There was another silence, and then Mistress Patrin's face changed.

"What is it? What do you remember?" asked Shamesh, unable to bear the waiting.

"It was in the last days before the Beysib left. . . . There was a mage called Keyral who was promising all sorts of things—wealth, love, the usual. Your husband, Darios, knew him—" Her rheumy gaze fixed Latilla suddenly. "He was in the Guild. Most people were too concerned to save their skins to pay attention, but there were some who found his schemes a distraction. That girl Elisandra was one of the ones he dazzled, and he encouraged her. She had no money, but she added class to his entourage."

"What happened to him?" Shamesh and Latilla spoke almost as one.

The old woman shrugged. "No one knows. He had invited everyone to what he called a Great Demonstration of Magic, something to do with the transmutation of jewels. But it went wrong somehow, and the house was destroyed—that was the same day the Beysa left, so no one paid too much attention."

"And Elisandra?"

"I can't recall seeing her after the Prince left Sanctuary. I always thought she went with him. But if she did not reach Ranke . . ."

Latilla sat back, trying to recapture her own memories of a time of more than ordinary confusion, even for Sanctuary. But since then so many more exotic traumas had shaken the city . . . It was Shamesh who recalled her to the problem at hand.

"If you do not know where this Keyral went, can you at least tell us where he was last seen?"

Mistress Patrin's brows bent. "His place was on the corner of Fowlers Street and one of those lanes a block or two below the Governor's Walk down at the end, but only the gods know what remains of the place by now."

"It's not a part of town I know," said Latilla. It was not a district any respectable woman should have been acquainted with. "But my son may be able to find it."

 Taran ran a hand through his dirty-reddish hair and cast an annoyed glance down first one and then the second of the streets that connected with the intersection in which they were standing.

"Come now, boy," Shamesh growled, "which way?"

Taran resisted the urge to spit out a snarl in return. *Mind yourself amongst your betters,* his mother had said. Manners were not one of Taran's usual concerns (they didn't go over well with the company he kept), but he held his peace. For an aristocrat, Shamesh wasn't that bad—not like the pompous fools out at Land's End—and he was intimidating enough to keep Havish's gang at bay.

Thinking of Havish brought back memories of Griff and the beatings. Corvi, one of the lads in Griff's little circle of would-be toughs, had told Taran that Griff would heal—he might not get back the full use of his legs, or ever again be the mammoth figure who'd led them when they swaggered down the street from one tavern to the next—but he'd still be Griff. The question was, would he want to be?

Taran hated it. Hated being afraid of Havish, and the way he and his boys had beat on Griff like a hammer on a nail, hated how his "friends" had stood by and watched. And most of all, he hated himself, because he had been so afraid he'd just stayed and watched with them.

A muddled mind makes a muddled life, his mother

would say if she were here, before giving him a friendly cuff to the head. Since that was all that seemed to be missing, Taran rapped himself twice on the back of his skull before pointing left.

"This way," he stated with a smile, hoping his voice showed more confidence than he was feeling.

In the old days, Keyral's house had stood three stories tall, with a garden in back where the wizard grew herbs and held parties now and again. Taran could almost see it. Almost.

Now the building's bones barely remained. Much of the stonework had been salvaged—by now the stones were likely part of the city walls or one of those houses Grabar and Cauvin had been building for merchants as trade revived. *The city consumes itself to rebuild itself*, Taran thought morosely. The rest of it lay in rubble on the ground.

Shamesh was staring at the ruins, looking as if he were sucking on one of those tart rock candies Taran got at holidays, except that he did seem to be enjoying the taste.

"What now?" Taran asked.

"I'm looking for an opening—a door to a cellar or basement . . ." Shamesh said at last. He picked his way through the rubble and began to heave rocks aside. Taran considered helping him, but the sun was warm and the rocks looked heavy. *Aristocrats need their exercise, and young men need their rest*, he told himself, stifling a yawn. It looked like a hopeless task anyway. In thirty years the rubble must surely have been picked clean. The overgrown remains of the garden looked far more inviting.

"I'm going to start looking over there—" Taran called as he made his way around the ruin, looking for a nice comfy spot where he would be well hid-

den from view. He brushed away a pile of dead
leaves and lay down with a sigh.

There was a rock digging into his ribs. Swearing,
he rolled over, pushing more debris away. But this
spot wasn't comfortable either. He sat up and
looked at the ground on which he'd been lying. He
couldn't see anything pointy, and even sitting up he
felt the irritation. It was in his head.

He ought to move, he thought then. But he was
tired, and if he got up Shamesh would expect him
to start working. Taran cursed again, then lay back
and began to breathe slowly in and out, letting the
annoyance flow out of him in the way his father had
taught him when he was a child. Taran tried not to
think about his father too often. Darios had been a
wizard too, but it hadn't saved him when the Dyareela cult came to power.

Taran could still feel—whatever it was—but it
didn't bother him so much now. He sighed again
and rolled over on his side.

His half-closed eyes focused on something in
front of him—a point of light that glittered where
he had pushed away the leaves. With dream-like deliberation, he reached out for it.

*D*arkness *falls again, in her forgotten world, the only
thing that changes in her endless days. She begins to count,
as she often does, a personal measurement of time. It is the
only kind she has, now.*

*A face appears behind her reflection—or has her reflec-
tion changed? But that's impossible. There are no changes
here. She looks again, and realizes that the face is not,
cannot be her own! She is looking at a boy, no, a young
man, with a mop of ginger hair, while hers is fair. He
looks confused.*

She laughs, then starts to weep, crying out to him, plead-

*ing, scratching at the barrier between them with desperate
fingers.*

*The darkness gives way once more to light and the face
is gone.*

*She pounds against the mirror, but only her own image
remains to reflect her agony.*

Taran sat up, heart pounding, as the vision faded.
What in hell was that? His visions were usually nightmares—they'd never shown him a beautiful woman
before. Had he been dreaming? The girl had looked
like one of those Rankan princesses from a marketplace storyteller's tale.

He felt a sharp point dig into his palm and realized that he was still holding something—it was a
jewel. Whatever he had seen, this was real enough,
and it looked valuable—an egg-shaped, faceted, in-
digo stone that left purple light on the ground
where the sunlight passed through.

"Taran!" Shamesh was shouting. With a start
Taran realized he'd been calling for some time.
"Drat you, where'd you get to, boy? There's nothing
here, and it's getting late. Time we were on our way
home!"

"I'm here, in the back. Just keep your britches
on." Taran slipped the jewel into the leather pouch
that hung around his neck, got to his feet and
dusted himself off.

I had better luck than you did, he thought as he re-
joined the older man. But he said nothing. There
was no point in getting everyone all excited until he
knew what it was he had found.

Dinner had been a silent meal. If the searchers had
been successful, the whole house would have heard
about it. But Latilla knew better than to question

men who were tired and hungry. Taran went off to his room as soon as dinner was done. He had that preoccupied look that usually meant he was trying to keep a secret. Likely he meant to sneak out to join his friends, and didn't want her to know. She frowned at the thought, but let him leave unquestioned.

It was her lodger, pouring himself yet another cup from the flask of wine of Aurvesh he had brought back with him, who was her primary concern just now.

"The place is a ruin," Shamesh said disgustedly. "You warned me—" He turned to Latilla. "I used to think that Ranke was past its prime ... compared to this ruin, the capital is blooming!"

Latilla realized that she was glaring and looked quickly away. Why it should gall her to hear someone else confirm her own opinion she did not know, especially when the flush on his cheeks showed he was finally being overcome by the wine.

"Not a scrap of paper ... not a smell of a spell ..." Shamesh drained his mug and poured another. "Don't know why I was so sure the answer was there! But there's nothing. Ever'one who might of known what happened is dead or fled. Vashanka! What'll I do now?"

He set down the mug with a thump that splashed blood spots of wine upon the cloth and rested his face in his hands. Latilla repressed an impulse to reach out and touch that bent head.

"You have done all that a man may," she said softly. "No one will blame you if you give up the search now. You don't have to go back—you could make a new life here ..."

"Think it's blame I fear?" He surged to his feet, swaying, and she stood up quickly to keep him from falling. " 'S my *family*. . . . We were great, once, you know? But m'grandfather, and father, they had a genius . . . for choosin' the losin' side!" He giggled a little at the rhyme. "All the money's gone, 'n most of the land. To Koron Eridakos, whose forefathers were kings!" He raised the wine cup, and with drunken deliberation, spilled the lees out onto the floor. "Last chance . . . last chance t' save m'name. . . ."

"Let's get you up to bed," murmured Latilla, draping his arm across her shoulders. Her husband had been a temperate man, but she could remember how her mother had dealt with her father in the days when he still had a weakness for wine. Some men got ugly when in drink. Shamesh, like her father, tended towards the maudlin. But these were more than sentimental maundering. The wine had dissolved the man's impervious aristocratic calm, and her heart ached as she realized the depth of his pain.

His coordination was a little improved by the time they reached his room, but not his control. As Latilla eased him down to the bed his hand brushed her breast and remained there. "Stay . . ." he muttered. His eyes were closed. "I don't want . . . to be alone. . . ."

He thinks I'm someone else, she thought, allowing her gaze to dwell on the finely cut features and mobile lips that had been haunting her dreams. His other hand closed on her shoulder. Even drunk, he was strong. Too strong to resist, she told herself as he pulled her down beside him, knowing even then it was a lie.

"*Please . . . Can't you hear me? Someone, I know there's someone . . . I will go mad, surely . . . it has been so* long. . . ." *She turns, battering against the glimmer of light that refracts around her. Something has changed, she is sure of it, something has changed the alternation of light and shadow in which she has lived so long. Hope, that fragile spirit she thought dead a lifetime ago, is stirring, frantic to be free.*

Blue . . . he is trapped in a maze of blue and purple light. Moaning, he struggles to get free. But wherever he turns his own reflection blocks the way, fair hair tossing, gray eyes wide with anguish. His senses reel, not least because in this nightmare he has somehow become a beautiful girl. He flails at the barriers that surround him, feeling the rasp of rough wool, and is confused anew, for all he can see is the polished prison of the Jewel. "Help me!" he cries. "Can't anyone hear?"

Someone is shaking him. He opens his eyes. Through shattering purple lenses he glimpses his mother's face and the familiar outlines of his room, and falls back with a moan of pain.

Taran shuddered, struggling to focus. His mother was bending over him, a lamp in her hand. Grasping for normal consciousness, he noted that she was still dressed, though she was disheveled as if she had slept in her clothes.

"Hush—" she was murmuring, "you've had a nightmare. You're home in your own room. You're safe here."

He flushed, sure he had outgrown the need for such comfort years ago. The other half of his mind was still throbbing with the sensations of his dream.

"Purple . . ." he muttered. "It was purple, and I was a *girl* . . ."

"Ssh . . ." said Latilla. "It's over now."

Taran shook his head. "But I have to understand. I was a girl, and I was a prisoner in the jewel . . ."

His mother stopped patting his shoulder. "What jewel?" she asked.

"I found it in the weeds. I was going to tell you—" he added quickly, "but you were talking to *him*, and—"

"Do you still have it?" she interrupted him.

"Yes . . ." he muttered. He felt almost himself again, and was already regretting having given up his secret. The girl had been so lovely! He heaved himself up on one elbow, unhooked his neck pouch from the bedpost and tugged it open. Violet refractions skittered around the room as it fell into his hand.

"I found it and I thought it was pretty, that's all. I thought it might be valuable."

"You know that's not all . . ." Latilla frowned. "There's magic in it—if you haven't sensed that already you're not your father's son, or mine! And you found it in a sorcerer's den. . . ."

Right, he thought, grimacing at his own stupidity. *And I just lay down in the middle of it to have a snooze!*

"Do you think this has something to do with that girl Shamesh is looking for?" he asked when her silence had gone on too long. He had agreed to help the Rankan. Did that mean he was honor bound to give up the jewel? "Are you going to tell him?"

After another long moment his mother sighed. "I don't know."

Will he remember? Latilla wondered as she ladled porridge into wooden bowls. The donkey-driver and the silk merchant who were her other guests this week were already sipping their tea. Shamesh had not yet appeared. She wondered if he would make it down to breakfast. She wondered if he would remember that he had not spent last night alone.

And if he does? If he looks at me, and remembering, smiles? If the quest that had brought Shamesh here failed, he would have no reason to go home. *We could be happy together,* she thought, *if happiness based on a lie could endure. . . .*

But the jewel might have nothing to do with his search, and she would not have to lie. Even if he did not remember, what had happened once might happen again. Her imagination started on its round once more.

By the time her Rankan lodger finally made his appearance, Taran had finished the morning chores he usually weaseled out of and had wheedled a second bowl of porridge—proof of her distraction. His eyes shifted uneasily from his mother to Shamesh as the older man sat down, squinting at the light flooding in through the eastern window. Behind him the fresco of Shipri, Queen of the Harvest glowed, the colors almost as bright as they had been when Latilla was young. Her mother was supposed to have modeled for that image. She found it hard to believe.

"Here's tea—" she said, setting a mug in front of him. His gaze passed over her unseeing as he groped for it.

Perhaps it was the hangover that made Shamesh so distant, she thought, but she did not think so. Keeping silent about Taran's discovery would be a fitting punishment for a man who could not even remember what she had given him.

As the tea hit his system Shamesh looked up, the fine eyes clearing. "That wine of yours was stronger

than I expected. I'm afraid I talked a lot of nonsense
last night—"

You talked about the things that matter to you . . . She
thought, gazing back at him, and understood that
though she had held his body in her arms, she
would never touch his soul. She sighed.

"Taran has something to show you," she said
aloud. Her son cast her a stricken look, his hand
going instinctively to cover the leather bag. *We are
both giving up a dream . . .* thought Latilla, but her
own pain made her ruthless. "There was something
left of Keyral's magic after all. Taran found a jewel."

For a moment Latilla wondered if her son was
going to obey. She could see the struggle in his face,
but after a few moments he opened the bag and very
gently, set the jewel on the mat. Violet coruscations
flickered across the walls as it caught the morning
sun.

"When I hold it . . ." he muttered, "I see a girl . . .
a beautiful girl with fair hair."

Shamesh sat back in his chair, the color draining
from his face and then returning in a rush. "The
transmutation of souls . . ." he whispered. "It must
be . . . But is she *in* the jewel, or is it only a gateway?"

"To an alternate dimension?" asked Latilla. He
looked at her in surprise. "My husband was a mage,"
she explained with a bitter smile.

"Exactly. Magecraft can create a container that is
bigger on the inside than on the outside. If that's
what we have here, then opening it will set Elisandra, if that's who it is, free."

"But if it's not, you'll kill her!" Taran cried.

"If the jewel holds no more than her soul," Latilla
said gently, "then her body died thirty years ago.
Would you keep her imprisoned here?"

Taran gaped back, gaze shifting between them. "Will you just . . . shatter it?"

"No! That would be destruction!" exclaimed Shamesh.

"You are a mage . . ." said Latilla, understanding what it was in him that had attracted her.

He shrugged. "I have learned a little about . . . jewels. It is heat, not force, that will relax the bonds that hold this spell together. A gentle heat that slowly grows, until the barriers dissolve and the prisoner is set free."

There are some sorceries that are best performed during the hours of darkness. But for this one, Shamesh deemed it best to make use of the radiant heat of noon. Within the circle he had drawn upon the ground in the garden, mirrors focused the pale spring sunshine around and beneath the jewel.

"Aren't there words you should say? Some kind of a spell?" asked Taran doubtfully.

"I will . . . that what should be, shall be . . ." murmured Latilla. "That each soul be free to find its own truth . . . that by my acts I may aid the forces of order in the world . . ."

"That's a Mageguild oath—" Shamesh looked at her with new respect.

Latilla nodded. This man and Darios had both poured out their souls in her arms, but with her husband, she had poured out hers in turn.

"Look!" exclaimed Taran, pointing at the jewel. It glowed like a purple egg in the sunshine. But now the flicker of refracted light was disappearing in a violet radiance that gradually grew.

"*Illin tan s'agariontë*—" Shamesh intoned, fingers rigid and quivering, arms extended towards the Jewel. "*Karistë! Karistë!*"

Violet light flared suddenly, then paled—no, the white blur was something that was taking shape within it, writhing in the churning light, then collapsing in a swirl of draperies as the glow, and the jewel, disappeared.

There was a moment of shocked silence. Then the huddled figure moaned.

"She's alive!" whispered Taran.

He started to move, but Shamesh was before him, reaching the woman in one swift step and gathering her into his arms. They were strong arms, as Latilla had reason to know. She watched in silence as Shamesh lifted her, noting the smooth skin, the corn-silk hair. Thirty years had passed, but they had not touched her.

"Elisandra . . ." he said in a shaking voice. "Elisandra Donadakos . . . You are free, Elisandra. Your sister is Empress now. I will take you back to her. Can you hear me, my lady? We're going home!" He gazed down at her, his face radiant with triumph, with ambition, with joy.

For a moment Taran watched them, jaw clenched. Then his thin frame seemed to sag. Head down, he turned and slowly walked away. Latilla opened her mouth to call him back, but let the words die unvoiced. Let him keep the illusion that he could run from his pain. She blinked back her own tears and folded her arms.

Elisandra opened her eyes and smiled, a prisoner no more.

Ritual Evolution

Selina Rosen

Kadasah was doing what she normally did towards the end of the early watch on an Ilsday night. She was holding up her end of the bar at the Vulgar Unicorn, her hand wrapped around her fourth glass of Talulas Thunder Ale, and trying desperately to ignore Kaytin who was as usual bugging the living shite out of her.

"Kadasah," he started in a sultry, silky voice. Kaytin was tall for a S'danzo man but still several inches shorter than Kadasah, and she had to look down at him when he talked to her. When she bothered to pretend to be listening to him at all that is. She could tell by the look in his eyes that he was about to feed her a line. "Your eyes are as dark as the blackest night, your lips like the reddest cherries, your hair like golden, liquid moonlight..."

Kadasah interrupted him with an uncharitable laugh. "You're so full of crap your back teeth are brown. And my eyes are blue. Gods! If you're going to sling such total horse crap about, at least have the good taste to get my coloring right. And just what the hell is 'liquid moonlight' supposed to mean?"

Kaytin smiled up at her undaunted. "Ah, my beautiful love, my tongue is as clumsy as my heart is true. I meant that your eyes were so darkly blue that they looked almost black. That your hair, the color of moonlight, flows around your shoulders like water . . ."

"Horse shite! My hair is braided like it always is." Kadasah laughed, genuinely amused. When he wasn't driving her completely crazy with his unbridled lust, she occasionally found his attempts to bed her entertaining. Besides, in a strange way, except for Vagrant, who was a red stallion and therefore an even worse conversationalist than Kaytin, he was really her only friend.

"Maybe so, but sincere horse shite at the very worst," Kaytin said with a smile. And then he started the touching.

Kadasah was a little surprised. By her reckoning they hadn't gotten that far into the evening's festivities. Normally he would have waited for her to drink at least three more ales before he felt safe enough to start manhandling her. He had wrapped his arms around her waist and was nuzzling at her neck. She was about to smack him hard enough to send him careening across the room when she realized that this wasn't his usual horny, loverboy move, but his, "I'm showing that I'm attached to the big blond mercenary with all the weapons so don't even think about kicking my ass move." She also realized that a strange silence had fallen across the bar. Apparently Kaytin had heard it before she had, which meant that he was expecting trouble. She wondered what the philandering little thug had done this time.

Kadasah turned slowly to see who had walked in and made a face of disgust in spite of her best efforts.

"All right, get off me before I knock you across the bar. Frogs! It isn't some angry husband, just that horrid, slimy, dead-looking guy. No doubt he's coming after his equally horrid toady." She shoved Kaytin roughly back, and he managed to catch and straighten himself without looking clumsy in a way that only Kaytin could do. No doubt because he'd had so much practice.

He smiled at her appealingly. "My own sweet love. What is this talk of a jealous husband? Kaytin has nothing to fear from any irate man who has an unfaithful wife, for I only have eyes for you, and I am saving myself only for the day when you will make me the happiest man on earth by agreeing to be mi—"

"I don't think your eyes are the problem. However, perhaps you're telling the truth. After all, I find it hard to believe that any woman could be stupid enough to believe the utter crap that springs forth from your mouth," she said, cutting a look at him from the corner of her eyes. He started to speak again, and she held up her hand. "Oh, enough already. Just shut up." She wasn't in the mood for any more of his flowery tributes, or his lies.

Kaytin had a tendency to lie when it would have been easier to tell the truth.

She watched the horrible abortion that had entered the bar warily as it walked over to the twisted hunk of flesh that sat at a corner table drooling into a mug of ale and touching any woman who came into his reach. He didn't seem to be bothered at all by the number of times he got slapped. In fact, Kadasah got the impression that he rather liked being slapped.

Kaytin followed her eyes and shuddered, obviously as disgusted by the creep as she was. "I wonder what it wants here?"

Kadasah shrugged. "Who knows what goes through the mind of something like that—or if it even has a mind. What motivates it? His ugly little friend is bad enough. One night I'm here slinging a few ales down, telling a story about one of my jobs, and that twisted little bugger comes right up, pulls his pants down and shows me his privates. I thought at first that the creepy little toad had a third leg, but no, and he's got a dragon tattooed on it. Damndest thing you ever saw."

"How dare he! Why, if that awful thing wasn't with him, Kaytin would march right over there and kick his twisted little butt and . . ."

"Like I need anyone to kick anyone's butt for me. I handled it," she said with only the hint of a brag in her voice.

"I bet you did," Kaytin chuckled. "So, what did you do?"

"What do you think I did? I laughed, said that had to hurt, and then when I saw he wasn't going away I kicked his dragon."

"Ouch!" Kaytin laughed.

The thing with no eyes turned its face toward her. Sightless or not, Kadasah knew—the way prey knows it's being hunted—that it could see her. Suddenly Kadasah was in no mood to finish out her usual routine, so she downed her drink and started to sneak out of the bar without paying—which was part of her ritual.

The bartender, Pegrin the Ugly, who'd earned his name the hard way, laughed, obviously more amused than he was angry. "You Irrune rogue! Get back in here and pay your tab."

Kadasah mumbled as she went back to the bar and grudgingly paid for not only her tab but Kaytin's as well.

"You're leaving early."

"You shouldn't oughta serve things like that," Kadasah said in a whisper nodding over her shoulder. "You know it's up to no good."

Pegrin laughed. "If I kicked everyone out of the Vulgar Unicorn that was up to no good, I wouldn't have a single customer . . . Why, some people tell me I shouldn't serve the Irrune," he leaned over the bar to whisper confidentially, "because they steal."

Kadasah smiled innocently. "Have I ever stolen from you?"

"More than probably," he said with a smile.

Kadasah feigned injury, then with one backwards glance at the creature that looked like death warmed up and his freaky-looking lackey, she left.

Kaytin followed Kadasah out. "He usually just comes in, gets his twisted idiot boy and leaves," Kaytin said, curiosity obvious in his voice. "I wonder what he was up to tonight?"

Kadasah shrugged. "Something horrible you can bet. He's obviously waiting for someone. I'd like to kill that horrid thing." A momentary look of confusion crossed her face. "But I'm not really sure whether it's still alive or not, and if it's dead . . . well how would you go about killing something that's already dead?"

"Besides . . . no sense in killing someone unless you're getting paid. Isn't that what you always say, my love?" Kaytin asked with a smile.

"For that thing, I'd make an exception. Besides,

I'm sure I could find someone who'd pay me to do it."

Kadasah was perturbed. Her usual ritual had been interrupted by that hunk of decaying flesh pretending to be a man, therefore it was now time to move on to her alternate routine. "So, Kaytin . . . I was thinking that since I didn't get to drink myself into a coma like I usually do on Ilsday night, that I might as well get some work done." Now she looked at him and turned on the charm, making it hard to believe that she was the same woman who had spurned him so harshly just a few minutes ago in the bar. "You want to help me? I'll let you in for a cut . . ."

Kaytin shook his head vigorously. "No, no, no, no, no! Every time you ask me to help you I wind up with the most dangerous part. Then when it comes time to pay me . . . well there is never any money, and there is certainly none of that which I want much more than money—which you have also on occasion promised me."

"Kaytin! Why, I'm cut to the very quick! When have I ever put your life in danger?" She hoped he didn't notice that she wasn't saying anything about stiffing him. There were deceptions and there were outright lies, and she froggin' well knew the difference.

He laughed and flung his hands around in front of him. "Too many times to count. You think I don't know what you're doing, but Kaytin isn't stupid. You are using me for bait. We go to the darkest, most horrid part of the ruined temple of Savankala or the Street of Red Lanterns, and you say 'Kaytin stand here,' or 'Kaytin stand there, and I'll tell you what to do next.' And I wait and I wait, but you never tell me anything else, and then when some Dyareelan spook is about to kill me you show up and kill them.

You always cut off a scar or a tattoo—I have no idea why, and then it's always . . . 'Kaytin be a good fellow and cart off this body and bury it and I'll go get my reward and meet you back at the Vulgar Unicorn and we'll split the money.' So I go bury the body and go back to the Vulgar Unicorn where I wait and wait, but you don't come back to the bar for days and when you do, there is no money!"

"Hey, I pay your bar tab . . ."

"When you don't manage to sneak out without paying at all," Kaytin reminded.

"Come on, Kaytin, quit being such a big baby. It isn't that dangerous. Who's the best bastard sword fighter in all of Sanctuary, maybe even the world?"

"Why you are, my love, but . . ."

"And who but me has killed three men with one swing of an axe?"

"No one but you, my love, but . . ."

"With me to protect you, you are as safe in the darkest, dankest part of Savankala as you were in your mother's womb, and I swear that if you help me this time, I'll deal with you fairly. Maybe this will even be the night that I find your advances irresistible."

"In which case . . ." He walked up close to her and took her hand. "Why waste any part of the night on death and killing? Let us spend the whole night making mad and passionate love to one another, and wake up in each other's arms to find our passion renewed."

"Kaytin—how many times do I have to tell you? I can really only get seriously aroused after I've killed someone," Kadasah said with an irritated sigh. "I suppose if you'd rather I go off into the night by myself, alone, into the very heart of the Dyareelan lair . . . To do not only my job, but to bring about

the death of yet another worshiper of the Lady of
Blood, to spare countless poor souls from a lingering, painful death . . ."

"Now who is full of horse shite!" Kaytin hissed.
"My mother has seen with the True Sight that you
are no good for me. That you only mean to use me.
That you care not even a small amount for Kaytin.
You use me only as a means to an end. I know this,
and yet I continue to allow you to use and misuse
me. But this time I say no! This very morning my
own dear mother did warn me about you yet again,
saying, Don't go to that horrid bar to see that *suvesh*
woman, for she will only bring you pain. That is
what she said, and being a good son I am listening
. . . Well to part of it anyway."

To Kadasah there was never any doubt that Kaytin
was at least part S'danzo, but she doubted seriously
that he was the full-blooded S'danzo man that he
claimed to be when he got very drunk and/or was
trying to impress her. For one thing it seemed to go
against everything she had ever been told about the
S'danzo that he would be bragging about his heritage much less about his mother's Sight—which was
remarkably something he apparently thought made
him more attractive.

The S'danzo were supposed to be a secretive people, and Kaytin was about as subtle as a fart in a
temple.

He kept complaining and going on about his
mother's visions, and how he wasn't going to be
lured into helping her even as she climbed onto
Vagrant's back and he climbed onto the back of his
mule and started following her down the road.

For the most part she didn't bother to listen; he
was going to come; he always did. He bellyached
and complained and moaned, and then did what-

ever she wanted him to do. She was sure this was due, in no small part, to the talisman of charisma she wore around her neck. She had stolen the charm from a wizard she'd once done a job for back before she started working for one of the "rich silk-sacked, so-called nobles living on the Processional," who now kept her in steady employment.

The talisman gave her a certain power over men, making her almost irresistible to them. When you lived by the blade you were always looking for anything that gave you any edge whatsoever. It was arguably easier for a man to kill an ugly woman than it was for him to kill a beautiful one, so . . .

Of course she hardly ever needed the charisma talisman since she'd started working for her patron, because the people she killed now cared very little about physical beauty. She continued to wear it because it made it very easy to manipulate most normal people—men in particular.

As she rode along ignoring Kaytin's moaning, she found herself once again trying to figure out just exactly who her employer was. She'd never actually seen the face of the man she worked for. He had approached her in shadows that first time, wearing a hood that covered his face, and she had never had any direct contact with him since. She left the pieces of skin with the tattoos or scars under a log in front of one god or another's ruined temple along the Avenue of Temples—as proof of her kill. When she came back the next day there was money. So she had no idea who her benefactor actually was.

She had laid in hiding once to see who would show up, but the person who came was obviously just a stable boy running an errand. She supposed she could have followed him. She knew it wouldn't be too hard for her to find out who her employer was, but she had long ago decided not to pursue it. This was a good job, and she didn't want to risk losing it.

Besides, she thought she probably knew, since at their first meeting he had told her his story. He was one of the few who had opposed the plan to invite the Irrune into town because he believed to the bitter end that he could negotiate with the Dyareelans. Then when Molin Torchholder led the Irrune into sight of the city walls, and the Dyreelans had only a little time to settle outstanding scores, they wreaked as much havoc as they could. They suspected, correctly, that the rich aristocrats and richer merchants had betrayed them, and sought vengeance against those they could lay hands on. Unfortunately, her benefactor didn't feel threatened because he'd argued against bringing in the Irrune, so he and all that was his were easy to "lay hands on." The day before the city fell to Arizak, the Dyareelans killed his wife and children and burned his house to the ground. Then to add insult to injury they proceeded to torture him, trying to get him to confess to his "betrayal," and give up other names. Ironically, it was only the arrival of Kadasah's people, the very Irrunes he had fought to keep out, that had saved his life.

He'd undergone a foxhole conversion. Since that day he had dedicated his life and his money to exterminating the extremist Dyareelans who hide by day in the tunnels under Sanctuary and only came out at night. Knowing her background and her skill, he had sought her out to be his instrument of their destruction. Since she already hated the horrid bastards anyway, getting paid to kill them was rather like getting paid to eat your dinner. It was something you wanted to do and would have done anyway, so getting paid was just a bonus.

What else did she really need to know? Of course it didn't stop her from wondering.

Soon they had reached their destination. She decided on this night to use Kaytin as a lookout instead of bait, just to make him feel better. With him watching to make sure she was unseen, she dropped a bunch of broken glass onto the ground hoping that in the dim light it would look like gems. She then made a simple snare around the "gems" using a measuring rope she had stolen from a carpenter's job site just the day before. Then she moved into the shadows with Kaytin to wait, and wait, and wait.

Some weeks that's all she did. Wait all night and go home empty-handed. Sometimes she'd go months between kills. They didn't always come up in the same place, and they were careful. In fact, the more of them she killed, the more cautious they became, so sometimes she'd give up hunting them until they got cocky again, or she ran out of money—whichever came first.

"They aren't coming," Kaytin whispered, putting his mouth right against her ear. "Let's leave this awful place and go back to your house for the night. I will take you places you have never been before."

She shoved him away . . . "Yeah, like to a healer to get a cure for some disease you'd no doubt give me. Still you're right, nothing's going to come this way tonight." She got up and started picking up the pieces of glass. She was about to gather up the measuring rope when she heard something. She grabbed her axe off her waist, twisted towards the noise just in time, threw it and dropped the nearest one.

"Vagrant! Go!" she called, and heard him running away as she drew her sword from her back. There were dozens of them, and they were obviously cultists, because no one else had any reason to come after her. Well, at least not in this section of town. But . . . this just couldn't be! The cult was supposed to be all but extinct. She killed a couple of them, then something grabbed her feet and she was falling. Too late she realized she had stepped into her own trap. The last thing she remembered was a foul smelling rag being pressed against her nose and mouth.

When she woke up the air was dank and filled with the smell of death and mold. She knew immediately where they had taken her—the tunnels under the Street of Red Lanterns. She was tied up and alive—which wasn't necessarily a good thing when one had been captured by a cult that delighted in nothing quite so much as torturing a person to death. As she became more aware of herself and her surroundings she realized that she was tied to someone, and she soon realized that a familiar voice was screeching at her.

"—safe as in your mother's womb, she says! I'm the greatest fighter of all times, she says! Killed three men with one blow from my axe, she says! Now we are going to die the death of a thousand cuts or be burned alive to death—"

"Yeah, that's what they usually do." Kadasah sighed. They had been tied up with their backs together. The bonds were so tight that she couldn't even wiggle her little finger without pain.

"I knew it, Kadasah. I knew you were going to get me killed. My mother told me. She tried to warn me, but my great love—"

"Lust," Kadasah corrected.

"My love blinded me. Now I am going to die. We're both going to die without ever consummating our love."

It was more than Kadasah could take at the moment. They had been captured and bound by the Dyareelan. She had never in her life been quite so sure of her own very immediate and horrible demise, and Kaytin was still whining because she hadn't slept with him.

"All right, dunderhead. Since you are more than probably right, and we are about to be killed, I'm going to let you in on a little secret. You don't love me. Hell, if you saw the real me you probably wouldn't even find me attractive. I'm wearing a talisman I stole from a wizard that makes me look beautiful, a froggin' charm."

"So that you can get men to do whatever you like!" he hissed accusingly.

"Well, what other reason would I have?"

"Always with you people it is with the stealing . . ."

"While your people are oh so virtuous."

"Quiet," Kaytin said quickly, and Kadasah remembered where they were and that the only people the Dyareelans hated worse than the Irrune were the S'danzo. Then he whispered turning his head. "Don't tell me that it is only some spell. I know what is in my heart, and I admit to you before we both die that I love you and only you." Then his voice changed, and he screamed. "You treacherous, lying, deceitful, harpy who is getting me tortured to death!"

"Me!" Kadasah spat back. "You were supposed to be keeping watch. You were supposed to tell me if you saw anything . . . You know, *anything*—like a couple of dozen worshipers of the Destroyer!"

"Shush! Don't say her name, you'll call her here."

"Horse shite," Kadasah said, shaking her head wildly since it was one of the only parts of her body she could actually move. "Gods, shmods! There are no gods . . . I knew it! I knew you were lying even about your damn heritage! Everyone knows the S'danzo believe in gods about as much as I do."

"I'm not listening, I'm not listening! I am S'danzo but . . . I . . . I can have gods if I want to. It couldn't hurt. I'm going to pray to some gods, and I'm going to ask them to forgive you for your blasphemy."

"You'll be wasting your breath, Kaytin. There are no gods; your people know that. It's all just froggin' crap the priests tell people to get them to give them their money. Did you ever see a god?"

For answer he started praying in his native tongue in a nearly inaudible whisper. He knew she, like his own mother, believed what she said; he'd heard her say it before. But he had learned differently from his father, and he wasn't going to listen to Kadasah right now. Not when they obviously needed some god to come and save them, and she was going out of her way to enrage them all. Perhaps she did have some magical talisman. He could certainly find no good reason to love this horrid woman at this moment.

"I tried to talk to my god once. Irrunega . . . He didn't talk back. Nothing in my life changed, either, so he obviously didn't listen. I tried talking to a dead relative—even an enemy. Finally I searched for my spirit guide. You know what happened? A big nothing. So go ahead pray your stupid head off, because it won't do you one damn bit of good."

"It couldn't hurt. Do you have any better ideas?"

"Well, we could—" She didn't really have any better ideas at the moment, so she looked around as much as she could. They were in a small, dank, wide space in the tunnel, with no doors on either side that she could make out. "All right—our legs aren't tied. If we work our legs up, maybe we could stand and try to get away."

Their first attempt only managed to land all of Kadasah's weight on Kaytin. He let out a groan and started praying again.

"No, no, now come on, we can do this. I'm taller than you, and we're tied at our backs, so we just have to remember that. I'll bend at the knees this time," she said.

The second time they succeeded in getting on their feet.

"Now what?" Kaytin asked.

It was a good question. It was black as pitch down either passage, and with their hands tied there was really no way to grab hold of the small candle that was lighting the tunnel where they'd been stowed. Obviously the light wasn't for them, it was there to keep any of their captors from stumbling over the pair in the darkness of the tunnel.

Suddenly—and amazingly, considering she'd been brain dead only a moment before—Kadasah had an idea. She pulled Kaytin over to the small table that held the candle. "We can burn the rope off!" she said forcing their hands over the flame.

"Ouch!" Kaytin screeched. "That's not the rope; it's my hand!"

"Sorry."

After a few more failed attempts the rope finally caught. A few scorched fingers and some ruined clothing later, they were free.

Kaytin grabbed the candle in its holder, and Kadasah smashed the small table, giving one leg to Kaytin and keeping another for herself. With the makeshift weapon in her hand she didn't feel quite as naked.

"Which way?" Kaytin asked.

"I don't know! How would I? It's not like I've been here before." She peered down both halls looking for any sign of light and found none. "But we've got to start moving. After all, they're going to come after us sooner or later and we can't stay here. In fact, I'm wondering why they haven't come after us already. You take a guess," she said indicating the two different passages.

"No, no. You only tell me to guess so that you can blame me when we wind up hopelessly lost. So you guess, and then I can blame you. Which seems fair since this is all your fault anyway."

"How do you figure?"

"Because all I wanted to do was make love. A painless, enjoyable pleasure, but no—you just had to go kill something."

Kadasah ignored him and chose. "This way."

They started walking. And walking. The longer they went without running into anyone the more worried she became. This wasn't right. Their captors should have come to get them and torture them to death way before this. They should have at the very least noticed they were missing by now, and how hard was it to find people in a tunnel? You could run down one way or the other, but that was about it. So far they hadn't come to anything jutting off from the main tunnel, although she was fairly sure such exits and entrances existed.

She was an excellent swordswoman—without a sword. She was experienced with an axe—though the "three men with one blow" was mostly a lie— but she had no axe, either. She was most probably the best horsewoman in all of Sanctuary, if not the world. But she was in a tunnel, and her horse was the gods only knew where above her.

She had a candle and a charisma talisman and a couple of table legs, and she was lost underground with possibly hundreds of Bloody Hand Dyareelans and of course Kaytin, who just kept praying to some gods even though he insisted he was S'danzo, and she constantly pointed out how useless it was.

She hadn't felt this helpless since her parents split up. Her father had chosen to take her with him while her mother had stayed behind with her younger siblings—she'd had no choice and no control then, either.

Her father had been a minor member of Nadalya's entourage, and she had grown up in the palace as basically his personal slave and housekeeper. But being in the palace gave her the chance to watch as Nadalya's guards trained, and they had taught her much. She became a skilled fighter because her father took her to live among fighters, and she became untrusting and uncaring because he took her away from the people she loved and who loved her.

Her father had disowned her when at the age of sixteen she left his service to become a mercenary. However, everyone knew whose daughter she was and she knew her father was occasionally asked to pay restitution for damage she'd done either while drunk, in a fight or both. It didn't bother her, if he chose to pay that was his problem not hers.

The mercenary life was a good one for someone like her, someone who had no ties and no commitments except to herself. Kadasah certainly never considered joining any war band. She might very well be good at giving orders—she certainly believed she was—but she sure as hell wasn't any good at all at taking them.

That one event that happened when she was only nine, had shaped her whole life—changed it totally from its original course. And here she was again with no control, basically helpless. Except that now she had a lifetime of experience behind her, and she wasn't a little kid that people could kick around. She made her own decisions now, and her destiny was in her own hands. All she had to do was use her head. This time her weapons skill wasn't going to be enough, though. She couldn't fight herself out of this one; she was going to have to think and think quickly.

Damn that creepy almost dead guy! He ruined my routine! Nothing is right! It's all his fault. I swear, if I get out of this one, I'm going to get that creep!

Suddenly she heard voices, and she threw herself and Kaytin against the wall and blew out the candle.

"What the . . ." Kaytin started in a whisper, but quieted down when he also heard the sound of voices getting closer. He seemed to be trying to actually crawl into the tunnel wall behind them and wasn't doing a half-bad job. Kaytin was of course a natural hider, just as she was a natural fighter.

There were at least two different voices. One most probably female, the other definitely male.

From the tone of their voices it was obvious that they were agitated and unhappy. She thought at first it must be because they had discovered that she and Kaytin were missing, but gradually it became clear that this wasn't the case.

Kadasah spoke both Wrigglie as well as Irrune, but these two seemed to be speaking in a tongue which was as foreign to her as the prayers Kaytin had been mumbling earlier. It was only as they got closer that she realized that they were speaking Wrigglie, just a slower more deliberate version than she was used to. Some people told her she talked too fast, and sometimes when she did this, she knew she stuck Irrune words in, making it impossible for people to understand her. As she listened to these two obviously agitated people, she wondered what they must sound like when they weren't excited.

"—cause she is an Irrune woman, a mercenary from her attire. Kopal swears he has seen her in the palace, that he recognizes her from Arizak's court. He thinks that Arizak may realize that we have infiltrated his court. That he may have sent her here to spy on us—to find out who our spies are," the woman was saying.

"Nonsense, how could they know? How would they? We have captured ourselves a couple of sacrifices. Nothing less and nothing more. I will talk to Kopal and calm him down. He worries too much . . ."

"But he wishes to question her before we sacrifice her."

"That shouldn't be too hard. We can use her little friend to get the information from her."

As she listened to them she was a little amused, and a whole lot of ashamed. She had been sure that they had been carefully hunting her, having figured out that she was the one killing them. Instead she and Kaytin had just been in the wrong place at the wrong time and had been picked up as sacrifices. It was more than a little embarrassing considering her profession, and she hoped that Kaytin couldn't understand what they were saying, or at least wouldn't come to the same conclusion that she just had.

They came into view then. They were covered in scars and tattoos, and all else was forgotten as the mercenary in Kadasah saw money—enough to buy new weapons.

She lay very still, barely breathing, and noticed that Kaytin did the same. When the pair were almost abreast of them she jumped out and plowed her table leg into the man's nose hard enough to bury it in his brain. Then she caught the stunned woman on the backswing, effectively and permanently silencing her as well. She grabbed their candle before it could go out and handed it to Kaytin. He took the candle and held it for her so that she could see to search their bodies, taking a long dirk from a sheath on the man's side, and collecting a trophy from each of the bodies. She then started walking in the direction the two cultists had been coming from, now carrying both the table leg and the dead man's knife. Part of her really wanted to search around and see if she couldn't find her own weapons, but she knew the chances of finding them were slim and staying in the tunnels one more second than they had to was just flat insane.

"But . . ." Kaytin scratched his head, as he followed her. "We were going that way." He pointed behind them.

"Yes, and so were they. Since they were going to meet with more of their kind."

"Back this way. But why didn't they notice we were gone?"

It was a good question, and she thought about it for a minute. "There has to be another tunnel that we missed, and that one will get us out of this hole. Hopefully to the surface."

Going back the side tunnel was visible. They had missed it before because of the angle, the bad lighting, and because they hadn't known to look for it. They followed the new tunnel, feeling more than seeing that they were moving up. They could just make out a faint light when they heard screams and running footsteps behind them. They didn't wait to find out what all the commotion was about. After all they were pretty sure that they knew. They just took off at a run, stumbling through the dark, and soon they were outside. Kadasah looked around for something they could knock back over the entrance, but there was nothing small enough for them to move, so they kept running and she started whistling loudly. In moments, Vagrant was at their side. They jumped on the horse and took off just as the first Dyareelans boiled up out of the hole.

It took them about an hour to find Kaytin's mule, and another to catch him. They were about to mount up when Kaytin turned to look at Kadasah. "So, let's see this enchanted talisman you use to confound men."

Kadasah went to pull the cord up out of the front of her shirt and found it missing.

"Damn, it's gone! Those bastards must have taken it as well."

"And yet you look no different to me, and I feel the same way about you." He kissed her cheek, got on his mule, and rode away.

"Frogs!" Kadasah cursed. "That wizard cheated me."

It wound up being easier for her to gain an audience with Arizak than it was to get him to believe the truth of what she'd heard. It didn't help that her father stood there the whole time insisting that she was an unworthy daughter who had gone away from the old ways, and was only there to tarnish his good name. In the end she consoled herself with the idea that they had been told now, and that maybe it would plant a seed of doubt and get them to open their eyes to the possibility at the very least.

She employed the skill of a whip of a man named
Heliz to write a letter to accompany the trophies she
left in their usual place, and against her normal
habit she actually paid him his fee without question.
In the letter she told her employer very briefly about
the events of the night before. She also told him
how many of the Dyareelans there actually were, and
that many were deliberately remaining unmarked
obviously so that they could infiltrate the population. She could only hope that he would listen better than Arizak. When she returned later to retrieve
her reward there was four times as much money as
normal, so she assumed that he believed her.

She used the money to buy new and better weapons, and spent a few days in quiet reflection just
hanging out in the outbuilding of an abandoned
red-brick estate in the hills beyond the walls. This
also allowed Vagrant to have a few well-earned days
of uninterrupted grazing time.

On Ilsday she rode to the Vulgar Unicorn and was
halfway through her fourth beer and her third em-
bellished telling of the events of a week ago when
Kaytin finally showed up.

"I . . . I thought maybe you weren't coming," she
said.

"I wasn't going to," he shrugged. "But I couldn't
stay away."

"Here," she reached in her pocket and pulled out
several coins. He held out his hand with trepidation,
and she dropped the coins into his hand, each one
falling a little more reluctantly than the one before
it.

"You . . . Kadasah! You're actually paying me." He
added with a laugh, "Are you sure you're all right?"

"Actually," she said with a smile, "I'm a little
miffed. I wouldn't have wasted my time stealing that

talisman if I had known it was worthless. And by the way it stank whenever it got wet."

"You are the most magnificent of women, Kadasah," Kaytin said with a smile. "Why would you ever think that you would need any sort of spell to make you more appealing?"

"I was just trying to get an edge."

"My love . . . Your eyes are like the bluest ocean, your lips are gentle like the curve of a bow . . ."

"Frogs, Kaytin!" Kadasah said in disgust. "You aren't going to start all that crap again are you? I almost got you killed! You have to stay mad at me longer than this."

"I cannot help it, Kadasah. Kaytin's love for you leaps within his chest at the vision of your loveliness, and . . ."

The dead-looking guy walked into the bar, and everyone got quiet. He turned to fix Kadasah with an eyes-sewed-shut stare, and her blood ran cold. She looked at Kaytin, did a quick rundown of everything that had happened the last time the creep had looked at her, and said, "All right, Kaytin, I give. Let's go make love."

She left without paying her tab, and Kaytin eagerly followed.

Duel

Dennis L. McKiernan

Cunning and guile oft proves fatal:
sometimes to the predator, sometimes to the prey.

"**A**gsh nabb thak dro . . ."

Arcane words wrenched out from the black hole of a cowl as the dark-robed man, the mantled creature, the cloaked thing on the pier, stood with his, its, the thing's arms outstretched toward the sea. Overhead the shadow-swallowed moon had turned ruddy, now wholly engulfed by the creeping darkness. Out on the sea a luminous mist coiled up from the brine, chill in the cool spring air. And still the chant went on, under the eclipse of the moon, the glimmering vapor thickening and thickening in the ebon depths of the night.

And behind the chanter, the canter, the caster, an ugly little man stood trembling, his hands clutching at his misshapen torso, his white eyes wide in fear. Rogi hated it when his master did such things, for Rogi's own mother had done likewise ere she had crumbled to dust . . . beneath a full moon as well, though not one in bloody eclipse. She had been chanting, too, but words different from these, just before she sprinkled the powder into the potion and drank it all, and then looked at him with an accusatory glare and croaked out "You little shite," even as she fell to ashes.

Rogi wrenched his mind away from remembrance of his mothe—no, not mother, though he still thought of her that way . . . rather the witch who had raised him— *"She plucked you from the sea, after you had been thrown in twice"*—or so the S'danzo El-emi had said as she read her seer's cards. Even so, had he not substituted that other green potion for the one he "accidentally" drank, perhaps his mother the witch would still be—

"It is done," whispered the ghastly, hollow voice of Rogi's master, a voice like dead leaves rustling in icy wind. "Now we wait."

With an awkward, stumping gait, Rogi hobbled around to face the enshadowed cowl; the mal-formed little man in an overlarge shirt peered up at the gaunt, six-foot-one necromancer, all the while hoping he wouldn't see the oh-so-terrible, painted-on eyes. "Now the champion will come, eh, Mathter Hâlott?"

"Yes," hissed the dead-leaves answer. "Now the champion will come."

In a dark corner of the Vulgar Unicorn, two men sat drinking brandy: one a fairly handsome young man, the other rather nondescript. "But I want that gemstone, Soldt, and I will pay well for its winning."

Toying with his glass, Soldt looked across at the fair-haired eldest son of Arizak. "You can enter the tournament yourself, Naimun. You have an adequate hand at swords."

"Ah, but contestants have come from all over—have you not seen the docks? Hardly a slip left open. And the stables are full as well, the inns near to bursting." Naimun gestured at the crowded common room. "And see these bravos, blades on their hips, surely the best of the Rankans and the Ilsigi as well as of the Irrunes. Aye, perhaps I could win a few, but I am not one to fool myself: I have no chance of reaching the final, much less of winning it. But you, Soldt, you are a master, a teacher of the dueling blade, and certain to win."

Soldt shook his head, his ragged-cut brown hair ruffling. "But for the lessons I give, Sanctuary is the place I come to get away from swordplay. I do not like to let blood within the city walls."

"But it's just to first blood—a simple nick, Soldt—and the prize well worth the risk. Ha! For you, there is no risk."

Again Soldt shook his head. "Naimun, whenever there's an edge or point involved, there is always a risk. Have you not been listening during your—?"

The blond Irrune shoved out a hand of negation. "Pah! You are the best swordsman in the city, Soldt, and I wager in the land as well. None can match your skill. Besides, when you win and I gift the gemstone to my father, I'll stand higher in his eyes, perhaps even on an equal footing with—" Of a sudden Naimun fell silent and stared into the dregs of his drink, and bitterness dwelled in his gaze, or so it seemed to Soldt.

Soldt's angular face remained impassive, and he continued to toy with his glass. Moments passed with no word between them, but finally—"What would it be worth to you?"

Naimun looked up. "What would you ask?"

Soldt peered across the crowded common room: men at every table, serving maids rushing here and there, doxies among them plying their trade, Pegrin the Ugly behind the bar, filling jacks and glasses and mugs. Among the tables a passed-out drunk slumped forward upon one, his mates ignoring him, as well as the one on the floor. Off in a corner booth two men furiously argued; perhaps it would come to blows or blades. Soldt's gaze returned to Naimun.

"Three things." He held up his hand and raised a finger. "First: For each one I face I get paid, whether or not I win, and thrice my usual training fee, since there is blood involved."

Naimun nodded. "Agreed."

Soldt raised a second finger. "If I am wounded, I am to be treated only by the best of healers—Pel Garwood will do, if Velinmet's not available—but I'll have no mages nor priests involved, and especially no witches . . . and you will pay for all."

Again Naimun nodded.

Soldt raised a third finger. "Lastly, I will be paid a fair price for the gemstone itself, as appraised by Thibalt the Rankan. Once the Dyareelans were done with their, um, offerings, there weren't many jewelers left, but Thibalt survived and is one of the few I trust to give a true assessment. It is his valuation we will use to set the worth of the stone."

"Agreed," replied Naimun. He waited, but Soldt said no more. "That's it?"

Soldt turned up a hand.

"Huah," grunted Naimun. "And here I was going to offer you a new sword to replace that smudged up blade of yours."

Soldt cocked an eyebrow at Naimun.

"I still will," said Naimun. "We'll go up to Face-of-the-Moon Street on the Hill, up to that new weapons dealer, um . . ."

"Spyder," supplied Soldt.

"Right. Spyder . . . he and that girl—a pretty thing—quiet as a mouse, but moves like a cat, she does."

A faint smile tugged at the corners of Soldt's mouth. "Familiar. —Her movement, that is."

Naimun looked at Soldt, but the duelist added nought. "Regardless, Soldt, my offer yet stands: a new sword. Rumor is that some of his blades are enchanted."

Again a fleeting smile crossed Soldt's face. "So they say, my friend."

"Then shall we add a new sword to your fee?"

Soldt gave a slight shake of his head. "The one I have will do."

"As you wish," said Naimun. He swirled then swigged the last of his brandy and glanced at Soldt's near-empty drink, then he caught the eye of a passing serving girl and raised his glass and signed for two more of the same.

Muttering to himself, Rogi waddled back and forth past a now-lit lantern sitting adock at the root of an empty slip, one of the many built after the great blow, there along the shore nigh Fisherman's Row. The small hunchback stopped occasionally to pull up a floppy sock, first on one leg and then on the other, but then resumed his awkward gait. As he passed by the lantern for perhaps the hundredth time, a pair of wharf rats scuttled across his path, and Rogi flopped back the cuffs of his too-long sleeves from his hands and clutched at the small blow gun on its thong about his neck and fumbled in his belt pouch for a dart along with his tin of special paste. "Ratth, Mathter," he said with a lisp, his overlong tongue getting in the way. "I'll put thom to thleep for you." But at gesture of negation from the necromancer, Rogi let loose the pipe and watched the rats disappear into the darkness. *Forthunate ratth*—even Rogi's thoughts lisped—*you will not awaken to be thkinned alive by my Mathter Hâlott*.

Rogi took up his pacing once more. Now and again the little hunchback peered past the slip and out into the eerie mist . . . for what? . . . he knew not. Occasionally he glanced at his Master Hâlott, seeking some clue as to what might come, or perhaps seeking confirmation that nothing would.

And the dark, blood-red moon was yet swathed in shadow.

And not a breath of air stirred.

But then . . .

But then . . .

. . . there faintly sounded the dip and pull of oars, and coming through the silvery mist, coming through . . .

"A thyip," hissed Rogi. "Mathter Hâlott, a thyip comth." Not knowing what to expect, the little man scuttled behind the tall, gaunt figure and peered around at the approaching craft.

Hâlott did not move.

Luminous mist aswirl with its passage, a small, single-masted ketch—its sail hanging lank, its oars creaking—eased through the chill waters and toward the pier, and Rogi could make out a huge figure plying the blades, while a smaller one sat astern at the tiller, both encloaked and hooded.

Onward came the ship, past others moored in the bay at anchor and toward the crowded pier, aiming for the light of the lantern, and as it neared the huge figure gave one last pull, then shipped the oars and stood and turned about; Rogi breathed a sigh of relief, for now he could see it was a man—what else he might have imagined, Rogi could not say. The man stepped to the bow and took up a mooring rope as the craft coasted into the slip. "Aid them," whispered Hâlott, and Rogi sprang forward, causing the man in the ship to frown in startlement at this scuttling misshapen creature. Nevertheless, he tossed the line to the small hunchback, and Rogi hauled the bow of the craft to the root of the slip and tied it to a mooring post as the man hung two tethered bolsters of hemp over the side to fend the craft from the jetty.

At the stern, the smaller of the two figures leapt to the dock and secured that end as well. Rogi's eyes lighted up when he saw that this second person was female, for she cast back her hood and looked about as the huge man lowered the sail and then took up a great sword in a harness and strapped it across his back. As he stepped onto the dock beside her, "This isn't Ibarr," said the woman in a flat, accented voice, an accent that Rogi knew not.

"It isn't even Azrain," rumbled the man, his own voice carrying an inflection different from hers, but one which Rogi could not place either.

The woman glanced at the dark, ruddy moon and the constellations in the starlit sky. "Nor are these the night skies of Arith."

Now Hâlott stepped toward the pair, gesturing at the lantern as he passed Rogi, and Rogi snatched it up and scuttled ahead of his master, lighting the way.

Soldt looked up from his third brandy. "Who is sponsoring this tournament, and why?"

Naimun shrugged.

Soldt's eyes narrowed.

Naimun took a deep breath. "The Rankans, that's who. There are rumors that Sepheris is mustering an army, ostensibly for an all-out attack on Ilsig's enemies to the north. But Jamasharem suspects that the Ilsigi army is going to march against Ranke instead. So, under the pretense of celebrating the Ten-Slaying—some Rankan festival having to do with one of their gods, Vashanka, I think, killing all ten of His brothers—the good emperor has sent an emissary, Badareen, to negotiate with my sire to convince him—to convince him, my dung-eating uncle, Zarzakhan, and my lout of a half-brother—to rally the Irrune against Sepheris should war come this way."

Soldt snorted and shook his head. "The Irrune are not likely to do so, not likely to take sides."

Naimun ruefully smiled. "Aye, not likely. Not even my half-brother the Dragon is that stupid." He took a sip of brandy and then said, "Regardless, as cover for his mission—rather flimsy, I say—Badareen has arranged for this tournament to be part of some bloody commemoration, as the Rankan would have this time of season be."

Soldt again shook his head and glanced out over the crowd. "Entertainment for the masses, while emissaries of so-called men of power—Emperor Jamasharem and King Sepheris IV—set the wheels of destiny in motion. —Ha! My father, Arizak, will play one side against the other to get whatever it is he wants from them both."

Naimun nodded, then fixed the other man in the eye. "Nonetheless, Soldt, I would have that jewel."

The door banged open, and one of the Vulgar Unicorn's patrons came staggering back in and shouted, "Oi! Come see! The moon has gone all dark and bloody!"

Down at the docks, the huge man gestured toward the icy water. "And that's not the Valagon Sea."

Hâlott came to a stop several paces away, Rogi at his side shuffling from foot to foot. "You are correct," whispered Hâlott, his hollow voice a rustle.

Now the big man turned toward the necromancer. "Where, by Tislitt, are we? And how did we get here?"

"Elsewhere," replied Hâlott. "I brought you here with the mantling of the moon, and I shall send you back with the shrouding of the sun, fourteen days from now."

Of a sudden there was a curved blade in the hand of the female, and she stepped forward into the light, the point of the sword held low. "You will send us back now."

Rogi gasped and stumbled back a step or two, not only because of the threat of the blade, but also because in all of his travels he had never seen such a woman before:

She was perhaps five foot two, with short-cropped, straight, glossy, raven-black hair. Under her gray-green cloak she was garbed in brown leather—vest and breeks and boots. Hammered bronze plates like scales were sewn on the vest; underneath she wore a silk jerkin the color of cream. A brown leather headband incised with red glyphs made certain that even the slightest wisp of her hair was held back and away from her high-cheekboned face. But none of that was what caused Rogi to gasp; instead it was her eyes and skin, for the eyes were so dark as to be black, and they held the hint of a tilt, and her skin . . . it was saffron—a tawny, ivory yellow.

Rogi was instantly in love. *Perhapth thshe will even want to thsee my dragon, perhapth even fondle it.* But at the moment she was too dangerous to even suggest such, for not only did she have a blade in hand, she also stood in a warrior's stance: balanced, ready. And Rogi could see the hilt of another sword peeking out from her cloak.

"I cannot send you back now," said Hâlott. "Not for fourteen days. Then I will act, but only if you do my bidding."

The woman growled and brought her sword to guard, but the big man stepped forward. "Ariko, wait, let us hear him out."

Now Rogi shifted his attention to the man. He was tall, very tall, perhaps six foot four or so, and muscular, and had to scale two-hundred-twenty or-thirty lithe pounds. He had sun-bleached auburn hair and ice-blue eyes. He, too, wore brown leathers beneath a gray-green cloak, but a metal breastplate covered his chest. The hilt of a great two-handed sword rode in a harness across his back. And although Rogi was no sure judge of age, he thought perhaps this man was in his early to mid-thirties, as was the woman Ariko.

Reluctantly, Ariko lowered the point of her blade, but caged fury lurked deep within the black of her tilted eyes.

"I am Durel," said the big man. He peered into the enshadowed, dark cowl. "And you are . . . ?"

"You may call me Hâlott," came the whisper.

Now Durel looked down at Hâlott's companion and waited. "R-rogi," stammered the little hunchback, flopping his hands about in his too-long sleeves. "H-hâlott ith my mathter."

Now Durel turned his attention back to the gaunt

figure in the black robes. "And why have you
brought us here?"

Hâlott turned his unseen face toward Ariko and
said, "There is this gemstone I would have. . . ."

Naimun was somber and silent when he and Soldt
returned to the table and took up their brandies
again.

"You seem pensive, my friend," said Soldt.

"It is an unfavorable omen," replied Naimun.
"Zarzakhan says that Irrunega is troubled whenever
the moon runs with blood."

Soldt smiled unto himself. Even so, he did not
gainsay Naimun's words, for gods surely visited both
banes and boons upon the world at large, and upon
Sanctuary in particular—or so it did seem.

"Perhaps He is disturbed by the thought that we
might ally ourselves with the Rankans," said Naimun.

"Or perhaps with the Ilsigi instead," replied Soldt.

Naimun nodded, his gaze on the table, and as if
speaking to himself said, "I will have to have word
with my sire about this bloodmoon, though I am
certain the shamans will seek audience as well. No
doubt they will tell him that Irrunega wishes us to
leave the city behind and return to the plains. Still,
if that were it, then why has He taken so long to
manifest His disquiet." He glanced up at Soldt and,
as if coming to himself, blurted, "—But this in no
manner affects our bargain. I want that jewel, the
moon's ill portent or no."

"Do you alwayth thail acrotht the othean in armor?"
asked Rogi, scuttling alongside Ariko.

Ariko looked down at the little man. And by the
light of the lantern he carried, and in the partial

glow of the now-recovering moon, she saw that Rogi
would perhaps stand some four and a half feet tall
were he to straighten up, assuming the hump on his
right shoulder would allow, but the way of his gait
put him a foot or so shorter. And speaking of gait,
there seemed to be something wrong with his feet—
either that, or he had stuffed his shoes with scraps
of leather or the like to make himself seem taller.
He wore woolen pants held up by a rope on which
was affixed a pouch. A shirt several sizes too large
graced his distorted form, the sleeves flopping down
over his hands. About his neck dangled a blowpipe
on a thong. His eyes were so very pale as to seem
almost white. Yet the most peculiar thing about him
was his hair: It seemed that he was completely bald
on the left side, while a long lank of reddish hair
dangled down on the right, though he wore an ear-
flapped, soft leather cap perhaps to disguise the
oddity. And he had but a single yet very shaggy brow
over his right eye, the left completely lacking. Ariko
could see the shadow of whiskery growth on his
right cheek and jaw, but nought whatsoever on the
left. Too, whenever the ends of his sleeves had
flapped aside, she had seen that the back of his left
hand was hairless and smooth, but the right was extremely hirsute. It was as if all of his hair had mi-
grated from the whole of his left side to double up
on his right. And from his slack mouth dangled a
tongue nearly long enough to lick his own bushy
brow.

"No," replied Ariko, "we do not sail armed and
armored. But we made ready when we thought we
were coming to the city of Ibarr along the coast of
Azrain, for enemies abound in that place, and we
would reduce their numbers." Ariko growled low in
her throat, and glared at Hâlott in the lead. "Now

we discover we are not even on Arith, but a different world altogether."

From the docks they had made their way leftward along the Wideway, then turned northwesterly along a narrow lane wending through the Shambles quarter. Over a bridge above a gash of water they went, and past a bazaar on the right and a jumble of hovels on the left, where they entered what had been a fairly large farmers' market and caravan square, now transformed into an arena, with high-rising tiers of planked benchworks ramped up all 'round a sandy flat. "Here is where you'll draw blood," whispered Hâlott, gesturing about with an all but skeletal hand.

Durel sighed and in a low voice said to Ariko, " 'Tis the only way back to Arith, my love."

Again Ariko growled, and from her savage mien and manner Rogi knew that it would be quite dangerous were he to show her his magnificent dragon, much less ask her to fondle it. Oh, no, it would not be like the times down at the Unicorn or the Yellow Lantern or any of the other inns and taverns sprinkled throughout the Maze, where he would get hurled into the street just for suggesting such to the serving girls and doxies and the like. No, if he asked this yellow woman to fondle his dragon, he might come up short one dragon altogether. Rogi vowed then and there to remain silent about his outstanding beast.

They passed through the Gate of Triumph and on up the General's Road, the warders at the gate shrinking back from Hâlott, the challenge dying on their lips even ere it were spoken.

Past a cemetery they went and along the road curving among temples and fanes. They trod across another bridge and through the area where the displaced farmers' market and caravan square was now

located. They came to the ford across the White
Foal, yet this they didn't traverse, but instead followed the eastern bank upstream for a goodly way,
the land canting sharply upward on both sides of
the river. Occasionally they passed the stubborn remains of former cabins swept away by flood, a chim-
ney here, a foundation there, marking where they
once had been.

The four entered into a relatively flat stretch of
woodland, and Hâlott turned eastward away from
the river and led them among the boles to come to
the ruins of a square-based tower, the whole of it
shielded by the lofty trees from the view of travelers
along the river and its banks. With vine-covered rubble about its foundation, four storeys tall, it was,
though the upper levels were but shells, for Ariko
and Durel could see partial walls here and there,
with stairs leading up to dead ends or gaps. The
ground-level floor, though, seemed intact, perhaps
even livable. Rogi scrambled ahead and opened the
weatherworn, heavy-planked, iron-bound door, and
Hâlott led them inward. They came into what was
once a welcoming hall, now all but dead of neglect.
Rogi set the lantern on a dust-laden table then went
about lighting candles. "Welcome to my abode,"
said Hâlott, and he turned and cast back his hood.

Durel sucked in air between clenched teeth and
he reflexively reached toward his shoulder for his
sword, only to let his hand fall back. Ariko's own left
and right grip rested on the hilts of her two blades,
but she drew them not.

Like Death did Hâlott seem, his entire head appearing to be nought but a skull covered with a
parchment-like skin, wisps of hair atop, his mouth
but a gash of desiccated blue lips drawn back from
yellowed teeth in a permanent rictus grin. Yet worst

of all, his eyelids were sewn completely shut, and painted in kohl upon them were representations of eyes, like the false eyes of a death's-head moth, dark and forbidding and baneful.

"Oi, they've got sixty-three entries," said Old Javan, his rheumy gaze on the posting, not that he could read it, but he could count the number remaining.

At his side Mava said, "I hear they had nigh a hundred, until Soldt threw his name in the hat."

"Ar, he scared many off," replied the oldster, nodding, "him being a dueler and all, teaching them as has got the coin. Not many'd want to go up against Soldt, 'less'n they knew no better. He's who I'll put my money on."

Mava snorted. "What money, old man?"

"Well, if I had any, he's who I'd back."

Mava nodded. "He'll be the favorite, all right. But there's somewhat afoot."

Javan looked at her, an eye cocked.

Mava peered about as if seeking lurkers and, finding none, whispered, "They say that that little Rogi, Rogi, Hâlott's man"—again Mava looked about, Javan peering 'round as well—"they say Rogi entered a name: Tiger it was, if them that can read got it right. And if Rogi's involved, well then, I'll wager that that Hâlott's got somewhat up his black sleeve."

"A poisoned blade, I shouldn't wonder," said Javan.

Mava grunted her agreement and then said, "Still, if I had any money . . ."

In the Vulgar Unicorn the only person trusted to hold the bets was Perrez—not because anyone particularly trusted *him*, but because Perrez's brother was Bezul the changer and Bezul was a man worth trusting. Off in one corner and for a small fee, Perrez took the slips and coinage—padpols, soldats, and even an occasional shaboozh—along with promissory notes and small deeds and occasional heirlooms—silver chains, pearl-handled daggers, and other such trinketry, all of which Bezul would eventually appraise for the bettors, to the not infrequent dismay of some—and placed all in the iron-bound lockbox he owned, a lockbox rumored to be trapped with poison needles or sorcerous fire or housing a deadly asp within, depending on who was telling of it.

As for the betting itself, Soldt was indeed the favorite, now that he had declared his intent. There were several who were disappointed that Arizak per-Arizak, better known in the Maze as the Dragon, had withdrawn, but with that bloody moon some eight nights past, nearly all of the entered Irrune had pulled out. . . . "Superstitious savages," went the whispers. "Everyone knows that Vashanka and a hundred other gods are exceedingly more powerful than Irrunega, even though His is the only religion sanctified in the city, but don't say I said that." Still, one or two Irrune remained on the list, though their kindred placed no bets on them; the ill-omened moon saw to that. They mostly placed wagers on Soldt or on a handful of others, though this "Tiger," whoever he was, drew some small stakes, for, after all, the tiger *was* and *is* the totem of the god Irrunega, though His tiger is two-headed and all black.

"Ha!" crowed Rogi. "Got you." Standing in the rubble at the base of the tower, he held the rat up by the tail, the creature's struggles waning rapidly.

Durel looked up from honing his great sword. "He's quite good with that blowgun."

At Durel's side, Ariko oiled one of her blades, then took a soft rag to it. "Rogi told me all about it. It seems our host uses live rats and other such to facilitate some of his . . . pleasures."

Durel frowned at the limp rat as Rogi bore it into the tower. "They're not dead?"

Ariko shook her head. "Merely asleep."

Durel sighted down the blade of his weapon, pale, spring sunlight aglance along the edge. He took to his hone once more, concentrating on a section. "The matches begin tomorrow."

Ariko didn't reply as she continued to wipe down her blade.

Close by the east quarter of the farmers' market, the dwellings along Shambles Cross had been co-opted as places for the contestants to prepare. Inside one of them sat Ariko and Durel. They could hear the roar of the crowd as one swordsman or another made a nimble maneuver, a skillful riposte, a deft parry, or drew first blood. Now and again the shouts grew louder as someone was wounded more severely, and occasionally a silence befell the mob when a thrust proved to be fatal. One such deadly quiet had just come to pass, when a knock sounded. "You're next, Tiger," said the man when Durel opened the door.

Ariko and Durel harnessed their weapons, and out into the sunlight they strode. They made their way behind the stands to come to the south entryway . . . and there in the aisle at the edge of the open arena they waited. They could see a tall Rankan, stripped to the waist in spite of the cool, swirling breeze, a blade in each hand, standing in the opposite aisle.

In the arena itself, bearers were lading a corpse upon a litter.

In the stands along the aisle and immediately above Ariko and Durel, gawkers turned their attention from the deader being carried off and looked down upon the pair and whispered among themselves.

"Oh, lor, but look a him. A giant he is."

"Ar, that sword across his back, why, it's as long as a man is tall."

"I thought this was supposed to be a duel, not a bloody slaughter. I mean, who can stand against such."

The murmurs and whispers and declarations went on, even as a herald stepped to the center of the field of combat and faced east, where the governor and ambassador and other notables sat on a high dais.

A hush fell.

"Lords and Ladies and guests," he called and gestured leftward, "to the north, Enril the Rankan!"

A shout went up from the crowd, interspersed with boos and whistles and catcalls, as the tall man stepped forth from his aisle to stand for all to see, and there he waited.

The herald held up his hands. And when quiet fell he gestured rightward and called, "And to the south, Tiger!"

A great roar went up as well as gasps at the size of the man when Durel stepped onto the sand and stopped. Then Ariko strode forth and paused; and Durel took her cloak from her and then stepped back into the aisle.

With her scabbarded swords strapped across her back, Ariko went on toward the center of the arena, and a murmur of wonder rippled through the crowd.

"This is 'Tiger'?"

"Vashanka, but she's a yellow woman."

"Why, this'll be a slaughter, tiny as she is."

"Look at them little square plates on her leather vest. Hmph, as if they'd stop a good thrust."

"Get the litter ready!"

Out onto the sandy square strode five-foot-two Ariko, as did Enril the Rankan, a full head taller or more. In one hand he held a rapier; in the other a main gauche—a sword-breaker.

They met in the center of the field, where both turned to the dais and bowed, then faced the herald.

"Are you certain you want to do this?" the herald asked Ariko, his gaze wide with amazement.

Ariko's only reply was to draw her two slightly curved blades, the shorter one in her left hand, the longer one in her right.

The herald shook his head and sighed. "Very well. Face the dais, weapons ready. Wait for the signal, and then it's to first blood." The herald bowed to each and withdrew.

From the corner of his mouth, tall Enril whispered to Ariko, "I shall try not to wound you too deeply, but one never knows, does one?"

Ariko did not reply.

At a gesture from Arizak, the Rankan ambassador called from the dais. "Let it begin."

The duelists faced one another and saluted with swords—Enril's gaze filled with haughty disdain, Ariko's impassive—then circled one another warily. Of a sudden in a whirl of steel, Ariko sprang forward, her blades but a blur—

—*cling-clang, shing-shang, chng-shng-zs*—

—and after but seven quick strokes she disengaged and stepped back.

Panting, frowning, Enril looked at her—"First blood," she said—and then he felt the warm trickle running down his right cheek.

Unbelieving, he struck his right hand to his face and wiped. His fingers came away wetly scarlet. An incredulous gasp went up from the crowd, and Enril, stunned, turned to the dais. "My lords, 'twas but an accidental—"

Enril's words chopped short as Arizak pushed out a hand for silence. "The combat is to first blood, and first blood has been drawn. Stand down, Enril the Rankan, you have been defeated."

A great roar went up from the crowd, and Enril growled but bowed to the dais, as Ariko did likewise. Then they went their separate ways, the Rankan to the north, Ariko to the south.

Grinning widely, Arizak turned to Emissary Badareen. "Bested by a chit of a girl, is this the finest Ranke has to offer?"

But off to one side stood Soldt, his eyes narrow as his gaze followed the retreating form of the yellow woman called Tiger.

In the Vulgar Unicorn that eve, many a past wager was paid and many a new one laid, and all talk was of the tourney and of the female therein. . . .

"Quick as a tiger she is, did you see?"

"Aye, she's aptly named."

"A golden woman at that."

"Bet she's a tiger in places other than an arena."

"You don't want to find out, Lamin . . . claw you to death, she would."

"Ar, I think that Enril was right: 'Twas pure accident."

"Do you think? I mean, she seemed, oh, I dunno, fast and deft, I suppose."

"Bah, she's just a girl; either it was an accident, or he wasn't ready."

"The next one she faces'll be on his toes, I'll wager."

"Speaking of wagers, what about tomorrow? Who you betting on?"

"Wull, with the bye and all, and as the favorite, Soldt didn't fight today. Even so, my coin'll follow him. What about you?"

"I think I'll put a silver on the golden girl."

"Ha! Dolt! Why don't you just throw your coin into the street? I mean, betting on a *girl* is just plain foolish, and . . ."

Many were the stakes proffered and accepted, odds shifting with each candlemark, Soldt yet favored to win. The Irrunes, however, bet on the one named Tiger; how could they not, for the tiger was their totem, and even though there had been a bloodmoon, how could that be wrong? Besides, they had now seen her fight. Mostly Rankans took on the Irrune wagers in ire, for, after all, this—this . . . this girl had accidentally beaten one of their best, and surely she deserved what she got.

"Five more," gritted Ariko, her black eyes flashing in the moonlight. "I must face five more opponents ere we win the jewel for this skeleton of a man—if man he is—and he sends us back to Arith."

Durel growled and glanced toward his great sword. "If there were a way we could get back on our own, I'd kill the bastard."

"To do so," said Ariko, "you would have to stand in line behind me."

Durel sighed and glanced at the moon riding

above in the cool night. Then he stood and held out his hand. "Come, love. 'Tis time we were abed."

Ariko took his grip and levered herself up. They went into the ruins of the tower, to the chamber with a bed so dusty that surely it hadn't been used in a decade or more.

Lurking in the shadows behind, Hâlott smiled to himself . . . if a slight twitch of his blue-tattooed lips could be said to be a smile. Beneath his robes, with a desiccated finger he traced the long, single scar running from his throat down the center of his cadaverous chest and hollow stomach and past his empty groin. *Little do they know I cannot be slain by the paltry weapons they have.*

"An Ilsigi emissary came today," said Naimun.

Soldt raised an eyebrow. "Oh? Come to woo Arizak, I suppose."

Naimun nodded. "It seems they fear my sire will throw in his lot with Emperor Jamasharem."

"What of perArizak, the young Dragon?"

Naimun gritted his teeth. "That hill bandit thinks to lead the Irrune once my sire is dead."

Soldt canted his head slightly. "He is your brother and the eldest of Arizak's sons."

Naimun's fist clenched. "Half-brother, you mean. Half the man I am, as well. Ariz the Dragon, they call him. Ariz the Unpredictable, I say. With his temper, he's likely to—" Of a sudden, Naimun chopped off. Then he stared into his drink and growled low. "Both he and my younger brother Raith, they each think to wrench rule from my sire, but I and my friends—" Again Naimun chopped short, and he glanced at Soldt.

Soldt thrust both of his hands palms out. "Tangle

me not in any intrigue, Naimun. I'm happy being what I am."

Naimun smiled. "Well and good, Soldt, being what you are. Tomorrow is your first combat. I trust you'll fare well?"

Soldt nodded. "It's Callenon I face. I watched him today. Drops his right shoulder just before beginning a beat. He will pay dearly for that tell."

The Irrune grinned at the duelist, for surely Soldt was destined to win the black onyx for Naimun, the stone a worthy gift for his sire. And yet, even if Soldt didn't win . . . well, there was more than one way to skin a cat. Of a sudden, Naimun broke out laughing, and when Soldt looked at him questioningly, Naimun merely laughed all the harder.

Amid the roars of *Tiger! . . . Tiger! . . . Tiger! . . .* Ariko walked away from the center of the arena. When she reached Durel she gritted, "Four more to go."

"Fast as a cat she is."

"Har! I think you have the right of it. I mean, did you see her eyes?"

"I did, and the eyes of a cat they are: slanty and black as a witch's cauldron."

"Where d'you think she's from, her being yellow and all?"

"Golden, you mean, or so they say. And as far as where she's from, perhaps it's that witch's cauldron after all."

"Conjured up you mean?"

"I wouldn't say yea nor nay. Instead I'll place a soldat or two on her tomorrow."

———

Arizak sat with the Rankan emissary on his right, and the Ilsigi emissary on his left—two who would exchange places on the morrow, and again in the days after, for the chief of the Irrunes would show no preference, no favorites, despite the urgings of Nadalya, Arizak's second wife, a Rankan herself. With a nod at the herald, Arizak signaled for the matches to begin. And at the herald's call, the first two of the sixteen duelists yet remaining entered the field, one of them a small female. *Tiger!* . . . *Tiger!* . . . *Tiger!* . . . roared the crowd.

Again Soldt watched the woman leave the arena, and now he knew it would take all of his skill, along with the power of his Enlibar blade, to defeat the one named Tiger.

"If there is any way to foil whatever plan Hâlott has and still get us back to Arith . . ."

Ariko in his arms in bed, Durel stroked her hair. "Shh, shh, my love. I know . . . I know. . . ."

"I hear she's almost drawn even with Soldt."

"As the favorite, you mean?"

"Yar. Did you see the way she took out that big Irrune? Flipped that blade right out of his hand and then pinked him in the wrist."

"Bah! He was grim-lipped, even half-scared, when he entered the arena, her being the Tiger and all and him being an Irrune, what with their god's totem being a tiger as well."

"Say what you will, but I'm putting silver on her if it comes down to her and Soldt."

"Well I hope it does that, for then you'll see just what a fool you have been, betting on a girl . . . hmph!"

"Ha! It's you who will be taught a lesson, my friend. I mean, look at the way things are going: Why, it's as if the gods themselves had arranged the pairings so that the final duel will come right down to Soldt and the Tiger herself."

"Feh! 'Twasn't the gods who arranged the pairings, but Arizak's own son Naimun who made up the list—or so it is I hear."

"Well, Naimun or gods or no, still I say it'll be Soldt and the Tiger blading it out in the end."

As if these words had been prophetic, over the next two days, Tiger won both of her matches, as did Soldt. And though on the eve of the final match, hammering rain and lightning and thunder and a windy blow came upon Sanctuary and travel was not fit for man nor beast, still the Unicorn was crowded, the storm within nearly as fierce as the storm without, many in the throng arguing loud and long over the merits of the two who would meet on the morrow. The odds were dead even on just which one would be the victor—would it be the man who was considered the finest duelist in all of Sanctuary, in all of Ranke, in all of Ilsig—as some stoutly avowed—or instead the black-eyed, golden woman, fast as a cat and a hundred times more deadly? Where was she from? No one knew. Beyond the sea it seemed . . . at least she and her large companion came in a boat, or so the rumor went. Regardless, speculation was rife, and mayhap even the very gods themselves didn't know what the outcome would be.

Ariko was awakened in the night by a *chuff*, and she opened her eyes to see what seemed to be the fading form of a large and low-slung black beast of sorts, yet ere she could get a good look, only shadows met her gaze. The storm was gone, or nearly so, for only an occasional distant rumble did she hear. Durel lay at her side, breathing softly in his dreams, and she lay awake without disturbing him. Moments later, above the swash of the nearby risen waters of the White Foal, there came the soft steps of someone entering the chamber, and Ariko reached under her pillow and grasped the hilt of her dagger as a tall, dark form glided to the side of the bed. Through slitted eyes, Ariko watched as first one of her swords and then the other were drawn from their scabbards, and something was smeared along the sharp edge of each blade. The weapons were restored, and the tall, dark form glided away, Ariko watching as Hâlott softly stepped into the hallway beyond.

Time passed, and once again Ariko heard a quiet *chuff*, and a long, black shape seemed to form out of the darkness and stand by the door. Without awakening Durel, Ariko slipped from the bed and, taking up her dagger and a small shuttered lantern, she padded softly after the shadowy form.

Awhile later she returned, a small tin in her hand, her feet damp, as if she had been walking in a dank place.

"Lords and Ladies and honored guests, to the north, Soldt!"

A thunderous roar went up from the crowd as Soldt stepped out onto the sands of the arena under the noontide sun. Dressed in soft gray leathers, he stood, a faint smile on his lips. On the dais Naimun signaled a thumbs-up, but Soldt didn't see.

When the clamor subsided, the herald called, "And to the south—" but the rest of whatever he

was to say was lost under the deafening chant: *Tiger!
. . . Tiger! . . . Tiger! . . .*

As Durel took Ariko's cloak he said, " 'Ware, love,
for this one is truly dangerous."

Ariko nodded, and to wild cheering she paced
forward and out into the arena. And in the stands
an ululating cry went up from a host of Irrune
tribesmen, all of whom had come to see the Tiger
be the best of the best even though she was a
woman, for after all, with such a name, how could
Irrunega Himself not favor her?

Forward she stepped across the still-damp sand,
wet from last night's rain. Even so, compacted by
water, the footing was firm, better than in the days
past. *This contest will not be decided by a slip of a boot.*

Ariko stopped mid-arena, Soldt opposite. She saw
before her a man in his thirties, with a nondescript,
perhaps even forgettable, face, a bit on the angular
side. His hair was brown and raggedly cut as was his
short and sparse beard, just enough growth to obscure his lower face without quite concealing it. His
even teeth were noticeably pale against the beard.
His complexion was weather-tanned. He had piercing, hazel eyes. In his left hand he held a long-
knife—not a sword-breaker, but a long, straight
blade, edged on both sides, with a brass-wire-wound
handle and a plain steel cross-guard. In his right
hand, he held a dark blade, dull in the sun, though
Ariko could see a faint tinge of green showing under what seemed oddly to be a coating of murky oil.

*Surely such a swordsman as this one would not so treat
his weapon without due cause.*

At a word from the herald, both faced the dais
and bowed, and then they awaited the signal.

Arizak signed to his son Naimun, and the twenty-
year-old smiled at his mother, Nadalya, then stood

and stepped to the edge of the platform. He glanced at his sire, and then faced the duelists and called out for all to hear: "May Irrunega look down upon you both and smile, for it is to His honor you strive. And may the best of the best be victorious. And, now . . . begin!"

A stillness fell over the crowd as Ariko and Soldt faced one another and saluted, and then in a flurry of blades Ariko sprang forward—*shing-shang, clng, tkk, dlang, tkk, dlang, dring-dng*—but with long-knife and dark-oiled sword, Soldt countered her every move, and a great roar flew skyward from the stands.

Now in a blur of steel, it was Soldt who attacked, and Ariko was hard pressed, yet she fended the blows of both of his blades with her own two flashing swords.

Now they both sprang back, their breathing coming in harsh gasps, and momentarily they paused. And neither seemed to hear the deafening howl of the crowd, almost as if the thunderous roar had faded into silence.

Then once more Ariko pressed forward, and the steel of her blades skirled and rang against his, as she attacked and retreated, parried and riposted, blocked and counterstruck; Soldt's power and quickness drove her back and back, and it was all she could do to fend, and whenever his dark-oiled blade met hers, a shock went through her arm. And she knew that there was something *special* about such a weapon.

And now Soldt drove her across the arena, and of a sudden—*Shing . . . !*—the sword from Ariko's left hand flew spinning through the air to land in the sand afar. *Shkk . . . !* The green-tinged blade sliced down and across through leather and bronze, but no blood welled from the diagonal cut high athwart her vest, for the silk jerkin below and the flesh beneath remained untouched.

Now she fended with but a lone blade, catching both of his on her one, and then with a fierce counterattack—*Cling . . . !*—Soldt's long-knife went spinning away.

Now it was but single blade on blade, as back and forth across the arena they raged, the skirl of steel on steel howling through the air. Yet, of a sudden, Ariko's blade—*shkkk*—slid down Soldt's and with a twist of her wrist—*ting*—she won past his guard. Astonishment flashed over Soldt's face, and he and Ariko disengaged. They stepped back from one another, and Soldt held up his wrist and slowly turned about for all to see: Blood trickled down his arm.

As with a clap of thunder, to Ariko's and Soldt's ears the roar of the crowd suddenly returned, and it was deafening: ululating howls from the Irrunes, and the chant of *Tiger! . . . Tiger! . . . Tiger! . . .* from the citizens of Sanctuary, as well as those visitors from Ranke and Ilsig and those from the lands farther north.

The herald escorted both to the foot of the dais, and Soldt looked up at Naimun and shrugged. But Naimun merely smiled back at him.

Ariko was presented with an onyx gem, a gleaming ebon stone the size of a plover's egg and faintly striped with a darkness slightly lighter than the dominant black.

Soldt was presented with a necklace of gold, and as this was done Ariko could see that his eyes held a faint glaze.

But in that very moment came a wailing from the stands, and all looked up to see that the edge of the sun was being eaten away by a black arc.

The Irrunes howled in terror, and some among

them fell to their knees in a plea to Irrunega. Many
in the crowd called out to Vashanka and Savankala
and Ils and others, and some voices even called out
to Dyareela, seemingly in exultation. None paid any
attention as Ariko and Durel led Soldt stumbling
away.

By the time they reached the chamber along
Shambles Cross, Durel carried Soldt over a shoulder. Once inside, Durel laid the man down on the
cot, and Hâlott whispered, "Well done—now the
stone, if you please."

Ariko gave over the striated ebon onyx to the necromancer and gritted, "Now our world, if you
please."

Hâlott nodded, then turned to Rogi. "Take Soldt
to the tower. You know where to put him. I'll be
along after the eclipse is done."

With a grunt, Rogi hefted Soldt over his own misshapen shoulder and bore him out and dumped
him in a two-wheeled cart standing just outside the
door. He covered Soldt with a blanket, and then he
stepped between the two shafts and took them up
and trundled away.

Slowly, slowly, the dark occlusion engulfed the waning sun, and now it was nearly gone. As if driven by
the heavens above, a fair but chill breeze sprang up
and blew southwesterly, sweeping off the land and
into the bay, its waters yet somewhat unsettled by
last night's storm. And down at the slips, Ariko and
Durel stowed their gear aboard the small, single-
masted ketch and made ready to cast off.

"In the depth of the darkness," said Hâlott, his
voice rustling like dead leaves stirring in the wind,
"sail for the ring of fire."

"Ring of fire?"

"You will know it when you see it," came the hollow reply. With his hideous, kohl-painted eyes, Hâlott glanced up at the sun. "Now go."

Using an oar, Durel pushed away from the slip, then with him rowing and Ariko manning the tiller, the little ketch moved away, while, behind, Hâlott began to chant:

"Agsh nabb thak dro . . ."

Free from the docks, Durel turned the ketch about, then shipped the oars and raised sail and angled the boom to make the most of the wind, and out into the bay they moved. To the fore, a luminous fog arose, a fog unaffected by the wind. And now the occlusion completely covered the sun, all but a ring of fire running entirely 'round. And reflected in the ghostly mist before them, a ring of fire appeared, and toward this ring they did sail.

And still to the aft, Hâlott's hollow voice yet whispered:

". . . dik dro ngar thebb . . ."

Into the mist they went, and through the ring of fire, and in but moments the occlusion passed onward and an arc of the sun appeared. The ring of fire had vanished, and so too had vanished the little ship along with Ariko and Durel.

"**H**ave you the stone?"

Hâlott turned. Naimun stood on the dock.

"Yes," whispered the necromancer, and he slid a desiccated hand into a voluminous pocket of his black robe and drew out the ebon gem.

"Ah, my sire will treasure this," said Naimun as he took the stone from Hâlott, trying to avoid touching the necromancer's skin. "Striped as it is, it represents Irrunega's black tiger, or so my sire said when he first saw it." Naimun glanced at the gradually emerging sun. "Are you certain that this marvel is natural, no matter what the shamans of my tribe say?"

Hâlott nodded and whispered, "Completely natural, though it and others like it greatly aid castings."

Naimun smiled tentatively, as if trying to come to grips with a new thought. But then he shrugged and said, "Well, thanks to our scheme we both got what we wanted: me, the stone; you, the body of Soldt to do with as you will." At this last, a shiver ran down Naimun's spine. He took a deep breath and, glancing once more at the returning sun, said, "If I need aught else, you will hear from me."

Hâlott bowed, and Naimun turned on his heel and left the necromancer alone on the docks.

As the young Irrune strode away, Hâlott sneered . . . if a faint twitch of a lip can be called a sneer. *Fool! Yes he got what he wanted, and so did I; yet it was not Soldt's body I desired, but that sword of his instead. In spite of my vital organs being secreted away in my enspelled canopic jars, that blade may be the only weapon in Sanctuary that can truly slay me.*

"**H**ow did you awaken when you did? I mean, Hâlott's step is like that of a feather."

"A tiger told me that danger was nigh."

"A tiger?"

Ariko nodded. "At least I think it was one, though it seemed made of shadow, and mayhap had two heads. It certainly sounded like one, *chuffing* as it did."

"And . . . ?"

"And I watched as Hâlott treated my blades."

"And then . . . ?"

"And then when Hâlott was gone, the tiger returned and chuffed once more and I followed it down a set of stairs, down through a laboratory of some kind, and on down into dank basements below, with water adrip, slime on the walls, and rats running everywhere. Three levels I went down, but not to the level below. On that third underlevel I found Rogi naked and asleep . . . all over his body the hair on his left side is completely gone, while on the right it seems doubled. —Did you know he has a tattoo of a dragon twined about his, um, rather lengthy member?"

Durel looked askance at Ariko, but said nought, though he motioned for her to go on.

"You know that I told you if there were a way to foil Hâlott's scheme, I would. And I guessed from Hâlott's late-night visit that Soldt would be dead should I nick him. And given he needed to appear dead for Hâlott to send us back to Arith, well . . . you know how Rogi used to crow about putting 'ratth athleep,' and he told me all about the paste he used, and how to judge the dosage needed for 'ratth' and 'catth' and 'dogth' and other such animals, some quite large. That given, I simply, um, borrowed a tin of Rogi's paste and, gauging how much it would take, I replaced the poison—I think it was poison—Hâlott put on my blades. . . ."

Durel's laughter rang out over the waters of the Valagon Sea as a gentle wind wafted the little ketch toward the city of Ibarr in the land of Azrain on the elsewhere world of Arith.

In a tower north of Sanctuary, Soldt awakened to find himself lying on a long metal table in a faintly lit laboratory. He swung his legs over the edge and stood, swaying slightly from the aftereffects of what-

ever had been done to him. And he took up his
soot-laden, oil-disguised Enlibar blade. Where he
was and how he had gotten there, he had not a clue,
but someone was about to pay.

Ring of Sea and Fire

Robin Wayne Bailey

The sea shimmered like a dark mirror, still and smooth as glass beneath a windless, starlit sky. The faintest sliver of a waning moon hung like a beacon low in the west. To the south, it was impossible to discern any demarcation between the water and the heavens. Not even the barest breath of a breeze teased the placid surface, and all the world seemed smothered in an unnatural hush.

Along the coast to the north and northwest, it was the same. The hour was late, and only a few lanterns and torches glimmered on Sanctuary's shoreline. The distorted shadows of warehouses and fisheries stretched over the wharves, and the masts of the few sailing ships anchored in their berths rose stark and unmoving.

Then from around the brief peninsula called Land's End, an Ilsigi trireme glided on banks of oars that broke the water with lumbering precision. The muffled throb of its master-drum, issuing from deep within the ship, counterpointed each sloughing oar-

stroke as the vessel rounded the point and eased
into the city's harbor.

A lantern brighter than the few that burned along
its deck suddenly appeared in the trireme's prow. It
cast a beam that rippled out across the black water.
A moment later, the beam winked out. Then it
flashed again, over and over in rhythm with the
drum.

At the end of Empire Wharf, another flashing lantern appeared, and a small skiff launched out across
the harbor. Following the now-steady beam of light
from the trireme, it approached the Ilsigi ship. An
old man, thin as a fish bone and weathered as drift-
wood, sat alone in the skiff. He worked the pair of
oars with the skill and strength of long practice.

A deep voice called down from the trireme's
prow. "Ahoy, Markam! Ahoy, the harbor pilot!"

The harbor pilot shouted back gruffly. "You're
Wrigglie-ass late."

"No winds, Markam!" came the answer. The
speaker could not be seen against the lantern's
glare. "We've been working the oars since noon this
whole damned day, and we'll have to put to sea
again by dawn to keep our schedule. But we've got
passengers and freight, and no matter the hour, our
berth is already paid for. So lead us in, and no more
of your flatulent mouth."

Markam grumbled a low curse, but turned his
skiff. The master-drum throbbed again, softer now.
A single bank of oars dipped into the water, and the
trireme slipped into Sanctuary's port. Guided by the
pilot, it nestled gently into a berth and dropped anchor. A dozen men leaped over the rails to the
wharf. Thick ropes sailed through the air, uncoiling,
and in no time, the ship was lashed and secure.

A gangplank slid down from the deck.

Regan Vigeles paused at the top of it and gazed from under his hood down the wharf toward the Wideway and the warehouses and the dark silhouettes of the rooftops beyond, and he wrinkled his nose. After days at sea with the sweet salt air filling his lungs, the stench of Sanctuary was a rude perfume. His black leather trousers, polished boots, and fine matching cloak marked him as a man of wealth. In one hand, he gripped a pair of gloves; in his other hand, a small purse.

A wagon drawn by a team of horses creaked slowly down the wharf as it approached the ship.

Footsteps on the deck behind him. Regan Vigeles turned slightly as the Ilsigi captain approached. The captain wore a smile as he chatted with the woman at his side. Her flawless skin was as black as shadow, her eyes large and dark over sharply defined cheekbones. Her full lips were parted slightly as if in a bemused grin, perhaps at some joke or comment of the captain's. She was dressed for sea travel, not in women's clothing, but in trousers of brown leather with a white silk tunic whose sleeves flowed at her easiest movement, as did the jet black hair that hung straight to her waist. On her belt, she wore a pair of sheathed daggers.

Arriving at the gangplank, the captain unfolded a brown cloak he'd carried over his free arm. In gallant fashion he draped it around her shoulders. She smiled and made the smallest courtesy.

"I believe you've charmed Aaliyah, Captain," Regan Vigeles said, looking down at the Ilsigi. He held out the purse in his hand and lowered his voice. "For your inside pocket. The voyage has been pleasant, and you've treated us well."

The Ilsigi captain bowed his head in thanks as he

quickly thrust the purse under his sash before anyone else saw it. "I'm loath to abandon you, Lord
Spyder," the captain said as he stared at the wagon
that pulled to a stop by the ship. "I've set into this
port many times, and it's no place by night for you
and your lady."

"No need to worry, Captain. We'll be quite safe."
Regan Vigeles took Aaliyah's hand. "Perhaps I could
impose upon you to have your men load my freight
into the wagon."

The captain patted the purse under his belt and
bowed as he backed away.

Aaliyah's vacuous smile faded. A look of alert concern took its place as she gazed toward the city.

"Nha su preo, shahana Aaliyah," Vigeles murmured
as he placed an arm around her shoulders and drew
her close. He pushed back his hood as he looked
down at her. His hair was black and cropped short,
and his tanned, strong-featured face was beardless.
She turned in his embrace to face him, and he
looked into the dark warmth of her eyes as he drew
a finger along the velvet line of her cheek.

A noise on the wharf below caught his attention
as crewmen began unloading his crates and stacking
them in the wagon. Each crate bore his seal, a
painted emblem of a black spider that was visible
even in the faint light of the ship's lanterns.

Regan Vigeles walked down the gangplank to the
wharf, and Aaliyah followed, her soft footsteps making no sound at all.

The driver of the wagon climbed down. His name
was Ronal, a short man, but powerfully built, in his
mid-fifties although he looked much younger. Disdaining a cloak, he wore only trousers, boots, and a
plain leather vest that laced across his broad chest.
An old burn-scar showed on his bare right biceps,

the brand of a slave-gladiator. It marked him as the property of House Donadakos. Years ago, however, he had won his freedom in the arena with fifty kills to his credit.

Ronal ran a hand through his short gray hair. "I'd nearly given up waiting, Spyder," he said quietly to Vigeles. "It's past the third hour of morning, but it's good to see you. Welcome to the anus of the empire." He ran an appreciative eye up and down Aaliyah. "Aren't you a beauty!" He gave a low whistle. "Where did you find her?"

"She's not a slave, Ronal, so watch your tone," Regan Vigeles, called Spyder, said stiffly. Then he relaxed again as he took her hand. "Aaliyah comes from a land beyond the western edge of any formal maps." He changed the subject as the last crate was loaded into the wagon. "I assume you've handled everything with your usual efficiency."

Ronal pursed his lips and nodded. "The renovations are completed. The shop and apartments are as you ordered, and the contracts are paid." He slapped one of the crates and walked around the wagon to make sure the load was secure. "It's on Face-of-the-Moon Street in the very armpit of Ils's temple. And except for the temple, it's the highest point on the Hill. From the rooftop, you have an unobstructed view of the harbor."

Aaliyah had strayed to the end of the wharf where she stood staring out toward the sea. The lanterns on the trireme's rails cast a nimbus of light about her that sent her shadow spilling across the old boards and over the water below.

Ronal's voice dropped a note. "There's something lonely and strange about that one," he whispered almost to himself.

Leaving Ronal by the wagon, Spyder came up behind Aaliyah. *"Shahana,"* he said softly, *"ven veiha ma elberath. Ten ki."*

She seemed to hesitate before she turned and came to his side. Together, they returned to the wagon, and he handed her up to the seat.

"What language was that?" Ronal asked. He had good ears. "It's beautiful—like the wind through leaves, or like water lapping the shore. I've never heard it before."

"Her language," Spyder answered, as he climbed up beside her. "You should know, however, that Aaliyah doesn't speak at all."

Ronal stood gape-mouthed for an instant before he, too, climbed into the wagon and took the reins. With a clucking of his tongue, he turned the team and headed into the city.

By mid-morning, the crates were unpacked and The Black Spider was open for business. Groups of rough-looking men, surprised to find a new and well-appointed shop in such a run-down neighborhood, ventured through the door with narrow-eyed curiosity. Most quickly exited to alert their compatriots. One or two lingered to scrutinize the shop for weaknesses, possible entry points, figuring the proprietor for a fool and the shop for easy pickings.

Swords of the finest manufacture and from many nations depended in their scabbards from pegs on three walls. Racks of bows, lances, and intricately worked staves stood along the fourth wall. There were barrels full of arrows and crossbow bolts. Tall wooden display shelves held daggers, knives, darts, and shuriken of various shapes. Expensive glass cases placed throughout the shop contained more exotic weapons—brooches with spring-loaded needles, belt buckles with concealed blades, still other objects whose surprises could not be guessed.

From a stool by the door, Ronal watched over it all, and throughout the morning, he broke only a single arm when a would-be thief, after examining a superbly crafted Rankan short sword, attempted to dash into the street with it.

"I suppose that made your day," Spyder laughed as the racket drew him down from the upper living apartments. He petted a small white cat that purred in the crook of one arm.

"I'm positively erect with pleasure." Ronal yawned as he hung the sword back in its place. "I see you've found a new friend. Named it yet?"

The cat meowed softly and leaped from Spyder's arm onto one of the display cases where it arched its back, circled itself twice, and gracefully curled up to lick its paws.

"Cat," Spyder said simply. "I want you to go upstairs to the roof, Ronal. Keep a sharp eye out for a Vasalan single-master entering the harbor from the west. Find me the moment you see it."

Ronal started for the stair, then stopped. "Vasalan? I thought they were coming from—"

Spyder cut him off. "They are. But they stole a ship out of the Vasalan Islands to bring them to Sanctuary."

Ronal mounted the stairs, then stopped again. "How do you know . . . ?"

"I know."

Shaking his head and frowning, Ronal disappeared up the stairs. Spyder watched him go with a thoughtful expression on his face. Ronal was a good man, a solid friend and ally, one of the few who knew Spyder's true name and heritage. But there were other things he didn't yet know, secrets that had to be kept. Perhaps in time . . .

Spyder moved to the doorway of his shop and watched the street. In years past, the Hill had belonged to Sanctuary's wealthy class. With the Temple of Ils crowning its peak and a panoramic view of the harbor and the sea beyond, it had been prime real estate.

Now, it was little more than a slum. The grand estates had been dismantled for their stone. Ramshackle shops and apartments now lined the streets, most thrown up too quickly after the great floods had destroyed the low-lying parts of Sanctuary and the poor district once known as Downwind. The wind that swept the Hill shook some of the older buildings, making them creak, and sometimes it collapsed one completely. Fortunately, it also blew away the stench that might have lingered otherwise.

The Hill, once a place for lords and ladies, had become the refuge for Sanctuary's poor, downtrodden, and luckless.

An old woman with a small girl child clinging to her skirts trudged up Face-of-the-Moon Street. She was probably no more than Spyder's age, somewhere in her twenties, but she looked sixty. Her face was lined and weather-beaten, her shoulders already slumped from hard work and constant hunger. Her clothes and those of her child were little more than rags, and her eyes were infinitely sad.

"Mother?" Spyder called out to her as he reached into the purse on his belt. She almost kept going, then stopped in mid-step, as if startled to realize that someone was talking to her. "Do you own a broom?" He held out a quarter piece of an Ilsigi shaboozh. The afternoon sunlight glinted on the silver metal.

She nodded slowly as she stared at the coin he

was offering. Then, eyes narrowing with suspicion, she studied his face.

"I need someone to sweep my shop each morning."

The woman hesitated. Bending down, she instructed her child to remain a safe distance back before she approached Spyder. She licked her lips, staring again at the silver coin, but she kept her hands at her sides. "That's too much pay for a shop-sweep," she said nervously.

Spyder smiled to himself. Despite her poverty, the woman had not lost all her pride. "One of these each week will adequately nourish yourself and your daughter. I am content to pay for a clean floor."

"The Hill is full of criminals and worse. What if I take your coin and never return?"

Spyder met her gaze with equanimity and said nothing as he held out the coin.

"Gray eyes," the woman grumbled. "Gray eyes always mean trouble."

"But not for you, Mother," Spyder answered. He closed his fist around the coin, then opened it again. The coin was gone. He reached toward her ear with his other hand, and the bit of silver rested between two of his fingers.

Her eyes lit up in brief amazement, then narrowed again.

"My name is Channa," she said, finally taking the coin. "And I have the finest damned broom in the city, Master Spyder. I'll sweep your shop every morning till the boards gleam and shine, and mop it, too. And I'll use it over your head if you ever get out of line with me or my little girl."

Though she tried her best to sound tough, she couldn't hide her excitement. Taking her child's hand, she hurried on her way and entered another apartment a short distance on.

Cat brushed against Spyder's ankle and made a soft meow as he continued to watch the street. "It didn't take much persuasion," he whispered as he picked Cat up and cradled it in his arms. "She needed the job and the money, and we'll benefit from another pair of friendly eyes and ears."

Cat meowed again, then jumped down and padded across the shop and up the stairs.

Word spread swiftly about the unexpected overnight opening of a new weapons shop on the Hill. The morning and the early afternoon might have been reserved for the curious locals and immediate nearby residents. But by mid-afternoon a seemingly endless parade of colorful characters from all classes and parts of the city passed through the door of The Black Spider.

Red-haired Raith, young and wide-eyed with curiosity, became enamored of an expensive White Hart bow. White Harts were rare and of extremely fine quality, made only by one artisan in the northern Rankan city of Tarkesi. Spyder, with a quiver full of arrows, escorted the young man to a narrow archery range behind the shop so that he could try it out. It took only five shots to clench the sale.

Eraldus and Gorge, two officers of the guard, arrived to introduce themselves and to remind Spyder of the dangerous location he had chosen for his shop. Neither the Guard, nor the City Watch, ventured onto the Hill after dark, they warned.

A dark-faced little gnome with a hunchback and a serious lisp wandered in just as Ronal descended the stair from above. The two shortest men in Sanctuary glared at each other, much to Spyder's silent amusement. Then the hunchback rushed off, muttering something about telling his "mathter."

Spyder introduced himself to all his visitors. To Soldt, a grim man with a professional eye for weapons. To Galen, another shopkeeper from the Maze, to whom Spyder took an immediate, if cautious, liking. To an arrogant young Rankan named Vion Larris, who despite disdaining and criticizing virtually everything in the shop, nevertheless bought and bought until his considerable purse was empty.

Despite the Hill's reputation, throughout the afternoon friendliness and courtesy prevailed—until the arrival of Naimun, the Irrune chieftain's second son, and his pair of burly escorts. Half of The Black Spider's customers, those nearest the door, exited at once. The other half backed into the far corners of the shop.

"Do you make all these weapons?" Naimun demanded as he took a Yenized sword down from its peg on the wall and unsheathed it. He ran his thumb along its edge.

"Of course not," Spyder answered calmly. "I'm a merchant. I, or my agents, travel the known world to find the finest merchandise made by the finest artisans and craftsmen."

"Then you're just a common shopkeeper," Naimun sneered. His two comrades laughed openly. "Tell me, shopkeeper, do you have any particular skill with the things you sell?"

It had been unseasonably warm for mid-winter in Sanctuary, warm enough that the shop's more elderly customers had muttered about a return of "wizard weather," and made finger signs against it; but with Naimun's question, the temperature in the shop dropped inexplicably. At the same moment, Aaliyah appeared on the staircase in a simple white dress with her hair spilling down her back. She paused there, her gaze fixed on the troublemakers. Though she had made no sound at all, every eye— even Naimun's—turned her way, as if sensing her presence.

"So we shall have a pissing contest," Spyder said in a low voice. His breath came out in a soft white stream, suggesting the chill in the air was no mere matter of nerves. "But then, pissing would make a mess of my floor, and the cleaning lady won't come until the morning." He reached toward a display case and drew down a pair of finely matched daggers. "I hear the Irrune have some skill with these." He handed one to Naimun.

Naimun looked at him with surprise. Though Spyder was actually an inch or two taller than the Irrune, the governor's son was far more muscular, not to mention backed by two friends. "You wish to fight me?"

Spyder shook his head and tapped the blade of the second dagger on his palm. "That, too, would make a mess of my shop, and I'd be all night cleaning up the blood." He paused as he looked around the shop. A young dark-haired boy in the unlikely garb of a S'danzo stood off to one side. In his hand he held a pear from which he'd taken a single bite.

"Kaytin," Spyder said. His breath no longer streamed white, and the chill seemed to have left the shop. "Would you mind tossing that into the air?"

Kaytin paled a little. "You want me to toss my lunch?"

"In a manner of speaking, yes," Spyder answered. He turned back to Naimun. "I'll bet this pair of daggers you can't skewer the pear in mid-toss."

Naimun sneered again. "Against what?"

"I'll name my price in a moment. Nothing too exorbitant."

Spyder nodded to Kaytin. The boy tossed the fruit and swiftly dove for the floor. Naimun's dagger flashed through the air, missing, embedding itself in the far wall. "It's impossib—!" he shouted. Before he could finish, Spyder's dagger flew as the fruit came down again, piercing the pear, cleaving it. A split-second after the first dagger, another one embedded in the wall, dripping juice.

"Not impossible," Spyder said quietly amid gasps and applause from the onlookers. "And now, my price."

Naimun's face darkened, and his two comrades stepped closer.

"Your friendship," Spyder continued. He extended his hand. "And perhaps your patronage the next time you're really in the market."

The governor's son hesitated, then grinned as he accepted Spyder's hand. "Well played, shopkeeper," he answered. "I'll pay your price and more." He turned to his escort. "Spread the word: This shop and its owner are under my protection. If anyone causes them trouble"—he glanced toward Aaliyah on the staircase—"especially this beautiful lady, they'll answer to me."

If Naimun expected an acknowledgment for his compliment, he received none from Aaliyah. She stood still as a black statue, her dark gaze unfathomable, until Naimun and his men turned and left. Only then did she finish her descent and place on the counter behind Spyder her own pair of daggers, which she had kept hidden behind her back.

"*Gilthona maha,*" he whispered, kissing her lightly on the brow. "My protector."

———

When the sun finally set, The Black Spyder closed. It had been a successful opening in many respects, and with the profits safely locked away in a concealed vault, Spyder and Aaliyah sat down on the rooftop to a supper of roasted pigeon breasts prepared by Ronal. She had changed into a dress of saffron-colored silk that hung off one ebony shoulder. He wore only a kilt of blue linen. Sesame oil burned in a lamp of pale alabaster. Its glow lent the rooftop an air of romance and tranquility.

"I don't understand it," Spyder said quietly as he sipped wine and stared outward toward the harbor. "I was sure they would arrive today. But you both kept watch, and I made what inquiries I safely could without arousing suspicions among the customers. No one has seen a Vasalan ship for a week.

Aaliyah reached across the table and touched his hand. It was meant to reassure him, but he could feel the tension in her touch. She was as worried as he was. More so, for she had more at stake. He met her gaze. "No, I can't be wrong," he insisted, answering her unspoken question. He raised his face toward the full moon that hung low and golden on the eastern horizon. "The eclipse is tonight or tomorrow night. They must perform the ritual before it's over, or all their hopes are lost."

Rising from her seat, Aaliyah came around the table and took his face in her hands. Her eyes were storms of anger, pain, fear, and doubt.

"*Silivren mi akare, Shahana,*" he said, wrapping his arms around her, pressing her head to his shoulder. "I will not let that happen! They will not take Lisoh from you, I swear!"

Swallowing, Aaliyah nodded and returned to her seat. They resumed supper, though neither ate much. Their eyes watched the harbor—and the rising moon.

When the meal was done, Spyder leaned on the rooftop parapet and stared impatiently outward. Aaliyah paced back and forth, her tread soundless, her eyes wild with worry and torment as the night grew later. Ronal was gone; Spyder had sent him to the wharves to learn what he could and to keep watch from there.

A light wind stirred Spyder's short-cropped hair and played on the back of his neck as he folded his hands together and leaned on the rough stone. The moon and the night mocked him, he thought. The streets, indeed the city as far as he could see, was a maddening patchwork of shadows lit only by Sabellia's wan smile and the occasional flickering torch.

The bay and the sea beyond were a silvery mirror where nothing moved. Merchant ships rested in their slips for the night; fishing boats bobbed lightly on their lines at the docks.

He had chosen these apartments just for this view. Jamasharem would be interested in the comings and goings in this city's harbor. The Rankan Empire yet regarded Sanctuary with suspicion, and in truth, even fear. Too much had happened here. The place was strange. Enchanted, some said. Cursed, said others. Whichever, gods and sorcerers and demons had left their marks here as they had in no other city.

Why did it surprise him, then, that Sanctuary had finally called his name? He was not the first of the Vigeles line to be drawn in by its arcane allure. Indeed, his family had a dark and shameful history here, a past that had cost House Vigeles its lands, much of its wealth, its very reputation. So great was the shame that to bear the name Vigeles was to be shunned throughout the Rankan Empire.

So he was Spyder, a man without heritage, without a nation.

And yet, for reasons he couldn't fully grasp, he served the Rankan emperor. Some lingering ember of loyalty still burning in his breast? Some minuscule hope of restoring the honor of the Vigeles?

It embittered him to deny his true name.

Aaliyah touched his arm, and he turned to her. Filled with a sudden need, he drew her close and pressed his head down upon her shoulder. The smell of her hair, the feathery brush of her fingers on his bare back—whether by his action or hers, his kilt fell away as their lips met. She tasted of honey and mint, sweeter and more intoxicating than the wine in his cup.

On the couch beside the table, in the open night, they made love. The soft illumination from the alabaster lamp highlighted the contrast between their bodies and charged the air with an eroticism and sensuality that, for a time, allowed them to forget Sanctuary and danger, bitterness and fear. For a time, they had no other mission, no other purpose, but each other.

Afterward, they lay side by side watching the moon. Spyder felt Aaliyah's breathing, the soft vibration of her body next to his. He knew that she was changing his life in a way that was both fantastical and disturbing. There was no room in his life for the feelings she stirred in him, and yet already in the short month since he'd found Aaliyah, he couldn't imagine being apart from her.

He kissed her mouth, then rose from the couch. The sesame oil burning in the lamp was beginning to smoke, so he sprinkled a few grains of salt in it to stop the smoking. As he did so, something in the flame caught his attention. He stared with puzzlement as a blood red shadow touched the edge of the flame and slowly engulfed it, turning blacker and blacker.

Spyder jerked his gaze away and rubbed a thumb and finger over his eyelids. Then he shot a glance at the moon. It floated in the sky over the harbor, effulgent. Next, he noticed Aaliyah. She stood at the parapet, her attention riveted on the moon, her fingers curled like claws on the stone, her body rigid, and her head thrown back.

The braided flax wick in the sesame oil crackled suddenly, drawing his attention once again, and the flame was just a yellow flame. But he knew, without understanding how, that he had seen a vision of the coming eclipse in that small lamp light, and that Aaliyah had shared that vision, or at least, in her own way, that she had sensed something.

He caught her shoulders and drew her against him. Her face was a mask of panic and desperation. He studied the harbor again for the Vasalan ship, then slammed a palm down on the parapet in frustration. Though it had only been a small vision, it had to mean something!

"Prepare yourself, *Shahana*," he said, leading her to the staircase. "They're here. They've gotten by us somehow. Now we have to find them."

They descended to their separate apartments. Spyder quickly donned garments of black leather and threw a cloak about his shoulders. From a chest at the foot of his bed he took a double-edged sword of medium length. The scabbard, though sturdy, was unremarkable, but before he strapped it on, he grasped the hilt and exposed a few inches of the blade. The candlelight in his room gleamed on fine

Enlibar steel. To this, he added a plain dagger, and closed the chest once more.

Dressed and armed, with one hand on the door, he paused and lingered beside one of the several candles that lit his room. He stared at the flame, tried to focus his attention on it in the unlikely expectation of another vision, a clearer message. It was a foolish effort: He had no powers of clairvoyance or foresight. Maybe what he'd seen on the rooftop had been a trick of light.

But Aaliyah had reacted, too. Something had plainly agitated her.

He hurried downstairs into the darkened shop and let himself out a side door into an alley that was barely wide enough for two men to pass through shoulder to shoulder. He followed it, pausing at the opening to stare both ways down Face-of-the-Moon Street. A few torches burned here and there. One burned in a sconce before the entrance to The Black Spider.

With his hood up and his cloak drawn close, Spyder moved into the street. He kept to the shadows and the dark places as he made his way down the Hill, his footsteps silent, his movements swift and stealthy. A gang of rowdy bravos passed him without so much as noticing his presence. A pair of customers stumbled arm in arm from a tavern almost into his path with no more awareness.

Once, a low animal growl caused him to pause in mid-step. With narrowed eyes, he searched the street and the darkness around him for some sign of danger, one hand going carefully to the hilt of his sword. Behind the poorly fitted shutters of a nearby shop he noted the furtive movement of faint light, a candle or perhaps a shaded lantern, which was odd at so late an hour. Thieves, he suspected, but it was no business of his.

As he neared the bottom of the Hill, he heard the rapid clip-clop of horses' hooves and the creak of wagon wheels on rough cobbles. From the shadowed recess of an alley, he measured its approach. As it rounded a corner, the moonlight fell full upon both wagon and driver. As it passed his hiding place, Spyder leaped aboard.

The driver, Ronal, jerked hard on the reins with his left hand. At the same time, he launched a backfisted blow toward his uninvited passenger's face. Spyder caught his arm before the blow could land.

"Such a swift ride must mean you have news," he whispered as he settled on the buckboard beside his friend.

Ronal's breath hissed between his teeth. "Damn it, you nearly gave me heart failure!"

"You've a stouter heart than ten men," Spyder answered, letting go of Ronal's arm. "To the point. The ring is here—I'm certain of it."

Ronal half-turned on his seat to regard Spyder. "How do you know that?"

"I just know," Spyder answered from beneath his hood. "A feeling."

"You may be right," Ronal said in a low voice. "In the Broken Mast a short time ago I overheard Markam telling a wild story. Seems there's a ship from Inception Island anchored at the easternmost end of the harbor, and some of its sailors were claiming they saw a ghost ship last night, all black with no running lights, off their starboard side hugging the shoreline. Sailed straight up the White Foal River, they claimed, before it disappeared in the fog. Markam was laughing about it. Impossible, he said. But I thought you'd want to know."

"Turn the wagon around," Spyder ordered quietly. "Take the Wideway at the best pace you can manage without drawing too much attention, and head for the White Foal."

Ronal complied. At a pace that was brisk without appearing frantic, the wagon moved back down the Hill, across the Avenue of Temples, down the Governor's Walk and the Processional. "What's on your mind, Spyder?" Ronal said as he worked the reins. "You've got *grim* on you like a pig's got stink."

Spyder didn't answer. He glanced over his left shoulder at the moon high above the bay. There was no trace yet of the eclipse Ranke's finest astrologers were predicting. And yet, there was that strange little trick with the candle flame on his rooftop. Out on the water near the pinnacles of stone called Hag's Teeth a number of ships were anchored. Lanterns burned weakly along their rails, in their bows. They were single and double-masted sailing vessels without oar-banks like the Ilsigi trireme he had arrived on.

There had been no wind last night. How could a ship have hugged the shoreline and sailed almost unnoticed up the White Foal? The river ran deep enough, but it was full of snags and tangles, particularly for the first few miles or so inland from the mouth.

They had come to the end of the Wideway. Ronal brought the wagon to a halt, and Spyder rose, standing on the seat to study the black ribbon of water. The river ran wide, but not so swiftly as in former days. It had washed out of its old banks and spread over the land, making bogs and marshes. "There is a name for that place," Spyder said with a sweep of his hand.

"The Swamp of Night Secrets," Ronal answered. "An evil place, especially at night."

Spyder climbed down from the wagon and turned slowly. Just behind them between their position and the sea were the low rooftops of Fisherman's Row. "Steal us a boat, Ronal. A skiff, a rowboat, anything that will get us to the other side. Hurry!"

Ronal turned the wagon and slapped the reins across the horses' backs to speed them along. Spyder watched him go, then drawing his cloak about himself, he moved into the shadow of a warehouse and turned back toward the river.

The Swamp of Night Secrets. An evil place, Ronal called it. What better place then for a coven of Nisi witches to make their sacrifices and work their damnable magic? He clenched his fists inside his leather gloves and swore silently. It was no longer enough to thwart their rituals and destroy the Ring of Sea and Fire—that much he had promised Jamasharem. He must also save Lisoh. That he had also promised.

The sharp, feline growl of a jungle cat sounded near the river's bank, interrupting his thoughts. He gazed in the direction of the sound, then sank deeper into the shadows and deeper into his thoughts.

The Ring of Sea and Fire.

Forty years before, two Globes of Power had been forged on Wizardwall in the land of the Nis, one each for the King and Queen of Night, who were the greatest warlock and witch of their day. Into those crystal orbs were poured the essences of the blackest sorcery, power magnified and amplified beyond understanding. Armed with such power, Nis looked with hungry eyes on the Rankan Empire, its neighbor.

A long and costly war followed, and though Ranke

eventually prevailed, the globes were not destroyed. As with so many things arcane and magical, they made their way to Sanctuary. Here, in the slum district once called Downwind, demigods and sorcerers and vampires and their masters, the strangest of allies, finally shattered them.

Spyder sniffed the air as he looked around. Downwind—he stood now upon its very edge, recalling the tales, how for a single night following that destruction every man, woman, or child with a mote of magical talent found their abilities elevated to drastic levels as the power contained in those globes diffused through the city. Then, like fire smothered under sand, the magic went out.

Not completely, of course. Embers of power still glowed here and there. But the gods had turned away from Sanctuary. Fearful of it, some said. Wounded by it, some said. Or most likely, Spyder thought, repelled by its corruption.

The creak of wagon wheels in the quietness alerted him to Ronal's return. The shorter man hopped down and threw back a tarp, exposing the small rowboat he'd appropriated. "I don't feel good about stealing from honest, hard-working folks," he grumbled as the two men together seized hold of the boat.

"Perhaps you'll feel better about it when someone steals your wagon and team," Spyder commented. "We'll have to leave them here."

Ronal frowned as they lifted the boat and carried it to the water. "And you're a right prick for mentioning it."

Again there came the feline cry that Spyder had heard earlier. Ronal straightened instantly. His startled eyes widened as he whirled and searched the darkness, and he gripped an oar like a club. "That came from behind us!"

Spyder gazed toward the sky again. The full moon hung directly overhead. Yet, there was a thin veil of clouds gathering over the sea, a moon-tinged grayness that had come up without warning out of nowhere. "Get in the boat," Spyder insisted. Climbing in first, he settled himself in the bow with his eyes fixed on the far side of the White Foal.

Ronal pushed off from the bank and seated himself in the middle of the boat. Quickly, he positioned the oars in the oar-locks and dipped them into the water.

A soft splash sounded off to their right. Ronal froze at the oars to stare. Spyder calmly turned his head for a moment. "You're nervous tonight," he said.

Ronal resumed rowing. "Swamps and witches," he muttered. "Witches and swamps. Why would I be nervous? This isn't your usual business, my friend. I've helped you count army divisions in secret, intercepted correspondence for you, watched you seduce information from the wives of generals. This is different."

Under Ronal's determined strokes they moved swiftly across the White Foal. Spyder remained silent, his jaw grim, his teeth clenched. All that Ronal said was true. This was not his usual business. This was far more dangerous, perhaps beyond his talents. Ronal was not the only nervous man under the moonlight. He felt the slight breeze upon his face like an evil breath. He listened to the water dripping from the oars, to the barely audible sound of something swimming off to the right just beyond the range of his vision. He smelled the industry of Sanctuary behind him and the rot of the swamp ahead.

And crawling at the edge of his senses, something more. Already in the air, the taint of Nisi witchcraft.

"When you get to the far side, row northward against the flow. Look for a tributary or a place wide enough to allow a ship to pass or to hide." He gripped the side of the boat until his knuckles cracked with strain and continued in a low voice. "We must stop them, Ronal. We don't dare fail."

Ronal shrugged as he rowed and answered with faint bravado. "It's only a ring," he said. "We break up their nasty little party and snatch the trinket, hopefully killing a few of the bastards as we go."

"It's no mere trinket we're after," Spyder whispered, careful now not to let his voice carry across the water. "And we don't know the number of enemies we face. Nis dreams of reclaiming its former might, and this ring is the key to their ambitions."

As they neared the western bank, Ronal turned the boat. Though the river lacked its former power, still there was a current, and his muscles bulged as he worked the oars. "There's more you haven't told me, though," he whispered. "Something worries you."

After a hesitation, Spyder nodded. "The ring is forged from minerals distilled from the sea, but it must also be tempered in fire." He hesitated again. "In the fire of a burning boy with sorcerous blood in his veins." He paused to listen again for the swimming sound that had followed them across the river. He could no longer hear it. "That sacrifice performed under a certain rare lunar eclipse on the ground where the globes were destroyed will complete their ritual."

"I'm a fool for misjudging you," Ronal said, his eyes narrowing as he regarded his friend. "It's not this bunch of mumblers and cauldron-stirrers that have you tied in knots. It's the boy, isn't it? They've got him already, and you know him."

"I don't know him, but his name is Lisoh," Spyder said. "He's fifteen summers old, and he's Aaliyah's brother. He was on a spirit-quest, something his people call *Vahana meh aaha diano*. It's a kind of initiation into adulthood. But he wandered much too far, and when he didn't return, Aaliyah went looking for him. I found her on the Nis border where I originally tried to stop this coven—and failed."

And you will fail again, Regan Vigeles called Spyder, just as you did then.

Ronal stopped rowing and looked nervously toward the shore. "That wasn't me," he whispered.

The jungle cat's cry sounded again, a shrill, high-pitched roar that chilled the blood.

From the east a sudden wind rose. It shook the leaves and the moss-dripping branches, shivered the reeds, and rippled across the water. The rowboat pitched and rocked. Spyder gripped both sides of the small craft and fought to keep it from overturning while Ronal struggled to do the same with the oars. "We're gonna flip!" Ronal shouted.

But just as suddenly as the wind arose it ceased, and the river became calm once again. Spyder crouched in the bow. "You're not in Nis now, Rime! Your powers are weak here!"

Laughter soared on the night, coming from everywhere and nowhere, and when it faded, the throb of coven drums replaced it, an ominous pulsing beat that came from deep within the Swamp of Night Secrets.

Ronal leaned on the oars, his powerful muscles visibly knotted, his face pale. "There once was a woman from Nis," he muttered, pausing to chew his lip, "who went into the forest to piss. Her soft little splash turned a boulder to ash, and lizards crawled out of her . . ."

The wind ripped through the swamp and over the river again, and Rime's voice took form on it. *Nasty little man, I heard that!* The rowboat rocked and bounced precariously on huge moonlit swells. Yet, the river seemed darker, the night less bright.

Spyder twisted around in the boat and shot a glance skyward. "The moon!" he shouted. "It's begun!"

The smallest sliver of the left side of the moon was gone. A faint arc of redness, like a trickle of blood, marked the slowly advancing edge of the black, light-devouring shadow that would soon consume its radiance entirely. Somewhere in the swamp, the coven drums beat louder even as the wind stilled once more.

The jungle cat roared again.

"Head for that sound!" Spyder ordered.

"I'd rather head for the Unicorn," Ronal shot back, "and for a couple of beers—I'd even buy!" But he angled the boat out of the main stream and into the reeds. "But no, before we ever find the witches we're going to wind up cat food."

A swarm of gnats, unseeable in the darkness, immediately surrounded them. Spyder pulled up his hood and covered his mouth and nose with one hand. Ronal, working the oars, cursed and sputtered, defenseless under the sudden onslaught. Then they were through whatever nest or insect home their passage had disturbed.

Spyder turned one shoulder toward his old friend. "Did you say gnat food?"

"No jokes from the bow," Ronal grumbled.

"You're only allowed to brood and look ominous under your big black cloak."

"Be glad they were gnats," Spyder answered, "and not bees."

Rime's laughter touched their minds again, not borne on a wind this time, but on a malevolent buzzing.

Ronal ceased rowing and looked up in horrible expectation. "I think I mis-remembered the limerick!" he hissed. "They weren't lizards that crawled out of her orifice. They were . . . ! Oh no!" Leaving the oars to rattle in their oarlocks, he flung himself over the side.

The bees came like a black wave over the tops of the reeds and through the tall river grasses. Clutching both sides of the rowboat to steady it, Spyder crouched down. He was not only cloaked and hooded, but also gloved. Still, he felt the weight of the creatures striking at his back, at his arms, trying to sting him. In only moments, hood or no hood, they would find his face and eyes.

"Get out of the boat!" he heard Ronal yell. "We can get under it!"

But there was no need for that. The buzzing diminished. Bees dropped out of the air into the boat, or into the water with little plops. Spyder shook one gloved hand, then straightened, shedding bees from his back and shoulders like droplets of water. Ronal's head broke the surface about three feet from the side of the boat. He shrieked and pushed wildly at the water with his hands, parting the bobbing curtain of insect corpses around him.

Then the panic left his face and a look of puzzlement replaced it. He swam to the boat, caught it with both hands, and peeked over the side at the unnatural cargo they'd taken on. "What the . . . ?"

He brushed a dead bee off the oarlock.

"The cold," Spyder said, balancing the boat while Ronal clambered back in. "Bees go dormant in the cold."

Ronal settled back between the oars, clutching himself and shivering. "It's been a warm winter . . ." He stopped as his teeth began to clack and chatter. "Until now." He hugged himself even harder and rubbed his bare arms.

It was Spyder's turn to laugh. "Is that the best you can manage, Rime?" he shouted. "Nis's Grand Witch reduced to conjuring *annoyances?*"

"I'm not just wet," Ronal complained with a disbelieving voice, "I'm freezing! How . . . ?" He stared at Spyder, then at the bees on the floor of the boat. With a vengeful determination, he began squashing them with his boots.

"You don't seem to be able to finish your sentences, my friend," Spyder observed as he unfastened his cloak and tossed it to Ronal. "Row, and you'll quickly warm up."

They didn't row much farther. Abruptly the bottom of the boat dragged, and the bow bumped up on land.

It couldn't be called dry land. They slogged through ankle-deep mud for the first fifty paces and forded a stream that cut suddenly across their path. Patches of dense foliage also impeded them, and strange groves of trees with willowy, whip-like branches and complicated, interlocking root structures sometimes blocked their way.

There was no sign of the Vasalan vessel. Spyder began to fear that the drums were a trick, a distraction intended to lure him in the wrong direction. He glanced repeatedly over his shoulder. Sometimes the thick trees hid the moon from him. But sometimes he could catch a glimpse of it—what remained of it.

"It—it—shouldn't be so c-c-cold!" Ronal muttered as he walked. His breath came out in a feathery stream. Spyder's cloak was much too long for him, so he wore the hood up and the rest of it clutched around his upper body.

Spyder didn't answer. He moved through the undergrowth with the speed and sureness of desperation. The drums were louder than ever in his ears—or were they just in his mind, an auditory hallucination sent by Rime to confound him? He pressed his palms to his ears. If the sound were real, wouldn't he be able to shut it out? He no longer glanced at the sky; he could feel the darkening moon on his neck. Far ahead he thought he spied a glow that might have been a fire.

He had no choice but to trust his natural senses as he plunged forward.

Rime's voice touched his mind again. *You cannot hope to succeed, Regan Vigeles. You didn't even get close to me in your first pathetic attempt.*

"You killed one of my agents on your border," he answered without slowing his pace. "For that alone I would hunt you to the ends of the world."

You are too late, fool. The boy is at the stake, and the torch is in my hand. The ring is already on my finger!

"You're a lying whore," Spyder answered. "The ring can't be tempered until the moon is completely eclipsed."

"Lying whore," Ronal repeated sarcastically as he hurried along on Spyder's heels. "I like that. It has a ring—oh, pardon me!"

You and your witless lackey are far outnumbered. If you do find us, I'll eat your heart with a spoon.

Spyder's eyes narrowed as he felt Rime's power

weighing down upon him. Her words were more than mere words; they were tiny spells designed to feed his doubts, to erode his confidence, to slow him. Despite himself, he glanced over his shoulder again. No more than a quarter of the moon remained. And in the instant that he diverted his attention from his path, he stumbled over an unseen root. Yet, he caught himself and did not fall.

"You're wrong, Witch," Spyder said through clenched teeth. Her power was subtle, but he resisted it with all his will. Yes, he had doubts—about himself and about his purpose. But he had no doubts about his abilities. "There are more than two of us stalking you tonight. I am numberless as the stars that grow brighter even as the moon dims. You speak to my mind, but you can't see me. I'm right behind you, and my knife is at your throat!"

He felt as much as heard her gasp. *Now it's you who lie, Rankan!*

A cold sneer turned up the corners of Spyder's mouth. "But it's you who flinched, bitch."

At last he knew he was on the right course. He heard the desperation in her words as she strove to delay him, and panic lent her thought-sendings a serrated edge. More, he was certain that the glow he saw ahead was firelight. It flickered among the trunks and branches, danced on the leaves. And yet with that sense of certainty a new fear came. Rime had said the boy was already at the stake!

"Spyder!"

Steel rang loudly on steel, and Spyder's eyes snapped wide at the sound of his name. For an instant, Rime had almost trapped him in his own web of doubt, and he had to admire the subtlety of her effort even as he shrugged off its effects.

Rime laughed inside his head. *You are surrounded, Rankan. In moments you will be dead!*

Three of Rime's coven brothers leaped out of the foliage and ran at him. Their nude bodies were painted with green mud and black slime. More mud dulled the metal sheen of their swords. The sounds of combat behind him indicated that Ronal was already engaged.

Spyder's hand went to the dagger on his belt, and the glittering blade flashed under the reddening moon as it flew straight to the nearest attacker's throat. A second Nisi rushed at him, swinging his sword in a horizontal arc. Spyder ducked low and side-stepped, and as he straightened he freed his own sword, raked it through the man's mid-section. Without pausing, he smashed his booted foot into the third Nisi's groin. It failed to have the expected effect—perhaps the man was a eunuch?—and Spyder dodged and parried a wild flurry of strokes.

"You'll learn not to meddle in the affairs of your betters!" the Nisi shouted, pausing to catch his breath.

"Here's a lesson for you," Spyder answered. He spun sharply, ripping a handful of leaves from a bush and flinging them at his foe's eyes. The Nisi recoiled, instinctively jerking his head away to protect his sight, and never saw the Enlibar sword before it bit deeply into his neck.

"And the witless lackey scores three on his own," Ronal said with mocking calm. At his feet on the muddy ground lay three more coven members. He tore leaves from a bush and wiped his blade.

Spyder turned toward the distant fire. "No words, Rime?" he shouted as he sheathed his sword. "Do you feel my breath on your neck, Witch?"

A pantherish roar sounded from the trees nearby.

Startled, Ronal jumped and stumbled over one of the bodies, landing on his back. "Shite!" he cursed as he scrambled to his feet again. "That damned beast is getting too close for comfort!" He kicked the body he'd fallen over. "Maybe this meat will satisfy its appetite. Here, kitty, kitty, kitty!"

But Spyder was already off again through the swamp, his gaze fixed on the fire. The ground turned muddy once more, slowing him, and he waded through a shallow stream. He brushed aside low limbs and vines and tried to brush away thoughts of quicksand. Rime spoke to him no more; the drums did her talking now, and he felt their power like waves on his skin. He glanced yet again at the moon. It was nearly gone.

He remembered the clouds he'd seen far out over Hag's Teeth. If Rime couldn't see the moon it might affect the timing of her spells. But that was too small a hope; those clouds were too thin and too far away.

What was worse, he wondered as he began to run. Failing to destroy the ring? That would mean another war with Nis, one that neither Ranke, nor Ilsig, could afford. Or losing the boy, Lisoh. That would break Aaliyah's heart. Why was he even asking the question now? He had his duty to the empire. No matter that it had ruined his family and declared him outcast—Ranke still commanded his loyalty.

Yet, it was Aaliyah, though, who commanded his heart.

He leaped a barricade of twisted roots, ducked under a low branch and dodged the gaping mouth of a hissing serpent that hung from it. Puddles splashed under his feet. He no longer valued stealth. Only speed mattered. A grove of willow trees loomed before him. A pale mist drifted over the grass, unnaturally thick, he thought, but there was no time to find a way around. He feared losing sight of the fire if he veered off course.

Clouds. Mist.

Perhaps.

The air turned chilly again, and a light fog began to eddy over the ground. Wispy tendrils swirled lazily upward, diffusing on the air. The stars, so bright in a crisp sky, began to waver and fade as a gray veil obscured their light. Stubbornly, the remaining sliver of moonlight lingered, yet moment by moment, the milky effluvium rose and deepened. The Swamp of Night Secrets seemed to shrink in upon itself as one by one the stars vanished entirely.

Spyder ran, narrowly avoiding trees and obstacles in his path. Only the barest hint of fireglow remained, and he focused his gaze on that and nothing else. He was sure Ronal was behind him, but he didn't know where. He didn't hear any sound of pursuit. Indeed, he didn't hear anything but those frantic drums and his own harsh breathing and his sloshing footfalls.

Then, he stopped suddenly, grabbing desperately at a slender tree to catch his balance as he found himself at the edge of a fifteen foot high embankment above a narrow tributary. A black Vasalan ship sat anchored on a river of mist at the opposite bank, its mast swaying ever so slowly. Not one, but three crackling bonfires burned on that far side. The lanky silhouettes of Nis witches danced around them, their shapes and movements twisted, distorted by the fog.

He stared for a moment, tasting desperation.

Again, he glanced over his shoulder through the branches above his head. There was no moon to see—only fog.

Securing his sword with one hand, he slipped and

slid down the embankment, finishing the descent
on his backside before he hit the water with a splash.
He didn't worry about the noise. The drumming
covered any sound he was likely to make. He began
to swim with fast, furious strokes.

Quanali pahabaril maha elberah yora. Aaliyah stole
into his thoughts like a warm wind, soothing and
reassuring him. *Each time we part, my heart cries.* He
remembered the first time he said that to her, how
she slipped her arms around him and laid her head
on his chest. It had become their ritual farewell, but
he had forgotten to tell her before he left the shop
tonight.

Quanali muriel maha elberah canta. She was in his
head, in his heart and blood. *Each time we meet, my
heart sings!* Only a month ago, he'd found her
searching for her brother along the Nis border.
She'd looked—Ronal had put it rightly—lonely and
strange, more than a little lost.

A splash interrupted his thoughts, and a moment
later, a softer splash. Under the muffling blanket of
fog he couldn't tell what direction the sounds came
from. It might have been Ronal behind him, or it
might have been one of the Nisi warlocks swimming
to intercept him. It might have been both.

He reached the opposite shore and crept out of
the water. With the enemy so near now, his natural
stealth reasserted itself. Crouched, he stole along
the edge of the bank and angled toward the fire,
stopping behind a thick tree trunk to observe. The
underbrush and foliage had been cut away or pulled
up by the roots to form a sizable clearing. Spyder
counted the dancers weaving among the fires, then
the drummers, who sat in a circle to one side. They
beat their drums with a hysterical passion, and their
bodies gleamed with sweat and fire-sheen. As if they

could see through the fog, all their gazes were turned skyward.

Regan Vigeles, called Spyder. Rime's voice slipped into his mind like a sharp knife. *Know that you have failed again. It is time. All the power of the Nisi globes will be mine, and there is nothing you can do to prevent it.*

He didn't know why he turned toward the Vasalan ship and caught his breath. With regal grace, the Grand Witch of Nis strode down the gangplank. Her beauty dazzled. Though bred in Hell, her form was something far more heavenly. Black hair swept down her back over her hips and to her knees. Large eyes glittered over perfect cheekbones and a lush mouth. A diaphanous skirt loosely encircled her waist. Rather than hiding her loins, it seemed to enhance and emphasize them. She wore nothing over her breasts but jewels. Dozens of necklaces sparkled with rubies, emeralds, diamonds, sapphires, nuggets of gold, and gold circlets banded her upper arms.

As she walked down the plank, she held her left arm rigidly at right angles with the back of her hand turned outward. The only jewelry that mattered tonight shimmered on her middle finger—a band seemingly of purest silver. But the firelight caught the metal and played strangely upon it so that at some moments it seemed liquid, not solid at all.

The Ring of Sea—and Fire.

As she moved into the clearing the dancers ceased their gyrations and threw themselves to their knees. Naked, they were covered in mud and filth, their hair matted. With their lips almost to the ground they chanted her name. *Rime! Rime! Rime!* As far as Spyder could tell, none of them bore any weapons at all.

"Looks more like *grime, grime, grime,* to me." Ronal whispered as he drifted from behind another tree to Spyder's side. "You want your cloak back?" He held out a wad of dripping cloth.

When Spyder put a finger to his lips for silence, Ronal shrugged and dropped the sopping bundle. He eased his sword from its sheath. "Is there a plan?" he asked.

"Kill everyone," Spyder said. "But not until I know where the boy is."

Ronal pointed. "You must have something in your eye," he said. "Look closely, there on the ground right in front of the fire where the lying whore is standing."

Spyder's gaze narrowed. On the ground right at the fire's edge, barely visible against the glow, was a white shape. It lay so still, but as he watched, the form twitched ever so slightly within the limits of its severe bindings. Lisoh—wrapped like a mummy!

He knew where the ring was. Now, he knew where Lisoh was, too. "Stay hidden," Spyder said to Ronal. "You'll know when I need you."

"You need me," Ronal muttered. "Wait until I tell 'em at the Broken Mast you finally admitted that."

Drawing a breath, Spyder walked into the clearing. The drummers saw him first, and the drums fell silent. When the drums stopped, the chanters also stopped and stared wide-eyed at him.

Rime also stared with disbelief and fear.

Then she laughed.

"I told you my knife was at your back, Witch."

"But how can that be," she answered, her voice deeply seductive, "when you are standing before me?" *Indeed, when you are kneeling before me!*

Her power hit him like a hammer, and he felt his knees start to buckle. But he resisted, drawing another breath, gathering his strength as he took a step forward. "My knives are many, Rime," he answered. A pair of her coven brothers seized his arms, but he ignored them. "They are everywhere! They strike from everywhere!"

She laughed again. "You're . . . !"

Her mouth gaped, and her eyes shot wide with pain before she could finish. One of the dancers screamed and leaped up to catch her elbow as she faltered and sank to one knee. Rime looked at the dancer. Then she looked at the bound form by the fire. A red spittle bubbled on her lip as she hissed, "Burn him!"

But the dancer was staring beyond Rime, and he wore a look of horror as he pulled the dagger from her back.

Indeed, Ronal always knew when Spyder needed him. The former gladiator ran into the clearing, his gaze focused on Rime. The witch was down, but not yet dead. The drummers leaped up. One of them threw a drum at Ronal's legs before he could reach his target. He dodged it, but they were on him. He cut and slashed with an expert fury.

Spyder twisted and drove his knee into one of his captors. He'd distracted Rime while Ronal worked his way behind her. Now, nothing but sheer ferocity would win the game. Freeing his sword arm, he drew the Enlibar blade and slashed through his second captor. Two more Nis rushed at him. He cut them down ruthlessly.

But a ring of witches had encircled Rime, and within that ring still another ring of witches. He rushed at them, then staggered under a chaotic assault of hastily cast spells. Some commanded him merely to stop; some ripped the breath from his body. Pain spells, blindness spells, even love spells.

For a moment, he felt himself drowning on dry land, the next moment he saw his sword turn into a serpent in his grasp, then back to steel. There was no order to the assault, and one spell interfered with another, so that all of them lacked sufficient power. Still, he reeled.

Then he screamed as a pair of witches in the inner ring lifted Lisoh's squirming, mummy-wrapped body.

A terrible cat-cry ripped the air, a scream louder than his own. High in a tree at the edge of the clearing, a pair of eyes gleamed with green anger. A panther, sleek and black, poised on a branch with its gaze fixed on Rime.

Spyder cried out, *"Shahana!"*

The panther sprang, landing on the back of an inner-circle witch. But that one was not its prey. In an instant, the creature was on Rime. Its jaws closed savagely on her neck. One powerful rear leg raked open the witch's belly. Necklaces broke, and jewels scattered like colored rain.

Still, the Nis sought to close ranks around their mistress. Two hurled themselves at the panther, oblivious to the death-dealing claws, and the two bearing Lisoh lifted him and threw him into the flames.

If the boy screamed, he could not be heard over the screams of the witches, the panther, and Spyder, himself. He waded into the witches, blind with hate and rage and shame. Even when the witches finally broke ranks and tried to flee, he chased them, cut them down mercilessly.

And the panther, with teeth and claws, claimed as many lives.

When no foes remained standing, his rage still not spent, Spyder seized a brand from one of the fires and flung it at the Vasalan ship. The flames caught in a coil of rope, spread along the deck, touched the furled sail and climbed the mast.

Only then, with the heat of the burning vessel scorching his face did Spyder drop his sword and sink to his knees. "I'm sorry, *Shahana*," he cried. "I promised you, but I failed!"

The panther padded slowly to his side.

"Regan! The beast . . . !" Ronal called from the far side of the clearing where he sat leaning against a tree unable to stand.

Spyder looked into the panther's eyes and touched its blood-matted shoulder. The beast hung its head and gave a low growl. Then, its form shifted, stretched, and transformed.

"I'll be damned," Ronal said quietly. "I knew there was something strange about her."

Aaliyah and Spyder fell into each other's arms and wept together, and Spyder wondered how they could ever share love again through so much pain. He hadn't known the boy, Lisoh, but he knew what Lisoh meant to Aaliyah. And he had promised—he had promised. Through his tears, he looked up. The fog had melted away. In the sky, the moon was past full eclipse.

With an effort, Spyder got to his feet and, picking up his sword, went to Rime's body. Her mouth, though caked with mud, seemed turned up at the corners as if the bitch were still laughing at him. For a long moment he stood there letting the rage wash over him again, then the grief, then a terrible emptiness.

He raised the sword once and cut off her right hand. The untempered ring went into his pocket. It was evidence for Jamasharem. Unless he decided to keep it.

A second time he raised the sword and cut off her head. That was for spite. Then he cast hand, head, and her entire body into the flames to burn with Aaliyah's brother.

The rest of them could rot in the mud.

"She's a shapechanger," Spyder explained quietly. He didn't feel obligated to tell Ronal that he was the witch, or rather, the warlock, and that the weird weather tricks had been his. Perhaps in time. It wasn't that he didn't trust his friend, but some secrets were best kept. Especially in Sanctuary.

Ronal sat on the couch with his swollen left leg in a swath of herbal poultices and bandages. "I'm getting too old for this," he said after a pause. "That knife-toss should have found the witch's heart."

"You did well, Ronal." He turned and stared from the rooftop parapet out toward the bay. Half to himself, he added, "My knives are always where I need them."

His knives. His agents.

After another long pause, Ronal asked, "Are you going to keep the ring?"

Spyder pursed his lips. Though the ring was untempered and would never be as potent as it was intended to be, it was not entirely without power. He wasn't sure yet if he wanted to hand that unexplored power to Jamasharem. "For now, it's safe in my vault. I may destroy it." He had no idea how to accomplish that, but he was certain it would take more than his meager talent.

Aaliyah appeared at the top of the stair with a tray of food and a fresh jug of wine. She set them on the table by the couch within Ronal's reach and went to Spyder's side. He slipped his arm around her and drew her close. *"Quanali muriel maha elberah canta,"* he whispered.

A sudden chill touched the air, but this time he wasn't the cause.

"It's beginning," he told her as he glanced toward the sky. Slowly the sun began to weaken and fade. He swept his gaze over the harbor below, then westward toward the Maze and the Bazaar, then toward the palace.

"Why do I have a feeling you don't mean the eclipse?" Ronal said as he bit into a roll.

"Witches, wizards, demons—even shapechangers." He forced a smile as he tilted Aaliyah's face toward his and kissed her forehead. "The Nisi covens are finished for good, but the things I've seen in two weeks' time. The things I've heard. We're all being drawn to Sanctuary again. It's as if we're being assembled for something. For what, I don't know."

The sky grew sullen and cool. Birds took to the air and flew in confused circles. Dogs barked. Everywhere Spyder looked people stood in the streets, on the docks, or on their own rooftops. They watched, too, with an uncharacteristic hush.

Slowly, the sky darkened, and the shadows of Sanctuary twisted into strange shapes as a black disk crawled across the sun. When it was finally in place all that remained where the sun had been was a flickering blood-red ring.

Spyder was not looking up, however. The placid, almost mirror-smooth surface of the bay held his attention. It reflected the spectacle in the sky with an uncanny precision. He wondered if anyone else saw it. He wondered if Aaliyah noticed.

On the bay was another ring of sea and fire.

Doing the Gods' Work

Jody Lynn Nye

"Thank you, healer," the gray-haired woman whispered as the potion took effect. Pel Garwood straightened his long back and stood up, taking the empty cup away from her lips.

"That should ease your back for a good week, until the full moon. You can chew this then," he held up a twist of green and gold herb strands, "to take away the pain for a day or two. I need the moon to make a potion that will last you a whole month. I can't cure what ails you, you know. I can only ease it."

"It's the penalty for living so long," Sharheya said. "I'm too old to expect miracles. I'm grateful for the relief."

"How much?" asked Carzen the sawyer, Sharheya's son-in-law, eyeing the apothecary warily. Pel's mass of black-and-silver hair and smooth face confused people as to his age, but his calm bedside manner gave him the air of a sage, too dignified to argue with.

Pel held up long fingers to count. "Nine padpols

for today, another for the twist. A bright silver soldat
for the month-long cure."

"A soldat! Too much!"

"Pay the man," Sharheya said, her eyes narrowing
as if the pain had returned suddenly. Pel knew there
was little love lost between his two visitors, but the
widow Sharheya owned the wood and the lumber-
yard attached to it that was the family's fortune. If
Carzen wished his wife to be disinherited and all
passing to Sharheya's scholar brother, all Carzen
had to do was infuriate Sharheya at the right moment. Accidents happened, especially in such a dangerous place as a sawmill. The woman was always
changing her will. Pel had been in and out of it for
a year. He had never cared whether a bequest was
forthcoming; he would have provided care for those
who genuinely needed his gift. If he liked them it
would cost them less than it cost Carzen. He didn't
like Carzen. The man had all the conscience of a
scorpion.

"What's in it?" Carzen asked, peering at the taller
man from under his shaggy brown eyebrows.

"Willowbark, dark-well water, cider, poppy, fever-
few picked at the new moon, sgandi leaf . . ."

"Sgandi? You mean stinkweed? I could make your
potion, for nothing!" Carzen snapped his fingers under the healer's nose. "I could throw those weeds in
a jug and save myself the price, as well as the trouble
of coming to you."

Pel just raised his salt-and-pepper eyebrow. "In
what proportions would you mix them? Too much
of one thing, not enough of another would be fatal.
And do you know the propitious times to gather
each plant? Where to get the most potent weeds?"
It had been so long since he'd been here in his
home city that the local Ilsigi—the Wrigglie—dia-

lect felt strange and slippery in his mouth. What was the commonplace insulting term they used to one another? Yes, that was it. "Pay up, pud, or take your problems home with you. Fair for fair. If you won't pay, then I have no obligation to you. I don't care." But he did. He could feel the suffering of the people who came to him, and he wanted them whole. His hand sought out Sharheya's, and held it tightly. All their pain resonated in him. It was part of his punishment, and his salvation. The old woman gave her son-in-law a disgusted look.

"Pay him and let's go home! I don't trust the apprentices to make that rosewood table for Lord Kuklos without supervision."

Grumbling, Carzen dug in his scrip. Looking up at Pel after each coin hit the table, he tossed out padpols one at a time. When he got to nine he started to put his purse away. Sharheya cleared her throat with meaning, the meaning being that if he didn't move faster she would call for pen and parchment right there. He put the tenth down for the herb twist, then very slowly produced a soldat. It wasn't very shiny.

"If," Pel let his voice interrupt the woodman's movements, "if you'd rather pay me in kind instead of in cash, I need a roof joist for the rear of my shop."

"How long?" Carzen asked. Pel pointed up. The wood-smith ran a practiced eye across the ceiling. "Uhm. Nine yards. You need more than one, pud. All that's holding up your roof is prayer. You need at least sixteen."

"I can't afford them all at once," Pel said. "I'm in no hurry."

"A good joist'll cost you more than one soldat. Four."

"Two. Add in next month's treatment as well," Pel offered, as the woodman started to protest.

"You've got a deal, foreigner," Carzen said. He spat in his palm and held out his hand. Pel gripped it. "I'll have my boys haul it up." He leered at the apothecary. "Labor's extra."

"Carzen!"

"It's all I expect," Pel gathered up the money in his free hand and tucked it away in his apron. "Thank you." He bowed over Sharheya's hand, a Rankan custom that he'd picked up from the courtiers of his more exalted clients. "I wish you healthy. If you have need of me, come back at once, or send a messenger."

Sharheya rose, chuckling. She stretched her back, arching it pleasurably. "I'd best come myself, healer. There are not too many boys in our yard who would willingly go running alone up the Avenue of Temples, no matter what kind of a beating I'd threaten them with for disobeying. Good day to you. Come, Carzen." She stalked out of the stone building and waited at the side of their donkey cart, waiting. The sawyer followed, still grumbling.

Pel watched them go, jingling his earnings in his pocket. The Avenue of Temples might not be everyone's idea of a choice address, but the muffling qualities of the empty buildings in between his shop and the next inhabited structure saved him many an explanation, especially at night, when guilt stalked him like a wolf.

The day he had fled Sanctuary he had never intended to return. The horrors he had left behind were more than any man's mind could have taken without breaking. The worst was that he was responsible for some of it.

He had been called Wrath of the Goddess, because his long reach and swift stride meant that none could escape him. His emotions ran to extremes, but especially his anger. He had believed with all his heart in the cause of the Mother. Humanity was corrupt, as anyone could see by the plagues that it had called down upon itself from the gods. To save it, therefore, required purification, freeing the mortal sphere from that which angered the divine mother goddess. He'd entered Sanctuary with the others of the Hand, determined to wipe out the stain.

But the purge had not gone as he had expected. The Mother had not caused the city and all of humankind to ascend into a new, pure age. Instead, over the next nine years came more of the corruption he had always seen before, some of it coming from the very priests he respected, coupled with a savagery that horrified him. When earlier only the unrighteous were being sought out and destroyed, he'd been able to accept that. But as the occupation continued, with anyone who held back a padpol or had an impure thought being considered irretrievably evil, Pel began to doubt. Then he grew frightened. If he was suspected of losing faith in the Mother he would be next on the flensing block. He was not afraid to die for his beliefs, but they were slipping away from him. He waited for a cleansing fire to come down and consume all the priests who were killing indiscriminately, who took offerings from the impure then killed them anyhow. None came. Sacrifices were held for no reason. Men and women were bled out for no other reason than they had angered one of the Hand. Then came the siege by the Irrune. The Servants of the Mother offered up desperate sacrifices to regain control. His own wife, sister-priest who had stood beside him when they swore themselves to Dyareela, caught the blood fever, and pulled their own child from the pits to cast onto the Mother's altar. The horror of watching their daughter die broke Pel's mind free. No longer could he wield his knife without thinking that beneath it was some father's son or daughter.

Then came the schism. Some of the priesthood rose up as the Bleeding Hand, challenging the traditional children of the Mother with their hideous vision of worship. Naniya went to the Hand and denounced him. Abandoned, betrayed and in mourning, Pel renounced his goddess.

Though he had pronounced them in silence, once the words had been said he could no longer remain with the other worshipers of Dyareela. Their stronghold was falling to the Irrune and Lord Molin Torchholder. Many priests had disappeared underground, ahead of the schism, and more ahead of the Irrune invasion. He told his masters that he was going into hiding, too. They gave him their blessing, thinking that he would continue secretly to do their bloody work for them. He let them believe it. As soon as he could, he fled Sanctuary.

He went as far as money would take him, then walked straight off the cart out of the last town into the countryside. He had no thought as to shelter or food or comfort. If his goddess had abandoned him, he had no choice left but to welcome death. But it didn't want him yet.

The door of his shop creaked open. Pel spun, hand automatically going for the knife he had worn at his side for so many years. It was not there.

"Garwood, how goes the day?"

The pounding of Pel's heart slowed when he recognized Siggurn, a regular at the Vulgar Unicorn.

The burly man had one hand on the battered, dusty stone lintel as if he needed help standing upright. His skew-nosed face wore a sheepish look.

"Well, man, are you going to berate me that my jewelweed potion wasn't strong enough?" Pel asked, feeling a touch mischievous.

"Strong enough!" Siggurn sputtered. "Why, it wouldn't go down for three days! I ... the girls thought it was a might funny, though they said I wouldn't pay until it did. After the first night they said it was sorcery and only that Twandan wench, Mimise, would stay with me. I made it worth her while, though. I'm no cheat."

Pel did some mental calculations and let out a hearty laugh, the first he'd had in days. "You don't mean to tell me you took the whole bottle at once? I told you, it's for a week's worth of nights. One mouthful at a time."

"You did! I ... well, I got nervous when nothing happened right away." Siggurn rubbed his nose with a knuckle. "I drank some more of it. Then, bang! And a mouthful's not much, is it?"

"It's meant to be a small draught," Pel said, still chuckling. "Many who've had ... trouble with potency ... aren't of a mind to drink down a great mugful when they want to perform."

The big man looked horrified. "You've asked them about it? You didn't mention me by name, did you?"

"No, no, of course not. When you pay my price you buy my silence as well. No, these are other men I've sold the same potion to—and I won't give you their names, either."

"I wouldn't ask," Siggurn said, relieved. "Only ... now I'm going to see Dolange next week, and I've none left of the first bottle, so ... would you?"

"With pleasure," Pel said. "Will you wait, or come back?"

Siggurn glanced out of the door. "I'll wait."

The carter sought out a comfortable place to sit. The shop looked like an abandoned mansion more than a going business concern, yet Pel had occupied it for several months. It took time to rebuild a structure so far dilapidated, and Pel was in no hurry. Nobody else wanted it. Except for bored street urchins shying stones through the cloth he'd stretched over the empty window holes on the street side nobody ever troubled him. Even in the crowded city of Sanctuary few liked to brave the empty places of worship on the Avenue of Temples. This was one of the smallest and least ruined, but that was not to say it might not have been improved by simply tearing it down and building it up again from its foundations. More than two decades of neglect and some active destruction wrought upon it by the adherents of Dyareela and, more lately, those of Irrunega, had all but broken the back of a structure meant to last thousands of years. No one alive remembered that this temple was once dedicated to a minor but necessary Ilsigi goddess named Meshpri, lady of health and healing, sister of great Shipri; and her son Meshnom, patron of apothecaries. If they had, they might have considered it coincidental that a newcomer to Sanctuary would have come to set up an herbalist's shop in its ruin, but there was no coincidence involved.

The structure was so derelict that not even lovers desperate for privacy would shelter there. The huge stone blocks comprising the walls had been cracked or shifted by gods-fire, earthquake, explosions and berserk men with hammers. As its supports had been attacked the roof decided to add to the debris

below by shedding plaster, tiles and finally shards of
wood. But Pel had found the place relatively sani-
tary. Deprived of donations and sacrifices for years,
there was no food to attract insects or vermin, other
than those attracted to the droppings of the birds
that nested in the rotting rafters exposed between
broken sections of roof. The weather had peeled the
gaudy paint from the walls and made mush out of
precious cedarwood and sandalwood incense boxes
next to the rectangular stone altar. That was still in
one piece, though incised all over its surface with
graffiti by youths who dared one another to violate
the haunted precinct. The air was cold, but after a
lifetime of fire he was grateful for the chill of nature.

Because the chamber was open to the elements
most of Pel's books, tools and equipment had to be
stored in heavy chests underneath braced tiers of
stone, to protect them from falling tiles and rain.
The first thing Pel had done, after cleaning the
building as best he could, was to bargain with Grabar, the local stonemason, to smooth out the surface
of the altar, eight feet long and four feet wide. Ostensibly he needed it as a mixing palette and oper-
ating table. Privately Pel intended it to be used for
its original purpose as well, though he could not tell
the stonecutter that. By order of Irrune law no worship might take place within the walls of the city. Pel
was willing to risk refreshing the temple, as part of
his personal penance, but in secret. He wasn't stupid, or ready to face the Irrune system of justice. He
washed out Siggurn's bottle with cleansing liquid
and sand, then chose a medium-sized mortar and
pestle. He knew instantly which among the myriad
of bottles, boxes, twists of paper and cloth, bundles
of twigs, herbs and flowers to choose. A little here,

a little there . . . he didn't need to look up the for-
mula. It had been only a few days since he'd made
it. Imagine drinking a week's worth of stimulants in
one night! He couldn't stop himself from grinning.

Siggurn propped himself up on half a lintel stone
to watch Pel grind herbs to powder. "Did you hear?"
he asked. "The Bleeding Hand has returned. They
were under the Promise of Heaven." Pel's heart
froze within him. He knew that warren well. If they
had returned, that would be where they would
congregate. Oh, Meshpri, keep me from their path!
Siggurn noticed that his hands had stopped. "Oh,
there's nothing to worry about now," he assured
Pel. "It's old news. I dunno what you hear, up here
all by yourself. The Dragon's men swept them all
away a couple of weeks back. They say they got them
all. Sewed them into bundles then stamped them all
to death under horses' hooves." Siggurn stopped
to swallow. "I didn't see it myself, but Dolange's
brother serves in the city guard. He said there wasn't
one man there who didn't puke his guts out at the
sight. You'd have done the same."

"Likely I would," Pel said, at the same time wondering if he would. He'd seen and done worse as a
priest of Dyareela. He was grimly thankful. In his
newfound faith he couldn't rejoice in the pain and
death of others, but it relieved him to know he
wouldn't have to face any of his former cohorts.

"You never saw what the Hand wreaked upon this
city," Siggurd said frankly. "I lost friends, families,
loved ones. I was even sorry to see my enemies go
to them. It was a terror you couldn't believe. Your
thoughts weren't your own."

"Are they ever?" Pel asked softly. He reached for
a beaker of water. No, not the well water collected
in the waning moon—that was to reduce swellings

and injuries. The other beaker, that one with the long neck, of running spring water gathered up under the waxing moon. That was for growing and increase. He splashed some into the mortar and dribbled a pinch of jewelweed powder into the mix. Not too much.

Siggurn watched him work with interest. "You don't make fun of me for my problem. Why not?"

"Why should I?" Pel asked.

"Well, the other healers won't do a thing for me. The herb woman in Prytanis Street said there's people aplenty with genuine ailments. The last thing she wants to spend her skill concocting for is an erection."

Pel shrugged. "I don't mind what anyone asks for, provided they can pay, and they take responsibility for what they do with it. If it puts your body or your mind at ease, so long as you do no harm to others, I have no reason to refuse. I serve." He glanced up at the ruined ceiling. Siggurn's gaze followed his.

"Better not talk that way where anyone else can see you," the carter warned.

The apothecary started. It had just seemed natural to want to pray at that moment. He'd forgotten the penalty, just like that. It was a quick way to get a beating, or catch his death of soldiers. "I was just wondering how you wished to pay this time."

Siggurn shook his big head. "Can't afford it twice so soon. All right, I was a frogging idiot. The tavern girls had a good joke on me. How much do you want? I'll raise it somehow, but I haven't got all of it right now."

Pel let one of his salt-and-pepper eyebrows go up. "Will you trade labor for your potion?"

Siggurn's shaggy brows matched his. "Doing what?"

Pel smiled. "Ever put in a roof joist?"

The remote Ilsigi village into which he wandered late at night on the last day he thought he'd live had only about twelve houses made of wattle and daub, set in a long oval about the market place and grazing green. Its wealth was in its goats. Pel didn't know any of that when he arrived there. At the end of his strength, too afraid of what he was fleeing to think about where he was going, he collapsed at the gate of one of the houses.

If the old man who found him wondered about the unconscious heap of black cloak he found at his doorstep, or about the heavy tattoos all over the body within or the red stain that covered the arms from elbow to fingertip, he never asked. That was the first gift Loprin gave Pel. He did not push to hear his visitor's name, tale, nor even his voice. A blessing, Pel always thought, because he could not have spoken. The second gift was a bowl of soup, then a blanket and a place to stay. Pel kept count of the gifts. They were the first he had received from outside the sect of the Chaos Goddess since he was a child. He had to fight his impulse to refuse them, coming as they did from a heathen. He recalled that he, too, was now a heathen.

The old man seemed happy for company. He didn't insist that Pel participate in his prayers or do chores or even talk to him. Food and shelter came with no obligation, something that Pel had never experienced before. Loprin let him sit against the wall with an eye on the door, making sure he was warm enough, dry enough, fed enough, as he went about his daily chores and devotions.

Loprin worshiped Meshpri the Healer. The image on the polished stone altar was that of a slender girl-woman whose mouth was set firm but whose kind, intelligent eyes, older than time, promised mercy. In her lap was a baby toying with a branch of lignum vitae: Meshnom. Loprin prayed especially during difficult cases. He sacrificed medicines, money, tools and offerings from his patients. The ingredients that went into his medicines were simple: herbs, water or liquor, minerals, bark, but it was the timing of the gatherings, the precision of his actions and instructions, and the deep faith he had in his god that made Loprin a successful healer. Pel was partly of Ilsig descent, partly not, the usual mongrel mix of Sanctuary's general population. He wondered if Meshpri or her lover-son Meshnom would listen to the pleas of a former murderer and torturer.

Repose and the lack of obligation allowed Pel to take time to think, and heal on his own. After a few weeks of having the blood taint out of his nostrils, Pel began to do chores for Loprin, rising before the dawn to draw water and light the fire. Because his appearance would have been remarked upon, he wore his enveloping cloak and gloves any time he went outside. During the day he cleaned and swept and cooked their simple meals. At night he followed Loprin's instructions on where to hunt for certain herbs and when to gather water from the streams and wells. After two months he found his voice again. Loprin seemed delighted he had decided to speak. Sensing that Pel didn't want to talk about what had driven him so far into the country, Loprin discussed his craft. He explained the names of all the plants he used: what their purposes were; when in the month, or even the year, one might be used, and how much of a dose to use for what ailments. Pel was interested in it all, but listened most closely to the last. Adherents of Dyareela abhorred the use of poison. Pel might have rejected everything else the Chaos Goddess stood for, but he felt strongly about that. They talked about the foibles of Loprin's patients, the difficulty of some treatments, and how each bore his suffering and recovery. The old man had responsibility for the well-being of every living creature around him, much like a god, but he bore it with humility. Pel respected that. Hearing about the problems of others was healing in itself. Listening to Loprin talk he found he cared about the people as much as his mentor did. He wanted them to live and prosper, with all their faults intact that made them so human. He rediscovered compassion, a sense of humor, and a sense of purpose.

Five months after he had arrived, he asked Loprin to take him as a pupil.

For the first time the old man held back immediate affirmation. "This is a serious thing you ask me," he told Pel. "The most important thing is to harm no one. If a patient is going to die, he will die. You can ease his going, if it is his wish. That is mercy. For the rest, do your best and trust in Meshpri. There will always be those who blame you for the loss of a loved one, but if you are honest they will understand you could did all you could."

He stayed with Loprin for several years, learning the old man's craft. He had discovered life-oriented gods to whom he felt he could honestly devote himself, but as it had been Meshpri who had led him to his new life, Pel gave her the greatest devotion. He had traded one goddess for another, and never regretted it for a moment.

As Loprin's apprentice the villagers had accepted his care, but he knew the robe, mask and gloves frightened them. They needed to see a human face, see human hands giving to them. He wanted to rid himself of the marks of Dyareela that covered his entire body, including his scalp. For that, Loprin explained, they had to turn to the gods. Still not judging, but with a twinkle in those kind old eyes, he began preparations.

Shaved as bare as a newborn, he lay on Meshpri's altar in the light of the new moon. Every tattoo, every word and number, every sacred whorl and scroll stood out in the silver light. The red on his hands glimmered like blood. The potion Loprin poured into his navel had taken many months to prepare. It was cold. Pel felt himself divided into three people: the one on the altar reaching out to his new goddess and taking everything very seriously, the watcher standing back and trying to save all these strange sensations and thoughts for later, and the little boy, stifled for so long, who wanted to giggle at the whole process.

"Be as a newborn," the healer had intoned. "Unmarked, untouched, at the beginning of your life once more. Clear your heart of what went before. As without, so also within."

Then the pain had begun.

"You should've froggin' asked me to come first," the large young man said to Pel, not for the first time, as he dodged a falling tile. It crashed on the floor between their feet. In spite of the cold of the day he was sweating, having just hauled in half a cart of stone blocks. He raised his voice to shout above the noises of sawing, hammering and talking, the busy sounds of fifteen other people who were present on an Anensday to work off their medical bills.

"Shoring up those pillars, resetting the walls—those ought to be done before anything on the gods' cursed roof!"

"Sorry," Pel said, brushing fragments off the front

of his tunic. "I don't know anything about construction. I can have them all stop what they're doing and help you instead."

"Why in the froggin' hell didn't you ask Carzen?" Cauvin asked, pointing to the woodman, who was standing near a wall with his arms folded. "He could've told you the same."

He wanted Pel to make a fool of himself, the apothecary thought, half-humorously. "He said labor's extra. I guess that included advice, too."

Cauvin spat, but he grinned, too. He knew Carzen well. "I won't charge extra for getting these puds workin', but Grabar wants paying for his stone. He says the sleep remedy didn't froggin' work!"

"It was one of two possible cures for the symptoms he described," Pel explained. "Loud snoring, sudden wakefulness, feeling like he's choking in his dreams, and so on. One condition's more dangerous than the other. I hoped it wasn't that. I'll send the other potion with you today."

"If it works the deal's on, but if not, you'll have to come up with the soldats," Cauvin said, folding his meaty arms. Pel nodded humbly.

"Done." Pel felt like a stripling beside the stonecutter. Because of his skin-renewal they looked to be about the same age, but Pel knew he was a good ten years older then Cauvin. Though the stoneyard put out that Cauvin was their long-lost son, Pel knew better. In fact, the man who had been the priest Wrath remembered when the Servants had dragged Cauvin in from the streets and dropped him in the pits. The boy had been big for his age, and in trouble a lot of the time. What a scrapper he'd been even then, determined to survive in the hell in which the adults had trapped him. Pel had had to haul him out for punishment once when a boy had died. The others had blamed Cauvin, but the other had been far larger and had fewer marks on him.

Thank all chance Cauvin didn't seem to remember him. To grow up so well, to become a respected man in this disrespectful town, was an achievement, twice so coming from such disadvantages. Pel rejoiced for him that he'd found a good sponsor, as good as Loprin had been for him.

"Friends!" he shouted. He picked up a mixing paddle and banged it on the altar to get everyone's attention. "Stop! There's a change in plan. Stop what you're doing and come down. Master Cauvin will tell you what to do."

With a curt nod to the apothecary the stonemason turned to his new workforce. Pel went back to his brazier, where a huge jug of water was brewing for tea. Some of the visitors had hinted that beer or liquor would have been more welcome, but there was no chance Pel was letting someone climb to the forty-foot ceiling with a skinful. Just in case of accident, he had prepared a load of bandages and salves. There was food, though. He'd asked the people who couldn't work to bring things to eat for the workers. A few of them had shirked it, like Ma Sagli, who'd brought half a dozen biscuits and called it her share. Pel was holding his ire until the next time she came in looking for her phlegm medicine. Others, like Chersey, the money-changer's wife, brought in a big basket of meat rolls, far more than she owed for the vial of flux medicine she had needed for her youngest. She was keeping one eye on the comestibles and the other on her two small children, who were playing with the scraps of wood near his herb baskets. A few others had come to watch the construction, huddles of blankets safely out of the way of the workers.

The place would be very fine when it was finished. He hoped the goddess would be happy with her refurbished temple. Every padpol Pel didn't use for food or the raw materials for his medicines was put onto the altar as offerings to be used toward remaking the goddess's house. He had sixteen strong new joists, some blocks of stone, and waterproof cloth that would go up on top until he could afford the right enameled copper tiles for the roof. That could take years, money being what it wasn't.

This was the third workday that Pel had organized. The first was only a couple of months after he had returned to Sanctuary. The idea had come about because hard currency seemed to be in such short supply everywhere. If the Rankan lords had plenty of money, they weren't spending it in the city. Nearly all businesses but the taverns were taking some of their pay in trade. What Pel needed more than anything was helping hands. Meshpri's temple needed to be restored, but before that could occur all the rubbish that had accumulated needed to be cleared out and the building shored up so he could live in it without fearing for his life. In spite of his rejuvenation by Loprin, Pel could neither move stone blocks nor hammer up buttresses by himself. He tried to be as fair as he could in estimating the value of his services, but quickly discovered that any man who didn't add a hundred or even three hundred percent onto the base cost was a fool, and an exhausted and resentful one at that. He'd ended up doing most of the hauling himself.

The second time he had grown wiser. Requiring hard labor or hard cash kept the idly curious from trying out potions for the fun of it. Having everyone come on the same day served several purposes: first, it amassed the necessary manpower for the work.

Second, it showed each patient he was not being singled out by Pel, and let some of them feel they'd gotten away cheap not having to fork over coin. Third, it brought people together in a cooperative effort of creation. Sanctuary needed healing. Even after the passage of years the place was filled with hidden wounds. The act of building up instead of tearing down was important to Pel not only actually, but spiritually. He'd been responsible for some of those wounds. He was ashamed to have run away instead of helping to heal them. His practical common sense butted in again to remind him that if he'd stayed he would have been killed, accomplishing nothing.

He scratched his head. It took six months from the day Loprin performed Meshpri's rite upon him until all his tattoos and scars had faded away forever, but where the crazy designs had crossed his scalp, his hair had grown in white instead of black. He wore his hair long so no one could distinguish the pattern.

He looked up at the cold, blue sky through the rafters, now cleared of plaster and tile. When he fled he thought he'd never be coming back. Loprin had been his teacher for five years, then the old man had taken ill. Pel nursed him devotedly, but Loprin's time had come. He was content to go to his god.

When the old man died Pel taken his place as village healer. The forty villagers had come to like him and accept him. He was content there for a time, but he missed his benefactor. Then, to his deep surprise, he realized that he missed the city. Loprin had taught him nothing worthwhile was ever achieved in a hurry. Pel had taken an apprentice: Taurin, the weaver's son, and taught the quick-eyed lad as much of his master's skills as he could. After four years the boy had encompassed all Pel could give him. With the purpose that had been lacking when he'd staggered into the village, he strode out, a new man inside and out, thanks to Meshpri and her servant Loprin. That's what he intended for this temple, to make it new inside and out. To finance it he made it known he'd sell any kind of philtre or potion to anyone who wanted it, regardless of its use. Poisons he would not make, claiming the ingredients were too hard to come by, disappointing a lot of disgruntled in-laws and would-be heirs who thought that an easy means had come their way of disposing of inconvenient relatives. On the other hand, love potions enjoyed a vogue, as did mixtures for enhancing eyesight and coordination. His reputation for giving the customers exactly what they wanted helped build his business up in a hurry. Men and women came from all over Sanctuary and outside, usually furtively wrapped up in cloaks, seeking their hearts' desire. Pel enjoyed it. Making "elective" potions that hurt no one and made others happy gave him something to amuse himself while waiting for genuine patients to seek him out. And those came. And here they were.

"Siggurn!" Cauvin shouted, standing on a scaffold high against the east wall. "Get that up right now!" The carter looked up from the barrel of mortar he was mixing to glare at Pel. The healer chuckled, but he lifted his hands to the shoulders, trying to school his face into innocent lines. Not his doing. Just a bad choice of words. Purely coincidence. But it was amusing to see the way the big man's face turned scarlet as if he feared his secret was out.

"Froggin' hell, hurry, pud! I'm bursting my froggin' back holding this block up until you get that froggin' mortar up here! Move it!"

Siggurn, now understanding the mistake, leaped to haul a bucket of cement up the ladder to the impatient stonemason. Pel couldn't stop laughing. Oh, if people knew what he knew! But he would never tell. He had too many secrets of his own to keep.

"Healer," a voice whispered to him. Pel glanced down at one of the blanket-wrapped heaps near the brazier.

"Yes?" he asked.

A gloved hand reached out of the mass of cloth to beckon to him. He could see nothing of the face. It was hooded by the heavy wool blanket. Good fabric, too, without a single patch or caught thread. Had a wealthy patron come here seeking his attention in the guise of a curious onlooker? Everyone knew the date of Pel's latest workday. Why, a handful of people who owed him had made a point of being out of the city today. Why shouldn't someone who wanted to see him come along?

"How may I serve?" Pel asked, crouching down.

"I hear you make the jewelweed potion."

"Yes, I do."

"I need some."

"For yourself?"

"Yes . . ." the breath came out in a hiss. "There aren't enough children in Sanctuary. I am called to make some. I cannot . . . try."

Icy fingers crawled along Pel's back. The way the huddled figure phrased his words alarmed him.

"What about . . . the mother?" he asked, very slowly.

"Ahh . . . so it's true," the voice breathed. The hand curled until the forefinger was pointing at his temple. A familiar gesture, one Pel hadn't seen in a decade. His heart contracted with fear. As surely as if he had torn it away to look, he knew the cloak concealed a body marked with red stain and tattoos. It came rushing back to him that he had told his former masters that he was going underground. He hadn't meant it then. He was even more determined now not to return.

"No!" Pel almost shouted. "I mean, you are sure the mother can have children? Is she old enough?"

"They are all old enough. My body will not obey the Mother's command." Now Pel could distinctly hear the capital letter.

"Ah, you must be an Irrune, sir," Pel said, carefully, still with his voice low enough so only the gloved visitor could hear, though he was tempted to shout out to the nearby crowd of big burly men with hammers and chisels, *There's a Dyareelan here! Kill him!* "We poor Ilsig only take one wife. So . . . you cannot raise your sword? Is that the help you wish from me?"

"Yes. As soon as possible."

"The potion takes but a short time to prepare, but I cannot do my work with so much dust in the air. Would you return tomorrow?"

"That will do," the blanket inclined its head. "After dark. I do not wish to advertise my . . . problem. Or my presence."

"As you wish," Pel said. "Many of my patients prefer to be discreet about seeing me. That means you'll be paying in cash, then? Otherwise, you'll be joining these," he gestured at the workers, "next workday."

"Cash."

"Healer!" Cauvin shouted at that moment. "Do

you want this froggin' pillar replaced with wood or stone?"

Pel started toward him automatically, then turned to look back toward the heap of blankets. It was not there. A shadowed shape was slipping out of the door. He'd been too surprised to take action; now it was too late. With an act of will he went to listen to an argument between Cauvin and Carzen.

The ringing of hammers and voices had long since died away. Pel huddled near the last orange embers of his brazier, alone in the echoing temple ruin. Night had fallen, and with it came a miserable, frosty drizzle. Sanctuary had always had terrible weather, Pel reflected. It had gotten worse since he had returned. The night was bitterly cold, but at least now the rain didn't come through the roof. The cloth could hold for a good long time, perhaps until another owner came to claim Meshpri's temple. The building would not fall down, thanks to Cauvin and Pel's other patients. It could house another servant of the healing god, one who would carry on the task of helping to heal Sanctuary . . . .

Visions of his former life came rushing back to him: the cleansings, the sacrifices, the dismal pits full of miserable children, and lastly the triumphant, mad look on his wife's face when she showed him the body of their daughter with the heart torn from it. No! He slammed his open hand down on the altar. He would not run away. Dyareela's priest couldn't have recognized him as Wrath. But there were other Servants hidden throughout the empire. Even if the man did not know him, he could think he was one of the others who'd gone underground.

But the important thing was that he knew the hooded visitor as a priest of the Bleeding Hand. Ar-

izak had not, then, wiped out the entire warren.
Like a cancer, the cult was growing back again somewhere in Sanctuary, and Pel might be the only one
who knew it.

His visitor must be gathering new devotees, probably street children. By what he'd told Pel there
were certainly a few girls old enough to bear, but
no boys old enough to impregnate them, leaving
him as the only one who could do the deed. That
meant the cell was small as of yet. Thank all chance
for that. But the priest was impotent. And so he had
come to Pel.

What a dilemma he was in! His conscience
wouldn't let the priest beget more babies to become
assassins or die as sacrifices, yet he must give the
man what he asked for. What could he do? Less than
a full day from that moment, just after nightfall, the
priest would return for his jewelweed potion. Pel
could go to the palace and bring guards to wait here
with him, to capture the man. But if he did, the man
would denounce him as a former Servant. Pel could
not hide the truth from his questioners. He and the
other would both die, trampled by a herd of horses.
He could—he had to steel himself just to think the
thought—he could kill the priest. He'd kept his
skills honed sharp all these years. But the man
might not arrive alone. There was a chance he'd
miss at least one defender, and his life here would
be over, one way or another. And if he succeeded,
there'd be the question of what to do with the body.

What was he thinking? Pel paced around and
around the brazier, now filled with cold ashes. He
was a healer now, a servant of Meshpri! He couldn't
spill unjust blood. He'd have to answer to his goddess one day. Poison . . . no! Absolutely not. Never.

Pel thought hard. There must be a solution that

would serve both his oath and his patient. He had
no good reason to refuse to make the potion. He'd
promised. But the Hand couldn't be permitted to
sire more innocent children. No more babies must
be born into the hell he'd survived. He just couldn't
bring himself to kill in cold blood, even for them.

A thought struck him, so hard he stopped dead
in the dark. What had he promised? He felt the slow
smile spread over his face. Yes, that was the solution!
He could keep his word. Hastily he felt his way back
to the altar, and scrabbled with sensitive fingertips
until he found his tinder and flint. Striking a hasty
light, he began to gather up bundles of herbs, piling
them on Meshpri's altar.

The buildings on the Avenue of Temples were re-
puted to be haunted. Anyone passing by the ancient
shrine to Meshpri late that night would have heard
the banshee cackling of restless spirits and hurried
home to lock their doors.

Night had just drawn its cloak over Sanctuary when
the hooded visitor returned to the apothecary shop.
Pel had been waiting impatiently all day. Unable to
think about anything but the impending meeting,
he couldn't trust himself to mix medicines, lest he
make an error that might prove fatal. Instead, he set
himself the backbreaking task of cleaning up after
his conscripted workforce. The bristles of his broom
were at least a handspan shorter than they'd started
out that morning, so vigorous was he in sweeping.
He had just bent to brush up a panful of stone dust,
when the low voice came almost at his elbow.

"Healer?"

Pel jerked bolt upright. The pan flew out of his
hands, scattering the dust all over. "You're here!" he
exclaimed.

"I am. Is it ready?"

"Yes, it is," Pel said, knowing he was babbling. "This way. It's ready. Seven uses' worth for one soldat. If you need more, I can make it. Any time."

Trying to keep his hands from shaking, he took the small bottle out from under the altar and placed it before the visitor. No gloved hand reached out to take it.

"Taste it," the visitor commanded.

"What?" Pel asked. He tried to peer under the hood to see his visitor's eyes, but it was too deep.

"I do not know you. There are poisoners in this city. Taste it."

"But I'll . . ." Pel began. Never mind. He picked up the bottle and uncorked it. With a glance at the door, Pel took a mouthful of the potion. He swallowed.

There was no way to disguise the effects of the jewelweed potion. They were immediate and long lasting. His member sprang against the inside of his trousers. Pel felt his cheeks burn. He hadn't had this sudden an erection since he'd been a boy just reaching puberty. It almost hurt. The hood appeared to study the reaction with intellectual interest. Pel thought he would die of shame.

"Satisfactory," the visitor said. He flicked his hand, and a soldat bounced on the stone table. With a sweep of the enveloping black sleeve, the small bottle disappeared. "I will be back for more when I require it."

"Welcome, I'm sure," Pel gritted, wishing he'd go.

The visitor laid a gloved hand on his arm for thanks. "You serve one greater than yourself." The cloak swirled out of the door, and Pel relaxed. Or tried to. It was going to be a couple of hours until things . . . calmed down.

He hadn't foreseen having to test the potion for the visitor, but it was unimportant. Pel never intended to sire a child again. The potion would do exactly what he had promised the visitor it would: allow him to mate with his new priestesses. Pel had not promised that it would allow him to sire children on them. He'd made the potion exactly as he always did, but added a special ingredient, a rare herb only found near graves and barrows. The priest might be full of new vigor and potency, but empty of seed. If he finished the entire vial, which Pel had no doubt whatever he would, he'd never be able to sire another as long as he lived.

The visitor was right: Pel did serve one greater than himself. Meshpri, and her son, would surely forgive the liberty, but it was all in the cause of saving lives. Babies who were never conceived would never die.

The Red Lucky

Lynn Abbey

Bezulshash, better known as Bezul the Changer, awoke to the honking of twenty outraged geese and a dream that something had struck the front door of his family's establishment at the nether end of Wriggle Way, deep in the Shambles quarter of Sanctuary.

"Bez?" his wife, Chersey, whispered. "Bez, are you awake?"

"I am," he assured her, despite the absurdity of the question: Nothing on Wriggle Way could sleep once the geese got going.

They both shucked their blankets. Barefoot, Chersey hurried to their children, four-year-old Ayse, and her little brother, Lesimar, both beginning to howl from the cradle they shared. Bezul spared the extra moment to find his boots and the antique, iron-headed mace he kept handy beside the master bed.

He was tiptoeing down the pitch-dark stairway when a patch of light appeared on the landing behind him.

"Bezul?" a woman asked, her voice gone deep with age. "Is that you?"

"It is, Mother." Bezul spoke loudly; the geese were still in high dudgeon. "I heard a strike against the door. I'm sure it's nothing, but I've got the club. Shut the door and go back to bed where it's warm."

By the lingering light, Gedozia did neither. The stairway shuddered beneath her unsteady footfalls.

"Mother—"

"It's them," she declared. "It's them come to steal what's left. Mind the shadows, your father says. They're waiting in the shadows. They came back. Came back with the bloody moon!"

Gedozia's body frequently awoke long before her mind. Her husband, for whom Bezul had been named, had been dead these last eighteen years, a victim of apoplexy, directly, and the Bloody Hand, indirectly. Gedozia had never recovered from his death. She was easier to deal with, though, when she was dream-addled. By the light of day, she lived on bitter tea and nostalgia.

"I'll mind," Bezul said. "You get back to bed, Mother."

She didn't, but the light from her lamp made it easier to shove through the geese milling at the foot of the stairs and find the door latch. Bezul trod precisely on a floorboard, engaging a well-oiled mechanism. A wooden post, barely ankle-high but stout and kiln-hardened, rose silently out of the floor a handspan away from the jamb. The post would halt the door's opening—for a heartbeat or two—in the event thieves were waiting on the other side. Bezul lifted the latch; the heavy door swung on its hinges and *thumped* against the post.

The slice of Wriggle Way visible through the partially opened door was empty save for the graying shadows of early dawn.

"Who's there?" Bezul called, his voice a trifle quavery.

Silence. Bezul noticed a pale lump near the threshold. He thought of the noise he'd remembered and bent to retrieve the object. The geese attacked his legs as he did. The birds were better than any dog when it came to watching a place, but they were completely untrainable and never did learn the difference between owners and invaders. Bezul swatted the nearest beak and, with his arms flapping wider than their wings, shooed them from the doorway. The birds retreated, noisier than ever. They'd be lucky if silence returned before sun-up.

"What is it?" Chersey called from the top of the stairway. She had a lamp in one hand, a wailing Lesimar tucked in the other arm, and Ayse clinging to her drab bed-gown.

"A piece of cloth knotted around a stone. Someone's sent us a message."

Bezul picked casually at the knots. They were well-tied with oiled cord and held tight against his curiosity. He waded through the geese to the counter at the heart of the changing house. Chersey was beside him, lamp and children in hand, when he laid the wrapped fist-sized stone down for closer examination.

"So, what's the message?" Gedozia asked from halfway down the stairs.

The geese nipped at Ayse who shrieked louder than all the birds together. Flapping and honking and shedding shite, the birds waddled into the maze of shelves and niches where the more valuable and vulnerable portion of the changing house's stock was stored. It would take the luck of Shalpa, god of thieves, to get the flock penned up before they opened for business, but Bezul couldn't worry about that yet. He couldn't get the knots loose, either.

Chersey deposited Lesimar on the counter and put his still-shrieking sister beside him. When a quick pass with the lamp failed to show any bloody nips on the little girl's flesh, Chersey took the stone from her husband's hands.

"What's the message?" Gedozia repeated from the other side of the counter. She slid her lamp beside Chersey's.

Chersey's slender, agile fingers traced a loosening path along the cord and the length of it fell to the counter.

"It's just cloth," Bezul observed, more than a little puzzled.

"Sewn cloth," Gedozia corrected. "Give it here," she demanded and snatched it before her daughter-in-law could obey. "The hem torn off a shirt," she concluded.

"Maybe there's writing on it?" Bezul reached for the cloth.

Gedozia wouldn't relinquish her treasure. She rubbed the seam between her fingers and held it close to her eyes. Bezul could see enough of the fabric to know there were no marks upon it.

"What manner of mess—?" he'd begun when Gedozia yelped and the cloth fell from her fingers. "Mother?"

"Perrez," she croaked, a look of sheer panic forming on her face. "Perrez! O, my husband, they've taken our son! They've taken Perrez at last! It was all for nothing! All for nothing!"

Perrez, the last member of the household, was Bezul's much younger brother, his mother's favorite son, and a man who put more effort into avoiding

work than into finishing it. He called himself a
scholar, which wasn't an utter lie. There wasn't a
musty manuscript in the changing house—in all of
Sanctuary—that Perrez hadn't memorized in his re-
lentless quest for treasure maps and clues. Perrez
hadn't been around when Bezul closed up for the
night, but *scholars* didn't keep workingmen's hours;
scholars needed the excitement only a tavern could
provide.

Chersey fetched up the cloth and met Bezul's eyes
with a worried frown.

"It's his," she confirmed.

"How can you be sure?"

"Marking stitches—"

"My stitches! My son!" Gedozia wailed, setting off
the children and the geese.

Chersey squared her fingers over a pattern of
dark-thread crosses embroidered into the cloth.
"The laundresses use these to sort their work. Most
of them can't read, you know, and one white shirt
looks like another."

Home-brewed soap and a wooden tub set up behind the changing house weren't good enough for
Perrez's shirts. Oh no—*his* shirts went clear across
the city to a woman in the 'Tween who dosed them
with bleach and blueing for two padpols apiece. It
wasn't that Bezul begrudged the padpols. Appear-
ances were important in a changing house. Though
the bulk of their business came from ordinary folk,
the bulk of their profit came from the aristocrat
trades that Perrez brokered. High-colored, handsome Perrez showed off a bleached, blued shirt far
better than Bezul, who took after his father's side of
the family, ever could. But Perrez would swear and
swear again that the laundress was a beldam liar
when she came to collect her fee, when it was Perrez

who lied as easily as the sun sparkled on the sea.

And now, a bit of Perrez's shirt had been thrown against the changing-house door.

What to make of it? Bezul wondered amid the cacophony. He lined up the cloth, cord, and stone on the counter. "They've taken him!" Gedozia keened. "They took him while *you* were sleeping!"

Bezul flinched. Short of tying Perrez to the bedpost, there was no way to keep him completely out of trouble and, by the thousand eyes of Father Ils, there was no convincing Gedozia that her most precious son drank and gambled his way into one tight corner after another.

Bezul had dreaded this night—had seen it coming for years. His heart was cold as he spun the cord between his fingers. Several moments passed before he noticed the sheen on his fingertips. Holding the cord to his nose, Bezul inhaled deeply. Fish oil . . . salt . . . wrack . . . the Swamp of Night Secrets on the far side of the White Foal River. He raised his eyes to meet his wife's.

They'd married young, in the depths of the Dyareelan Troubles, and waited fifteen years to start a family of their own. That had given them the time to learn each other's ways. Bezul didn't have to say a word, nor did Chersey. She kissed Lesimar lightly on the forehead, took the lamp, and disappeared into the warrens. The geese honked and flapped as she passed.

"What was that about?" Gedozia demanded when she was alone with her elder son.

"Good chance you're right about Perrez. Did he happen to tell you where he'd be last night?"

Gedozia pursed her lips tight and shook her head. By those gestures, Bezul recognized a lie. He could badger the truth out of her, but Chersey was already returning.

"No sign of him among the manuscripts," she admitted, "and the latch to his room is drawn from the inside."

Meaning Perrez had left the changing house through his private entrance and had expected to return the same way. Even Gedozia could grasp the implications of that. Her lips worked silently. The bond between his mother and her lastborn child was nothing Bezul could understand; its strength brought out the worst in both of them.

"Whoever's got him, he sent us a message," Bezul mused aloud. "He wants something . . . wants to *exchange* something. That's what we're here for, isn't it? Setting values, brokering exchanges. Getting Perrez out of trouble . . . again." Bezul was mildly astonished by his own lack of panic or despair. "Put the tea on, Chersey, and keep it hot. Sun's nearly up— Ammen and Jopze will be along soon to keep an eye on things while I'm gone."

By training and temperament, Jopze and Ammen were soldiers, Imperial soldiers. They said they'd served their terms in the unsettled northern reaches of the crumbling Rankan Empire and that, five years ago, they'd decided to retire in Sanctuary because it was a quieter place these days. Bezul imagined there was more to the story; he didn't press for details. The pair could have joined the city guard, maybe commanded it, but between them they'd had six children when they arrived and at least a dozen children now. They did better swapping time for shoes, cloaks, and other household goods at the changing house than they'd have in the barracks.

Without comment, Chersey lowered her eyes. She lifted the children off the counter and herded them toward the kitchen where geese and Gedozia were forbidden. Bezul locked stares with his mother, fairly defying her to wish him well or warn him to be careful.

"It's not his fault," Gedozia said instead. "This isn't what your father meant for him . . ." She caught herself—"For either of you—" but the correction, as always, came too late.

"You've done him no favors, Mother, reminding him every day."

Bezul was angry to the bone, but what good was anger in a family that the Hand had broken? Someday Bezul feared he might lose control and ask how his father had truly died. And where would he be if his mother told him the truth? No closer to his father, that much was sure.

The eastern sky had taken a sunrise glow when Bezul strode onto Wriggle Way. He was dressed as befitted his station in life: plainer than the best of Sanctuary, but better than most in homespun breeches, loosely fitted boots, a linen shirt and a bit of Chersey's fancy work on his half-sleeve coat. He'd left his cloak behind. It had been a warm winter thus far—no appreciable snow and very little ice—and though the air was chillier this morning than it had been for a month. Bezul believed in the sun. He believed in the short-bladed knife sheathed at his waist, too, and another, longer knife tucked into a boot top. The latter was a weapon, not a tool, and he'd made good use of it once or twice, though no one would mistake Bezul the changer for a fighting man.

There were signs of life all around—Wriggle Way was a workman's street and workers rose before the sun in winter—but no strangers. Bezul dug the cord, the stone, and the cloth out of his scrip. He held them out for anyone to see. People hailed him left and right—the master of the changing house was known to nearly everyone in the Shambles—but no one noticed the cord, not in the quarter, nor on the Wideway where the wharves were empty, the tide was out, and the air smelled like the cord dangling from his left hand.

From the Wideway, Bezul headed northwest, toward the bazaar and past streets that would have him quickly back to the changing house, had he been returning home. Toward the raw, knocked-together tournament stands as well. Perrez, that epicure of rumor, claimed that both Ranke and Ilsig had put up the gold and silver to host a first-blood tournament—short of the old gladiator matches the Vigeles clan used to run in the Hill, when it was still the estate quarter. If Bezul believed Perrez, Sanctuary's importance in the minds of kings and emperors was growing daily. If Bezul were ever fool enough to believe his brother.

What Bezul did believe was that his brother's great scholarly talents were currently being employed as oddsmaker and bookkeeper for scores of ordinary folk who were squandering their savings on one duelist or another. Bezul didn't care a tinker's damn who won the tournament; he'd made a point of ignoring it, even forbidding Jopze and Ammen—inveterate gamblers, like all career soldiers—to mention it inside the changing house. Time enough for that when the tournament was over, debts were due, and the losers trooped into the changing house to sell their clothes, their tools, anything short of their wives and children.

Bezul reminded himself he needed to visit the palace soon to do some changing himself: a sack of their valuable, but slow-moving, jewels in exchange

for a chest or two of Sanctuary's near-worthless shaboozh for cutting into padpols.

He came to the footbridge below the bazaar that
connected the Shambles with the fishermen's quarter where knotted, oiled nets hung by the armful
over every fence and wall. The bridge-keeper held
out his hand for a padpol. Bezul dug the smallest,
blackest bit of pot-metal from his scrip and crossed
the footbridge, holding his breath against the
stench rising from the midden ditch beneath.

The men and women who crewed Sanctuary's
fishing fleet lived by the tides, not the sun. Their
boats were out and had left their moorings long before the stone thumped against the changing house
door. But there were other ways to harvest a living
from Sanctuary's waters. Across the White Foal
River, the Swamp of Night Secrets sprawled as far as
the eye could see.

Night Secrets Swamp was larger than it been when
Bezul was a boy. He could just about remember how
this part of Sanctuary had looked before the Great
Flood rechanneled the White Foal River. The slum-
quarter his father had called Downwind had stood—
or slouched—where thickets of swamp-scrub now
grew. "Good riddance," Bezul's father had said
when he'd brought him to see the damage. Of
course, Sanctuary wasn't truly rid of Downwind. The
Hill quarter—every bit as treacherous and squalid—
had sprung up before the flood waters receded and
the swamp wasn't exactly empty.

A hardy breed they called the Nightmen eked
their livings from the shifty waters. They were trap-
pers, mostly, and not particular about what they
snared: fish and crabs, plume-y birds, soft-furred
predators, or the occasional man. When the Hand
couldn't find better targets or victims for their mad-

ness, they'd combed the swamp; and the people of
Sanctuary—Bezul included—had heaved guilty, but
relieved, sighs: Better the Nightmen, than kith or
kin.

For their part, the Nightmen did nothing to im-
prove the impression they left behind. They stood
out in any crowd—if only by the tang of their un-
washed flesh. The Irrune shaman, Zarzakhan, in all
his fur-clad, mud-caked glory, looked no more un-
kempt than the average Nighter. And as much as
the Imperials complained about the guttural belch-
ing of the Wrigglie dialect or the Wrigglies complained about high-pitched Imperial chatter, both
agreed that it was impossible to converse intelli-
gently with anyone reared in the swamp.

Still, Nightmen—their women almost never
crossed the river—in their reeking leathers were
regular visitors at the changing house. They found
things in the mud—old coins or bits of jewelry—
that weren't useful until traded away. Bezul gave
them what they wanted, Chersey gave them a little
more, but the changing house showed a profit either way. Fact was, a good many thieves had lost
their hoards when the White Foal flooded and there
were rumors—undying rumors—of riches hidden
in the Swamp of Night Secrets: the beggar king's
hoard, the slaver's mansion, the treasure troves of a
half-dozen immortal mages, to name only a few.

Perrez—Father Ils have mercy on his greedy
heart—believed every rumor and Gedozia encouraged him. She wouldn't forget that the family had
once been jewelers—goldsmiths and gem-cutters—
on the Path of Money. They'd never been as wealthy
as their clients, but they'd lived very comfortably,
indeed, when she was young and beautiful. Bezul
kept food on the hearth and their heads above

water, but a changing house on Wriggle Way could never salve Gedozia's wounded pride.

Perrez believed Gedozia when she told him that fate *owed* him, that their dead father was looking out for him, and that he was too good for labor and better than any ten other men rolled together—especially ten Nightmen who, by her reckoning, weren't really men at all.

Bezul stopped short of cursing them both as he trod carefully down the planks to the White Foal ferry—a rickety raft festooned with cleats and ropes. A blanketed figure of no discernable age or sex slouched against the mooring post, the shadow of the summoning bell across its head. The figure stiffened as Bezul approached and he glimpsed the face beneath the shadow: beardless, wide-eyed . . . *young*.

Bezul loosed his silent curse: When his luck went bad, it went very bad. There were no rules in the Swamp of Night Secrets—except the ones experience taught. An honest man could negotiate with a practiced criminal if he knew what he wanted; but a raw youth with no sense of the possible—? Bezul drew the cloth through his fingers.

"You the changer?" the blankets asked with a voice that was surprisingly deep.

He nodded. "And you're the man who threw a stone at my door this morning?"

Flattery soothed the Nighter who shed the blanket and rose. He was a fine specimen of his breed: dark, dirty, scrawny, and, above all else, surly, with his head cocked over his left shoulder and all his weight on the same leg.

"Got the red lucky?"

At least, those were the words Bezul thought he'd heard. Between the dialect slur and the snarl, he couldn't be certain. "The red lucky?"

The youth grunted. "Perrez. He said, see the changer. Said you'd have it."

Bezul's imagination swirled with countless unpleasant possibilities. "Take me to Perrez first," he demanded.

"Can't," the youth replied after a fretful glance toward the swamp.

"Nothing happens until I know my brother's safe," Bezul adopted a softer, conspiratorial tone.

Another swampward glance, more furtive than the first. Bezul guessed he was merely a messenger and already over his head.

"Who gave you the cloth?"

"Him."

"Who? Not Perrez?"

A unexpected nod. "Him. Perrez."

"Why?" Bezul asked, bracing himself for another of his brother's bollixed schemes.

"We swapped," the youth replied. "For the lucky, the red lucky. We was to swap back when we met up again last night. He said it was earnest. After the other night, when the moon went red an' there was fire in the swamp."

"Great Father Ils!" Bezul sighed as he deciphered the Nighter's revelations. "You don't *have* Perrez. You're looking for him."

The youth hesitated, then nodded. "He *swore*. Come midnight, he'd be right here. I waited 'til it weren't midnight no more then I come to the changin' house. Perrez said, aught went wrong, the changer'd have the lucky." He stuck out his hand.

There'd be hell to pay when Bezul caught up with his brother who, as Father Ils judged all men, had never intended to meet the Nighter but, first things first: "You've been—"

Before Bezul could finish his explanation, the

youth lunged for his throat. It was a foolish move, not because Bezul was prepared—he most certainly wasn't—but because the youth was more crippled than surly. His right leg betrayed him and he'd have tumbled on his face, if Bezul hadn't caught him. The youth fought free, snarling threats and lashing out with his fists. Bezul countered with a forearm thrust that unbalanced the young man. He went down with a groan that owed nothing to Bezul's strength.

"Whatever your dealings with Perrez," Bezul said sternly, "he didn't share them with me. I don't know what's become of your 'lucky.' "

"No," the youth insisted, his chin tucked against his chest. From the way he shook, Bezul guessed there were tears dripping onto the mud. "I gotta get the lucky." He swiped his face with a leather sleeve. "Got to." Then the youth hugged himself tight. "Shite," he muttered and repeated the oath as he swayed from side to side.

Bezul had seen misery too many times in his life not to recognize it in a heartbeat. Knowing that his own brother was the cause didn't make it easier to bear.

"Stand up," he urged the youth. "Tell me your name and tell me about this 'lucky.' What does it look like?" There was, after all, a chance that the changing house had an identical "lucky" or two stashed in its warrens.

"It's red."

"Your name or the 'lucky'?"

"Name's Dace. Lucky's red. Reddest red."

"And it belongs to someone else?"

Dace raised his head. "Not Perrez!" he snarled.

"No, not Perrez, and not you, either, by the look of things. But you gave it to Perrez—as earnest.

Why? What was Perrez planning to do with it before midnight?" And what had either to do with last week's moon eclipse or perhaps the first-blood tournament? Frog all—he should have been paying more attention to his brother's activities, should have known Perrez would find a way to get in trouble.

The Nighter shrugged, recapturing Bezul's attention. "Said he'd find out if'n it was true lucky. Told him it was. We been usin' it for years."

"For what?"

"Baitin' crabs."

"I thought—" Bezul began, then returned to his first question: "What does your 'lucky' look like, Dace? Not just its color, but how big? Is it shiny—?"

Dace clambered to his feet. He framed his fingers around a nut-sized hole. "This big, drop-shaped, and shiny. And *smooth*. Hard-smooth and cool in your hand."

Glass, Bezul decided. Heated once for clarity, then cooled into a solid bulb and stored for a future use that never came. There weren't many glassblowers left in Sanctuary and most of what they blew was milky yellow, but years ago it had been different. Years ago, master craftsmen had blown their glass clear as sunlight or colored like rainbows, glass brilliant enough to earn a goldsmith's respect.

Perrez knew where they kept their father's storage chest of jewel-colored bulbs, so why had he swindled a Nighter out of his precious "lucky" . . . ?

Bezul shook the question out of his thoughts. "Come along," he told Dace, "we'll find you a 'lucky,' " and when that was settled, by all the gods, he'd have choice words with his brother.

Dace followed Bezul from the ferry. The Nighter

threw himself into every stride, swaying precariously on his weak leg. Bezul wondered why the young man didn't use a crutch—until he imagined a crutch sinking into a swamp's endless mud. He offered to pay their way across the footbridge, but Dace wanted nothing of charity—or the narrow bridge. They took the long way, instead, shouldering their way through the crowds at the tournament, then hiking uphill, upstream through the bazaar. Dace was gasping when they reached the palace wall, but much too proud to call a halt, so Bezul called one for himself at the top of Stink Street.

"What do you get out this, Dace?" Bezul asked. "Why loan your 'lucky' to a stranger?" He'd tried, and failed, to keep the critical tone out of his voice.

Dace stared long and hard at his grimy sabots before answering: "No stranger," he admitted between deep breaths. "I been workin' for him all winter. Showin' him places in the swamp, old places, like the one where my uncle found the lucky. I told him how the lucky's the best bait ever. Ever'thing comes to it, even birds and snakes, but crabs is the best, even in winter—specially *this* winter when nothin's froze. Put the lucky in a crab-trap at sunset and it's full-up with a mess o'crabs come morning. Eat 'em or sell 'em, nothing better than crabs. Perrez, he wanted to bait a trap over here. Said it was dangerous, but if the lucky caught what he was lookin' for, then him and me would be partners and I could live over here with him." The Nighter met Bezul's eyes. "You being the changer, you've got to help me. Perrez said. If I go home without the lucky—" Dace drew a fingertip across his throat.

Bezul wasn't a violent man, but words might not be enough when he came face-to-face with Perrez. Dace was a Nighter: crippled, wild, and utterly unsuited for life anywhere but the swamp where he'd been born. Telling him otherwise—giving him hope—passed beyond swindling greed to cruelty. And leaving Bezul to sort it out, that would be the last—the absolute last—in a long string of insults a younger brother had heaped on his elder. He started down Stink Street with Dace lurching along beside him.

Nighters with their furs and leathers, not to mention their swampy aroma, attracted attention at the best of times. A gimpy Nighter trailing after a respectably dressed merchant attracted extra attention. Someone, seeing them and recognizing Bezul, had run ahead to the changing house. Jopze had left his comfortable post inside the changing house and taken up position beneath the baker's awning a few doors up Wriggle Way. A barrel stave leaned in easy reach against the wall.

Bezul caught Jopze's eye and shook his head twice, assuring the old soldier that, however strange it looked, he wasn't in need of protection. Jopze picked up the stave and followed them to the changing house where Ammen, their other guard, had remained with the family and customers.

"Any sign—?" Bezul began as he stepped across the threshold.

Before he could finish, Chersey ran from behind the heavy wooden counter. She was all smiles and clearly hadn't noticed Dace.

"It was all for nothing," she told him. "Your brother showed up not long after you left—shirt and all. I told him what had happened—how frightened we were and how you'd gone after him. He laughed, like it was nothing at all, and said it had to be the laundress; he was missing a shirt . . ." Cher-

sey's voice trailed. She'd gotten an eyeful of Dace.
"What—? Who—?"

"Meet my brother's laundress," Bezul said bitterly
and began his own version of the morning's events.

He was cautious at first, expecting Gedozia or Perrez himself to challenge him from the shadows, but
Chersey had said—when Bezul paused for breath—
that Gedozia and the children hadn't returned from
the farmers' market—held this week, on account of
the tournament, in the cemetery outside the walls—
and Perrez had stayed at the changing house only
long enough to "borrow" three shaboozh.

"He said he had work to do," Chersey explained.
"Something big—isn't it always? He was meeting a
man. I couldn't tell whether he was buying or selling—but it wasn't anything to do with the tournament. Your brother was beside himself, Bez. All
bright-eyed and high-colored, as though he'd been
drinking. I didn't know what to make of him so I
gave him one shaboozh and told him to come back
later, when you'd gotten back, if he needed more."

One shaboozh was two more than Perrez deserved.

There was more that Chersey wasn't saying. Bezul
knew that by the way she fussed with her silver-gray
moonstone ring. It was a magical ring—not particularly potent, but useful for assessing intentions,
useful when you made your living buying and selling. He watched his wife take Dace's measure with
a casual gesture, lining the ring up with the Nighter's face as she tucked a stray lock of hair behind
her ear.

They needed to talk and if Bezul had been thinking he would have helped Chersey clear their customers out of the shop before they talked further
about Perrez's indiscretions. Or perhaps not. Bezul

had restrained himself far too long on his brother's account, and his mother's. Suddenly, he no longer cared. Let the gossips spread the tale of how the changer's brother had swindled a crippled Nighter out of a lump of red glass throughout the quarter, throughout Sanctuary. Let Perrez feel their eyes burning his neck and hang his head in shame for a change.

Words spilled out of Bezul, honest and acid, until his belly was empty and he asked, "I don't suppose he left that damned red lucky here?"

Chersey shook her head. Mistress Glary—the greatest snoop in all Sanctuary—slipped out the door, careful not to let the hem of her dress brush against the slack-jawed Nighter. Her departure broke the spell of curiosity. The other customers clamored to complete their business. Bezul joined his wife behind the counter: twenty padpols exchanged for a pair of boots with patched soles, a copper-lined pot exchanged for four shaboozh, one of them a royal shaboozh minted in llsig, not Sanctuary; and a child's fur-lined cloak swapped even for a larger one of boiled wool and a pair of woolen breeches.

Dace blinked often enough, but he didn't move, didn't say a word as the changing house conducted its business. As birds flew, the Prince's gate on the east side of Sanctuary was farther from Wriggle Way than the Swamp of Night Secrets, but Dace might just as well have fallen from the moon for all he seemed to grasp of ordinary trade.

"I'll see him back where he belongs," Jopze volunteered. His hand fell heavily on the Nighter's shoulder and spun him effortlessly toward the door.

"No, we owe him—" Bezul rubbed his brow. He'd acquired a headache between Stink Street and home. "We owe him a 'lucky.' " He turned to Chersey. "That chest of my father's. The one with the glass bulbs Ayse loves to play with, it's—?"

"In the woodshed behind the annex, under the porphyry urn we're holding for Lady Kuklos. The key's in the flowerpot."

Bezul leaned forward to kiss his wife on the cheek.

She whispered, "I knew Perrez was lying about something, but I couldn't get him to say what. That's why I wouldn't give him three shaboozh—I'd guessed he wanted it for wine. I never thought—"

"Who could?" Bezul replied in the same tone. "There'll be a reckoning this time, I swear it. The children are getting old enough to notice."

"What about that one? The Nighter . . . the boy."

"We'll give him a 'lucky' and send him back to the swamp." Bezul sighed. "I don't know which I find harder to believe: that my brother stole crab-trap bait or that he promised to take that poor, frog-eating bastard on as a partner."

Chersey put an arm's length between herself and her husband. "Could you be wrong about the bait?"

"I could be wrong about everything, Chersey. Why?"

"It's just—"

She twisted the moonstone ring and revealed an oval patch of reddened skin on her finger. Bezul gasped. The ring had been in his family since their goldsmithing days. It had kept them safe—almost—from the Hand and even in the face of Retribution himself, Dyareela's right hand in Sanctuary, the ring hadn't harmed the slender finger that wore it.

"I was suspicious," Chersey confessed. "So I kenned him—Perrez. I didn't see the aura—no malice—but, it hurt, Bez, and, afterward, all I could think about was the pouch hanging from his belt.

That's how I knew . . . how I knew it wasn't anything to do with the tournament."

She blushed and Bezul tried to reassure her while asking, "Did you see which way he headed?"

"Out, that's all. We've been busy all morning. Maybe Jopze saw something. He was near the door, but I doubt it."

Bezul's headache was getting worse by the heartbeat.

"I'll go down to the tavern after we're done with Dace—the Nighter. I'll talk to him, get to the bottom of this."

He left his wife smiling and went outside to the woodshed where the dusty air aggravated his headache and the big urn was at least twice as heavy as he remembered. Bezul had his arms full and his cheek pressed against the porphyry when he heard footfalls behind him.

"Give me a hand, here," he said, expecting that Chersey had sent Jopze or Ammen out to help, but the arms that slid around the polished stone were Gedozia's.

His mother was a strong woman, despite her gray hair and missing teeth. Between them, they got the urn to the ground without crushing anyone's toes. Bezul brushed his sleeves and waited for her to start the conversation because, sure as the sun rose in the east, Gedozia hadn't shown up by accident or to help with manual labor.

"You won't find your brother in any tavern around here."

Bezul raised his arm—in anger or sheer frustration, he couldn't have said which. After a moment, it dropped to his side again. "You knew," he accused her. "This morning, I asked you where he'd gone and you said you didn't know."

"And I didn't!" Gedozia insisted. "Oh, Bezul, this has nothing to do with that Nighter stinking up the front room. Perrez found something—"

"A bulb of red glass!"

"Some glass bulb," Gedozia retorted, "if there's an Ilsigi trader willing to pay *seventy* royals for it."

Bezul blanched at the sum, though, surely, if something were worth seventy golden royals in Sanctuary, it would be worth seven hundred in the king's city.

"Perrez came by to tell me this morning. Seventy royals! He's been working with this trader all winter. Yesterday the trader finally got serious and offered some earnest money. Today Perrez said he was turning it over—the red glass—and getting the full seventy royals. Seventy! He was so excited. He swore me to secrecy because he wanted to tell you himself, Bezul, to show you what he's made of. But you were already gone—chasing that Nighter—and he had to meet the Ilsigi at midday. Think of it: *seventy royals!* I told your father, 'Bezulshash, it's not enough, not what he deserves, but it's a start.' I went to market to buy food for a feast—tried to, the city's up to here with people who think they're going to win more than seventy royals tomorrow and are spending their winnings today!

"Your father came to me at the fishmonger's: 'Gedozia,' he says. 'Gedozia, he can't be trusted!—' "

"Praise Ils! It's about time—"

Gedozia seized Bezul sharply by the wrists. "Not your brother, the Ilsigi! The Ilsigi means to cheat Perrez out of the seventy royals! He's too sweet-natured, my Perrez. He'll never suspect a thing, until it's too late. Find him, Bezul. He's your brother. It's up to you to do what his father would have done.

Bezulshash would have beaten this Ilsigi with a stick."

Bezulshash would have done no such thing and Bezul would have dismissed everything his mother had said, if it hadn't made a sour sort of sense when compared with the tale Dace had told.

Bezul broke free of Gedozia's grasp. "Hard to cheat a thief, Mother. He tricked that glass from the Nighter. Good as stole it—"

"The Nighter's a halfwit—and who's to say where he got it, eh? If he got it. If it's even what the Ilsigi trader wanted to buy. You're the one talking about *glass.* I thought it was a manuscript."

"You—" Bezul caught himself. The sun rose and set on Perrez, always had, always would, and telling Gedozia anything else was a waste of time. Best to go back to the beginning, to what *she* wanted. "You said I wouldn't find Perrez around here. Where will I find him?"

"Uptown . . . in the Maze. The Unicorn."

Just when Bezul had thought he'd heard the worst, Gedozia astonished him. But if she knew the Vulgar Unicorn's reputation as a den of thieves and ne'er-do-wells, she kept it hidden. Bezul shook an iron key out of a painted flower pot, unlocked his father's chest, and sorted through its contents until he'd found a bulb of blood-red glass as big as his fist.

"You can't be serious," Gedozia complained. "That's irreplaceable. It's worth four shaboozh, three at least—"

Bezul locked the chest. He tucked the key inside his jacket and left the urn where it was. "Don't say another word," he warned the woman who'd birthed him. "After I've settled with the Nighter, I'll go uptown, looking for Perrez. Don't convince me otherwise."

"You—" Gedozia began, but Bezul's darkest stare convinced her not to finish.

He returned to the front room where Lesimar was sitting in Ammen's lap and Chersey tended a desperate-looking woman trying to exchange an apron of windfall apples for three fishhooks. Had Bezul been the one behind the counter, he would have given the woman a single metal hook for the brown, wrinkled fruit that even the geese wouldn't eat. Chersey parted with two and a length of light silken thread pulled invisibly from the hem of a lady's dress left in the shop on consignment. Their eyes met as the woman departed.

"Has the Nighter gone?" Bezul asked, saying nothing—wisely—about his wife's generosity.

"The kitchen," she replied, meaning that she'd decided to feed him.

Dace sat on the floor beside the hearth, ignoring the chairs and table. He cradled a smallish bread loaf and a bowl of whey in his lap. By the looks of the whey as he dipped a morsel of bread in it, Chersey had fortified the weak milk with an egg. Thanks to their flock of night-watchmen, the changing house always had extra eggs. Four-year-old Ayse sat cross-legged in one of the chairs, her wide eyes not missing a thing as the Nighter ate with his fingers— something she was no longer permitted to do.

The young man wiped his hands on his breeches before taking the glass bulb Bezul offered. He seemed pleased, though a bit overwhelmed. Bezul's gift was bigger, he stammered, redder, and heavier— solid where the missing bulb had been hollow, but it was Ayse who got to the heart of matter:

"Is it lucky, Poppa? It's got to be lucky, doesn't it?"

Bezul answered with hope, not honesty, and got out of the kitchen.

Despite Gedozia's statements, Bezul didn't strike out for the Vulgar Unicorn. He clung to the hope that Perrez wasn't *that* foolish until he'd finished poking his head into every tavern and wine shop in the Shambles without meeting anyone who'd seen his brother recently. With his hope exhausted, and feeling quite foolish himself, Bezul plunged into Sanctuary's most infamous quarter.

It had been a year, easily, since Bezul's last encounter with the tangled, narrow alleys that passed for streets in the Maze. He'd nearly convinced himself that he'd missed a critical turn and would have to start over (getting in and out of the Maze wasn't nearly as difficult, by daylight, as finding a particular place) when he caught sight of the Unicorn's signboard. The sign was to Bezul's left, not his right, where he'd been expecting it, so he had missed a turn or two, or perhaps the gossips were correct and, in the Maze, all paths led to the Vulgar Unicorn.

The Unicorn's shutters were open, not that it made a difference. The air in the commons was as thick and stale as the shadows. Bezul leaned against a wooden upright, looking for Perrez, waiting for his eyes to adjust to the haze. A woman hailed him by name—

"Bezulshash! Bezul the Changer!"

The woman coming toward Bezul was taller than him by a handspan, heavier by at least a stone. Her red hair fairly glowed in the twilight and her bodice was cut so snug and low that her breasts jounced above her corset like fresh fish on a trawl line. She came to the changing house every month or so to change a sackful of padpols into fewer, better coins. Bezul knew her name; he might even remember it, if he concentrated on her face.

"Frog all, Bezulshash, what's brought you to the Unicorn?"

They were considerably less than an arm's length apart. Bezul would have retreated, but he had a post at his back. Clearing his throat, he stammered, then said, "I'm looking for my brother, Perrez."

That name meant nothing to her (and Bezul hadn't remembered hers . . . It was Mimmi, Minzie, something like that), but his description of Perrez's scrupulously clean clothes, neatly trimmed hair, and his love of someone else's largesse rang a bell.

"You froggin' missed him, Bezulshash. He was here when I came downstairs—talking with the aromacist."

"The what?"

She shrugged, a very distracting gesture. Bezul missed her first words. "—of winter. Set himself up off the Processional. Froggin' fancy place: fancy bottles, colored oils, silks and tassels hanging from the walls."

"A perfumer?"

She shook her head and everything else. " 'Aromas' he called them, better than perfume. Said no man could resist his 'aroma' of passion. Frog all, Bezulshash—do *I* look like I need help attracting men? He never fit inside the Unicorn; a little like you, Bezulshash: You don't belong here. But he came by, every few days, late morning or early afternoon, when it was slow and quiet. He'd take one of the side tables, buy a whole ewer of ale, leave it, too—unless he got company—your brother, a handful of others. Come to think of it—they left

together. First time, I think, for that; first time I noticed: Your brother, he was tipsy, noisy. Don't think
he'd've made it outside by himself—"

"A fancy shop off the Processional?" Bezul asked
and tried to keep the rest out of his thoughts for a
few moments longer. He was ready to leave, but
found his way blocked. In his concern—his anger—
he'd forgotten something more important than her
name. "Stop by the changing house," he urged.
"There's a pair of earrings tucked away with your
name on them."

She grinned and let him depart.

The Processional between the harbor and the palace was neither the longest nor the widest street in
Sanctuary. With the tight-fisted Irrune in the palace,
it wasn't even the busiest street. Mansions, some of
them still abandoned after the Troubles, lined both
sides of the street. When the residents left their
homes, they traveled in clumps. A solitary man was
marked as a visitor and ignored.

Lord Kuklos—a bearded magnate with an over-
sized cloak, a bright-red hat, and a flock of aides—
rushed past Bezul without a by-your-leave. Probably
on their way to the tournament. A slower clutch of
nursemaids and guards surrounding a pair of children stopped when the better-dressed boy threw
himself into a tantrum. Probably wanted to go to
the tournament.

As Bezul wove around them—stepping carefully
over one of the two gutters running from the palace
to the harbor—he took note that the second child,
equally winsome but less lavishly dressed—received
the thrashing his companion deserved.

The third procession bore down rapidly on Bezul
from behind. A man with a clanging bell and a loud
voice ordered him out of the way. Prudence, rather

than obedience, launched Bezul up on a curbstone.
He clung to a pedestal that had long since lost its
commemorative statue while a woman wrapped in a
sea-green mantle and seated in an open chair
charged toward the harbor. A whiskery dog with jewels in its ears yapped at Bezul from the lady's lap.
The rest of her retinue—a brace of underdressed
porters that might have been twins, three breathless
maids clutching their skirts with one hand, their
mantles with the other; five guards whose legs were
taking a beating from their scabbards, and the lead
man with the bell—spared him not a single glance.

Watching them sweep around the corner that was
his own goal, Bezul offered a quick prayer to any
nearby god that the lady's final destination not be
the aromacist's shop. Someone listened. The lady
and her retinue were rounding the next corner
when Bezul turned off the Processional. Perhaps the
lady knew something the corseted wench at the Unicorn had not: The aromacist's shop—its business
proclaimed in both Ilsigi and Rankan script on a
bright signboard—was shuttered tight from the inside.

"Perrez," Bezul called, giving the handle a firm
shake. "If you're in there, open the door!"

He shook the handle a second time and kicked
the door. When that produced no response, Bezul
berated himself for imagining that his quest would
end any other way. He should return to the changing house: His own business was suffering and his
brother would return. Men like Perrez landed on
their feet and on the backs of their families.

Bezul turned away from the shop; and as he did,
he noticed that the door beside it—the alleyway
door between the shop and its left-side neighbor—
was not completely closed. By Ils's thousandth eye,

Bezul was a cautious man and, to the extent his profession allowed, an honest man. Undoubtedly, there
were objects on the changing house shelves which
had not been placed there by their legitimate owners, but Bezulshash, son of Bezulshash, did not
knowingly trade for suspect goods. He did not venture into another man's domain uninvited, or he
hadn't before. After glances toward the Processional
and away from it, Bezul slipped into the alley and
pulled the door back into its almost-shut position.

The alley proved to be a tunnel running beneath
the upper floors of the aromacist's building. Bezul
scuttled as quickly as he dared through the darkness, emerging into a tiny fenced-in square with another door to his right. This door had been properly
closed and bolted, but the bolt was on Bezul's side.
The aromacist, then, was more concerned about escape than invasion. After listening for sounds of life
on the far side, and hearing none, Bezul slid the bolt
from its housing. Still gripping the bolt, he lifted the
door so its greater weight was in his hands, not on
its hinges, then eased it open.

Bezul stuck his head into what looked, at first, to
be a long-abandoned garden, strewn with discarded
barrels, crates, and overturned furniture. On second
glance around, Bezul realized that while the garden
was, indeed, abandoned, the other wreckage was
more recent. Perhaps very recent: There were puddles in the dirt around a broken barrel. Bezul eased
the rest of the way into the garden. He grabbed the
nearest chunk of sturdy wreckage and used it to in-
sure that the door remained open.

Bezul was taking his time, assessing everything in
sight, when he spotted a broken barrel-stave with a
scrap of red-stained cloth caught in its splintered
end.

"Perrez?" he asked himself, then, louder: "Perrez?"

He heard the sound of a heavy object thudding to the ground. The shop's rear door, Bezul realized, was open and the sound had come from within. He ran across the garden.

"Perrez! Per—!"

Horror, relief, and anger were only three of the emotions that bottled Bezul's voice in his throat. He'd found his younger brother, found him alive, but bloody. Beaten bloody, bound with ropes and rags, gagged, and hung from a roof beam where he swayed like a dripping pendulum, an overturned bench beneath. Not—thank all the gods that ever were—hanged by a noose around his neck, but slant-wise with from a noose that passed under the opposite shoulder. The shoulder-slung noose wouldn't make much difference, if Bezul didn't cut through it quick. Perrez was already wheezing for air.

Bezul righted the bench and went to work with his knife. He freed his brother's wrists with a single slash, then hacked through the hanging rope. Bezul meant to keep hold of the loose end and lower Perrez gently to the floor, but the rope wasn't long enough. Perrez hit the floor with a moan—but he was breathing easier even then.

"Hold still!" Bezul commanded as he slipped his knife beneath the gag and for, perhaps, the first time in his life, Perrez obeyed.

"Bez . . . Bez!" the battered man gasped. "Father Ils! Never thought . . . you'd find . . ."

"Save your thanks." Bezul had gotten a closer look at his brother. On the ground, it was clear that none of Perrez's wounds was close to mortal and that meant Bezul could vent his anger. "I don't know which is worse: that you cheated the Nighters or that you got cheated by some Ilsigi fly-by-night yourself."

Through the bruises and blood, Perrez protested his innocence.

"I've talked to Mother," Bezul snapped. "I've talked to a wench at the Unicorn who seemed to remember you well enough. And I've done more than talk to that Nighter."

"What Nighter? What are you talking about, Bez?"

"Don't 'Bez' me. You knew he'd come looking when you didn't show up to return his damn lucky so you pointed him at me. What did you expect? That I'd keep him out of your way until you had your seventy royals? Or was that just a number you threw at Mother? Did your aromacist friend make you the same sheep-shite promise you gave the Nighter: Give me what I want and I'll make you my partner? By Lord Ils's thousandth eye, what *else* have you been doing besides making us the guarantor for every bet in Sanctuary?"

"I'd have split the royals with you, Bez . . . with you and the frackin' froggin' Nighter!" Perrez studied his torn, stained sleeve before cursing softly and swiping his face with the cloth. He ignored the jibe about his oddsmaking activities. "It was a fair deal, Bez, a good price. That 'lucky' wasn't any ordinary piece of glass. It's an *attractor*. The fish-folk made them: hollow bulbs filled with their magic. If you want something bad enough it'll bring it to you, or lead you there. Worth their frackin' froggin' weight in gold when the fish-folk made them and ten times that now. Nareel—"

"Your buyer? The aromacist? The man who strung you up?"

Perrez hesitated, then nodded. "Nareel will get a thousand for it up in Ilsig . . . once we'd gotten the crabs out of it. Shalpa! Those Nighters were using a fish-eye attractor as bait in their crab traps! Now, there's a waste, Bez, a true crime. Once we got it focused on gold—"

"What '*we*,' Perrez? I should think it would be clear—even to you—that this Nareel has plans that don't involve you."

Perrez wanted to disagree; Bezul could see the arguments forming, then fading on his brother's face. It was painful to watch, but Bezul did, in icy silence, until Perrez broke.

"I should have come to you," he admitted. "As soon as I realized what the Nighter had baiting his traps, I should have come to you and let you handle everything: getting it away from the Nighter and finding a buyer, too. But it was going so well . . . I was going to come to you with the seventy royals, Bez, I *swear* I was. I'd lay them down on the counter and you'd be *proud* of me. Shalpa, Bez—I don't want to be Nareel's partner. I want to be yours. I want you to trust me with the changing house. You've done so well, and what do I have to show for myself?" From his knees, Perrez reached up to take his elder brother's hand. "Help me, Bez. I know where Nareel's gone, I think. If you confront him, he'll honor his bargain. I'm begging you, Bez. Our honor's at stake, here. You can't let Nareel get away with what he's done."

It was a good speech and it might have melted Bezul's heart, if he hadn't heard similar speeches too many times before. He withdrew his hand. "Nareel's robbed a thief. Where's the honor on either side in that? That glass never belonged to you. No, it's over. The aromacist's made a fool of you, and there it ends. Stand up. We're going home. Be grateful you still have one . . . and *pray* you've figured the odds right. What little I hear, it's not going the way anyone expected."

With a whimpering groan, Perrez rose unsteadily. His brother could not tell how much was genuine pain, how much just another part of the act.

"What about Dace?" Perrez asked. "If the attractor wasn't mine, then it belongs to the Nighter, not Nareel. We can't walk away, Bez. We've still got to get it back."

Bezul scarcely believed what he was hearing. "Don't you—" he cut himself short. The aromacist's workroom was no place to continue an argument with Perrez, who would neither listen nor change. "I gave Dace one of Father's glass bulbs to replace his 'red lucky.' "

He returned to the garden. Perrez followed.

"You can't do that, Bez. You can't replace a fish-eye attractor with a bulb of ordinary glass. It's not going to catch crabs. I mean, a few nights, and he's going to know it's not their frackin' froggin' lucky."

"Maybe; maybe not."

"No maybes. The attractor's got *pull*, froggin' fish-eye sorcery. There's nothing in Father's chest to compare with it, nothing in the whole shop. Dace'll be back . . . with his relatives. I've seen 'em. The gimp's one of the *normal* Nighters, Bez. You've got to think they've been screwing rats and trolls—"

Bezul opened the gate. He had the impression of a face and a yell, then he was reeling as something surged past him. The fence kept Bezul upright. Perrez was not so fortunate. He was on his back, bellowing panic and pain, beneath not the mysterious aromacist, but Dace, who attacked him with wild fury. Bezul seized the youth's shoulder, hoping to pull him off Perrez, but he underestimated Dace's determination, not to mention his skills and his strength. The Nighter broke free with an elbow jab between Bezul's ribs.

With greater caution and an eye for self-defense, Bezul tried again and succeeded.

"He can't say that!" Dace growled while struggling to get his fists on Perrez again. "He lied. He stole the lucky."

Realizing that he couldn't break free, Dace twisted about and attacked Bezul. Bezul successfully defended his groin and his gut, but lost his grip when Dace stomped his instep. Still, he caught the Nighter before he laid into Perrez.

"Enough!" Bezul gave Dace a shove into the fence that nearly toppled it and quieted the youth. "Yes, he stole it and lost it, because he's a frogging fool, but, you're no better. You gave it to him for a scrap of cloth and a promise! Let it be a lesson to you both." He shoved Perrez, who'd just gotten his feet under him, at the open gate. "Start moving."

Perrez, who hadn't actually lost anything that could have been called his in the first place, went through the gate without protest. Not so Dace. The Nighter retreated toward the aromacist's workroom.

"I'm stayin'. That Nareel comes home, I'm gettin' the lucky back. Don't care 'bout no royals."

By that Bezul assumed Dace had overheard his entire conversation with Perrez. "You don't need sorcery to bait crabs, Dace. The lucky's not worth dying for," he told the youth and silently chided himself for caring. He turned around and nearly walked into Perrez.

"We don't have to wait. I know where Nareel's gone—he'd brought a map with him from Ilsig. He was looking for some dead shite's hoard. Fastalen— something like that. The map didn't match with what he found in the quarter. There's not a house up there now that was standing when whoever drew Nareel's map. That's where the attractor came in. He and I were going to use it to find the hoard. Said it had to be today—couldn't wait 'til tomorrow, something about the sun. He's up there now—I swear it—and we don't need an attractor to find a man rooting through rubble."

"We don't need anything," Bezul replied. "We're going home to Wriggle Way." But Bezul stopped short of shoving his brother toward the gate again. He wasn't blind to the allure in Perrez's argument. "Look at yourself," he said in one last attempt to free them all from temptation. "Clothes torn. Face bloodied. And don't tell me you've got full use of your right arm. The aromacist has already beaten you once today, Perrez—"

"Because I wasn't ready. This time, I'll be surprising him . . . and you'll be with me."

"No."

"Bez—"

"No."

"You're getting *old*, Bez. Ten years ago, you'd have led the way."

"Not a chance," Bezul said confidently.

Children hadn't changed him, marriage hadn't changed him, even the Troubles hadn't changed him. He'd changed the day his father abandoned their uptown shop for Wriggle Way. Perrez couldn't remember that day; he'd been a toddler, younger than Lesimar; but Bezul had been old enough to see the despair on his parents' faces and it had burnt the wildness out of him forever.

"Let it go, Perrez. Come home. Chersey will bind up your ribs and cuts."

"No. It's the Nighter's lucky and *our* gold, not Nareel's. Tell Mother I'm coming home rich, or not at all."

Dace—Father Ils bless his limp and his stubbornness—had hobbled out of the workroom to stand beside Perrez, all but announcing that they were partners again. Bezul closed his eyes. He imagined himself returning to Wriggle Way: sober, righteous . . . alone. Wealth had never tempted him. It still didn't, but the tide had turned regardless.

"If we're going," he conceded, "we'd best get started."

Between Dace's withered leg and Perrez's bruises, the three men crossed Sanctuary slowly. Bezul considered that their prey might be flown by the time Perrez got them to the right quarter. He kept his thoughts to himself. If they missed the opportunity, then they missed the danger, too.

"Not far now," Perrez assured them as they trudged up one of the steepest streets in the city.

They'd paused for water at a communal well where Perrez had washed the worst of the blood from his face, which only made the bruises more noticeable, and the swollen kink in his nose. Bezul was a grown man with children of his own, but he'd always be the elder brother. He reserved the right to pummel Perrez; he conceded it to no one, especially not an *aromacist* from Ilsig.

Perrez led them down a treacherous alley to a courtyard that had seen better days, much better days, a generation or more earlier. Patches of fresco murals clung to the weathered walls, none of them large enough to reveal a scene or subject. The windows and doorways were empty, stripped of everything valuable or moveable.

"Where to?" Dace asked.

There was no need for Perrez's answer. They

could all hear a man shouting, "Slowly . . . Slowly,
you worms!" with the rounded accent of old Ilsig.

"Nareel!"

Perrez grinned and Bezul had to move quickly to
stop his brother from racing to a confrontation.

"Slowly's a damn good idea, Perrez. Slowly and
quietly. He's not alone."

"You first," Perrez urged and Bezul obliged.

There was a sameness to the ruins of Sanctuary.
After beams burnt and walls fell, it could be difficult
to say if the ruins had been a mansion or a hovel.
For Bezul, it was enough that there was rubble to
hide behind and see around in a deeply shadowed
corner not far from the gaping doorway. He motioned to Perrez and Dace and they joined him.

Perrez clapped his brother on the arm and
pointed at a tall man with gray-touched hair. His lips
shaped the word *Nareel*. Bezul nodded and wished
he could have asked Perrez if the aromacist regu-
larly dressed in long black robes or tied an antique
bronze breastplate over his chest—though, judging
from the puzzled expression on his brother's face,
the answer would have been No.

The "worms" at whom Nareel shouted were a pair
of laborers—the ragged unskilled sort who sometimes showed up on Wriggle Way, hoping to
exchange their sweat for a few padpols. They'd dug
themselves a pit a few paces north of the ruins' center. Beyond them, three sell-swords who, together,
wouldn't be a match for either Ammen or Jopze, if
Ammen or Jopze weren't still in the Shambles. A
sixth man stood east of the pit. Younger than Nareel
and possibly his son, the sixth man also wore a long
black robe, though without the shiny breastplate.
He held a wicker-work triangle between his hands.

A bright-red lump dangled from the triangle's

peak. Although the light wasn't good and the angle was worse, Bezul could see that the glass teardrop wasn't hanging straight down, but strained toward the pit, pulled by an invisible hand. Bezul's breath caught. Neither Perrez nor Dace had lied; the red lucky was filled with sorcery and, shite for sure, Nareel wasn't hunting for crabs!

"See? I told you!" Perrez whispered excitedly. "Fish-eye sorcery. We're rich!"

Bezul raised an arm to clout his brother, but before the blow landed, he had worse problems to contend with. The Nighter was up and on the move toward his damned lucky. Without thinking, Bezul lunged and tackled the youth. He'd swear the ground shook when they struck the ground and thunder was not half so loud. Bezul pinched his eyes shut, convinced that when he opened them, he'd be looking up into the face of his death.

"Sorry," Dace said, the merest breath of voice in Bezul's ear. "Can't breathe."

So Bezul moved and there were no sell-swords standing over him, no death awaiting him. He and the Nighter crawled back to Perrez. The reason for their survival was simple enough: Nareel and his men had been moving, making their own noises, at precisely the right moments.

The two diggers had climbed out of the pit. They and the sell-swords now stood together on the opposite side of the pit. The sell-swords had their hands on the hilts of their weapons, but they weren't looking into the shadows where three spies were hiding. They were watching the pit and even at this distance, Bezul could see that they were afraid.

Bezul couldn't fault them. When he looked, there were faint bluish flames rising from the hole and he was frightened, too. The younger man who'd carried the attractor had exchanged it for a plain, bronze disk, polished to a mirror shine, which he held before his face like a shield as he slowly circled the pit against the sun. Nareel had his back to Bezul, but he was also circling and his face would come into view—or rather, his mask, because it was clear that he, too, had a disk in front of his face, tied around his skull rather than held in his hands. Both black-robed men were chanting, not in unison, not in Ilsigi. Bezul didn't recognize the language at all, and he'd heard a good many in the changing house. That added to his fear.

The bluish flames rising from the ground got brighter and sound, like a chorus of cicadas on a hot, summer night, emanated from them. Bezul looked at Perrez; Perrez was already looking at him. They didn't need words: The aromacist hadn't come to Sanctuary to look for gold, he'd come for sorcery and, thanks to Perrez, he'd found it. The world was full of sorcery, but sorcery that put fear in a man's heart wasn't welcome in Sanctuary. It was the one thing everyone agreed upon. Perrez had the decency to hang his head.

That was all Perrez did: He hung his head. He didn't run, he didn't hurl stones, didn't do anything to make the rubble near them shift; but shift it did and this time the noise attracted the sell-swords' attention. They advanced, drawing their weapons. Bezul grabbed his brother and the Nighter.

"Run!" he commanded them and shoved them toward the doorway as he cast a warning—not a prayer—to Father Ils in Paradise: *Take care of Chersey; make her strong for the children. Don't blame her for my sins.* Then he pulled the fighting knife out of his boot. It wouldn't serve against three swords, but it might give Perrez and Dace time to reach a street where the presence of passersby would protect them.

Bezul saw the sell-swords choose the doorway, not him, and somehow got in front of them, then desperation took control of his mind. He parried for his life—there was no thrusting with a knife against three swords—and parried a second time and a third, because he wasn't dead yet and he wouldn't stop fighting until he was. There were more swords, then fewer swords, screams, and a thunderclap so loud it flung Bezul into the wall.

His head cracked against the plastered brick; he lost consciousness for a heartbeat or two, just long enough for his heels to sink to the ground. A sell-sword charged toward him. Bezul could see his knife, flat across his palm, but his arm belonged to someone else when he tried to clench his hand around the hilt. It didn't matter. The sell-sword wasn't interested in him; he raced through the doorway without stopping to kill a defenseless man. The diggers staggered along behind the sell-sword which left two men standing in the ruins. Neither was a man Bezul had seen before.

The nearer of the pair, a man about Perrez's age with a hardened face and a brawler's body advanced toward Bezul. "You hurt?"

Bezul shook his head. With the wall solidly behind him, he pushed himself upright and looked around. One of the sell-swords lay motionless in the rubble. By the angle of his head and the size of the blood pool beneath it, he wouldn't be getting up again. Nareel and his companion were down, too. The other victorious stranger—another man who preferred a one-color wardrobe: black boots, breeches, cloak, and tunic—prodded Nareel with his sword, trying to loosen the mask.

"What drew you here?" the brawler asked.

Bezul spotted the lucky red attractor, apparently unbroken. "That," he said, pointing to it.

The brawler's eyes all but disappeared in his scowl. "You're the Shambles changer, right? What's your tie to the sorcerer or a Beysib attractor?"

"It's a long story," Bezul answered with a weary nod. "I have a troublesome brother—"

A third stranger entered the ruins through the doorway. Short, shapeless and unbearded, Bezul decided the stranger was a man simply because he didn't want to believe that a woman could be so ugly. The new arrival dipped his chin to the brawler and the man in black then, with more agility and speed than Bezul expected, leapt into the pit and out of it again, a deep blue enameled chest clutched like an infant in his arms.

"It's all here," he announced with a eunuch's boyish voice.

"You're froggin' sure?" the brawler asked.

The eunuch patted the chest lovingly. "Have no doubts, Cauvin. We're safe for another day . . . more than another day."

Cauvin. Bezul knew a Cauvin . . . knew of one, anyway. The stonemason's son from up on Pyrtanis Street, rescued from the palace after the Irrune slaughtered the Bloody Hand. The gossips said he was good with stone, better with his fists and not at all reluctant to use them.

But, perhaps, there was another Cauvin in Sanctuary.

His prize in hand, the eunuch waddled toward them. "One less problem to worry about, eh? No one stealing the sun, trapping it in a box?"

Cauvin didn't answer, didn't look like he particularly agreed. The eunuch giggled and for an instant his eyes glowed red, then he was gone.

"Wh—?" Bezul began.

"Don't ask," the brawler snarled, leaving Bezul with no doubt that there was only one Cauvin in Sanctuary.

"What do you want to do with the bodies?" the black-booted swordsman called from Nareel's side.

"Shite if I know or care," Cauvin muttered as he turned his back on Bezul.

The way out of the ruin was clear. A wise man—an ordinary man with a wife, children, and a business waiting for him—would take a few sideways steps and be gone. Bezul even took one of those sideways steps, before choosing against wisdom and striding toward the pit.

"This *thing*," he said, pointing at the red glass. "It belongs to a young man who lives out in Night Secrets. I'd like to give it back to him. Apparently, it keeps his crab trap full."

Cauvin and the swordsman stared at Bezul then at each other.

"Your call," the swordsman said and, to emphasize the point, busied himself untying the mask from Nareel's corpse. "Make up your mind. I can't stay here. They're expecting me across town. Never should have let you talk me into that one. Goes against my principles *and* then you tell me I've got to lose."

Cauvin paid no attention to his sarcastic companion. "Froggin' crabs?" he sputtered. "A froggin' Nighter's using a froggin' attractor to trap froggin' crabs?"

Bezul nodded. Against all expectation, the stonemason's brawler-son was giving orders to swordsmen and sorcerers. He'd have to make inquiries after he got back to the Shambles. Until then, Bezul could sympathize with Cauvin's frustration. "Probably the smartest thing you or I could do is break it into little pieces, but the Nighter wants it back. I don't know if he eats the crabs or sells them; as Father Ils judges us all, I'm not sure if it's his or his whole family's. Either way, he calls it the 'red lucky' and my brother tricked him out of it. Then my brother lost it himself to that one there—"

Bezul gestured toward Nareel just as the swordsman lifted the mask. The black-clad man swore an oath in a language Bezul didn't recognize and cast the mask aside. Nareel had died a hideous death, and not from the swordsman's weapon. His face was blackened—cracked, curled, and peeling, like a log left to char at the back of a hot fire. A breeze not strong enough to lift a lock of hair, set an ashy flake adrift. Bezul leapt backward to avoid contact with the flake; the other men did likewise as other bits of Nareel lifted into the quiet air.

The corpse began to crumble from within, shrinking and losing form. Bezul watched, transfixed, for one or two heartbeats, then forced himself to turn away. He steadied himself by breathing in through his nostrils and out between his lips—the way he'd learned years ago when the Bloody Hand of Dyareela summoned the city to public executions.

Not since the Troubles. Not since the Troubles. The notion tumbled in Bezul's mind along with *Who?* and *Why?* and *What manner of darkness has Perrez stumbled into?* He concentrated on the mask: a shallow bronze disk, polished smooth, without holes for sight, breath, or speech; but touched with gold and ringed with stylized flames. *A sun god,* Bezul told himself, not one he recognized, but not the Bloody

Mother, Dyareela, either; and for that he was relieved.

Bezul's relief was interrupted when the corpse of Nareel's companion collapsed with a sigh, like air released from a bladder—a foul, rotting bladder. He recoiled from the sight and the stench; the swordsman did the same. But Cauvin leapt across the hole, seized a shovel the diggers had abandoned, and went to work with more effort than effect until the remains of both corpses were either in the hole, covered with a layer of dirt, or floating in the city breezes.

"Shite for sure," the young man swore as he leaned, sweating and gasping, on the shovel, "I didn't froggin' ask for *this*!"

The swordsman said nothing and Bezul judged it was time for proper gratitude: "I owe you my life, and the lives of my brother and the Nighter, Dace. I think it would be us in that hole, were it not for your timely arrival."

"Froggin' shite, we were already here, waiting for Yorl to show up. You never know what he's going to look like, so I thought, maybe, he was you—until nearly too late. Lucky we weren't all froggin' killed."

Confused by the explanation, Bezul asked, "You were waiting for Nareel?"

"Yorl, Enas Yorl?" Cauvin paused, clearly expecting a reaction to the name, which Bezul didn't provide. "You saw him. He's the one who claimed the chest." Cauvin shook his head. "He's under some froggin' curse that changes him every day, but his eyes give him away . . . most times. Sometimes, you froggin' just don't know."

Bezul hadn't heard the name, Enas Yorl, since before the Troubles started. Gedozia and the other gossips said the mage's mansion had vanished one long-ago night with him in it—Come to think of it, the mansion had been up on Pyrtanis Street, same as the stoneyard where Cauvin worked with his father. Maybe that was the connection—

"You work for him?" Bezul asked and realized, before he'd finished asking the question, that he shouldn't have.

"What's the one true thing about Sanctuary?" Cauvin asked. He didn't wait for an answer. "We've had our froggin' fill of miracles and magic. A froggin' priest comes to Sanctuary, he better talk about what his god does for us, not the other way around and a magician better keep to himself, if he knows what's good for him. We like our froggin' gods quiet and our froggin' sorcerers even quieter. If they're not, we'll froggin' run them out. And if we can't, then there's froggin' Enas Yorl."

The swordsman offered his opinion: "Better one man you can't quite trust than a score of them?"

They glared at each other a moment before Cauvin insisted, "I froggin' trust froggin' Yorl."

"But you knew about Nareel?" Bezul asked quickly, hoping to distract both men. "You know about that shop he has—had—off the Processional?"

"Anyone asks that many questions is bound to attract attention. He was wasting his time and his shaboozh until he got lucky—" Cauvin looked down at the red glass teardrop. He'd come close to breaking it with the shovel, but—luckily?—he'd missed every time. "Crabs? Frog all."

"That's what the Nighter said. They've been using it for years. Your Enas Yorl left it behind—"

"He said an attractor was just a tool," the swordsman said, then added: "Don't let it fall into the wrong hands."

Bezul couldn't tell if the man was speaking for himself or the absent magician, to him or to Cauvin.

Cauvin picked the red glass up, pulled it free of the triangle, and gave it to Bezul. "Yorl didn't know there was an attractor loose in Sanctuary until it left the swamp. See that it gets back to the swamp and stays there. Tell your brother to forget he saw it."

Bezul slid the glass carefully into his scrip.

"See to it," Cauvin warned. "Remember: You owe your life."

Suddenly, Cauvin. didn't sound like a foul-mouthed brawler. Bezul met his eyes and quickly turned away from the depths he saw there. "You have my word." He left the ruins without a backward glance.

Bezul found Dace in Chersey's kitchen, watching the children while she stirred the kettle. He took the red lucky from Bezul's hands with a joy that bordered on reverence and, though the sun had set, the Nighter left at once for the ferry and home. By contrast, Perrez hadn't returned to the changing house. He had missed supper which, Bezul admitted, was unusual and cause for concern, especially as Bezul had decided against telling his mother the unburnished truth about his adventures in the uptown ruins.

Dace returned the next day, his worldly wealth knotted into square of plaid cloth. The red lucky was back where it belonged, he swore, luring crabs to the trap, same as ever. But, after a day on dry, solid ground, the youth was determined to put the swamp behind him. And Chersey's stew was the best-tasting food he'd ever eaten.

Chersey thanked Dace for the compliment . . . and for helping her with the children. Bezul sensed the inevitable coming his way. He gave the Nighter a place in the changing house and enough padpols for a *long* soak in the quarter's bath house.

It was a long afternoon and an unnerving one. The sky darkened at midafternoon. The geese got restless and, as a black disk cut across the sun, big Ammen dropped to his knees in the dirt outside the changing house, bawling like a terrified child. Coming so soon after a similar disk had eaten the moon, it was enough to make a man brave the crowds at the fanes outside the walls.

Bezul got home from Ils's temple as the beleaguered sun was retreating to the western horizon. Perrez had returned while he was gone, reeking of wine he swore he hadn't drunk. He hadn't forgotten his promises. He truly did intend to devote himself to the changing house, but the aromacist had left behind a thriving business in the best part of Sanctuary. Perrez had already found three partners—men who'd won their bets at the tournament—to help him run it, if Bezul would put up enough money to appease the landlord . . .

Apocalypse Noun

Jeff Grubb

Heliz Yunz, linguist of Lirt, moved between the documents scattered across his work desk with the furtive passion of a gambler closing in on a straight flush. He moved hunch-shouldered back and forth beneath the front window of his tiny garret, comparing notes and referencing texts. Three separate primers were propped open along the back of the bench, and another trio of heavy grimoires fortified one end of the desk. The subject of his attentions, a pair of weathered, dissimilar documents, were sprawled out, surrounded by foolscap notes in Heliz's own hand. The lean young scholar had a predatory grin, and his eyes were nearly white in the light of the tallow candles. He was oblivious to the world around him. He was on the hunt.

The precise nature and purpose of the two documents were immaterial to the linguist's quest. One was a stained legal transcript written in the scratchy alphabet of the Rankan court language, rescued from an excavated midden. The other was an erotic poem on perfumed parchment, transcribed in a florid hand in Beysib script, originating far to the south and later imported to, then abandoned in, Sanctuary. What was important, as far as Heliz was concerned, was the words. Most importantly, a grouping of verbs about halfway down the Ranke document, and a similar group in the closing stanzas of the overheated Beysib sonnet.

Heliz checked a primer, then returned to the two documents. Then he was off again to a Beysib dictionary, really little more than a phrase book, then back again. Then back to his shelves to pull one of the Crimson Tomes down to double check, then pulling some detail from one of the grimoires.

The grin deepened. Yes, there were no less than three points of convergence between the two phrases, indicating a deep connection between the transoceanic languages that was previously unknown. The fact that both documents predated Beysib presence in Sanctuary indicated that the common root had to be much older than either document.

And there, cradled within each similar phrase like a pearl was a diminutive suffix, identical in both cases. A piece of hard, firm evidence that this small suffix might have once appended the greater words of power, the words that made the universe itself. He took a small leather-bound book from inside his stained ruddy robe, from the pocket over his heart, and slowly inscribed the phrase and the diminutive suffix together. There were only about a dozen entries in the book, but it held more power than any other tome in his cramped quarters. Indeed, more power than any tome within Sanctuary.

As he finished the last stroke of an accent mark, a heavy footfall creaked on the landing of the outside back stairs, and like a morning dream the revelation snapped apart and elation was shattered. Heliz scowled, his single great eyebrow dipping down towards the bridge of a hawk-like nose. He wanted to ignore the sound, dim the lamps, ignore the guest, but once the remarkable state of discovery was broken there was no return. Snarling mildly to himself, he spun towards the back of the garret, crossed the distance in a matter of three steps, and flung open the door on the surprised and unwelcome client.

The client was a big man, big in a bad way, with a sagging belly that spilled over the top of a wide belt straining at its last notch. A small face surrounded by waddles of fat, masked badly by a spotty beard. Knee-length cloak of good material, but well traveled. Other garments a mishmash of whatever was in fashion at the time they were purchased. A merchant, then, one hand still raised to knock.

"Help you?" snapped Heliz, sincerely hoping the answer was No.

The merchant reached inside his cloak, and pulled out a crumpled bit of paper, the last bits of sealing wax still adhered. "I was told you could read a letter for me."

The merchant's language was Rankan, but his bucolic tones identified him as from Berucat, far to the north. There was just a trace of dialect (clinging to his words like mud on a boot) that revealed he had spent a lot of time recently on the far side of the Shadowfoam.

"It's from my wife," added the merchant, as if it made any difference to the linguist.

"I'm sorry, you have the wrong garret, goodbye," said Heliz, but the merchant had already oozed a foot into the doorframe. He hefted the letter in sausage-heavy fingers and said, "The cooper said you'd do it for a fair coin."

Heliz glowered at the merchant, but the fat man failed to evaporate. Reaching out with a thin hand he snatched the letter from the merchant's hand and retreated back into his lair. "My landlord," said Heliz, "is much too impressed with my capabilities. I'll need my light."

The merchant lumbered in after him. Along the back wall were about a two dozen books, half of them acquired since Heliz Yunz's arrival in Sanctuary. None of them, of course, printed here.

"You're a man of letters?" said the merchant.

"No, I'm a collector of multi-volume paperweights," said Heliz. The linguist held the letter near his study lamp. "Rankan, of course, in execrable handwriting and missing half the prepositions. Masculine hand. Whoever wrote this for your wife carries themselves about as being a 'learned' man."

The merchant shifted from one foot to another, unsure if the analysis was part of the service.

"One silver soldat to read it," said Heliz, holding a hand out. "In advance." The merchant fumbled with his pouch.

Upon pocketing the pay, Heliz said, "It *is* from your wife, though she enlisted someone else to write it. She says that she hopes this letter finds you in good health. One of her pearl earrings went missing the week previous to when she sent this, and she sacked one of the maids as a result. She asks you to respond as to when you are coming home. She implores you to be careful in your journey. She says she misses you, offers her passionate love and signs her name. There."

The merchant grunted and reached out for the letter. Heliz jerked it back in his hand.

"That's what it says," said the linguist, the sharp smile returning for a moment. "For another soldat I'll tell you what it *means*."

The merchant looked confused, then fumbled for his purse again. Pocketing the coin, Heliz regarded the letter again.

"The signature is different than the rest of the letter. Your wife knows no more of writing letters than you know of reading them. She's very comfortable with the dictation, and her scribe is trusted enough to write down intimate words. She's sleeping with whomever wrote this letter, and wants to know when you're coming home so she can hide her paramour away. Given the time it takes for you to get the letter, it's quite likely that more than the pearl earring will be missing by the time you get back to Berucat."

The merchant turned a florid crimson, wheeled, and stormed out of the garret. His boots thundered down the rickety stairs in the back of the cooper's shop.

"Which is *why* I ask to be paid in advance," said Heliz to empty air, a nasty smile breaking across his face. He turned back to the study lamp with the note, examining the paper. The other side of the note was perfectly usable, and even the side the message was written on could be salvaged with a little scraping.

Another footfall on the landing, this one just as heavy, but firmer and more assured. Heliz did not need to reach for the door. Lumm the staver owned the garret, the barrel shop beneath it, his own quarters and the small yard behind the building. He was a good-natured man, a tolerant man, and as far as Heliz was concerned, an ideal landlord. Lumm the staver was also as unlearned as the rest of the town's population, and left the linguist to his studies. Unless he was trying to be friendly. Unless he was trying to be helpful. In which case the larger man was a royal pain. But still, he was the landlord, and it paid to cozen him.

"What did you say this time?" said Lumm, managing to wrap the entire sentence in a sigh.

"It is *not* my fault if people write bad news," said Heliz, "Basic rules for translators—you don't blame the speaker for the words."

"It was something you said, I'll bet," said Lumm, mild irritation in his voice. "I found him at the Unicorn, you know. Told him you knew your letters. Figured you could have gotten a bit more out of him, say, writing a letter back. You passed up an opportunity."

"I don't need the sad cases you find in taverns, thank you," Heliz said in a mild tone. "I just wish to be left with my studies. Without interruptions."

"It seems to me . . ." said Lumm.

Heliz shook his head. "I am not some flat-back girl, Master Lumm, and I do not need you to serve as my monger."

"What I want," Lumm began, more strongly than he intended, then stopped. He took a deep breath. "I want a tenant to pay his rent. And I don't feel right taking silver buttons in trade."

Despite himself, Heliz's thin hand went to the buttons on his travel-stained robe. When he had left the tower, the entire row of buttons, thirty in number from hem to collar, had been silver—now all but three were replaced with wooden fasteners.

Still, the linguist said, "Do you think I should sit in the courtyard and scribe for anyone with the proper coin?"

"If it will pay your room and board, what of it?"

said Lumm, his voice calm again, his eyebrows raised to make his point. "Another thing. The neighbors are complaining. You're boiling rags again."

"I'm making paper," said Heliz. "It's a necessity for my craft."

The landlord held up a protective hand. "So you told me, and I said you could do it, but it kicks up a stench that makes even the Hillers sit up. You might want to wait for the day afore market day. That's when most of the hogs are slaughtered and your stench won't be as noticed." Lumm was at the desk now, looming over the volumes and notebooks.

"I'll take that under advisement," said Heliz, but his eyes tracked Lumm's hands as they moved over the scattered notes and pages.

"So many different ways of writing," said Lumm, admiring the various scripts.

"Different languages," volunteered Heliz, hoping the man would soon grow bored and return to his drinking. "Different alphabets, often alien and mutually exclusive syntaxes. Some languages include more vowels, some do without them, some indicate tense by umlauts and carets . . ."

Lumm touched the small open notebook and Heliz's words died in his throat. "These are interesting. Poetry?"

Heliz reached out and grabbed the booklet from out in front of the stunned Lumm. Despite himself, the larger man staggered back, as if threatened.

Heliz held the small notebook to his chest. "Sorry."

"And what was *that* about?" said Lumm, truly irritated now. "It's not as if I can read your damned poems."

"I'm sorry," said Heliz, suddenly realizing he was

in very real danger of losing his quarters. "They're not poems. They're words. Powerful words. Dangerous words."

Lumm's face clouded. "Dangerous? You mean like spells? Don't care for magic around here."

Heliz shook his head. "Not spells. I mean, not quite. These are the words that spells are made of. Wrapped at the heart of all spells are parts of these words, or at least cognates." He looked at the cooper, but only got a blank, puzzled look. "Um, similar words that sound like them. These words of power are the building blocks of the world. Using them, even unknowingly . . ." Heliz's face clouded for a moment in memory, but he shook it off. "Speaking them *can* be dangerous, in certain circumstances. Sorry if I startled you."

Lumm tried to look as if any of that sunk in. "But they're not spells," he concluded.

Heliz thought about trying to explain again, then said, "No. They're not spells, though a spellcaster might be interested in them."

Lumm looked at the linguist for a long moment. "People don't like spellcasters much in Sanctuary."

"I know," said Heliz, letting out a relieved sigh that nothing had really sunk into the barrel-maker's thick-spackled skull. "That's one reason I came here. Less danger of some wizard wanting to take my work. Privacy for my studies. That and there are so many languages that people have used here."

"Hmmmpf," said Lumm, looking at the collection of writing, and dismissing it. Heliz let himself relax. "I'll leave you to your work, then. But I hope you stung that merchant enough to make the rent. I don't want any more buttons. I'm going back to the Unicorn. You want to come?"

Heliz managed a modest shrug that would only

fool someone like Lumm. "I cannot. I have my studies."

Lumm shook his head and galumphed down the
back stairs, taking most of the air with him.

Heliz was suddenly aware that he was still clutching the booklet tightly to his chest. Carefully he
opened it, as if the words caught within could escape. There were about a dozen. A verb that softened the earth for plowing. An adjective that caused
fire to ignite. A turn of phrase that helped lambs'
birthing.

Words that any mage would slay for, if he knew
they existed.

And a single word, a noun, that Heliz had spoken
aloud only once. A word that had devastated his
home monastery and killed every one of the other
Crimson Scholars. There had been fifty of them,
members of his order, in a hillside tower a day's ride
north of Lirt, all led by his great-grandmother. He
had grown up there. He had studied there. And he
had researched and toiled in its great libraries. And
he had discovered this word there. And after he had
spoken the deadly word, the tower lay in wreckage
at the foot of the hill, and only he managed to pull
himself from the wreckage.

And he had fled to the most illiterate, backwards,
unmagical spot he could find to avoid ever having
to deal with it again.

Lumm stalked through the streets, heading back to
the Vulgar Unicorn. He wasn't angry at the little
scholar as much as confused. Why would anyone
turn down a bit of coin, especially for a skill that
didn't require any heavy lifting? This scholar was a
good tenant as tenants go, but his mule-headed devotion to words completely bumfundled him. If the

lad would just get out a little, he wouldn't be so tightly wound.

Above Sanctuary, the sky grumbled a warning curse. The cloud cover was heavy and low tonight, such that the reflections of fire-pits could been seen illuminating the rounded bottoms of the clouds. It looked like a trickster's storm, more like a summer storm than a winter one. A storm that could drench the town in an instant, or could equally pass over Sanctuary for more promising locations. As Lumm looked up, a spidery thread of lightning crawled along the cloud base, followed by the deep toll of thunder. Definitely a summer trickster's storm.

For the first time, Lumm wondered if Heliz was really a sorcerer. He didn't seem like one, in that he didn't turn into things or have curses or anything. He didn't do any chanting, or dancing, or summoning. And he didn't have the animals, the familiars, stalking about. He wouldn't rent to someone with pets.

Maybe Heliz was a sorcerer—a spellcasting wizard, in fact—but he wasn't a very good one, and that's why he came here. But why be a wizard if you don't want to cast spells?

For that matter, why would a scholar be in Sanctuary? It was not as if the town had a university, or a library, or even other people interested in languages.

Of course, the easy solution would be just to leave the smaller scholar alone, take his silver buttons, and then turn him out on the street when his funds were exhausted. That would be the easiest solution.

Lumm shook his head. Without proper coin, this town would kick the small man into the gutter in a week's time. Heliz was right that Lumm looked for sad cases. Heliz was one of them.

The common room of the Unicorn was as smoke-ridden and murky as usual. Old Thool, the Unicorn's resident sot, was lurching from table to table, cadging what change and dregs of drinks he could manage. The two waitresses, known to all as Big Minx and Little Minx, threaded through the tables, grabbing empties and avoiding hands with equal deftness. Half the people in the room were watching the other half, and malice hung in the air with the smoke. A typical night, then.

Lumm himself scanned the room, looking for the Berucat merchant. No sign of his heavy frame. But Lumm's eyes stopped for a moment at one of the back tables.

At first he could have sworn that Heliz was a wizard, and had gotten to the Unicorn before he did. On second thought, the table's occupant could have been the scholar's sister. She was dressed similarly to the linguist, though her red robes, running from neck to ankle, were cleaner, newer, and still had all of their silver buttons. Yet her hair was as dark as the scholar's, swept back instead of in the bowl cut that Heliz wore. They shared sharp features: dark, heavy eyebrows and a thin, raptorish nose. Yes, she could have been his sister.

And Lumm was staring long enough that the newcomer realized she was being watched. She gave Lumm a smile and beckoned him come over.

"Help you?" she said in a pleasant, soothing voice.

"Sorry to stare," Lumm stammered. "You just remind me of someone." There might be another reason, he realized, that the linguist was in Sanctuary. It would not be the first time someone came to the town to lose themselves of pursuers, family, creditors, or all three.

"No offense taken," said the young woman. She

looked a few years younger than Heliz. A younger
sister? Surely not a daughter. Heliz did not strike
him as either being old enough or bold enough to
spawn any young. "Sit and tell me about it," she continued.

"Sorry to disturb you," said Lumm.

"I said sit and tell me about it." And she said
something else as well, something low and wispy that
the staver did not catch, that brushed against his
mind and was immediately forgotten.

Lumm suddenly found himself in the chair opposite, though he did not remember sitting down.

The young woman in the red robes leaned forward, and Lumm could not help but notice that,
unlike Heliz, the newcomer did not use the top
dozen buttons of her garment. Yet it was her eyes
that most caught his attention—wide, deep, and
green. Eyes you could wander around in.

"I remind you of someone?" she said.

"Another fellow," said Lumm. "I mean, not that
you're a fellow and all. Dressed like you. The fellow.
And you."

"These are the robes of my order," said the young
lady. "I am a Crimson Scholar. Have you heard of
them?"

Lumm felt the hairs stand up on the back of his
neck. "No," he managed.

"Really?" she said, and added that breathy, low
word again. Lumm felt the words surge up his throat
like a bad egg sandwich.

"I've never heard of your order," he said, almost
like it was a single word. It was the truth, of course,
but he felt compelled to say it. "You just look like
someone else I've seen."

The young woman raised a glass of mulled wine,

the spices heavy even at Lumm's distance. "So you said. Friend of yours?"

Despite himself, Lumm laughed. "I don't think he has any friends. A very private person. Wants to be left alone. Spends most of his time in his room. Reclusive, that's the word."

"Indeed," said the young woman, "that's the word. You know where to find him?"

"I should," said Lumm, "I'm his landlord. Maybe I should go get him, if you're looking for him."

"Maybe you should tell me where he is," said the young woman, and for a third time added a breathy addendum.

Again, Lumm felt the need to tell her, felt the words vomiting upwards. But as he opened his mouth, Old Thool slammed into both him and the table, hard. The young woman dropped her glass on the table, sending shards and wine everywhere. She raised her arm to keep it from getting in her face.

"Padpol for an old veteran?" slurred the drunk.

"Go jump off the dock," snarled the young woman, her face suddenly a mask of rage. She added something as well, that struggling fish of a word that kept avoiding getting tangled in Lumm's mind.

Thool stood bolt upright and started lurching towards the door.

Lumm rose as well, suddenly realizing he was sweating. He didn't look directly at the young woman, but instead said, "Let me get a rag to clean all this up. Won't take a moment." Without waiting for an answer, he headed for the bar, and grabbed Little Minx by the arm.

He pressed slivers of pot-metal into her hand. "Get a clean rag for the young woman in red. And another drink. And keep an eye on her until I get back. And don't talk to her."

Little Minx responded with a coquettish nod and a wink, and Lumm was gone as well, out into the night.

The barmaid turned and regarded the young woman with the hard, practiced eye of a Sanctuary native. A few years older than she, but only a few. Wine-spattered robe, but otherwise in good apparent financial shape. Definitely first time in Sanctuary.

Little Minx headed over towards the back table, a slim smile on her lips. She wondered how much more she could get from this fat pigeon by telling her whatever Lumm didn't want her to know about.

Heliz sighed deeply. Of course the moment, the thrill of discovery, wasn't coming back again. Once the path of reasoning was upset, there was no recovery. He had managed the diminutive form, but the two documents were just that—pieces of paper with writing. They held their secrets.

Still, he did not pay enough attention to the heavy footfalls up the back stairs, and jumped in his seat when Lumm, without preamble or politeness, burst into his garret.

"Your sister is here!" the large man blurted out.

All Heliz could manage was a startled, "What?"

"Your sister," said the staver, gulping for air. He had run the last block, or at least tried to. "At the Unicorn. I think she's looking for you."

"I never had a sist . . ." started Heliz, then caught himself up short. "A woman in red robes?"

"She said she was a Crimson Scholar," said Lumm, "I suppose you are too. You never said."

Heliz waved a hand to silence the larger man.

"Black hair, worn long? Green eyes? Almost as tall as I am?"

"Yes, yes, and yes," said Lumm, Heliz Yunz turning paler with each answer.

"I'll need my satchel," said Heliz, launching over to the desk to pull out a heavy bag.

"I left her at the tavern, and said I would go get you," said Lumm.

"Not enough room," said Heliz, looking into the depths of the bag. "Need to take the base primers, and the Ilsig grammars. And the Beysib phrase book. I'm never going to find those again. But what to leave behind?"

"Are you in trouble with your sister?" asked Lumm. "Perhaps if I told her . . ."

"She is *not* my sister," said Heliz, turning on the cooper. "Her name is Jennicandra. She is my Great. Grand. Mother. And Yes, I am in trouble with her."

Lumm stood there, a puzzled look on his face, as Heliz started throwing bulky volumes into the satchel. "Now wait a moment. She's younger than you are . . ."

Heliz was choosing which tome to take and which to abandon. "I know. She's very powerful."

"Powerful? I don't . . ."

"I told you about the power of words. Jennicandra knows these words. Each morning after she rises, she speaks a word of power that keeps the demons of age at bay. She's looked that way for a century. She has a lot of words. More than me. I thought she died when the tower fell, but no such luck. She's tracked me down." He put both tomes aside and dumped his scribe's pouch into the satchel, then touched the notebook resting over his heart. "I have to go. Here's the silver. Sell the books and whatever else I've left behind."

"You said they weren't spells," said Lumm.

"I said they weren't *like* spells," said Heliz, his voice rising. "They are the hearts of spells. The bits that connect for their powers. They are words that should not be spoken. Ideas that should not be evoked. And she knows more of them than I do."

Lumm continued to block the door. "I think you two need to talk."

"I blew up her tower!" shouted Heliz. "I found a very, very dangerous word and uttered it like a damned fool, and blew up the monastery! She's going to want me dead! Now out of my . . ."

The words died in Heliz's throat at a sound in the street out front. It was a single string of syllables, chanted softly. The linguist's face went white and he pressed both palms against Lumm's chest, forcing the larger man backwards in surprise.

Lumm recognized the voice.

"Back! Out the door! She's here!" shouted Heliz.

The front of the garret was already losing all color, turning an ash white that spread from the window overlooking the street. Desk, books, and shelves all slowly were drained, turning first white, and then a pebbly gray. Then, like burned ash, it began to fall in on itself, cascading downwards, striking the whitened floor like dumped flour. Then the floor itself turned gray and began to dissolve as well.

"What is—?" began Lumm, looking as the front of the house disintegrated.

"Out. Now!" shouted Heliz, grabbing his satchel and pushing the cooper out the door onto the back landing.

Both men were now in flight, hurtling down the back stairs. Behind them the house continued to collapse upon itself, becoming nothing more than a cloud of silent gray ash.

"What was that?" gasped the barrel-maker.

"A collection of syllables," said Heliz. "It pulls the energy out of wood and stone without burning, leaving only the ash behind. It's one of her favorites."

"She's a sorceress!" muttered Lumm.

"Worse," said Heliz, clutching his bag of books. "She's a thesaurus."

The clouds of settling ash thundered behind them. "Heliz!" shouted a female voice from the ashen cloud. "Show yourself! I won't harm you!"

"How do we fight her?" asked Lumm.

"With our feet. Put distance between us and her. What's the best way out of town?"

Lumm thought a moment. "This way. There are some abandoned manors north of the city. You could hole up there until she moves on. Follow."

The two darted down the alleyway behind the house. Above, the pregnant clouds were just starting to spit a hot drizzle, and the sky rumbled like a dyspeptic deity.

At the end of the alley, the pair dodged out on the street. The rough, dirt-packed road was blocked to the south by a surging billow of ghostly dust.

A huge shadow loomed up in the dust, resolving into a great, animated statue. It was in the form of a great ape walking on all fours, its stone knuckles leaving deep imprints in the muddy road. Its maw burned with a fiery, greenish light that shone like a beacon. Riding on its shoulders was a raven-haired young woman in crimson robes.

"Heliz!" she shouted, and it seemed she could outshout the thunder itself. "Surrender now! You don't want to make this worse than it is!"

By common, unspoken consent, both men turned and fled down the road. The warm rain began in earnest now, and felt like tears on Heliz's face.

Somewhere else there was a shout, and a slamming of shutters behind them.

They passed two alleys and dodged down the third. Heliz was already breathing hard, and his chest was tight and his arms tired from carrying the satchel. He plastered himself again a wall.

"Change in plans," he huffed. "Let's go to the heart of the city. Maybe go to the Maze. The docks. Hells, head for the Unicorn. There'll be more people there. Someone who can handle her."

Lumm the staver shook his head. "No. We bring sorcery to the heart of the city, and there will be a mob all right, but they'll be after our heads as well. Don't you know any spells to stop her?"

"They are *NOT* spells," Heliz Yunz said testily, "they are words. Words the gods used when they built the world."

"What about the big word, the one that blew up her tower?" asked Lumm.

"That noun destroyed an area about a half-mile in radius," said Heliz. "Would you wish that on Sanctuary?"

The staver did not get a chance to respond, for they were transfixed in a beacon of greenish light issuing from their pursuer's maw. Perched behind the stone ape's head, Jennicandra laughed.

Lumm cursed, invoking several Ilsig gods.

The malediction made a connection in Heliz's mind, reminding him of another string of words. He pressed his hands against the hard-packed dirt of the roadway and spoke a scattering of syllables.

It was the earth-softening phrase, the one that would help speed the plow at planting time. Here, in the increasing rain, it had a greater affect.

The rock-ape lumbered towards them, but its knuckles sank deeper into the road than before. It lurched forwards, off-balance, and almost threw Jennicandra from her seat. Now the softening had spread down the alley, and its hindquarters were sinking as well, mired in the newly softened earth. It raised one hand, pulling up tarry strands of dirt and debris with it. The creature bellowed, and its flaming cry was met by thunder.

Lumm grabbed the satchel of books and shouted at Heliz, "Manors! Now!" And he was gone, not looking back.

Heliz looked back at the trapped rock-ape. There was no sign of Jennicandra, and now the rain was heavy and black, worsening its situation. He started off after the staver.

The rain was small hot spears now, spattering the road and driving even the hardiest natives to shelter. The pair stopped talking, taking refuge in the low overhangs and doorways, working their way north and east towards the manors. The closed shops and shuttered houses began to finally give way to open, empty lots and rubbled buildings, and finally to the rolling slopes of the manors themselves.

The worst of the rain had abated now, and had settled into a sullen, pounding patter. Both men were drenched to the skin and breathless. They dodged into the nearest of the old manors, a rotted manse than had only seen thieves and other fugitives as its tenants for over a decade.

They sat in the darkness for a while, the only sound the pounding of the rain on the upper floor. The roof of this manor had disappeared some time earlier.

"What now?" said Lumm.

"I can't stay," said Heliz. "She found me here. She wants vengeance. I can head across the Shadowfoam, work my way north again to the Ilsig capitol.

Maybe lose her there." There was a pause, and Heliz added, "Sorry to be such a poor tenant."

"I'm going back," said Lumm, rising to his feet. "See what the damages are. Salvage what I can. I'll get you some food and water, if you can wait until morning."

Heliz nodded, and Lumm's shadowy form moved towards the door.

"Lumm?" said Heliz. The older man stopped in the doorway.

Whatever Heliz was going to say was disrupted by a blast of greenish light. It struck Lumm like a hammer, knocking him from his feet. Lumm bellowed, covering his eyes as he fell.

"Heliz!" came Jennicandra's voice from outside. "Show yourself."

Heliz pulled himself to his feet. Cursing himself. Cursing his great-grandmother. Cursing Lumm and the gods and words and Sanctuary itself.

He moved into the doorway.

Outside, the rain had stopped, but only in the immediate vicinity. It formed a curtain around the manor's front drive. Standing before the main doors was the red-clad form of Jennicandra, Mistress of the Crimson Scholars. Behind her loomed the green-mawed ape made of hewn rock.

"Heliz," said Jennicandra, the corners of her mouth turned up in a smile.

"Great-grandmother," said Heliz, his throat tightening.

"You've caused me a lot of trouble, child," she said reproachfully. Her mannerisms were careful now, those of an old person. She looked like a child playacting.

"I'm sorry," said Heliz, feeling his knees tremble and threaten to go out. "I didn't mean to destroy

the tower. I didn't know the word was that dangerous. Don't kill me."

The smile blossomed fully on the young/old
woman's lips. "Kill you? Hardly. Not while you have
that useful word in your mind."

"But the tower?"

Jennicandra laughed harshly. "What of the tower?
Fifty scribes. A word that powerful is worth five hundred. I've been looking for words like that. Original
words. Words of Destruction and Creation. Show me
the word you learned, child. I'll be happy to leave
you in this hole of a town if you just show me the
word."

She said something else, something that Heliz
heard and then forgot immediately. Something that
slid off his brain, leaving a muzzy residue behind.
He wanted to speak, but his throat tightened at fear
of his great-grandmother. He shook his head, more
in confusion than in negation.

"Come now, child," said Jennicandra. "You wrote
it down, didn't you? Of course, you're a good
scholar. I taught you to be one. So you would find
the right words for me. Now I want you to show me
your devotion to your Great-grann-nanna. Show me
what you did, child. Show me the word."

Again she added something else, the extra syllable
that strained at the gates of Heliz's mind. Heliz
made a gasping whisper. "I'm sorry," he managed.
Despite himself, he clutched at the notebook resting
over his thundering heart.

Jennicandra took another step forward. "You dis-
appoint. All those deaths are meaningless, child, unless I get the word. Unless I get the power. It's your
purpose in life. It's in your notebook, isn't it? I can
take it off your body. Don't fight me, child. Your

blood comes from me. You owe it to me. Give it to me. Give me the word."

This time the syllable struck like a blade against the bounds of his mind, and the torrent came loose. He felt the sudden need to pull the small notebook out, to show his Great-grann-nanna what he did, to make her proud of him. He reached for the book.

And something large and heavy slammed into him, knocking him against the side of the door. Something sharp broke inside Heliz's mind, and he realized that he had fallen beneath one of Jennicandra's own words of power.

Lumm, rubbing his shoulder, bellowed, "Use it, Heliz! Use it on her!"

Heliz looked at the staver. "But the town . . ."

"Will be my first test of power," said Jennicandra, and she shouted, "NOW, GIVE ME THE WORD!" and added her word of power. Behind her, the rock-ape bellowed in chorus.

Heliz opened his mouth and screamed, bellowed the word of power that had been unspoken these many months. It was a short word, but charged with the power of sun and stars and earth and creation. It pulled fury with it, and detonated right where Jennicandra was standing.

And as Heliz shouted the word, he changed it, twisting it in his mind and his throat to merge it with the diminutive form he had discovered earlier in the evening. He appended it more as a hopeful prayer than as a real attempt to control the damage.

A bright light flashed, one that Heliz had seen once before, long ago in the tower. It blossomed outwards, encasing his great-grandmother, the rock-ape, and licking at the entrance of the manor itself. Yet it was contained, folded back upon itself by its diminutive suffix. It looked as if a massive ball of lightning had detonated among the manor houses, turning the region to brief, sudden day.

And as suddenly as it appeared, it diminished again, collapsing like energy without matter to house it, pulling itself inwards and evaporating in a single point. The area in a fifty-foot circle was blasted black, and the stone front of the manor house was charred and blackened. All that remained of the rock-ape was a pair of roughly hewn feet, which could be imagined as being anthropoid only with a vivid imagination. Of the Great-grandmother of the Crimson Scholars there was no sign. The rain was falling again in the courtyard, and the thunder grumbled in the sky like a god disturbed from its slumbers.

Lumm helped Heliz to his feet. The linguist had not realized he had collapsed.

"You got her," said Lumm, self-satisfaction in his voice.

Heliz shook his head. "I did this to her before. She survived that."

"No, you got her," assured Lumm. "If she lived through that, she's a better thesaurus, or sorceress, or whatever, than she should be."

Lumm thumped down the broad steps of the manor house, then turned. "You coming?"

Heliz was quiet for a moment, wrestling with his thoughts. "Yes. Let me take you to the Unicorn. I suppose I owe you a drink."

Lumm shook his head, then spat, "You owe me a *house*, linguist." He growled, "And I just hope you like working in the central courtyard, because that's where you're going to be until you pay me back."

And with that the barrel-maker headed down the slope, listening as he walked for the footsteps of the linguist behind him.

One to Go

Raymond E. Feist

The flea moved.

Jake the Rat held motionless, ignoring the irritation as the tiny bloodsucker sought out another location where he could visit more misery upon the old thief. Jake could feel the tiny parasite hop down his right calf toward his ankle, already covered in scab-capped welts. Slowly, with a patience born of a lifetime spent being patient, he moved his leg, bringing it to a point where his gnarled fingers could lash out and seize the tiny malefactor.

"Ah ha!" he shouted in triumph as his still nimble digits struck downward, fetching up the flea between calloused forefinger and thumb. "I have you!"

"Wot?" asked Selda.

"Damn flea that's been biting me for the last hour. I got it!"

Selda had been tending her knitting. She put down the two bone needles and sat back in the rickety chair she had appropriated for that purpose approximately five seconds after entering the hovel for the first time, seven years earlier. Fixing her hus-

band with a baleful gaze she said, "Ain't that wonderful! Now you can set about catchin' the other
thousand or so wot's still in residence with us."

Ignoring her sarcasm, Jake held the tiny creature
up for inspection. He moved it closer and farther
away under the dim light of the lantern above the
table and couldn't quite seem to get it into focus.
"Damn," he muttered. "Are these fleas smaller than
they used to be?"

"No, you old fool. It's your eyes wot ain't what
they was."

Not taking his eyes from the tiny bloodsucker, he
muttered, "Nothing wrong with my eyes, old
woman. I can still spot a watchman a mile away." He
rolled the flea between thumb and forefinger, very
hard. "You've got to mess them around a bit," he
said as if conducting lessons on the execution of
vermin. "They've got hard shells and if you just try
to squash them, they'll leap away. But if you roll
them hard, it breaks their legs or something and
they just sit there." He did so and deposited the flea
on the table. He couldn't be sure, but he thought
he saw the insect twitch. Deriving satisfaction from
the thought that the thing might be suffering in retribution for the misery inflicted upon others, Jake
hesitated a moment, then drove a bone-hard thumb-
nail into the wood, bisecting the tiny creature. "And
there you have done with it!"

"Well, pleased as princesses on a shopping trip
about decapitating a bug, isn't he?" said Selda. "Why
you go to such lengths about it when most people
just swat the damn things is beyond me."

"It keeps me relaxed while I'm waiting," he answered.

She knew that. She knew everything about Jake.
Selda and Jake had been together for thirty years.

They'd even had a child together once, though the boy had run off when he was twelve. They had called the boy Jaxon. They'd heard he'd become a sailor, but didn't know if it was so. Neither had mentioned his name to the other since the day he had left. Both knew to do so would be to open the debate as to who had been responsible for the boy's leaving, and both knew that would be the end of them. So they remained silent on that one matter.

But on any other subject, they had argued so often and so repeatedly that each could hold the argument even if the other was off somewhere. But tonight was different.

Jake looked over at Selda and said, "Wot? You ain't going to say something about relaxing?"

She put down her knitting. With a scolding tone she said, "And wot good would it do? None at all. It's a sad situation we're in, in'it? And there's nothin' for it but for you to go off and get yourself killed, you old twit."

He stood from the other chair, as he always thought of it, her chair and the other chair, and made his way around the table to where Selda sat, clutching her needles in hands so tight her knuckles showed white. "Who you callin' an 'old twit,' you old shrew?"

She jabbed at him with the needles and shouted, "You, and you are an old twit, you old twit." Eyes rimming with tears she said, "You're going to get yourself killed, then where'll I be?"

He easily avoided the jabbing needles and bent over her. She turned her head aside and tried to brush him away with both hands, but he would have none of it, circling her in his arms as he had tens of thousands of times in the past. "It'll be good, you'll see," he said.

Tears ran down her cheeks and she said, "I'm frightened, old man." Suddenly she leaned into him and clung to him as if fearful of letting him go. "Must you?"

"I must. I told you, old woman, three jobs and we'd be out of this pest hole."

Showing the resiliency he had known for most of his adult life, she pulled away and shouted, "Aye, and whose bit of thunderous wisdom was it brought us to this pest hole, this 'Sanctuary,' out here at the edge of nowhere, in the first place?"

"Now, don't you go starting up with me on that, old woman," he admonished.

"We should get out of the Empire, he says," she mimicked his voice. "We should head out to Sanctuary. I hear it's lively out there, with all manner of people wot never been this far east before. Easy pickin's for the likes of us, he says. No Imperial thief-catchers chasing us for bounty. No merchant's guild hiring assassins to stalk us in the night, he promises. No revengeful nobles sending soldiers out by the dozens to cut us down in the city square like bowmen slaughterin' lambs in a pen.

"No, he says to me, it'll be fun, lots of interestin' folks, and some easy days." She held up her hands to describe the hovel in which they lived, one table, two chairs, a lamp, a tiny brazier over which they cooked their meager food, and a sleeping roll on the floor they had shared for the last seven years. It was located at the darkest end of an alley abutting a wall on the other side of which lay the city's busiest slaughter house. "Does this look like easy days?"

He started to speak and she held up a silencing hand. "No! If it's not drunk Ilsigi soldiers trying to kill us because someone's grandfather died fighting the empire, it's Rankan mercenaries who just happen to think we look like easy prey. And for the last two years we've had those wonderful Irrune body-guards of Chief Arizak all over the place looking ready to kill if you happen to be looking in the general direction of their master's house.

"An' let's not forget the Cult of Dyareela wot's running around killin' people 'cause they think it's holy. Lovely bunch they are. Then there's that lot over at the Vulgar Unicorn."

He let his head sag, knowing that he wasn't going to get any peace until she had finished her rant.

"You've got sorcerers who'll turn you into a toad for a giggle. People who are I-don't-know-what carvin' each other up for all manner of odd thingies, runes, books, gems, and the like, except I think a couple of them are already dead and you can't carve them up unless they want you to, but they do get by with having pieces fall off now and again! Freeboot-ers and rogues, murderers and scoundrels, and some of 'em aren't even human, I wager! And the way they talk—can't hardly understand a word. They're *all* foreigners!

"And you've got more thieves in the Maze than who've been hung on the Imperial Gallows in Ranke since the first Emperor was a pup! You can't bend over to pick up one of their greasy little coins with-out bumpin' your head with a thief, and your arse with another behind you. You pick a man's pocket and discover he's the fellow who'd picked yours five minutes before!"

He'd heard the rant nearly every day since the end of the first year after they'd arrived in Sanctuary and was always astonished at how little it varied, though the part about Chief Arizak's bodyguards had only been added about a year and a half ago.

He resisted the temptation to join in as she finished—

"And for this misery, what do I get? Do I get riches and good food, my ease as servants stand idly by waiting for my merest whisper to do my bidding? No, I get this!" And as always, she stood up, with her arms outstretched on the word "this!"

Squelching a sigh of relief the last of the rant was now over, he stepped before Selda and put his arms around her. "Hush, old woman. I know you're frightened. But I told you, three more jobs and we're done with Sanctuary. I boosted the Jade Cat from the royal caravan just as it left, to square my debt to Bezul the changer, and to get these!" He showed her a leather packet, the contents of which were known to her. "Then I lifted six full purses in one night on the first day of the tourney to give to the caravan master for passage back into the Empire and to give to Pel Garwood, to concoct a mix for my chest, so I can do tonight's job without a coughing attack."

"We've already paid our passage. Why another job?" she asked him for the uncounted time.

Patient as always he answered her as he always had, "Because we have passage only to Ranke, and I want enough after getting there that we can live quietly in something better than this." His hand described the hovel.

"But Lord Shacobo, the magnate?"

"He's the obvious choice."

"Then why has no one has ever boosted his place?"

"Hetwick the Nimble did!"

"An' they hung him for it! Or do you think that was a success, just having gotten in for a bit and wanderin' about?"

"Woman, I've told you all this before. The night before Hetwick danced the gallows, his woman came to see him in his cell and he told her something, something she told me for a price, and it's the reason I'll succeed where Hetwick didn't."

"Oh, and you're a man of vision and genius and Hetwick was just another fool, is that it?"

"Woman, remember who was the greatest thief in the Empire!"

"You old fool, most nights you weren't even the greatest thief in the room!" She held up her hand before his nose and wiggled her fingers. "These beauties boosted a fine number of fat purses in their day, you can't deny it, can you?"

He hugged her fiercely and said, "You did that, old girl, you did that."

"You're not going to tell me what it was Hetwick's woman told you, are you?"

"No. You'll just worry over it." He kissed her cheek. "You remember wot I told you?"

"Yes," she said with frown. "I 'member wot you tol' me. I wait here until the final tournament starts. Then I take what I got"—she waved to a small bundle of personal goods—"and gets to that little inn out by the old ford across the White Foal. Wait there until you come by, just afore dawn."

"I talked to Landers—he runs the Hungry Plowman—and he'll let you bed down under a table in the commons for a padpol or two."

"Then we makes for the fields where they're unloading caravans 'til the tourney stands come down—which we won't be here to see, will we?—and head out to Ranke at first light."

"Remember, as my old mentor said, 'Timing is everything.'"

"Mentor? You never had no mentor. You 'prenticed with Shooky the Basher. Not much craft in bonkin' a mark over the head wif a club and rifling his purse as he lies on the ground moanin'. Got himself hung, remember?"

"True, but he knew a thing or do, did old Shooky. And he was right about timing; if he'd been out that door after he murdered that bloke one minute earlier, they never would have hung him."

He grabbed up a shoulder bag from a peg by the door and slipped his head through the noose. Picking up the small leather package from the table, he slipped it into a pocket sewn into the inside of his shirt. He adjusted his rope belt, as if concerned for his appearance, and said, "That's it, then. Remember, something odd's about to happen this afternoon, but it'll be all right. Don't worry about it. Just wait until it's time to go, then head for the Hungry Plowman. I got to go now."

Without another word he slipped through the door and into the alley.

As Jake anticipated, the streets were deserted. The final day of the tournament was on high, and if he judged his timing rightly, the crowd was at its maximum capacity this moment, with Master Soldt, acknowledged the greatest swordsman in Sanctuary, if not most of the known world, facing the mysterious woman called Tiger. Jake had chanced being spied by the local guardsmen, who might or might not have noticed him—but why take unnecessary chances?—just to see the previous day's matches. The woman was unlike any Jake had ever seen and Jake had seen a lot of women in a lot of different places, from a lot of different places. Under all that armor she looked lithe and slender, and she was a tiny thing. Wonder if she was pretty? he absently added.

Time was he had a practiced eye for beauty. Jake liked women in all forms, tall, short, ample, thin. Dark, fair, it didn't matter much; if they had some beauty in them somewhere, he'd find it. He'd been quite the lad with the girls until he'd met Selda.

Now she'd been something, he thought with a smile, as he scampered down a twisting street leading through the Maze. Not a thin girl, but not thick either. Just right. Brown hair, again not too fair or dark. Clear blue eyes and an odd bit of a nose, just slightly too big for her face, but again not by too much. He liked it. He had liked her first time he put eyes on her. She must have liked him, as well, for they were in his bed that first night, and she'd been in it every night since for thirty years.

Not that he didn't look at other women. He was a bit past fifty years, but he wasn't dead. He still appreciated a slender leg, rounded rump, or a wicked smile. But no matter how tempting another woman looked, he'd still not found one to match his old Selda.

But as fascinating as the woman called the Tiger was, his reason for attending the semi-final bouts was to see where Lord Shacobo would be. As hoped for, while the otherwise penurious trader might stint in most things, he liked the reflected glory of being located near the great and near-great. His box was the first to the left of the true nobility and must have cost him enough to have made him wince when he paid over the fee to the stadium managers. Jake was certain Shacobo would be back in that box today.

For an absent moment, Jake wondered at how much the Rankans were paying for that thing they had built in the old market and Caravan Square. It was no Imperial arena, but it took a lot of men and lumber to build the damn thing. Seemed a shame to start tearing it down tomorrow.

He focused his attention on a particularly problematic corner, the one where five streets, or slightly larger alleys really, almost came together in a muddle, which had a couple of complete blind spots. He'd used it in the past to shake a follower, but it also was a good place to hide in waiting. He automatically moved to the left side of the street, moved diagonally across the first portion of the three-way intersection, then cut to his left again to enter the farthest turn, giving him the best advantage of seeing someone before being seen.

No one was there.

As he anticipated, everyone who could was at the tourney this day. When first hatching his plan to rob Shacobo's, he had planned on being there already, lurking in some nearby shadow as the fat merchant, his wife, dimwit son, obnoxious daughter, and far-too-pretty serving girl all marched off to their precious little viewing box.

But a passing remark by Heliz, the linguist of Lirt, made one night at the Vulgar Unicorn had eaten at the corner of his memory for a week. He had found an old text a while back while boosting a trader's stall at the Market, and had almost tossed it. But by chance he had not, and when he presented it to Heliz, in his office above Lumm the staver's, he thought the man would melt with pleasure. The odd document was something Heliz called a Beysib script, whatever that was, but he certainly seemed thrilled to have it.

In exchange for it, he had explained his passing remark to Jake, who had instantly put his mind to how he could turn this to his advantage. Soon after the tourney ended, there would be an eclipse.

Jake had managed to get a good ten minutes of solid information out of Heliz, which wasn't all that bad considering it had come embedded in about two hours of sarcasm, insult, and condescension. Jake wished Heliz had something worth stealing, because he loved victimizing people who assumed they were smarter than he, simply because he was a thief, or less well born, or older, or for any reason.

Jake the Rat was many things, but stupid wasn't one of them.

Jake had seen a couple of lunar eclipses and once, when he had been a very young boy, a solar one, but Heliz said none had been seen in Sanctuary since the oldest living man's grandfather had walked the streets, and had mentioned that "most of the locals will probably run around like demented chickens, in anticipation of the gods' wrath." Heliz talked like that.

He was from the heart of the Empire, too, as far as Jake could tell. Not Ranke from his accent, but somewhere close by. Jake had him pegged for a Crimson Scholar, except word was, they'd all died in some sort of violent explosion. He was, Jake was certain, capable of magic, simply because being around those people made Jake's butt itch, and Heliz made Jake's butt itch.

Jake had heard Heliz's sister had been in town looking for him yesterday. He turned the corner and walked quickly past Lumm the staver's place. Noticing the still smoking fifty feet of destruction before the building, Jake judged that family reunion hadn't gone as well as it could have.

Jake pushed aside the thought. Time to turn his full attention to the job. He reviewed what he knew of the locks at Shacobo's and patted the picks he had purchased from Bezul, then remembered what Hetwick's widow had told him for a price: Beware of the dog. Patting the bag of meat gleaned from the slaughterhouse next door, Jake grinned. "No problem," he muttered.

"Nice puppy," Jake said for the fiftieth time to the slavering monster below. The thing sort of looked like a hound, big and loose jointed, covered in dark brown and black fur, but it had a square muzzle and ears that perked up.

The creature—Jake refused to think of this monster as merely a dog—had an incredible array of teeth, all currently set to remove large hunks of Jake from Jake's bones.

The caper had gone exactly as Jake had anticipated. He had gone through the locks like a blade through parchment. He was standing in Shacobo's lock room within ten minutes of entering the building and had selected several items to remove; he concentrated on the small and portable, while less experienced thieves might have been lured by the pile of gold coins. He had taken a few of those, for certain, but the jewels and a couple of curios with precious stones would set him and Selda up for life. Not just a modest hut somewhere, but a lovely little home on the river south of Ranke, with a servant, perhaps even two.

He had taken one step out of the strong room when he had confronted the monster. The dog stood flatfooted and looked Jake in the eyes. It growled and Jake understood why Hetwick had preferred being captured. The creature had been trained to keep the invader in the strong room until guards could be summoned.

Feeling brilliant, Jake had produced the meat and

tossed it through the door. As he had anticipated, the dog's training was overcome by hunger, and Jake had a chance to cut through the door to make his getaway.

What he hadn't counted on was the dog being the size of a small pony and eating everything Jake had brought along in two bites. Jake had earned about a thirty second headstart.

So now Jake hung from a pole used to run out laundry from a second-floor window. The rear wall of the estate was temptingly close, a mere twenty feet away, and his only means of transverse a slender cord used to hang the wash. Jake kept his knees tucked up as the dog would occasionally leap and take a bite at Jake's exposed toes, which could feel hot breath.

Not having the wit to call up the appropriate god for this circumstance, Jake started praying to all of them. He vowed as soon as he got to Ranke he would make the rounds and put a votive offering on every alms plate in every temple of every god, no matter how minor, if he could just get to that wall.

Reassuring himself with the observation that wet laundry was quite heavy and the thin cord was probably a great deal stouter than it looked, he began his move, first one hand then the next.

The dog started barking and Jake was suddenly afraid the noise might alert someone. Then the sky darkened and other dogs in the area also started to howl. Jake knew better than to glance at the sun, but the fading light told him the eclipse was now in progress. That should keep this situation under control a few minutes longer, Jake judged, as he moved slowing across the courtyard.

The dog stopped barking and looked up, his eyes fixed upon Jake. For no better reason than hedging his bet, Jake crooned, "Nice puppy! Sweet puppy! Puppy want to play?"

For an instant, Jake swore he saw the dog's tail twitch as if on the verge of a wag, then the creature's hackles rose and it growled.

"Oh, you don't mean that, puppy-wuppy," said Jake, sounding like a demented granny. "You're a nice puppy." Jake glanced over and saw he had reached the midpoint, which meant the cord was now hanging at its lowest point.

The dog leaped. Jake jerked his knees up around his chin and could feel the air move below his toes as jaws like iron traps slammed shut less than an inch away.

"Nice puppy!" Jake almost shouted. The dog turned in a circle, looking almost playful, before attempting another leap. *Snap!* went the jaws and again Jake could feel the creature's hot breath.

And in that instant the cord broke.

Jake fell, butt first, his knees around his chin, as the dog hit the ground. The dog looked up just in time to see Jake's posterior blot out the sky, the instant before Jake landed upon its head.

The hound's jaw slammed into the stone courtyard surface with a lethal-sounding crack, and Jake felt the shock run up his spine, rattling his teeth.

For a second, Jake sat on the dog's head, unsure if he should move, then he scrambled off the creature as quickly as possible.

Could it be? Was the hound from hell dead?

Not waiting around to find out, Jake stood up and did a quick inventory. All his body parts were still attached and in their proper locations, so he turned and made for the wall.

Just as he reached it, he heard a *woof* from behind. Spinning, he saw the still dazed dog advancing on him, a low inquisitive *chuff* sound coming from its throat. Grinning, Jake said, "Nice puppy!"

That's when the dog leaped.

"You could have told me we was walking," scolded Selda as she trudged along behind a rug merchant's wagon, an hour after sunrise and their departure from Sanctuary.

"I didn't have enough coins to buy better at the time," Jake answered. "I'll see what I can do about arranging a ride when we break for the midday meal."

"Harumph," she answered. After a minute, she said, "And I still don't know why you had to bring that along." Her thumb stabbed behind them.

Jake tugged on the laundry cord he had tied around the dog's neck after it had leaped toward him and started licking his face. "Look, old woman," said Jake. "You want to go back and tell that beast he can't come with us?"

She glanced back at the huge dog, its tongue lolling out of its mouth as its tail wagged.

"Nice puppy," Jake crooned and the dog's tail wagged even faster.

"What are we going to feed it? It's licking its chops and eyeing the horses!"

"We'll buy some meat," said Jake. "We have means."

"We do?"

"Better than I thought, old woman. We'll find a proper fence in Ranke, who'll give us more than young Bezul ever would, and we'll be set for life. Riverside house and a servant, m'gal."

"A servant?" she said in wonder.

"Like I told you, one to go and we're done." He grinned. "Well, we're done."

"Wot we going to call that thing? Ain't no proper puppy."

" 'Shacobo' seems fitting?"

"But what if someone who knows him in Sanctuary shows up in Ranke and puts it all together?"

"Slim chance, but then maybe you're right. What about calling him 'Hetwick'?"

"Never liked Hetwick, or his wife."

So they trudged along until the midday break, arguing over what to call the dog, who remained "Puppy" until he died of old age seven years later. Selda and Jake actually wept when they buried the beast in the garden behind the riverside house.

And they lived happily ever after, until a thief name Grauer broke into Jake's strong room and stole most of his wealth, and Jake had to steal it back—but that's another story.

Afterword

Lynn Abbey

Who says you can't go home again? When home is the city named Sanctuary, anything is possible.

A lot of water has flowed under the bridge since that Boskon dinner in 1978 when Thieves' World was conceived. We had a great run—twelve anthologies, a couple of novels, some graphic adaptations, games, and some great music you never got to hear—and then times were changing, not just in publishing, but in private lives as well.

We boarded up Sanctuary in the late 1980s—put it in "freeze-dry mode" with the hope that the great wheel of fortune would spin around again. Without going into great detail, Robert Asprin and I got married not long after Thieves' World began and we separated a few years after it ended. By the time the divorce was final, the great wheel had pretty well come off its axle and, when asked, I'd answer that pigs would fly before there'd be another book with Thieves' World on the cover.

Bob moved to Houston, then New Orleans. I moved to Oklahoma City, then central Florida (odd places both, for someone who hates heat and humidity). Years went by and my answer never changed. Then it was May 1999, and I came home to find my answering machine lit up like a Christmas tree: A line of tornadoes of unprecedented strength had ripped through the Oklahoma City area. My stepdaughter and friends were all calling in to tell me they were safe—for which I was most thankful—and to inform me that along with the roofs and the trees, the cattle and the cars, there were pigs in the air and I had never said they had to walk away from their landings.

Oops.

I guess I'd started thinking about it a year or so earlier, when I realized I was signing (and resigning) battered copies of *Thieves' World* and *Tales from the Vulgar Unicorn* that were older than the readers handing them to me. Maybe a reprint program, I'd thought, but no publisher was interested in reprints only. Frankly, they weren't interested in resurrecting anything that seemed as tightly associated with the 1980s as, oh, Michael Jackson and Ronald Reagan.

Enter Brian Thomsen, editor extraordinaire and proverbial longtime friend of the family, and Tom Doherty, who'd been the man-in-charge at ACE Books when Thieves' World began its run and is now the man-in-charge at TOR. Brian was looking for a project he could sink his fangs into and Tom, in a moment of weakness, agreed that if anyone was going to bring back Thieves' World it should be TOR—but not as a reprint program.

They wanted new material—new anthologies that got back to Sanctuary's grungy roots and a novel (a "James Michener-esque epic novel"—it said so right at the top of the contract) that would recap all twelve previously published anthologies while leveling the playing field for the new stories. I, of course, would write the "Michener-esque epic novel" that we honestly thought TOR would be publishing in the first half of 2001.

Oops.

Thieves' World has always been a lot like an iceberg: What's visible on the surface is only a fraction of what's really there. Contracts had to be written and rewritten. The authors who wrote for the original incarnation had to sign off on the parameters of the new one. New authors had to be selected, invited . . . *persuaded* that their professional lives would not be complete until they'd written a story set in the renovated Sanctuary. And there was that little matter of turning more than fifty often contradictory (often deliberately contradictory) stories into that "Michener-esque epic novel."

Little by little, Thieves' World came together. All the first-generation authors signed off on the changes necessary to bring Sanctuary into the twenty-first century world of electronic publishing and multi-media exploitation rights; many of them signed up to write new stories. I read and re-read the old stories, stared at maps, dove into obscure histories until the boundaries blurred and I began to think I knew what had happened in Sanctuary, what was happening, and what needed to happen in the future.

The novel was late . . . very late. By the time the authors in *Turning Points* got a chance to read it, their stories were also—technically—very late. I owe them, and everyone else connected with *Turning Points,* my thanks for their patience. At least this time around we had e-mail. (I think back to the late seventies, when overnight mail was just getting a foothold, and I marvel that Bob ever managed to get the anthologies put together.)

Mostly, I give thanks to the fans of Sanctuary, to everyone who read a Thieves' World story and wanted the pigs to fly.

Welcome back—I hope you'll agree it was worth the wait.